Winner of the Ron
Choice Awards
in U

"Arthur is positively
authors in print

"Keri Arthur's imagination and energy infuse everything she writes with zest."—Charlaine Harris

Praise for the Souls of Fire series

"Amazing. I love the world building and character development. . . . I am hooked."
—The Book Pushers

"With the plot, the characters, the steaminess, and the rhythm of the writing, this series is bound to be a hit. . . . Keri's talent for steaming up the pages is definitely in there as well."
—Awesomesauce Book Club

"An epic journey . . . a series that I can't wait to see more of."
—Much Loved Books

"A fresh new urban fantasy series that will please fans of the genre and Keri's writing alike. This one will definitely be staying on my keeper shelf."
—A Book Obsession

"Expertly builds on the tensions and conflicts from the series debut and expands both the world of this urban fantasy series and the alluring cast of characters that populate it."
—*RT Book Reviews*

"Another gripping series from Keri Arthur. She seems to always find a different spin on urban fantasy . . . an original take with stellar writing and plotting."
—Just Talking Books

"A red-hot new series that's destined to become an urban fantasy favorite; if you're tired of the same ol', then look no further than Keri Arthur's Souls of Fire."
—Rabid Reads

ALSO BY KERI ARTHUR

THE SOULS OF FIRE SERIES

Fireborn
Wicked Embers

THE DARK ANGELS SERIES

Darkness Unbound
Darkness Rising
Darkness Devours
Darkness Hunts
Darkness Unmasked
Darkness Splintered
Darkness Falls

THE OUTCAST SERIES

City of Light

FLAMEOUT

A Souls of Fire Novel

KERI ARTHUR

SIGNET SELECT
Published by New American Library,
an imprint of Penguin Random House LLC
375 Hudson Street, New York, New York 10014

This book is an original publication of New American Library.

First Printing, July 2016

ISBN 9780451477903

Printed in the United States of America
10 9 8 7 6 5 4 3 2 1

I'd like to thank all the usual suspects who help make this book a reality:

My wonderful editor, Danielle Perez, copy editor Janet Robbins Rosenberg for making sense of my Aussie English, and the fabulous Tony Mauro for continuing to provide awesome covers.

I'd also like to add an extraspecial thanks to my agent, Miriam, my crit group (and best buds), the Lulus, and my lovely daughter, Kasey. Thank you all for your continuing support.

Chapter 1

The throaty roar of machinery shattered the peace of the cemetery. Deep in the old trees and on the other side of the road that channeled drivers up to the mausolea, light shone. It was fierce and bright against the thick cover of night, but it oddly cast the man who stood at the very edge of its circle into shadow.

I paused on the side of the road and took a deep breath. It did little to calm either my nerves or the churning in my stomach. I had no right to be here. No right at *all*. And I certainly knew that shadow wouldn't be, in *any* way, happy to see me.

But I couldn't stay away. I had to see with my own eyes the lack of a body in the grave the excavator was digging up. While it might have been only a few days ago that I'd physically confronted the man who was *supposed* to be buried there, some insane part of me couldn't help hoping that it *hadn't* been Luke, that it had instead been some sort of doppelgänger. Not for my sake, but for the sake of the shadow ahead.

After another useless deep breath, I crossed the road and walked as silently as possible through the old eucalypts that dominated this section of the cemetery. Although given the man ahead was infected by a virus that had basically turned him into something of a pseudo vampire, I'm not sure why I bothered. He'd sense my presence long before I actually got there.

Whether he'd acknowledge it was another matter entirely.

The excavator's engine suddenly cut out, and the ensuing silence was eerie. It was almost as if the night was holding its breath, waiting to see the outcome of the grave being opened.

As I neared the site, the shadow turned. Despite the darkness, his blue eyes had an almost unnatural gleam, and, as ever, I felt the impact of them like a punch to the gut. But if he was in any way surprised to see me, it wasn't showing.

But then, Sam Turner probably knew me better than almost any human alive, given our rather intense—if altogether too brief—relationship five years ago.

"Evening, Emberly." His voice gave as little away as his expression, yet it ran over my senses as sweetly as a kiss. "I was wondering when you'd turn up."

"There was always a chance the sindicati were lying when they said the leader of the cloaks was your brother." I shrugged. "I needed to be sure."

He raised an eyebrow. "Why would you disbelieve them when you confronted Luke face-to-face?"

"I know. I just . . ." I paused and shrugged again.

"You just keep hoping that you're wrong, that it's someone who looks like my brother in charge of the red cloaks rather than Luke himself." A bitter smile momentarily twisted his lips. "I know the feeling."

"The red cloaks" was the nickname given to those infected by the Crimson Death virus—or the red plague, as it was more commonly known—and it was a virus

Sam had running through his veins. Those infected generally fell into two categories—the ones who were crazy and kept under control only by the will of the red cloak hive "queen," and the ones who kept all mental faculties even though they were still bound to the hive and its leader. No one really understood why the virus affected some more than others, although the powers that be suspected it very much depended on whom you were infected by. Of course, there *was* a third, much rarer category involving people like Sam and Rochelle—Sam's lover and another member of the Paranormal Investigations Team. They might be infected, but they had no attachment to the hive, and did not fall under the will of its leader. How long that would last, no one could say.

All anyone really knew for sure was the fact that this virus had the potential to become a plague even worse than the Black Death. It wouldn't just *kill* millions; it would change them, thereby making them an even greater threat to those who remained uninfected.

Unfortunately, the two scientists who'd been leading the charge for a vaccine were now infected themselves, and under the control of the hive.

As situations went, it was pretty damn dire.

And it wasn't helped by the fact that the sindicati—the vampire equivalent of the mafia—were also after both the scientists *and* the missing research notes. Vampires could be infected as easily as humans, but I suspected their interest in a cure was more monetary based than self-preservation. The government had already gone to great lengths to keep this outbreak a secret, so it was a given they'd pay billions to get either a vaccine or a cure.

The man who'd been operating the small excavator climbed out of the cabin and walked to the edge of the grave where a second cemetery worker already stood.

He looked down into the hole for a second then glanced at Sam and said, "Do you want me to start the opening procedure now, sir?"

Sam nodded, the movement sharp. Abrupt. Tension rolled off him in waves and held within it hints of fear and resignation. He might not want the leader of the cloaks to be Luke, but he, like me, had all but come to accept the fact that *this* time, the sindicati had been telling the truth.

Not that Anthony De Luca—the leader of the faction currently trying to wrest control from the vampires they considered too old-school and out-of-date to be running the sindacati, and who'd given me the information—had had any reason to lie. He'd thought he was safe simply because he had sole control over both Mark Baltimore's and Professor Wilson's original research notes and that it would protect him from both his red cloak partners and from his opposition in the sindicati. He'd been wrong—at least when it came to the latter.

With De Luca now dead, the notes he'd so carefully guarded were out there somewhere in the wider world to be found, as, apparently, were the backups of Professor Wilson's notes. Of course, the two sindicati factions and PIT weren't the only ones currently scrambling to find those notes. The red cloaks undoubtedly were, too. They might control the two scientists, but their job would be made far easier if they didn't have to start from scratch.

The cemetery worker climbed into a harness and was lowered into the opened grave. There was a soft thud as he landed on the coffin's lid. It wasn't a wooden sound—it was metallic.

I glanced at Sam in surprise. "You buried him in a metal coffin?"

"It's lead-lined rather than mere metal, and the choice was out of my hands." His voice was grim. "The government didn't want to risk toxins leaching into soil—not when we have no real understanding of the virus."

I frowned. "But isn't the virus transferred via a bite or scratch? Besides, it can take twenty years or more for a normal coffin to decompose, so it's doubtful whatever is left of the body by then would actually infect the soil."

"Maybe. Maybe not." He shrugged. "I can understand them not wanting to take the risk, however, given there *are* toxins out there that remain viable basically forever."

"Yeah, but this is a virus, not a toxin."

"A virus that transforms cells in a way no one yet understands. In *any* case like this, it's better to be safe than sorry."

"So why not cremate him?"

"Luke didn't believe in it."

I frowned. "I didn't think Luke was religious."

"He wasn't. He had this weird fear of being declared dead only to wake up as he was going into the cremator." Sam shrugged. "I know that wouldn't have happened, but a regular burial was the least I could do for him."

If the authorities were so worried about contamination, I had to wonder why they hadn't insisted. But then, maybe they'd also feared this thing could mutate and become airborne.

As the worker aboveground tossed what looked like a bolt cutter down to his partner, Sam made a low sound deep in his throat and strode into the full circle of the nearby floodlight. It gave his short black hair an almost bluish shine, and somehow emphasized the leanness of his athletic frame. There wasn't a scrap of fat on him these days; it had all been eaten away by the virus he was still fighting. But while all that was left was muscle and bone, he was still a very good-looking man.

Of course, given the fact that the heart of a phoenix is fated to find love only once each lifetime, and Sam was my allotted love *this* time around, I'd be attracted to him no matter what.

I trailed after him. The metal coffin gleamed in the shadows of the grave pit, its surface untarnished by time or earth. There was no indication of damage or attack from either within or without; it could have been buried yesterday rather than over a year ago.

The worker inside the grave seemed to be struggling to get the casket open, even with the use of bolt cutters. The padlock was *huge*. The government really *had* been serious about not letting any contaminants out.

So how the hell had Luke escaped?

"Is that the same padlock he was buried with?" I asked.

Sam shrugged. "It looks like the same type, but I guess we'll know for sure when the damn thing is opened."

I could have gotten it open in half a second. Even if

the lock were made of tungsten metal, it would have melted quickly enough under the full force of the flames that were mine to call. But that would have meant revealing myself as something other than human to the two cemetery workers, and I wasn't about to risk that. Vampires and werewolves might be out and proud, but the rest of us remained well and truly closeted—and with damn good reason. While humanity had, on the whole, accepted the presence of vamps and weres in the world with surprising calm, there were still many who figured their very existence was a crime against nature, and one that needed to be dealt with. Nightly hunting parties were a growing problem, even if it was one the vamps and weres had so far ignored.

If they ever *did* decide to react to the situation, heaven help humanity.

The lock finally snapped. The coffin was unlatched, and then the bolt cutter was exchanged for a rope. Once it was securely tied to the lid portion of the coffin, the worker was hauled out.

"We've been ordered to stand well clear of the grave when the coffin is opened." He tossed the rope to Sam. "Give us five minutes before you do so."

Sam nodded. His grip on the rope was so tight his knuckles were white, but his expression remained as neutral as ever. He hadn't always been this calm, this controlled. And while it would have been easy to blame the virus, I doubted *that* was the true source. Any man who'd killed his brother, and who felt a personal obligation to hunt down as many of the cloaks as he could, would have both witnessed *and* caused much bloodshed. In that sort of situation, you had two choices—control your emotions or go crazy. The former was always a better option than the latter. I knew that from experience.

The two men climbed into the excavator. A heartbeat later, the machine was turned and began to trundle away, its bright headlights piercing the shadows.

Once it was out of sight, Sam moved around the grave then glanced at me. "You ready?"

I nodded and took my hands out of my pockets. Sparks danced across my fingertips, tiny fireflies that spun into the night and quickly disappeared. Just because I knew Luke wouldn't be in that coffin didn't mean someone—or some*thing*—else wasn't. Luke had never been stupid; he'd know he couldn't possibly keep his resurrection a secret forever and that, eventually, his grave would be checked. He'd have something planned—of that I had no doubt.

Sam took a deep breath and released it slowly. His tension echoed through me.

With a quick but powerful motion, he yanked the rope back. With little sound, the lid opened.

The coffin was empty.

Nothing waited within. Not a body, not a trap. The sparks died as my tension slipped away.

"Well, the sindicati weren't lying. Neither were your eyes." Sam's voice still held little in the way of inflection, yet I could feel the rise of anger in him. It wasn't, in any way, aimed at me, but it was fierce, dark, and thick with the desire to hunt, to kill. Goose bumps fled down my spine, and it was all I could do to stay where I was and *not* run from the sheer force of it. "Luke *is* alive."

"Not only alive, but in charge of the red cloaks." The words were out before I could stop them, and I silently cursed. I really *didn't* need to poke the proverbial bear any further, if only because the darkness within him—the darkness that was the virus—had risen along with his anger, and *that* was very, very dangerous. He might not want to harm me, but who knew what would happen if that darkness ever gained full control.

"Yes." His gaze rose to mine. In the blue of his eyes, grief shone. Grief and disbelief. Despite the evidence, despite his words, despite me telling him what I'd seen, he still didn't want to believe his brother was capable of so much chaos.

"What will you do now?" The desire to go around and comfort him was so strong I actually took a step toward him. But while the Sam of old might have welcomed such an action, *this* one certainly wouldn't. Not from me, at any rate.

"I'll do exactly what I've been doing." The grief had disappeared from his expression, but the anger remained. "And this time, when I find him, I'll make sure he stays dead."

"Good luck with that," an all-too-familiar voice said. "Because you certainly haven't had much success so far with your quest to erase us."

I jumped and swung around, flames instinctively burning across my fingers as I scanned the night. Luke's voice had come from the trees to the left of the floodlight, but there was absolutely no sense of him. As far as I could tell, there was no one and nothing nearby in that section of the cemetery.

"Come out and face us, Luke." Sam's voice was low

and very, *very* controlled. "Or are you still that same little coward hiding behind excuses and the strength of others?"

"My, my, we have gotten bitter since the infection, haven't we?" There was an almost jovial note in Luke's cool tone. "But then, I guess hunting a killer that is little more than a ghost will do that to anyone."

"You're no ghost," I snapped. I desperately wanted to unleash my flames, but it would be a pointless action until I actually had a target. "You're not even immortal. And you certainly bleed as profusely as anyone else when shot."

"You're right." His voice was still amused, but the edge of ice was stronger. "I do owe you one for that shoulder wound, you know. And bringing that building down on top of me was *very* impolite of you."

I snorted. "Next time we meet, I'll make sure the damn building *actually* kills you."

"Oh, I have no doubt that the next time we meet *will* be the last time—but for you rather than me."

"Says the man who's currently hiding behind shadows and trees," Sam said. "Come out and face us if you're so damn confident."

"I would love to, but, unfortunately, the aforementioned building collapse has seriously curtailed my movements in the short term."

Which suggested he wasn't actually near. I frowned and glanced over at Sam. He half shrugged and motioned me to keep on speaking.

"I can assure you, Luke, that *wasn't* my intention."

Sam stepped out of the floodlit area and merged

with the deeper darkness of night. It was a vampire trick, one the virus had gifted him. I wasn't sure if all those infected with the virus got the ability, as few of the madder red cloaks—the ones who had the scythe-like brand burned into their cheeks—seemed to use it. Luke *did* have the ability, but even if he were using it, I should have sensed him—unless, of course, he was using some form of magic to distort my senses.

But if he *was* close, why hadn't he said anything about Sam leaving the grave site? Was that exactly what he wanted—me and Sam separated—or was there something else going on here?

"Oh, you made your intentions clear enough." The last shreds of amusement had left Luke's tone. All that remained was ice and fury. "Now let me make mine clear—"

"We're all *very* aware of your intentions," I cut in. The quickest way to annoy Luke had always been to interrupt when he was speaking—and when he was angry, he tended to react without thought. Right now, with Sam off in the trees trying to find him, keeping his attention *and* annoyance on me would hopefully mean he wasn't paying attention to everything else that was going on around him. "But history is littered with would-be dictators like you, and each and every one of them was doomed to failure from the beginning. Just as you are."

"They weren't in possession of a virus capable of infecting the world and making it mine," he spat back.

"The world would be yours for only as long as it takes to make a cure or a vaccine." I crossed my arms and wondered why the hell Sam was taking so long. Surely, given the clarity of Luke's voice, he couldn't be *that* far away.

"By the time *that* happens—if it ever happens—my army will be vast," Luke growled, "and not even your flames will be strong enough to stop my rampage."

"I wouldn't be so sure of that, Luke. You've only had a very small taste of what I'm actually capable of."

"Ah, but now that I have, I can work on ways to counter it."

A chill ran through me. The flames of a phoenix certainly *could* be curtailed, and one of those methods had been employed by the sindicati only a few nights ago. The last thing I needed was a psycho like Luke getting his hands on *that* sort of magic.

"You might want to talk to Parella about how well that worked out for him," I snapped back, glad my voice was absent of the fear churning my gut.

"Oh, if I ever get near *that* piece of vampire scum, talking is the last thing I'll be doing with him."

Meaning Parella had better watch his back, because I needed him alive. I had no love for vampires *or* the sindicati, but Parella and I had something of a truce going—he'd agreed to keep his men off my tail until I found Wilson's backup notes. It gave us breathing space—not much, granted, but at least it meant there was one less group we had to worry about. If he got himself killed, there was no guarantee his replacement would keep that agreement.

My gaze swept the tree-filled darkness beyond the floodlight. I still had no sense of Luke, though I was aware enough of Sam's position. His presence reminded me of a winter storm—filled with ice and the promise of fury. So why was it taking so long to uncover where Luke was—or wasn't?

"Look," I said, my tone holding a hint of the frustration that swirled through me. "It's been nice catching up with you again, but is there *any* point to this whole conversation? Have you decided to hand yourself in or what?"

He laughed. It was a high, not altogether pleasant sound. He might not be one of the crazy ones, but he sure as hell wasn't far off it, either.

"There is a point to *everything* I do," he replied. "And you had better remember that."

I snorted. "Yeah, okay. If you say so."

He made a low sound that was an odd mix of a growl and a curse. "Perhaps a small demonstration—"

"Oh, don't feel obliged," I said. "Because we both know it will seriously hamper your domination plans if you lost any more of your soldiers right now."

"Oh, I have no intention of losing soldiers." His tone once again held an edge of smugness, and the flames flickering across my fingertips flared brighter. "After all, we both know that if you're incapable of making fire, you're of very little threat."

And with that, an unnatural force began to unfold around me. It was a wash of energy that stung my skin and had the hairs at the back of my neck standing on end.

Because it wasn't *just* energy—it was magic. The type of magic that could restrict a phoenix's fire.

And not only would it curtail my ability to create fire, but it would also hamper my access to the earth mother, and the mother was the only force capable of utter and instant annihilation of the cloaks—or anyone else I decided to direct her against, for that matter. She was the heat of the earth, the energy that gave life to the world around us, a power that was dangerous and deadly to even those of us who could call her into being. But the risk was often worth it, especially in a case like this. My own flames, while they burned the cloaks, took longer—and that was never a good thing when fighting against greater numbers.

And I had no doubt that, despite his words, Luke would throw more than a few red cloaks at us. He'd always favored having the odds on his side.

I reached for my fire form, but even as I changed from flesh to spirit, the magic tore at my skin, trying to restrain me, to stop me.

It failed.

I surged up, away from the ground and the net seeking to encase me. Threads of energy briefly chased me then snapped away. I paused and turned, but didn't relax. The magic was still active, even if it couldn't get me right now. What I needed to do was find the source of the damn spell and deactivate the stupid thing.

My gaze swept the ground, but I didn't immediately see anything odd or out of place. I moved out of the floodlit area, my flames casting an orange glow across the ground.

That's when I saw them. Four stones, each gleaming a soft, almost blue-black in the darkness. Spell stones—stones that provided both a base for the magic to latch onto and a means to restrict and control the size of the spell. While the use of stones was common among witches, the color of these suggested the creator of the spell walked a darker path with his magic. White witches drew on the energy of the world around them in conjunction with the strength that came from within, and the stones they used tended to reflect the purity of that. Those who used black magic—or blood magic, as it was more commonly known these days—often didn't need them, but when they did, their darkness was reflected in the stone's surface.

A twig snapped in the trees behind me. I spun, my flames surging in response. But it wasn't Luke or the cloaks, as I'd half feared. It was Sam.

"Luke isn't here," he said, his voice vibrating with fury. "He was using a fucking speaker."

He threw some wiring on the ground, then stopped abruptly as he spotted me. "Emberly? What the *fuck* is going on?"

It was pointless answering, given only another phoenix could actually understand me when I was in my fire form. Instead, I spun and surged toward the nearest stone. I had no idea how the spell was constructed, but I knew it could usually be undone if one of the stones was dislodged.

But even as I moved, figures erupted from the trees behind me. They were twisted, ugly beings with scars that resembled death's scythe burned into their cheeks.

Red cloaks. The *mad* kind.

They didn't run at me. They ran at Sam.

"You always were an untrustworthy bastard, brother dearest," Sam muttered. With that, he pulled out a gun and began firing. Blood and brain matter sprayed across the nearby tree trunks, but it didn't stop the tide.

There were far too many of them for one man, and one gun.

I cursed and reached for the force of the world, for the mother herself. She answered immediately, her energy wild, powerful, and difficult to contain. Not that I wanted to do that right now. I flung my hands wide and aimed her force at the cloaks. She surged through me and leapt almost joyously into the night, separating into multiple streams of flame that burned with all the colors of creation. Each finger hit one of the red cloaks and wrapped almost lovingly around them. Her flames pulsed, briefly darkening, as if in distaste.

Then she burned.

In an instant, the cloaks were little more than cinders fluttering gently to the ground.

When they were all gone, I released my hold on the mother. Her flames shimmered brightly for several seconds, then dissipated, the energy of them returning to the air and the earth itself.

Weakness washed through me. There was always a cost to calling such power into being, and this weakness was just the start of it. If I ever held on to her for too long, she would drain me until there was nothing left—no heat, no flame, and no life. She would take me into her bosom, into the earth itself, and there would be no escape. No rebirth.

Not something I ever wanted. I might be tired of the curse that bound phoenixes to endless lifetimes of having their hearts broken, but I wasn't yet tired of life itself.

I spun, dropped to the ground, and, even as the magic surged toward me, sent a lance of fire at the nearest black stone. Its surface began to glow as my flames hit it, but it didn't immediately move out of alignment. I swore and pushed harder; the color of my flames changed from orange to white, but it seemed to make no difference. Then, just as the magic began to twine around the fiery edges of my spirit form, the stone exploded. Sharp splinters speared through the night and a shock wave of energy sent me tumbling. I hit the ground and skidded along the dirt for several yards, ending up in flesh form and hard up against the trunk of an old pine.

I winced as I rolled onto my back. "That fucking *hurt*."

"Hitting a tree *that* hard generally does." Sam squatted beside me. "You okay?"

I opened one eye and glared up at him. "Do I look okay?"

The smile that briefly teased his lips was a pale imitation of the one that sometimes haunted my dreams, but I was nevertheless happy to see it. It meant that, despite the shadows in his eyes, despite the darkness I could almost taste, he was in control.

"You look pale, tired, grubby, and your lovely red hair rather resembles a bird's nest." His smile grew a fraction, briefly touching the corners of his bright eyes. "But other than all that, yeah, you look okay."

I snorted and sat upright. His hand hovered near my spine, not touching me, but close enough that I could feel the chill radiating from his skin—another gift of the damn virus.

"If Luke wasn't actually here, how did he know we were? Was there a camera attached to the speaker?"

"No, but there was a microphone." He rose and offered me a hand. "There must have been some form of alarm in the casket that let him know when we opened it."

I gripped his fingers and allowed him to pull me up. "But how did he know we were going to be here tonight?"

Sam released me and stepped back. I couldn't help noticing that the hand that had held mine was now clenched, as if to retain the lingering heat of my touch. Or maybe *that* was just wishful thinking by the stupid, deep-down part of me that refused to give up hope.

"He couldn't have. I checked both the perimeter and the cemetery itself before I gave the go-ahead to exhume the body. There was no one and nothing here."

"Then how did those red cloaks get here so fast?" I tucked my shirt back into my jeans. Thankfully, the magic that allowed us to shift from one form to another also took anything that was touching our skin—clothes, watches, etcetera—with it. Unlike werewolves, we didn't end up wearing rags after shifting shape.

He shrugged. "The virus endows many vampire-like qualities, including speed."

"Not even Superman could have gotten here on foot from Brooklyn so fast," I said. "There were barely ten minutes between us opening the casket and them attacking."

"Maybe he had a small squad of them on standby. There are plenty of drain outlets nearby, and that seems to be their chosen method of moving about."

That was certainly possible, but part of me doubted it. He had to have known Sam, at least, would be here tonight. And he would have guessed that curiosity would also drive me here, if only to support Sam.

"You don't believe that any more than I do." I paused, then added softly, "He knew we were coming, Sam."

"It wasn't Rochelle."

"Are you sure?"

"Yes, because I didn't tell her. Only my boss knew what was going on tonight."

"Your boss, and the security team who monitors your every move."

He hesitated then nodded. "They wouldn't have given her the information, though."

"Are you sure of that?"

"Yes." His voice was flat. "It wasn't her, Em."

I let it go. It was pointless arguing, because he was never going to believe that the woman he was sleeping with would betray him that way.

Which was odd given his belief that I *had*.

Of course, my betrayal had come out of necessity rather than choice—something he'd refused to hear back then. He knew the truth now, when it was all far too late.

"Then there's the magic—"

"Magic?" he cut in. "Where?"

I waved a hand to the black patch of soil that had once held the spell stone. "And it was a strong spell, too, but it's one that can't be set up too far in advance."

His gaze swept me, and it was a cold, judgmental thing. "Since when did you become an expert in magic?"

"I'm not, but I've been around a very—"

He clapped a hand over my mouth, the movement so fast I squeaked in surprise. He released me almost immediately and motioned me to remain silent as his gaze swept the night and his expression grew dark.

"Fuck," he said, his voice a low growl. "That's all we need."

"What?" I kept my reply low and studied the trees around us. I couldn't see anything out of place, nor could I sense anything or anyone approaching. But the senses of a vampire—or even a pseudo vampire—were far sharper than those of a phoenix. I might be able to sense the heat in others, but if they *had* none, or if it was concealed in some way, it left me as blind as any human.

Which meant, if there *was* a threat out there, it could really have only one source.

His next words confirmed my fears.

"Vampires," he said. "Six of them. And they're coming straight at us."

Chapter 2

"Why the fuck are *vampires* here?"

Surely Parella wouldn't have gone back on his promise? Not yet, anyway. He was smart enough to realize the notes wouldn't be found here, in the grave of a man who'd been buried over a year ago. Granted, it would make a brilliant hiding spot if you *did* want to hide something, but it wouldn't be an easy place to access—and De Luca had said he'd doled out the research notes on an as-needed basis.

"Until we know which faction they belong to," Sam bit back, "it's kinda hard to say."

My gaze jumped to his. "So you do think they're sindicati?"

"Who else would they be?" He began reloading his gun. "They're the biggest crime syndicate in the city—human, wolf, *or* vampire. And while the rest of them might know there's a problem in Brooklyn, they're not—as far as we know—aware of its source."

Because PIT was keeping them—and everyone else—in the dark about both the virus and the red cloaks. The trouble in Brooklyn had certainly been in the news of late, but everyone still blamed the crooks and the homeless who'd once called that place home. "That doesn't mean it can't be someone else. Hell, for all we know, it's just a random gang of vamps out for bit of fun and bloodshed."

He snorted. "Most vamps these days know better than to try something like that. Besides, no one else but the sindicati have links to the cloaks. I doubt it's coincidence they're here at the same time."

I scanned the night but still couldn't see or sense them. "Can you tell the mood they're in from this distance?"

"They're vampires, so no. But I suspect they're not coming here to discuss the weather." He gave me a somewhat deadpan look, but the hint of a smile once again teased the corners of his lips. "Let's move into the middle of the clearing. It'll give me more shooting time."

Only by a fraction, given the speed with which vampires could move. But I guessed a fraction was better than nothing. I didn't immediately follow him, however, but instead walked over to the floodlight to shut it down. The darkness might be more the vampire's friend than mine, but I didn't need my eyesight compromised by the brightness of that light if I happened to glance at it, either.

"How are we going to play this?" I stopped beside Sam once more and flexed my fingers. Heat burned through my body, but I kept my weapon leashed.

He raised an eyebrow, the amusement stronger. "It's simple. You burn them; I'll shoot them."

"And if they're not here to actually harm us?"

"If they aren't here to harm us, they wouldn't be coming at us full speed and in stealth mode." He paused, gaze narrowing. "They've just split up. Three of them are circling around behind us."

Coming at us from two directions was definitely better than coming at us from all sides—although *that* might yet be their plan. "You know, it might be a whole lot more sensible right now to get the hell out of here."

"Probably."

"Then why aren't we?"

"Because while you're a spirit capable of speed and flight, I'm merely human."

"Not when you're infected by the virus, you're not." I studied him, eyes narrowed. Saw within him the desire to stand his ground and fight. "This is stubbornness and pride: nothing more, nothing less."

"Perhaps." The amusement faded. "But—infected or not—I'm not as fast as those vamps. Faster than I once was, yes, but they *will* run me down. I'd rather stand my ground than be hunted like an animal."

"Which is a logical enough excuse, but we both know I was right the first time."

I flexed my fingers again. My skin glowed a vivid red, but I continued to keep the sparks and flames in check. I wasn't about to waste energy, not when I'd already expended a lot calling up the mother to crisp the red cloaks.

"You can hardly call me stubborn when there's nothing stopping you from doing the sensible thing and getting the hell out of here." That hint of amusement was back in his voice and it sent a warm shiver down my spine.

"Sensible never was one of my better traits." *Especially* when it came to this man. "Besides, I didn't save your butt from the red cloaks just to have vampires turn around and kill you."

"Death doesn't frighten me."

"Does anything actually frighten you these days?"

His gaze met mine and something within me stilled. Just for an instant, everything we'd once shared—all the heat, the passion, and the love—surged between us. But it was gone just as quickly, leaving in its wake the bitter ashes of memory and regret.

"Yes." He looked away. "I fear becoming what my brother is. Or, worse, one of the mad ones."

"If that was what fate intended, you would have turned down that path by now."

"Maybe." His voice was flat. "But the poison still crawls through my veins, Em, and every day it grows stronger."

"But so do you." Thankfully, my voice was free of the fear that surged at his words. "You're in far greater control now than you seemed to be when I first met you."

"Because I finally gave in to the inevitable." His voice was edged with bitterness, but before I could question what he meant, he added, "Back-to-back. They're almost on us."

I obeyed. Even through his clothing, I could feel the coolness of his skin. But there was strength there, too, and determination, and both were very comforting. He might fear becoming what Luke was, but he wouldn't go down that path easily.

I took a deep breath and slowly released it. It didn't do a whole lot to ease the tension riding me, but then, it never did. I waited, listening, but couldn't hear anything beyond the occasional rustle of possums in the nearby trees.

"Half a minute, if that," Sam murmured. "Be ready."

"If I were any more ready," I bit back, "you'd be soot on the ground right now."

He chuckled softly. "You know, I really miss your snark."

And I really miss you. But I held the words in check. Missing my sarcasm was *not* the same as missing me. This man had broken my heart once already. I couldn't let it happen again, no matter what that stupid part me that refused to let go might want.

"And," he murmured, "the fun begins."

With that, he fired. The gunshot echoed through the otherwise hushed cemetery, meaning that *this* time, he wasn't using a silencer. I briefly wondered why, then raised a hand and sent a rope of fire spinning forward. Though it didn't connect with anything, darkness briefly blocked my vision of the tree to my right—a vampire, cloaked in shadows. I narrowed my gaze, formed my fire into a lasso, and flicked it after him. One of the others shouted a warning, but it was already too late. As my lasso settled around his shoulders, I snapped it taut. He screamed and went down, and the smell of burning flesh began to stain the air. But I had no intentions of killing him—or even burning him any more seriously—because a dead man could answer no questions.

I snapped the flames away, but left him entwined in fire and pinned to the ground. Another shot rang out, and this time someone cursed—a sound that was cut off as Sam fired again. *He* obviously wasn't too bothered about uncovering the reason behind the attack.

Another shadow swept past the trees, this time to my left. I flung a stream of fire after him but caught nothing. Maybe he'd ducked behind a tree trunk. I looped my fire around, intending to flush him out, just as another shot echoed. But this time, it didn't come from Sam's gun.

It came from the vampires.

Sam jerked and swore, the sound a mix of anger and pain. I had no doubt the next shot would either take him out completely, or perhaps even me. Because when I was flesh, I was just as vulnerable to bullets as anyone else. Nor could my flames actually *stop* them—not unless it was a wall of fire thick enough to melt them.

Even so, flames exploded from me. I quickly pulled them back so that I didn't burn Sam and then cast them into a high circle around us. It might not stop bullets but would at least prevent the vampires from seeing where we were and what we were doing.

With that done, I spun and pushed Sam into the open grave.

Though I had to have taken him by surprise, he nevertheless landed on his feet and with little noise.

"What the fuck . . ." He cut the sound off as I landed lightly beside him. A heartbeat later, a bullet pinged off the top edge of the grave, showering us with dirt and grass.

"Unless they want to chance my fire or they've suddenly developed bullets that can turn in midair," I said, "we're at least safe here."

"But for how long?" he growled. "You can't hold the fire forever, Em. You're just delaying the inevitable."

"Let me worry about that. You just stop the fucking bleeding."

"I won't die of blood—"

"You're only a *pseudo* vampire," I interrupted. "Unless you've experienced bleeding out before, you can't be sure of that. Now tend to that wound while I take care of these bastards."

I called again to the mother. As her power surged, I quickly wove her into the net that already surrounded us, providing not only a backup barrier against the vampires, but one that would protect Sam from the bullets.

But she was also the only thing beside daylight that could force shadows away from vampires. To hunt these bastards quickly and efficiently, I needed to be able to see them properly.

"Em, don't . . ."

But he was talking to air. Or rather, fire. I was already streaking out of the grave and into the wall of heat that was the mother's flames. They wrapped around me, cocooned me, drawing me deeper into the heart of her, where it wasn't only fire but the force of the world, of life itself. It was an intoxicating sensation for any being made of fire and, just for a second, I let it roll through me. God, it would be so easy to let go, to remain forever in her embrace . . .

It was a thought that cut like ice through the growing haze of rapture. I'd never merged with the mother so completely before, and really had no idea just how dangerously alluring it could be. I tore myself free from her grip, even as the tendrils of her energy clung to me, trying to draw me back.

I moved farther away, until those tendrils no longer threatened, then spun. The mother's light had indeed torn the shadows away from the vampires.

Four of the remaining five stalked around the barriers

I'd raised, randomly firing into the flames. Either they had no idea the bullets were melting long before they ever reached their target, or they just didn't care. The fifth vampire was striding toward the vamp I'd lassoed, his gun held loosely by his side. I had no idea if he was about to attempt to release my captive or kill him, but either way, he had to be stopped.

I flung fire at him—not the mother's fire, but my own. It was deadly enough in its own right, but I didn't actually burn him. I just grabbed him, raised him, and threw him—hard—against the nearest tree. Vampires might be able to heal themselves of almost any wound, but they could be knocked out just as easily as humans. There was a loud crack as he hit the tree, suggesting I'd broken either his ribs, an arm, or maybe even both. Not that I really cared—not when our death had obviously been *their* intent.

More shots rang out. Multiple bullets hit me, the metal cold as it tore through my spirit form in an almost endless stream. It seemed whoever had sent them here had failed to tell them guns were an ineffective weapon against spirits of *any* kind.

I cast four streams of fire and sent them spiraling forward. The vampires immediately ran in the opposite direction, but they never had a hope. I caught each one, flung them into trees, and knocked them out.

Once I'd checked that they were all out cold, I released the mother and regained flesh form. My knees hit the ground hard, and a mix of shock and pain reverberated though the rest of me. My whole body shook with the force of it, and I couldn't seem to suck in air fast enough. *This* was the price I paid for merging—however briefly—with the mother. Had I stayed a few minutes longer, I might not have had the strength to return to my flesh form at all.

And *that* was not only scary, but would have seriously pissed off Rory.

He was my other half, the phoenix I was forever linked to, and the only man I could ever have children with. He was as vital to my continued existence in this world as I was to his, because a phoenix could be reborn only by a ceremony performed by their phoenix partner.

And he really wanted to get through a lifetime without one of us dying before our allotted one hundred years was up.

Given all the shit currently being flung our way, I wasn't sure it was a wish he was going to get in *this* lifetime.

A grunt of pain caught my attention. I sucked in more air then forced my eyes open. Sam had climbed out of the grave and was standing—somewhat precariously—on one leg. Though he'd torn off a shirtsleeve to use as a tourniquet around his left thigh, the stain that darkened his jeans still seemed to be growing, even if at a slower rate.

"You need to call an ambulance," I all but croaked. "That wound looks bad."

"And you look even worse." His voice was grim. Angry.

Help, it seemed, wasn't on his agenda right now. Not for either of us. I briefly felt a little sorry for the vampires.

But only briefly.

I pushed upright. The world spun madly around me, and I thrust a hand against the nearby tree to steady myself. "The one encased in flame is awake. You want to question him?"

"Questioning him *would* be the sensible option." He hobbled forward, one hand on his wound and blood oozing slowly through his fingers.

The vampire looked up and snarled, revealing somewhat stained yellow teeth. Given he didn't look any more than twenty in human terms, he'd obviously never taken any notice of hygiene lessons before he'd become a vampire. While turning made humans as close to immortal as they were ever likely to get, it didn't alter whatever problems they'd had as humans. Bad teeth would always be bad teeth, and the wheelchair bound would forever be so.

"You're fucking dead meat." Weirdly, the vampire's gaze was on me rather than Sam. "This won't be the end of it."

"You want to wrap those flames a bit tighter around this bit of scum?" Sam's voice was remote. Disinterested.

But then, he faced death—or worse, madness—every day of his life. The threats of vampires were hardly likely to concern him.

I took a somewhat shuddery breath and did so. But the mother's demands had seriously compromised my strength, and keeping the vampire contained was taking more juice than I really had. My flames reached higher, briefly searing his rather pointed chin before I allowed them to die down again.

The vampire swore; it was a low, vicious sound.

"Next time," Sam said, "we'll burn your fucking face off. You may be able to heal such a wound, vampire, but you'll suffer in the process."

The vampire glanced from Sam to me then back again. "Fine," he growled. "What do you want to know?"

"Who sent you here, and why?"

"No one sent us. We came of our own accord."

"Vampire, you don't look old enough to make such heady decisions by yourself." Though Sam's expression remained neutral, that dark edge had crept back into his voice. The wise *wouldn't* be playing games right now. "Tell the truth, or this could get very ugly."

"It *is* the truth. And it's not like we have any other fucking choice right now, do we?"

"And why would that be?"

"Because *she* fucking killed our maker, didn't she?" He glared at me. "And it left us not only rudderless, but without the protection of an elder."

I raised my eyebrows. Newly turned vampires ran under the protection of their "creator"—the vamp who turned them—for the first twenty or so years of their "after" life, although it wasn't unusual for most to continue in their creator's den until they were ready to start their own. And *that* didn't happen until they were at least two hundred years old. Even then, the vampire elders—vamps who hit the "magic" one thousand years—kept very close control over who could and couldn't form their own dens. Vampires who ignored their ruling, or those who figured they could simply run outside it, very quickly learned otherwise. And their deaths were never pleasant, if what I'd been told—that they were torn apart by said elders—was right.

The strictness didn't come so much from a fear of humans—who for many older vampires were nothing more than a food source—but rather, the rest of us: the dark fae, the shifters, and the spirits. The elders knew from past experience that it really wasn't wise to annoy the supernatural community by allowing their numbers to get too out of control—that by doing so, they were endangering the existence of everyone. Humans might be weaker physically, but that didn't matter so much when they had both numbers *and* technology behind them.

Of course, this also meant elders had no time for vamps who'd lost their maker, and that generally meant they became little more than fodder for the rest of the dens. No master ever invited the spawn of another into his or her lair.

So *this* vampire's anger and need for revenge was understandable. I just didn't understand why he was blaming *me*.

Sam glanced at me. I half shrugged at his unspoken question and said, "As far as I'm aware, I haven't killed any masters of late."

"So you're denying you were at the recent Highpoint bust-up?" the vamp snapped. "That it was another fire witch, not you, who destroyed so many of my den mates?"

It was interesting that he'd called me a fire witch rather than a phoenix. Luke knew I was the latter, as did Parella, so that surely meant this vamp belonged to a different den entirely. But whose? Aside from the two sindicati factions, the only other vamp who appeared to be on our tail was the mysterious Professor Heaton. We had no idea who he was or what he actually wanted, and he hadn't been at Highpoint as far as I was aware.

I certainly *had* been, and I sure as hell had killed some vamps. But they'd been trying to either capture or kill me—I still wasn't sure which—so it was quid pro quo as far as I was concerned. None of them, as far as I knew, had been masters—and it wasn't like masters put themselves on the front lines too often anyway.

"If you're aware of that fight, then you're also aware that I was there at the invitation of Frank Parella." Which was something of a white lie, as I'd been the one who'd demanded that meeting, not Parella. "And you'll know that Parella walked away unharmed."

"I wasn't talking about Parella."

The way he said his name was a revelation in itself. "De Luca," I said. "You're from his den?"

"And, thanks to you, we're now without hearth and home." His fury was so fierce his whole body vibrated.

"Like I really care," I replied evenly. "But you're wrong about one thing—I didn't kill De Luca."

He snorted. "Liar. We know the truth."

"And were you there?" I said. "You saw De Luca die?"

I knew for a fact he *hadn't*. Beside me, the only people who had been there were Parella, whoever Parella had watching from a distance, and De Luca's men—both of whom had been either dead or unconscious.

"The red cloaks' master told us it was so," he spat back. "He has no reason to lie."

I snorted. Lying was part of Luke's nature, but it was interesting that he was lying in *this* particular case. And why wouldn't he tell his allies the truth about what I was? Or was it simply a matter of De Luca not passing the information on to everyone in his den?

"Given *he* wasn't there," I said, "you can hardly take his word as gospel."

"He didn't have to be there. His hive was, and they are one."

"Actually, no," I said. "There were no red cloaks there, either. And it was Parella who killed De Luca, not me."

The vampire's gaze narrowed. "Parella would not be so foolish."

"Why not? It's not like he and De Luca were on friendly terms, was it?"

"One master cannot kill another without a sanctified challenge," he spat back. "If he'd sought such a sanction, we would have heard."

"Maybe the rules changed when the sindacati split into factions."

"They did not—"

Sam made a low, almost animalistic sound then grabbed the vampire by the throat and lifted him off the ground. It was both a show of strength and an indication of just how inhuman he now was.

"Enough," he growled. My flames cast an orange glow across his pale features and made his blue eyes gleam with ruddy fire. "If you value your life, you will not come after either of us again. If you do, I will ensure every last one of you is hunted down and destroyed."

The vampire bared his teeth. It was a contemptuous action more than fear filled. "As if PIT has the people for such a task given the current situation."

Sam shook him. Hard. "If you or your den mates believe the current situation will benefit you in the long run, then you have no understanding of my brother."

The vamp's gaze narrowed slightly. "Your brother?"

"Luke Turner, erstwhile leader of the cloak hive. My brother."

"*That* is information we were not told."

"Oh, I'm betting there's a whole lot more that you're not being told, vampire. I suggest you go back to your den mates and seriously consider your options."

The vampire glanced at me. Though his expression gave little away, I very much believed the only option he'd be considering was how he and his den mates were going to kill me. He might fear PIT and Luke, but he feared being left without the protection of a den a whole lot more. Maybe he figured that killing me would somehow gain them respect and the possibility that the sindicati would, at the very least, consider them of use.

It was a very long shot, but I guess in his situation, I might have done the same.

The vamp's gaze returned to Sam. "I shall share the information with my den mates."

Which certainly wasn't a promise to back away. I half expected Sam to simply take him out, but he surprised me.

"Release him," he said, without glancing at me.

I hastily did so. Weakness washed through me, and I had to seriously concentrate on locking my knees just to remain upright. I really hoped the night wasn't going to throw any more surprises at me, because there wasn't all that much left in the tank.

Sam threw rather than released the vampire, but he landed catlike, his fingertips briefly brushing the ground as he found his balance.

Once upright, the vampire gave a somewhat mocking bow and said, "Thank you for your understanding."

Sam snorted. "Go, vampire, before I change my mind."

The vamp hesitated, then said, "And my companions?"

"Will live as long as they're also sensible and leave."

The vampire glanced at me then spun on his heels and walked away. I looked briefly at the other vamps. None of them appeared to be approaching any level of consciousness. I really *had* knocked them out cold.

My gaze returned to Sam's. "Why did you do that?"

He frowned as he walked over. "Do what?"

"Ask me to release him. You know as well as I do that this won't end here."

He grimaced and waved a hand in acknowledgment. "Yes, but as much as I sometimes might want to, I can't go around killing vampires willy-nilly."

I raised my eyebrows. "I thought PIT had carte blanche to bend the rules and apprehend crims in any way deemed fit?"

"Bend, yes. Break—well, that depends on the situation and what might be at stake."

"So the mere fact they attempted to kill us both isn't enough?" I shook my head and wondered what in the hell those vamps would have to have done before Sam disposed of them. I wasn't normally an advocate for skipping the whole law, order, and fair trial business, but in this particular case I was willing to make an exception. "PIT has some very strange ways, let me tell you."

"You don't know the half of it." His gaze swept me as he stopped. "You okay?"

I nodded. "Just tired. I need to go home and get some rest."

"Is your car nearby?"

I shook my head. "Rory's picking me up over near the main gates in . . ." I hesitated and glanced at my watch. "Fifteen minutes."

Other than the bitter smile that briefly twisted his lips, there was little in the way of reaction to Rory's name. He might still blame Rory's presence in my life for our breakup, but perhaps he was at least beginning to accept that he was a *necessary* presence.

I hoped so. It might be too late for the two of us, but it would be nice if at least in *one* lifetime I could remain friends with the man fate had decreed I would love and lose.

"Then I'll escort you." He half raised a hand, as if to touch my elbow, then dropped it again and simply motioned me forward. "So tell me, why the hell were you meeting with Parella?"

I hesitated then shrugged. There was little point in lying given PIT was undoubtedly aware of what had gone down at Highpoint, even if they didn't know the finer details.

"We exchanged some information for a pledge not to come after us until we found the missing research notes."

His expression darkened dangerously. "What sort of information?"

"Not the sort you're thinking," I replied evenly. "We told him that that De Luca was working with Luke and the cloaks, and that Rosen had been murdered."

Rosen was the man behind Rosen Pharmaceuticals—the company who'd hired Jackson—the dark fae I'd met during my investigation into Baltimore's murder, and the man who'd recently offered me a partnership in Hellfire Investigations, his PI agency—to find both Professor Wilson's murderer and the backup of the professor's research notes. We had thought Parella might have been behind his death, but his surprise at the news had squashed that.

"I'm surprised he didn't at least know the former."

"Apparently not, because he refused to believe me until De Luca himself confirmed it."

"And did you shoot De Luca?"

"No. Parella did." I hesitated again then added, "But not before De Luca had boasted that while Luke controlled the two scientists, *he* controlled all the research notes. And that he was the only one who knew where they were or had access to them."

Sam stopped me. His grip was fierce, but he almost instantly released me. "So Luke *hasn't* got either Baltimore or Wilson's notes?"

"No one has. They're still out there in whatever hidey spot De Luca put them in."

"*That* is good news."

Indeed it was; it meant the notes PIT held—the ones that had come from the books Mark Baltimore had given me to transcribe just before he'd been murdered—were currently the only ones available.

And hopefully, that gave whatever labs were now working on a vaccine a head start against Luke and his scientists.

"The only problem being Parella is well aware the notes are out there, and believes he will find them before the rest of us."

"Parella can believe what he wants." He motioned me forward again, and then fell in step beside me. "De Luca's offspring are not likely to ease off their quest for revenge. It might be better if you and Rory left the state until all this is over."

"I'm not running any more than you are."

"But as you noted earlier, it *is* the sensible choice."

"This is a very different situation." I squinted up at him. "Are you going to report the attack?"

"A leaderless den intent on revenge is a threat to *everyone*, so yes. Both the Australian Vampire Council and the local elders will be informed and action will undoubtedly be taken. They can't afford to have a leaderless den on the loose, if only because it would be a public relations nightmare." He half shrugged, an action that had his arm brushing mine ever so briefly. "You wouldn't have to leave for very long."

"Which doesn't alter the fact that I'm not doing it."

"What if they come after Rory?"

A chill ran through me; it wasn't fear but something else. Instinct. Foreboding. I tried to ignore it. It was pointless worrying until I had something more concrete than a vague feeling. I might be cursed with the ability to foresee death, but it usually came in the form of prophetic dreams. And while foreboding was sometimes a precursor to them, I'd learned a long time ago that the dreams would come when they're good and ready, and not before.

"Luke has already threatened that." I lightly rubbed my arms to erase the lingering chill of apprehension. "It resulted in me bringing a building down on top of him."

"Which *didn't* stop him. Nothing but death will stop him, and you know it."

"But at least I've come closer to achieving that goal than PIT has." Anger gave my tone bite. "What in the hell is your mob doing?"

"I don't know."

It was softly said, filled with repressed anger, and my gaze jumped to his. "What in hell is *that* supposed to mean? You're lead on this case—how could you *not* know what's going on?"

"It's simple. Rochelle and I are now under house arrest until this whole red cloak mess is sorted out."

I stopped abruptly and stared at him. "What?"

He grimaced and pressed a cool hand all too briefly against my spine, lightly pushing me on. "While I do not believe there's any sort of telepathic connection between Luke and myself—"

"There's not," I cut in. "He said that himself. He can read your emotions, not your thoughts."

Bitterness briefly crept into his expression. "You know as well as I that *anything* Luke says can't really be trusted."

"But in this case, I don't think he was lying—"

"And *we* cannot take a chance on your uncertainty,"

he said. "Especially given he *does* appear to have some sort of line into PIT. If not myself or Rochelle, then someone else."

"So by locking you two up, you can see whether or not there's another player in PIT's midst?"

"And Rochelle and I can keep an eye on each other."

Meaning they were locked up *together.* Annoyance—or maybe even jealousy—flitted through me. It was a useless emotion, given the situation, but one I instinctively couldn't help.

I briefly looked away. "That being the case, why were you allowed out tonight?"

He shrugged again, and again his arm brushed mine. Awareness and desire cascaded through me, and I silently cursed both Luke and fate for bringing this man back into my life.

Because, really, who was I kidding? I couldn't remain friends with him—not if I wanted to retain any sort of sanity. I might not be human, but I wasn't without a heart and a soul, and there was only so much pain I could stand in one lifetime.

"It wasn't a PIT mission, as such. It didn't really matter if Luke was aware of our actions."

Was there a hint of awareness in the soft rumble of his reply? Perhaps even a sliver of yearning? Or was that merely my endlessly hopeful heart hearing what it wanted to hear?

I took a breath and slowly released it. "That almost sounds like you were being used as bait."

"In many respects, I was."

I raised an eyebrow. "So where is the backup team?"

"There wasn't one. As the vamps noted, this whole situation has stretched PIT's resources to the limit."

"It hardly makes sense to use you as bait, then leave you without a backup team if the wolf comes calling."

He smiled, but it was a cold thing, containing little in the way of amusement. That hint of awareness and yearning—if indeed it had even existed—had very definitely fled.

"In this particular case, the bait is very capable of taking care of himself."

"In normal circumstances, yes, but there were too many red cloaks here tonight for even you to handle. They would have taken you—"

"Maybe not," he cut in. "Maybe they only attacked because *you* were here."

I blinked. "Why on earth would you think *that*?"

"Because of the vamps."

"I'm not seeing the connection—"

"They came here to kill *you*. And the information that you were here could have only come from Luke."

"Yes, so?"

His gaze met mine, blue eyes gleaming like ice in the darkness. "Given the speaker and microphone I found, Luke was obviously aware of both my presence at the grave site and the fact that I was all but alone. If snatching or killing me *had* been his sole goal, he could have ordered the cloaks to attack earlier. But he didn't—not until you arrived."

Given Luke had already told me his plans to capture—and torture—me, that was certainly more than a possibility. "Either way, PIT basically hung you out to dry, and that's not particularly nice of them."

He half smiled, but again, there was little in the way of humor in it. "You can hardly expect them to worry about the safety of someone who may be giving information to the enemy, even if unknowingly."

"If they thought *that*," I snapped, "they'd have killed you."

He didn't immediately say anything, but when he did, his voice was oddly wistful. "*That* option is still very much on the agenda."

Another of those almost prophetic chills ran through me. "You can't be serious! If anything, you're their best means of *capturing* Luke. If he's using a link to gather information, surely you—and they—can do the same?"

"He's the hive master, not me." He wasn't looking at me, wasn't looking at anything, really. Whatever he was seeing, it was internal rather than external. "I see nothing. Nothing beyond what he wants me to see."

The chill got stronger. "Meaning what, exactly?"

He glanced at me. Just for an instant, the darkness flared and all I could see, all I could taste, was the bitterness of death and destruction. Mine, his, the world's.

But it was gone in a nanosecond. He stopped and half shrugged. "I'll leave you here."

I glanced around. We were at the gate already. Obviously, Sam wasn't the only one not taking much notice of his surroundings.

"Sam . . ." I reached out to touch his arm, but he stepped back so swiftly he practically blurred.

I dropped my hand and clenched my fingers against the bitterness and anger that surged through me. It was a stupid response and one that deserved no time or thought.

"Keep safe, Em." His voice was remote. "And for god's sake, keep away from the cloaks and the sindicati."

That wasn't going to happen—not when our search for the missing research notes was now so entwined with both the cloaks and the vampires.

But he knew that as much as I did, so it was pointless replying.

A small, somewhat bitter smile briefly touched his lips, but he didn't say anything. He simply turned and hobbled away, his body merging with the night in an almost ghostlike manner.

Leaving me wondering if I was seeing his future.

Chapter 3

Rory had parked our small rental car just down from the gates. His gaze swept me as I climbed in, and concern flared in his amber eyes as his smile of greeting faded.

"I take it there was a problem?"

"You could say that." I leaned across the center console to kiss his cheek then quickly filled him in on not only the attacks, but also what the vamps had said. "It appears we now have something *else* to worry about."

He snorted softly. "I doubt whether another mob joining the *let's hunt the phoenixes* party is going to make *that* much difference to us right now."

"Maybe not." I thrust a somewhat shaky hand through my hair. "But it's not like we need an extra reason to be watching our backs, either."

"True." He started up the car. "Where to next?"

Home, I thought wistfully, because right now, I really wanted nothing more than to sleep in my own bed. But that wasn't an option given the aforementioned bad guys after our butts. Home was being watched by both the sindicati and PIT. And while we trusted PIT—up to a point, anyway—the same could not be said of the sindicati. Not even of the faction we had a temporary truce with.

"I need to sleep," I said. "But more than that, I need to recharge."

Recharging was something phoenix pairs had to do on a regular basis or face diminishing powers and death. It was a process that involved completely merging our energy and our spirits to both reinforce our connection and rejuvenate our strength. It was also the reason we could never let each other go. No matter how much we might love someone else, we could never remain completely faithful to him or her. Not if we wanted to live.

After a quick glance in the rearview mirror, Rory pulled out of the parking spot. "We can't risk doing that at the hostel. Even if we're careful, the place is a tinderbox."

Fire might be ours to control, but it wasn't something that was upmost on our minds when we were in the midst of recharging. Which is why we had a specific, fully fireproofed room in our apartment. But that option had gone by the wayside when we'd decided to go "off grid" a few days ago. We'd not only dumped our cars and our phones' SIM cards, but had also quit using our credit cards—and that meant most high-end hotels were out. Hell, even cheap motels required some form of card for security these days. Thankfully, Jackson had used this particular hostel before, and knew it had no such qualms as long as cash was paid up front.

"We could just drive up past Kilmore," Rory said, "There's plenty of open space up there."

I nodded and, as a familiar golden M came into

view, said, "But you can pull into McD's first. I'm in desperate need of a cup of tea and some fries."

He immediately headed into the drive-through to order my food and drink, as well as a coffee for himself. As he swung back out onto the highway, I carefully pulled the lid off the cup to let the tea cool then started munching on fries.

Rory leaned over to snag several then said, "Jackson's planning to do an early-morning raid on Rosen's house."

I groaned. "How early is early?"

Rory gave me a somewhat amused look, and my stomach sank. Obviously, this was *not* going to be a good night for catching up on sleep.

"He's talking four a.m."

I groaned again. "Why so early? It's not like it's going to make much difference if we go later. Besides, PIT will have searched the place already, and if anything was there to be found, it would now be gone."

"Actually, PIT hasn't searched it. The cops apparently did."

"What? Why?"

He shrugged. "Maybe they're short staffed. I actually suspect they're also using us to do some legwork for them—it's the only possible reason they haven't warned us away from Wilson's case. They want us to uncover the missing backup notes—if, indeed, they actually exist—so they can swoop in and snatch them."

Given what Sam had said about PIT being stretched to the limit, that was more than possible. Especially given our investigations were the only reason PIT currently had a copy of Baltimore's notes.

Of course, I also happened to be the reason De Luca's section of the sindicati had also gotten their hands on most of those same notes, but I could hardly be blamed for that when PIT and Sam had been reluctant to tell us not only about the virus, but also how important the notes were in trying to find a cure—or, at the very least, create a vaccine.

"But Rosen lived in a high-security apartment on Southbank. How the hell are we going to even get in there, let alone avoid all the surveillance? We won't be able to cut the alarms—that'll just bring everyone running. And we can't cut the power, because all systems have battery backup."

"All of which I said when he mentioned it."

"Did he also mention a plan to get around those two—rather major—problems? Or is he just planning to set fire to a substation, thereby cutting power to the entire area, and hope for a miracle?"

"Two questions I also asked, and was met with a *do I look that crude to you?* comment."

"I bet you said yes." Amusement ran through me. "I certainly would have."

Rory's grin grew. "A friend apparently works for the security company that looks after Rosen's building. He or she has access to a pass card for building and override codes for the apartment."

I blinked. "But won't unauthorized use of the override code raise all sorts of alarms back at the base?"

"Not if the person who has that code is scheduled to do an in situ maintenance check on the system."

Trust Jackson to know someone with *that* sort of

pull. I offered Rory some more fries. "Are you accompanying us on this venture?"

He shook his head at the offer and plucked his coffee from the holder instead. "I think it's safer if I remain in the background, at least when it comes to this sort of investigation or anything unrelated to the cloaks."

"You just like the idea of riding to the rescue if something goes wrong."

He chuckled softly. "Old habits do die hard."

I grinned. Rory had been a cavalry officer during several of his lifetimes, the last time as a redcoat in the British army during the eighteenth century. I'd managed to be one of the women chosen to follow their man into war during that period, but I'd hated my time there. As a camp follower, we wives had been expected to only cook and wash for all the soldiers, but we'd often acted as nurses. It was hard, dirty, and dangerous work, and lots of women died, as much from disease as from the war itself. Thankfully, as the military became more mechanized, the cavalry lost its appeal to Rory, and neither of us had seen action in any of the world wars.

We hit the Northern Highway and cruised on through the night, eventually finding a suitably barren-looking spot several kilometers north of Kilmore. Rory pulled off the road and stopped between two old trees. I climbed out and breathed deep. The air was cool but rich with the scent of eucalyptus and an approaching storm, and it went some way to washing the lingering tease of Sam's scent from my nostrils.

Rory walked around to the front of the vehicle and

held out a hand. As I clasped it, his fingers became flame, sending a shudder of longing running through me. Merging might be a necessity for us, but fate had at least allowed it to be pleasurable.

He led the way through the scrubby grass then held down the top couple of strands of the old barbed wire fence so that I could climb over. The paddock beyond was a wasteland of rocks, browned earth, and old eucalypts. There were no houses to be seen, nor was there any livestock—not that cows or sheep would hang around long. Not once we became full flame, anyway.

He came to a stop in the middle of a wide rocky circle and tugged me a little closer. "So," he said, his breath warm on my lips. "Fast or slow?"

"That's a main highway down there," I said, voice dry. "With the way our luck is running, someone will spot us and come running up with a fire extinguisher."

He chucked softly. "Fast, it is, then."

With that, he became flame. I threw back my head as the heat of him burned through me, my nostrils flaring as I sucked in the fierce glory of him. Desire surged, primal and hot, and my own fires ignited. They were a firestorm that ripped through every muscle, every cell, breaking them down and tearing them apart, until my flesh no longer existed and I was nothing but fire.

"Oh lord," he murmured, "that feels *so* good."

It certainly did. He was life, need, and necessity, and his essence flowed to every corner of my soul, reaffirming the connection between us and assuring that life went on.

But this dance wasn't *just* about affirmation. As we

moved, the fiery threads of our beings entwined, intensifying the pleasure, heightening the need. Soon there was no separation—no him, no me, nothing more than a growing storm of ecstasy. And still the dance went on, burning ever brighter, until the threads of our beings were drawn so tightly together it felt as if they would surely snap. Then everything *did*, and I fell into a fiery pit of bliss.

"That," I said, once I'd regained flesh form and had breath enough to talk again, "was a damn fine way to end an evening."

"That it was." He dropped a kiss on the top of my head then stepped back and offered me his hand again. This time, it was flesh rather than flame that met my fingers. "Shall we go?"

I nodded, and together we made our way back to the car. It took little more than forty-five minutes to drive back to Collingwood and The Journey Man, the old hostel that was our temporary home. It was actually a two-story pub on Johnson Street, with accommodation in the two floors above the bar, as well as several small apartments in the rear yard. Its exterior was as basic as the accommodation—the concrete walls were an odd green-gray color, and the ground-floor windows had been painted black. Though they were large, each one was made up of at least twelve smaller panes, some of which had been broken over the years and replaced by different-colored glass. The upper floor had smaller sash windows, and many were either stuck open or in serious need of repainting.

Rory swung into the street that ran along the side of the building and found parking only a few doors down from the rear entrance gate. We both climbed out and headed for the two-story shoe box the Journey Man's brochures rather grandly called "an apartment with all the mod cons." Which wasn't a lie if you considered something out of the last century modern.

I opened the screen door, then the somewhat battered main door, and walked in. The room inside was a combination of kitchen and living room, and was clean and functional despite its run-down, last-century facilities. I flung my purse on the nearest sofa and headed for the stairs.

"You're not stopping for tea?" Rory asked.

"Not if Jackson's intent on waking me at an ungodly hour." I blew him a kiss over my shoulder. "I'll see you tomorrow."

"Sleep tight. Don't let the bedbugs bite."

"They try, and I'll sizzle the little bastards."

With his laughter following me, I headed up the stairs, stripped off my clothes, and then collapsed into my allotted bunk. And not even Jackson's soft snoring could prevent sleep from claiming me.

A warm, rich aroma invaded my slumber. It took several minutes to register that it was tea and toast, and my mouth started watering even before my eyes were open. I might have eaten a large bag of fries before Rory and I had recharged, but my stomach was something of an endless pit. Thankfully, a phoenix's system ran far hotter than that of humans, and as a result, we could basically eat mountains of food without fear of putting of weight. Fate hadn't been a total bitch when it came to us, it seemed.

I scrubbed at the sleep clinging to my eyes then opened them. Though Jackson's body was little more than shadow, his emerald eyes gleamed brightly in the darkness. He was squatting in front of my bunk, a plate of buttered toast in one hand and a mug of steaming liquid in the other. Obviously, breakfast was being delivered bedside to make up for the obscene hour.

"Morning, sunshine." He looked altogether too bright and cheery, considering it was—according to the clock on the wall opposite—three o'clock in the goddamn morning.

"I thought you were planning a four o'clock raid?" I grumbled, keeping my voice as soft as his. Rory was asleep in the bunk above the one Jackson used, and I didn't want to disturb him. One of us might as well enjoy a good night's sleep.

"Which is why I'm waking you now. We need to be there by four to meet the tech who'll get us inside."

"Just as well you bought me tea, then."

I reached for the mug, but he pulled it out of my reach. "Nope, no food or refreshment until you get your lovely butt out of bed and into the shower. Oh, and wear dark blue. We leave in ten minutes, whether you're ready or not." He paused, and amusement glimmered in his eyes. "Personally, I'm hoping for not. It's been far too long since I've seen you in all your naked glory."

"You," I said darkly, "are positively evil."

"And you love it." He leaned forward, dropped a quick kiss on my lips, and then rose. "The clock is ticking."

I muttered something decidedly unpleasant at his

retreating back even as I was admiring the long, lean length of him. Dark fae in fiction bore very little resemblance to reality. They were neither small nor winged, and the only ones who were ethereal in *any* way were the air fae.

With another soft curse, I flung the covers off and got up. The night air was even colder at this hour, and goose bumps skittered across my skin as I padded over to my bag to gather fresh clothes, then headed for the shower.

I made it downstairs with a minute and a half to spare. Jackson's gaze scanned me critically; then a smile split his lips. "Luscious enough to eat."

"But definitely not on the menu, given we have time restrictions."

"Unfortunately, that is all too true." He handed me a plate of hot buttered toast smothered with jam and a travel mug of tea, and ushered me out the door.

"So who is this tech we're meeting?" I asked, munching on the toast as he put Rosen's address into the GPS. "I'm presuming it's a woman."

He gave me an offended look, though the gleam in his bright eyes somewhat gave the game away. "And why would you presume that?"

"Because you seem to have a number of lovers in very useful professions." Or, at least, professions a private eye might find useful.

"I do have male friends, you know."

"Yes, and I've met a couple of them. But that doesn't answer the question on the table."

He pulled out of the parking spot and followed the GPS's directions into the city. "Well, as it so happens, yes, Shona *is* female—but not, as you're obviously presuming, one of my current lovers. I only have time for one right now—and she has been sadly elusive of late."

I leaned across and patted his leg. His skin jumped at my touch and warmth flared—both in his eyes and in the air. Jackson was a fire fae, and they generally couldn't produce their own flame—they could only control fire that already existed, even if only as a spark. But that restriction had been shattered when I'd allowed Jackson's spirit to merge with mine in an effort to burn the red cloak virus from his body and save his life. We had no true idea yet what other ramifications there might be from the merging, although we could occasionally catch each other's thoughts now. Not all the time, and certainly not when it would be advantageous to do so, but it was still happening.

"Yes," he all but growled. "And if you're catching my thoughts now, you'll know it might be wise to remove your hand from the upper portion of my thigh."

I shook my head and, with mock sadness, said, "A fire fae with so little control that an innocent touch will set him off is a very sad thing indeed."

"So is a fire fae who hasn't had sex in days. Trust me, we're entering uncharted territory here."

I grinned. From what I knew of the fae, there were four groups—earth, air, fire, and water—each able to fully control their element. While all fae tended to be loners—and certainly didn't do either monogamy or love—they were great sensualists, existing to experience pleasure both within and without their elements. Fire fae, in particular, not only had a rather high sex drive, but apparently delighted in introducing innocents to the more seductive pleasures of this world—something Jackson had yet to achieve with me.

"Which is not surprising," he commented. "Given you've been alive quite a few more centuries than me."

I frowned at him. "You appear to be catching my thoughts a whole lot more than I'm catching yours of late."

"Maybe you're just not trying hard enough." He grinned suddenly. "Or maybe you're afraid you'll discover just how much a fire fae really *does* think about sex."

I snorted. "I'm already well aware how often you think about it."

"Well, yeah, I guess you *are* the main recipient of those lustful thoughts of late." His smile faded. "I wonder if we could converse telepathically if we actually tried?"

"Maybe. But now is *not* the time to try. Concentrate on the damn road, please."

He swerved to avoid the pedestrian who'd rather unwisely decided to jaywalk, then said, "Yes, ma'am."

I smiled. "I'm gathering Shona is a former lover?"

"Not former. Just on hold until this whole sindacati and red cloak mess is taken care of. I'd hate to get anyone caught in the middle."

I raised an eyebrow. "Just how many fillies do you actually have in your stable?"

The smile that touched his lips was decidedly wicked. "Just one, as I said."

"I meant normally."

"Ah." He paused, as if considering the question. "Five that I see on a semipermanent basis, and probably three or four others less regularly."

I blinked. "How in the hell are you managing to juggle that many women without them getting madder than hell at you?"

"I am a fire fae," he said simply. "It's all part of the charm. Being honest helps, too."

"So you tell them you're not human?"

"Well, no. There's honesty, and then there's stupidity. One or two of them have a less than stellar opinion of weres and vampires, and I enjoy their company too much to admit I'm not actually human."

"*That* is an all-too-male response."

He snorted softly. "When it comes to honesty, *that* is a case of the pot calling the kettle black if I ever heard one."

I grinned and didn't bother denying it. "So she's not likely to get antsy about you turning up with another woman?"

"No, because I've explained who you are."

"I'm betting you didn't admit I was another of your lovers."

"And *that* is a bet you would lose." His expression was smug. "I told you, I am, at all times, almost totally honest."

"I also take it she's not in danger of getting in trouble by doing this?"

"Only if she's caught, and that won't happen unless the night guard reports her. Which he won't, because he has the hots for her."

I shook my head. "The information you can get your hands on is sometimes truly amazing."

"Loving lots of women well does have its advantages." He slowed the car and flicked on the blinker to turn right as instructed by the GPS, then added, "And no, the security guard isn't a woman."

He flashed me another of those cheeky smiles and heat stirred through me. He wasn't the only one suffering. I might need and enjoy Rory's loving, but I also rather enjoyed flesh-to-flesh contact—especially when it came to someone like Jackson, who was a very good lover.

And so was Sam, my traitorous inner voice whispered. I ignored it. Him being civil was the closest thing to a miracle I was ever like to get. I very much doubted we'd ever step beyond that.

"However," Jackson added, "we only have between four and four thirty. She has to be out by then."

I frowned. "That's not giving us much time to search an entire apartment—"

"We won't have to search the entire place. The cops have already done that, remember? What we need to do is search the less obvious places."

"Oh good—that'll be *so* much easier."

"Do I detect a trace of sarcasm in your voice?"

"Hardly a trace."

He chuckled softly. I ignored him and studied the building up ahead that was, according to the GPS, our destination. It wasn't much to look at—just another tall glass box in a growing landscape of them. Even at street level it wasn't all that inspiring—at first appearance, it really didn't seem all that different to any of the nearby office buildings. But given its location right in the heart of South Bank, I was betting it had million-dollar views—and a price tag to match.

Jackson found a parking spot on the opposite side

of the street then reached around and grabbed a backpack.

I raised an eyebrow. "And that is?"

"Equipment to hurry things along."

With that, he climbed out. I followed suit. Across the road, just to the left of the building's main entrance, a blonde waited. She was tall, slender, and, even in her somewhat nondescript blue security uniform, rather stunning.

She pushed away from the hood of the Corolla she'd been leaning against when she spotted us and smiled. "Jackson Miller, if you get me into trouble for doing this, your ass is grass."

Jackson laughed, drew her into his arms, and kissed her soundly. Then he swung her around and waved a free hand toward me. "Shona, may I introduce the lovely Emberly Pearson."

"Pleasure to meet you," she said. Her blue eyes scanned me but held nothing more than friendly curiosity. "I hear you're keeping our boy on the straight and narrow these days."

I smiled and shook her extended hand. "As if that is *ever* possible. It's the case, not me. Expect a return to normality once it's dealt with."

"So he said." She bent to pick up the black pack at her feet. "I've told the guard to expect three of us tonight. You're trainees."

She handed us passes similar to the one she already had clipped to her breast pocket then led us toward the building. The guard inside opened the door as we approached, his smile wide and friendly. He was a middle-aged man with thick black hair, warm brown eyes, and the beginnings of a paunch under his crisp white shirt.

"Shona," he said, voice warm. "It's a pleasure to see you again."

"And you." She slid the sign-in book around and picked up the pen. "How's the divorce going?"

He shrugged. "The lawyers are involved now. It'll cost the idiot more than she'll gain." His gaze flicked to Jackson and myself. "These the trainees?"

"Yeah." Shona scrawled our names into the book. "We'll only be half an hour, Frank."

He nodded and handed her a keycard. "Elevator two, as usual."

"Thanks." She flashed him a warm smile then headed off. We trailed after her.

"I take it you're not the cause of the divorce," Jackson said as the elevator doors closed.

Shona swiped the card through the reader then hit the button for the twenty-fourth floor. "No, but he's definitely hoping I might provide warm arms to fall into after it."

"Any chance?" I asked curiously.

She shrugged. "He's a nice enough guy, but I'm not after anything serious."

"After the divorce, he probably won't be, either," Jackson commented, amused.

Shona raised a pale eyebrow. "Are you trying to get rid of me?"

"Never. I love your athleticism too much to do that easily."

She snorted and glanced at me. "Whoever said the way to a man's heart is his belly was totally off the mark."

"I have no heart," Jackson commented. "But I do have a very large appetite."

"*That* is a statement I doubt any of us could deny."

The elevator came to a halt, and the doors opened. Shona led the way out. The hall was wide, with a rich mix of wood, lushly painted walls, and thick carpet. The lights were muted, but brightened in sequence as we moved along the hall, lighting our way even as the shadows closed in behind us.

Rosen's apartment was down the far end of the hall, and was surprisingly barren of anything official. "Why isn't there any police tape around the door?"

"Maybe because he wasn't murdered in the apartment," Jackson said.

Shona glanced over her shoulder. "Where *was* he murdered?"

"We don't know," Jackson said. "And the police certainly aren't telling us."

It was an honest enough answer because we *didn't* know where he'd been murdered. We just knew where his body had ended up—in the middle of our office.

Shona grunted and keyed in the security code. A heartbeat later the door clicked open. "The clock starts now, folks."

We slipped past her and entered the apartment. The living and kitchen area was one vast, open space, and crowned by a sweeping curve of glass that overlooked the bright lights of Melbourne itself. The colors in the room were a mix of creams, browns, and blacks, which should have looked stark but somehow didn't. Splashes of bright color were dotted here and there in the form of large artworks, and the place was pin neat—which was odd considering the cops had searched the apartment from top to bottom.

Jackson dumped his bag on the circular white coffee table and undid the zip. The device he pulled out looked rather like a handheld speed camera.

He obviously caught my confusion, because he said, "It's a frequency-modulated continuous-wave imaging radar."

I blinked. "That makes me a whole lot wiser."

He grinned. "Basically, it'll capture people or objects hidden behind walls."

"And you're using this because you're expecting bodies behind the walls?"

"Well, no, but safe places, maybe."

"The cops will have talked to his son and sourced out any safes."

"Yeah, but it's totally possible senior had secrets junior didn't know about."

Given junior's opinion of his father had been less than stellar the one time we'd talked to him, that was all too possible. I waved a hand airily. "By all means, then, continue. I'll search the laundry and other unlikely places, and see what I can find."

He nodded and flicked a switch on the device. As the small screen came to life, I went in search of the laundry. If Rosen *had* installed secure storage in this place, I very much doubted it would be somewhere obvious, like the living area. I hadn't known Rosen well, but it had been long enough to not only dislike him, but to know that beneath the bluster and arrogance there was a very cunning mind.

The rest of the apartment was as vast as the living

area. There were three bedrooms—each one large enough to hold a king-sized bed, although only one of them actually did so. The second one was used as a storeroom, and the third had been turned into an office, complete with one wall of rather masculine-looking striped wallpaper. Rosen obviously hadn't believed in having guests staying over. I quickly checked each room for any signs of alterations or additions, but couldn't spot anything. There were no safes hidden behind any of the paintings, either. I moved on to the bathroom. It was opulent—all white marble and glass—and had a walk-in double shower as well as a spa bath. I checked the cupboards under the dual sink, but again, couldn't spot any alterations. The laundry netted the same result. This was looking like a waste of time, but it needed to be done. While it was unlikely Wilson's missing research notes would be found here, we still had to rule out the possibility that Rosen might have hidden information about the virus research here. After all, he'd not only been feeding the wererats—who ran most of Melbourne's underground gambling dens, and to whom he'd owed big money—information, but had been selling it to both the wolves and the sindacati. And he'd been wily enough not to do so from his office at Rosen Pharmaceuticals. Of course, if he'd blabbed the location of said information to his killer before he'd died—and that was certainly possible considering someone had been drugging information out of him for months before his death—it was likely that anything hidden here would be long gone.

"Em," Jackson called. "You might want to come in here."

"And where is 'here'?" I walked out of the laundry and headed in the general direction of his voice.

"The third bedroom."

"You've found something?" Something I'd missed?

"Just come and see."

I walked into the room to see him standing in front of the huge desk, frowning at the wall behind it. I stopped beside him. The wall hadn't changed in the few minutes since I'd been in here, and there still wasn't anything out of place that I could see.

"What are we looking at?"

"The wall."

"Yes, but why?"

"Because it's straight."

I blinked. "Most walls are straight. In a place as expensive as this, you'd be up in arms if they weren't."

"Unless, of course, they're deliberately curved, like the dividing wall in the living area is." He pointed a finger. "This bedroom backs onto the living area, and that wall should therefore be curved."

Damn, he was right. I hadn't even noticed that. "What does your device say about the wall?"

"That there's a void behind it that's larger at the left end, where what looks like shelving has been built."

Meaning Rosen *did* have something to hide. Whether it was related to a case or not was the question that now had to be answered. I frowned and studied the small bookcase. Now that Jackson had mentioned the existence of a secret hidey-hole, it did strike me as odd that Rosen had built a bookcase on one side of the room but not the other. In an apartment that was all about clean lines and symmetry, the balance was definitely off here—especially when the bookcase held only a scattering of dusty-looking books and nothing in the way of knickknacks.

I walked closer and ran my fingers along the wall just above the bookcase's top shelf. At the right edge of the there was a hairline break. It was barely noticeable thanks to the wallpaper's vertical stripes, but it ran from floor to ceiling, and I very much suspected it was one edge of a door. It was a similar story on the other side.

I glanced at Jackson. "You've already looked for locks, keypads, or pressure points, I gather?"

He nodded. "There's a small thumbprint scanner under the top shelf."

I looked. It was tucked into the very edge, right next to the joint between wood and plaster. "Can Shona get us into it?"

"No. It was installed after her company took over management of apartment security, so she can't legally help us access it."

"What about illegally?"

He shook his head. "We need a copy of his prints."

"Which we can't get." I paused, frowning. "What about short-circuiting it with fire?"

"Might work, but it could set off other alarms."

"That's a chance we might have to take."

He nodded in agreement. "And it's not like we have many other options anyway. Not if we want to find out what he's hiding in there."

"Which might be nothing—nothing we need, at any rate." I held up my hand to stop his protest. "But I agree: We need to try it."

"Shall I do the honors?"

"By all means." I grabbed the biggest of the books sitting on the shelf then stepped back and made a sweeping *after you* motion.

With a grin that was filled with anticipation, he placed the scanner on the desk then walked over to the bookcase. He studied the thumbprint box for several seconds, and then energy surged and flames flickered across his fingertips. The heat of them rolled across me, and the need to draw them into my body stirred. He might be a fire fae, but I was a spirit of flame. It was who I was, *what* I was, and fire—any sort of fire—was a siren's call I found hard to resist. Even the heat of the living could draw us—especially if our strength was low—but taking *that* path was an extremely dangerous one. It was all too easy to get lost in sensation and kill. Thankfully, that was something I hadn't ever done—not unknowingly, anyway.

Jackson shaped his flames into a thin, powerful lance then hit the scanner with it. As the plastic began to melt, I sucked in the radiating heat and waved the book to disperse the small amount of smoke. The inner circuitry was quickly exposed and, as Jackson's flame hit it, there was a short, sharp explosion. A second later, the whole apartment plunged into darkness.

In the ensuing silence, there was a soft click and a small gap appeared.

"What the fuck are you two doing in there?"

Shona appeared at the doorway, her expression less than pleased. Thankfully, Jackson had already shut down his flames.

"I just short-circuited the scanner." He rose and

stepped back. "Sorry—I didn't expect it to be connected to the main power."

"Well, it's hardly going to run only on batteries." She paused as her phone rang. "That'll be Frank. You've probably only got a few minutes to play with, as he'll come up and check why the circuit breakers went off in the apartment."

She unclipped her phone from her belt and walked out. I grabbed my phone and switched on the flashlight app. I might not be able to make calls or send texts without the SIM card, but that didn't mean the phone couldn't be used for other purposes. The bright light cut through the shadows, highlighting the newly created gap. Jackson squeezed in his fingers and pulled the door open. The void behind it was about three feet wide at this end but got gradually smaller as the curve of the original wall swept around to meet the false wall. In the larger portion there were multiple shelves built onto the original wall, each one stacked with a mix of artwork—small paintings and sculptures, both new and old—as well as several safes that had been secured to the concrete floor.

"I may not know much about art," Jackson commented, "but I'm betting some of those pieces are worth a fortune."

"Considering there's at least one Bernini bronze in there that I recognize, that's a bet you'd definitely win." I ducked under his arm and swept the flashlight down the other end of the void. As the space got smaller, the artwork gave way to a collection of boxes and files. "We're not going to have the time to search all those."

"No," Jackson said. "Our best bet is to hope he moved with the times, and started storing important stuff on USBs. And given you're shorter and more agile than me, the job of checking falls to you."

I raised an eyebrow. "You're a fae. Agility comes with the territory. You just don't want to go in here."

"Because tight spaces and me don't mix well." He paused, and mischief suddenly gleamed in his eyes. "Unless, of course, there's a woman involved."

I snorted softly and headed in. The phone's light cast crazy shadows across the walls and highlighted the dust and cobwebs—a sure sign Rosen hadn't used the deeper recesses in recent weeks. At the end of the shelving units there was a small filing cabinet. Unlike the boxes beyond, there was only a sprinkling of dust on the top of it—an indicator, perhaps, of more recent use. I pulled the first drawer open and scanned it. The contents seemed to be personal: household bills, medical records, and divorce paperwork—stuff like that. Though why he'd store that sort of information in a place like this, I have no idea.

"Anything?" Jackson said.

"Not yet."

I closed the first drawer and opened the second. This one held a mix of personal and business stuff. I was just about to close it when a file stuffed right at the back of the cabinet caught my eye—CORRESPONDENCE FROM FUCKWITS.

I grinned and reached for it. Inside the folder there was a collection of notes, and one name immediately jumped out of me—*Reginald Heaton.*

Heaton was the surname of the vampire who'd supposedly been bought in to replace Mark Baltimore at the Chase Medical Research Institute. Of course, that had been a lie, as the only reason he'd been there was for me. What he'd actually wanted I had no idea, because I'd done what any sensible person would do when instinct was screaming something was off—I ran.

Instinct hadn't been wrong, either, as Heaton had turned up again a few nights later, this time in our office. We'd caught his somewhat brief appearance on the security tapes when we'd played them back to uncover who'd delivered Rosen's body to our office. Heaton had come in sometime between Rosen's arrival and ours. While his actions there made it obvious he hadn't been involved in Rosen's murder, I doubted it was a coincidence that Rosen happened to have some correspondence mentioning him. And given we had no idea who he actually was, or how he was involved with either the sindicati, the red cloaks, or the missing research notes, anything we found on him could only help. Even if it was nothing more than a few malicious notes made by a man seemingly intent on destroying the empire he'd built from scratch.

"Em, come out," Jackson whispered. "The guard just arrived."

I slid the cabinet drawer closed, pulled a sleeve down over my hand and quickly swiped it over the cabinet's handles to blur any prints, then scampered out. Jackson grabbed the file and put both it and the infrared scanner in the backpack, then threw the pack over his shoulder and headed out. I pushed the hidden door back to its original position, repeated the hand swipe, and then followed him out. Shona and the guard were walking down the hall toward us.

"Found the problem," Jackson said, tone nonchalant. "There's a fused thumbprint scanner in here. Must be aftermarket, because it's not mentioned in the specs we have."

"Typical." Shona's cross tone was at odds with the mix of amusement and relief in her expression. "They own million-dollar apartments, yet don't want to spend the extra money to install additional devices and link them to the full system. Then they whine when it all goes ass-up."

"At least you won't have to listen to Rosen whining," Frank said. "He's dead."

"So says the boss. Have you heard anything about it?"

"Only gossip." Frank strolled over to the panel. The damage was easy enough to spot in the harsh glare of his flashlight. "Any idea how that happened?"

Shona followed him. "Looks like an electrical short circuit. I can get the boss to send in a qualified sparky to check it out, if you'd like."

"Nah. If it's aftermarket, it's not your responsibility—especially if your firm had no idea it was here. I'll inform the cops and they can deal with it."

"Why the cops?" I asked, surprised. "Surely whoever is handling Rosen's estate would be more appropriate?"

"Normally, yes, but we're under strict instructions to report any and all events related to this apartment."

I shared a brief, somewhat concerned glance with Jackson. "Why would the cops be interested in a fuse blowing, considering they haven't even placed crime tape at the front door?"

Frank grimaced. "The order didn't actually come from the regular cops. It came from some specialized unit."

PIT, undoubtedly. Which meant they'd be keeping an eye on the security tapes and would become aware of our presence here. I hoped like hell we hadn't gotten either Shona or Frank in the shit with them.

"You finished here?" Frank added, looking at Shona.

"No, but we can't do anything more until the power comes back on," she said. "I'll report what happened, and will probably be back once the power is restored."

"Can't be sad about that." Frank's smile crinkled the corners of his eyes. He made a motion with his hand. "After you."

"What rumors did you hear about Rosen's death?" I asked as we headed out of the apartment. "The gossip at the office is that he was attacked by a vampire, but that can't be right, surely?"

Frank shrugged and punched the CALL button. "The men from the special unit didn't say much, but the two cops who initially searched the apartment did say it was a vampire."

"I wouldn't have thought a man like Rosen would have much to do with vamps," Jackson said.

The elevator appeared and we all stepped in. "You'd think so, but he seemed to get a lot of visits from them."

I raised my eyebrows. "Really?"

Frank nodded. "Yeah. None of my business, of course, but it's hard not to notice things like that."

Instinct began to prickle, and I wasn't entirely sure why. "Can you describe any of them?"

As the elevator began its descent, Frank shrugged and said, "The one who visited most was tall, with gray hair, thin features, and these weird old-fashioned rimmed glasses that seemed precariously perched at the end of his nose."

Which was an almost exact description of the vampire we knew only as Professor Heaton. That prickle of wrongness got stronger. I glanced at Jackson and saw him surreptitiously open the backpack then roll up the file I'd taken.

I stepped forward, blocking Frank's view of him as the elevator came to a halt and the doors slid open. "I don't suppose you know why he visited so often, do you?"

"To be truly factual, I have never *actually* visited Rosen here," a new voice said. "But if I had, it would be for the same reason as now. For information."

Fear surged, and I had to clench my fists against the fire that instinctively sparked across my fingertips.

Because the man who was now blocking our exit was none other than Heaton himself.

Chapter 4

"What the fuck is going on?" Shona said, her tone a mix of outrage and fear. "Frank, do you know this man?"

"No, he doesn't." Though amusement touched Heaton's lips, there was nothing warm or pleasant about his smile. "As I've already said, this is the first time I've appeared in this building."

"Then why would he give such an accurate description of you?" The fear was stronger in Shona's voice. She glanced at Jackson, then at me, obviously seeking some sort of clarification.

"I'm afraid Frank was just relaying what Heaton here wished him to say," I said softly. "He's under Heaton's control."

"He's a vampire? Oh shit," she muttered, and took a step back.

"To put it mildly." Jackson placed himself in front of Shona. "Let them go, Heaton. Neither she nor the guard know anything about our purpose here."

"Oh, that much I already know." His smile gained a predatory edge. "Nor will they remember this little encounter. They are, however, excellent hostages against your good behavior."

He made a brief motion with his hand, and both

Frank and Shona collapsed. Jackson swore and somehow managed to catch Shona before she hit the ground *and* keep his back to the wall.

I stared at Heaton, the unease becoming full-blown fear. While most vamps *could* read the minds of others, they rarely had carte blanche access, let alone the capability to take over the minds of their victims so completely that they could control body functions.

And I was suddenly very, *very* glad that both Jackson and I were immune to such mental invasions.

"They're fine." Heaton's low, almost pleasant tone was totally at odds with the thick waves of viciousness rolling off him. "I have merely ordered them to sleep. Of course, I could also order them to stop breathing . . ."

"Do that, and you're ash," I ground out. My fists were clenched so tight my nails were drawing blood.

"Oh, I'm *well* aware of your capabilities, Ms. Pearson, but the second I see flame, I *will* kill them. Do you really wish to test whether your fires are faster than my order?"

No, I didn't, and he was obviously banking on that. "What the hell do you want with us?"

"Information, as I said. But first, please hand over that backpack."

Jackson did so. Heaton opened it up, pulled out the scanner, and frowned. "You found nothing behind the false wall?"

"No," Jackson growled. "The fucking fuse blew and we had no real chance to examine anything before Frank appeared."

"Unfortunate." Heaton tossed the pack back. Jackson caught it in his free hand. "What were you looking for?"

"The same as you, undoubtedly," I said. "Why did you risk coming here? If you wanted information from us, it would have been easier to confront us someplace PIT *isn't* monitoring."

"This place is as secure as any other, given I had Frank switch off the security system before I entered the building."

I snorted. "Like PIT won't think *that's* suspicious."

"Oh, they undoubtedly will, but they won't get anything from Frank." He paused, then added gently, "Of course, if *you* report my appearance here, I would be forced to kill them both. You wouldn't wish that, now, would you?"

I had a momentary vision of his ashes falling like black snow all around my feet, and wished like hell I could make it a reality. But while I could flame in the space of a heartbeat, I really couldn't risk his thoughts being faster than my fire.

So I took a deep breath in an effort to calm both instinct and anger, and simply said, "Why worry about the security here when you didn't appear concerned about it at our office? Or at Rosen's office? You *were* the reporter who visited him there, weren't you?"

"Yes, and more than once. The sindicati and the rats may need cruder methods such as drugs to get information, but I am above that."

"And modest, besides."

He smiled. It wasn't a pleasant thing to behold. "Modesty has no purpose or use in this day and age."

But violence did. Though Heaton's demeanor was urbane and pleasant, he was anything but. "And our office?"

"That was a mistake. I was not aware then how closely PIT was monitoring you."

Which begged the question—how had he become aware? Given I hadn't spotted whomever PIT had assigned to tail us recently, I doubted Heaton would have. PIT had been careless twice in that regard; I didn't think there would be a third time.

But if Heaton was now aware of PIT's interest in us, did he also know about my connection to Sam? I suspected he might, but again—how? Aside from Jackson and Rory, the only people who were aware of my past with Sam were Luke and Sam's current lover, Rochelle. I doubted Heaton was involved, in any way, with Luke. He didn't seem the sort to play second fiddle to *any* man. Or, in Luke's case, monster.

Which left Rochelle. While I suspected she might be Luke's source of information, I couldn't see her being connected with a vampire like Heaton. PIT was keeping too close an eye on both her and Sam now for that to happen.

But if Luke was reading her from a distance, why couldn't Heaton? While most vampires had to be close to their target to gain information, Heaton was obviously an unusually powerful telepath.

But which faction was he connected to? Or was he connected with neither, and simply playing his own particular game right now?

Once again instinct was suggesting the latter, and, if that was right, it wasn't good news. The last thing we needed was another competitor throwing his hat into an already overcrowded ring.

"If you were in such close contact with Rosen, why are you seeking the notes?" Jackson said. "I would have thought you'd already have a copy of them."

"No, because as a recent arrival in this town, I'd been wary of stepping on too many toes until I'd established a base. And that meant, by necessity, not showing too much interest in Rosen, given the rats already had their claws in him." He flashed a smile that held very little in the way of warmth and civility. "Of course, now that I *am* established, I can lay my cards on the table and start pursuing my interests."

"I'm betting the sindicati won't be pleased about *that* decision." Nor PIT—although they undoubtedly knew about him, as I'd given Sam the photo I'd taken of Heaton after I'd fled from him at Chase.

"Oh, I'm betting you're right. Now, back to the matter at hand . . ." Heaton paused, and his gaze swept my length. There was something very unclean about its touch, and distaste crawled through me. "Where are the research notes Baltimore gave you to type up before he was murdered?"

"PIT has one of the notebooks. One of the sindicati factions has the rest of them." My smile was brief and cold. "And who said Baltimore was actually dead?"

Heaton raised an eyebrow. "The coroner I interviewed just after his death."

"Yeah, well, you might want to revisit him. Baltimore walked out of the morgue a few days ago."

"He undertook the vampire ceremony?"

"*That* is entirely unclear."

"Meaning he could also be infected." The elevator doors began to beep. Heaton leaned a shoulder against them and crossed his arms. A second later, Frank rose, pulled out his keys, and locked the doors open. There was no animation in his face, no life in his eyes. I shivered.

"If you want those notes," Jackson growled, "then go have a chat to the sindicati and the cloaks. In fact, please *do* go speak to the cloaks."

Heaton smiled, but again there was little in the way of humor or warmth in it. Another chill ran through me. I really, *really* wanted to cinder this vampire—so much so that flames burned through my veins and it was taking every ounce of control to not only hold them back but prevent my skin from glowing. I had no doubt Heaton would make good on his promise if that happened.

"Oh," he drawled. "I have no intention of revealing my presence to either party at the moment."

"The cloaks appear to have a source within PIT," I said, unable to keep the slight hint of satisfaction from my voice. *Anything* that inhibited this vampire's plans—whatever the hell his plans were—could only be a good thing. "And given your previously mentioned appearance on our security tapes, *that* horse might well and truly have bolted."

"Which would be unfortunate, but not as disastrous as you are apparently hoping."

"Pity." I crossed my arms, hiding fingers that were beginning to glow. I was a creature of fire, and sometimes instinct got the better of control. "You didn't risk coming here just to ask about those notes, Heaton. What else do you want?"

"Rest assured I'm after nothing more than what I have already stated." He paused, and something very dark and even more dangerous stepped into his gaze. I'd seen such a glint once before, and it had been in the eyes of a very old, very *insane* vampire. Heaton obviously wasn't insane, but old? Yeah, he was that. "At least that is the case for the moment."

I really, really didn't want to know what else he might want. But, given that look, I had suspicions, and they would undoubtedly give me nightmares for nights to come.

"We've already told you we don't have the notes," Jackson said. "There's nothing else we can give you, because we don't *know* anything else."

"Yet," Heaton said. "But I've been keeping an eye on all players in this particular little game, and I believe you two have the most chance of finding what is currently missing."

"Well, I'm glad you have faith in us," I bit back. "Because few others do. Not even us."

"Ah, but PIT would not be monitoring you so fully if they did not think you could help them with their own investigations."

"That monitoring isn't going to make it any easier for you to contact us," Jackson noted. "And you certainly can't go about erasing the minds of security guards without drawing unwanted attention."

Heaton waved a hand. "That is simply a matter of logistics and planning. I doubt, for example, that they are aware that you have already met with several of my men."

"Your men?" Jackson and I shared a glance as he

added, "And which of the many psychos we've interacted with of late were yours?"

He raised an eyebrow. "They were in the BMW—"

"Ah," I cut in. "Yes. The ones who attempted to shoot the crap out of me."

"Well, you *did* have them trapped and ringed by fire. It was a somewhat justifiable reaction, even if an unwise one."

"Especially given you wanted information out of me. Me being dead wouldn't have helped your cause."

"No, it would not. But luckily for them—and you—phoenixes are capable of rebirth."

This vampire knew entirely *too* much about me. I shifted from one foot to the other, my skin so damn hot sweat was trickling down my back.

"It's not as easy as that, Heaton, believe me."

"Oh, I do believe." He gave me another of those cool, threatening smiles. "But that is beside the point at this particular moment. I wish your help and you will provide it. Otherwise, I will kill everyone in PIT, including the man who was once your lover."

I raised an eyebrow. "And what makes you think I'd care about the death of a former lover? Or about an organization that has caused us nothing but problems?"

"Because, my dear phoenix, you are a creature of fire, not stone, and if there is one thing I have learned over the last few weeks, it's that you care. You would not want those deaths on your conscience." He paused again. "If, however, that is not threat enough, then I'm more than willing to add Miller here and the man you share your apartment with."

Man, not phoenix. Heaton might know more than

he should about me, but he didn't know the truly important stuff.

"Please ease up on the threats," I growled. "Because I'm seriously battling the urge to smite you right now."

"Which only proves my assessment was correct. Had this situation been reversed, I would not have hesitated."

"That's because you're an unfeeling monster."

He bowed his head, the movement regal. It was almost as if I'd paid him a great compliment. "I expect daily updates."

"How? We've gone dark in an effort to dodge our tails."

"And quite successfully, too."

"Not successfully enough, if you found us," Jackson noted.

"Ah, but I merely did what was logical. If a target cannot be found, then you need to cover the places said target is likely to reappear." He waved a hand toward the foyer behind him. "This is one of five we are watching."

"The others being what?" In some respects, it was now a pointless question, but it would at least give us insight as to just how much he knew.

"Both Rosen's son and Professor Wilson's place are covered, as is your apartment and office. There was no need to keep a watch on Baltimore's building, as you were holding the only information of value—the notebooks—but we *are* also keeping an eye on the movements of a certain rat, given your recent altercation with him."

Meaning Radcliffe, whose responsibility it was to

look after the everyday running of the rats' various businesses, had better watch his back. Otherwise, he might lose not only control, but maybe even his life.

But the question that really needed answering was, where was Heaton getting his information from—especially if he was new in town? He couldn't have had people following us to all those places, because if he knew about those, then he'd have known about our current hidey-hole. And if he'd known about *that*, he wouldn't have risked a confrontation here.

I doubted he was getting the information from the sindicati, and I couldn't imagine the city wolf pack dealing with him given they already had a business relationship with the sindicati. But there again, if they deemed Heaton and whoever—whatever—was backing him stronger than the sindicati, then maybe they would. It wouldn't be the first time a wolf pack had placed bets on both sides of the field.

"To repeat an earlier question, how are we supposed to contact you when we have neither phone nor computer access right now?" We *could* actually contact him if we used one of the Wi-Fi apps that allowed free text and phone calls, but I wasn't about to admit that.

"There are such things as public phones," he said mildly. "They are an outdated technology, granted, but still usable in this sort of situation. And they can't easily be traced. It's a win-win for us both."

He pushed away from the door and pulled out a rather ornate silver card case from his jacket pocket. He flipped a card out and handed it to me.

It was totally black, with simple white writing that sat on the bottom right of the card. It said, JOSEPH

RINALDO, MARKETING MANAGER. Of what, it didn't say. Underneath that was a phone number.

I flipped it over but there was nothing on the other side. I handed it to Jackson, then said, "So is Rinaldo your real name, or just another pseudonym?"

"That is a question I'm disinclined to answer." He smiled benignly, and if I'd had hackles, they would have raised. "I will expect a call between seven and eight every evening. Be late and people will start to die."

"If people die, then I have no reason not to hunt you down and cinder your ass." I said it no less pleasantly than him. "You might keep in mind that you really are playing with fire here."

"Yes," he said. "It is a somewhat exciting prospect, too. And please do not attempt to follow me from this building or harm me as I leave. Remember, I am well able to kill these two from a distance."

He gave us a nod, then turned and walked away. His movements were casual, unconcerned, and flames flared across my body, eager for release. God, it was so, *so* tempting, but he'd judged me altogether too well. I wouldn't risk harming either Frank or Shona just to satisfy anger.

"It's hardly *just* anger," Jackson growled. "The world would be a far better place without the likes of *that* bastard staining it."

"Granted, but I don't see your flames chasing his ass, either."

I stepped into the foyer and watched Heaton—Rinaldo—leave the building. The minute he stepped into darkness, he shadowed and disappeared. Frank stirred, unlocked the lift, then walked over to the security desk.

I followed, watching as he turned the security system back on.

A heartbeat later, life came back into his eyes. Behind me, Shona said, "What just happened? Why are you holding me?"

"Because you fainted," Jackson said. "I figured you wouldn't appreciate hitting your head on the floor."

"Damn right." She straightened but didn't immediately step free from his grip. "Though I'm not sure why I would have fainted."

"Maybe your blood sugar is low," Frank said. "It used to happen to the ex when she was on one of her diets."

Shona snorted. "The one thing I *don't* do is diet. I love food too much."

"Pleased to hear it." He sat down and scanned the monitors. There was no indication that he'd noticed a good chunk of time had passed. "This has certainly been a more interesting evening than usual."

Jackson and I shared a glance. No memory of events, as Heaton had promised. "The short circuit upstairs wouldn't have affected anything down here, would it?"

"No, we're on a separate system here, and everything is up and running." His sudden smile was warm, and aimed at Shona. "I'll report the problem, and we'll see you again very soon."

"You will." She glanced at her watch and frowned. "We'd better run, as I'm late for the next client. Thanks, Frank."

We headed out. Jackson tossed me the car keys then escorted Shona over to her car. I jumped into ours and started it up.

"I've decided someone upstairs hates us right now," he said as he climbed into the passenger seat. "Because they certainly seem intent on making our lives ever more difficult."

"Yeah." I pulled out of the parking spot and merged into the traffic. "The first thing we need to do is find out more about Heaton."

"I doubt PIT will give us any information," Jackson said. "Not that you can really risk asking Sam about him anyway. Not until we know if he has a source at PIT or not."

"I can't imagine he has. Surely PIT would have taken measures against the possibility of agents being subverted or psychically invaded."

"Probably, but where else could he be getting information from? They're probably the only ones who have a complete picture of what the various chess pieces are doing in this particular game."

"We could ask the sindicati." Heaton might not have much of an opinion of them, but I doubted they were oblivious to the fact that there was a new player in town. "It might also be worth contacting Baker."

Scott Baker was the alpha of the werewolf pack who'd claimed Melbourne as their territory. Even if the sindicati didn't know about Heaton, the wolves surely would—especially if Heaton did plan to take over what the sindicati currently controlled. Any such action would fracture the black market operations deal the wolves apparently had with the sindicati.

"Baker might be the easier option," Jackson mused. "He's certainly the less dangerous one."

I snorted. "I wouldn't be so damn certain of that."

"We saved his life. He owes us." Jackson glanced at me, amusement crinkling the corners of his eyes. "He may not like us, but he'll feel obliged to help us until he considers the debt paid. Wolves are weird like that."

"There's nothing weird about being honorable."

"I agree, but you have to admit, it's a rare commodity in this day and age."

Actually, I didn't think it was any rarer now than at any other period of time. Maybe it simply said more about the people he generally associated with than anything else. And, as a PI, he certainly knew a lot more about society's underbelly than most "regular" people ever would.

"Where are we likely to find him?"

"The pack owns a building on Collins Street. Most of their business deals are handled there."

"Will they be there at this hour of the morning?"

Jackson glanced at the clock on the dash. "Maybe. From what I understand of the deal between the pack and the vamps, the wolves run operations during the day, the vamps at night. But I can't imagine they wouldn't be monitoring what the vamps are up to twenty-four/seven. The sindicati have never been the most trustworthy lot."

I did a quick, illegal U-turn and headed back into the city. "How long has the deal between them been running?"

He shrugged. "For the ten years I've been working in Melbourne as a PI, at least."

"You've been here ten years, and we didn't run into each other until a few months ago?" I said. "There's no justice in this world."

"No," he agreed, tone grave. "Because if there was, I'd be in bed loving you senseless right now."

"There, there." I reached across and patted his thigh. Once again his muscles jumped under my touch and heat stirred. I drew in a deep breath and let it fill me, tease me. "All good things come to those who wait."

"Those who wait," he growled, the amusement dancing in his at odds with the gravity in his voice, "will need to come more than thrice before their need is, in any way, slaked."

"Only thrice?" I said, amused. "Need can't be all that severe if that's all it will take."

He snorted. "Oh, trust me, it'll take more than that. But it is, at least, a good start."

And I, for one, couldn't wait. But I wasn't about to start a fire until we had the time to *take* time, so I withdrew my hand and turned my attention back to the road. "Has the city pack always lived here in Melbourne? Or are their traditional lands elsewhere, and this is just where they do business?"

"This is their traditional home, though I believe they own vast tracts of land up past Macedon."

"So why would they allow humans to develop the area so completely? Most packs I've come across have tended to keep traditional lands solely for pack use."

"I suspect they did it for the same reason as they now deal with the vampires—money. Not all wolf packs need or want wild, free spaces in which to run. Some are more than happy with city life and the facilities it brings."

I frowned. "But if they sold the land, they can't legally call it theirs."

"Ownership has nothing to do with a title. It's more about place. A feeling of kinship and belonging." He shrugged. "As for the deal with the vamps, nobody wins if the two parties go to war over the right of control. It is far better to reach a satisfactory compromise for them both."

Except at least one of the sindicati factions had decided that the deal was no longer relevant. Maybe that was why Heaton was here—he was using the current uncertainty between the former allies to establish his own power base.

"Which end of Collins Street are the wolves?"

"Spencer Street end, just before King Street."

It didn't take us long to get there. I found a parking spot just down the street then got out and studied the building. It was a gray slab-sided, modern building that lacked the charm of the older buildings in the area and had none of the polished finish of the newer ones. But each corner of the building was equipped with cameras, and I had no doubt there would be additional security measures inside.

"They're infrared cameras," Jackson noted as I joined him on the sidewalk.

"It makes sense, given who they're dealing with." I studied the nearest camera as we walked toward the main entrance. "How can you actually tell?"

"The shape of them. Infrareds tend to be more bulbous because of the extra technology they need." He climbed the steps and opened the door, ushering me through with a sweep of his arm.

"You'd think that with a building bristling with

technology, they'd actually take the extra step and install auto doors," I said. "It's not like they can't—"

The rest of the sentence was lost to a roar so loud it left my ears ringing. I half turned to see what was going on, and caught a brief glimpse of something that was half-man, half-wolf, and fucking huge.

He hit me with the force of a truck and sent me crashing back into a nearby wall. Pain bloomed and, for several seconds, I couldn't move, couldn't breathe, and all I could see was a mist of red. I wasn't sure if it was blood or fire, and didn't really care, because the air was screaming and the scent of wolf filled my nostrils. Flames rose, thick and hard, my body instinctively protecting itself even though I was half out of it.

But the approaching mass of fur and fury never hit. There was a grunt of pain; then the wall behind me shuddered as something big smashed into it.

I drew in a shuddery breath that hurt like hell, sucked my fire back in, and forced my eyes open. The furry man mountain was slumped, unconscious, at the foot of the wall ten feet away. Security guards were running toward us, their expressions of mix of wariness and surprise. I'm guessing it wasn't every day visitors were attacked before they'd stepped three feet into the foyer.

But then, it wasn't any old wolf who'd attacked me. It was Theodore Hunt, a hit man who'd promised to kill me because I'd apparently ruined his reputation by preventing him from murdering someone. Twice.

It was tempting, so *very* tempting, to unleash the fires that still burned within, and turn his ass to ashes.

But cindering someone as a precautionary measure wasn't exactly a civil thing to do, even when it came to someone like Hunt.

Several security guards unceremoniously picked him up and hauled him away, but no one approached us. Wolves were notoriously savage when it came to defending pack territory, so the mere fact they were keeping their distance and not even questioning us suggested they'd been ordered to do so.

Jackson squatted beside me, his expression anxious. "Are you okay?"

"Nope. I think I've bruised every muscle in my body." And there was blood trickling down my face. I swiped it away and pushed upright, but my breath caught in my throat and pain rolled through me. I sucked in several breaths that hurt—although not as much as they would have had I broken something—and said, "What did you do to Hunt?"

"Picked up a planter and hit him with it."

I glanced past him. The planters were almost as large as Hunt. Jackson certainly wasn't lacking in the muscle department, but that was still an impressive act.

"Yeah," Jackson said, "but it's amazing what a body can do when adrenaline is racing."

"Just our fucking luck to enter the building just as Hunt is leaving it." I paused and winced again. Things were bad when even talking hurt.

Jackson glanced at the guards and said, "I don't suppose you boys have medical facilities in the building, do you?"

"Yes, we do."

The voice was deep, cold, and it wasn't coming from any of the watching guards. As one, they parted, and Scott Baker, alpha of the pack, strode through. He was a big man with close-cropped brown hair and sharp brown eyes. And he didn't look pleased to see us.

He stopped several yards in front of his men and crossed his arms. It was an action that seriously tested the seam strength of his shirt. "Muscular" wasn't often a term used to describe wolves, because they tended to be lithe, but the city pack seemed to be the exception to the rule.

"Whether we offer you the use of them," he continued, "very much depends on your reasons for being here."

"Well, we didn't fucking come here to be blindsided," Jackson growled.

"You are well aware of Hunt's passion to kill you both." Baker's expression and tone were mild, but the gleam in his eyes was animalistic. The alpha was ready to defend his pack, and he'd do it with teeth and claws if necessary. "So you're either foolish or desperate to come here unannounced."

Anger flashed through Jackson, so fierce it just about blew my senses. I placed a hand on his knee in warning. His gaze shot to mine, and though the anger didn't recede any, his tone was polite as he said, "We came here to ask you some questions."

"About what?"

"Not what," I said. "Who."

Baker half raised an eyebrow. "Information costs. We are a business organization, not a library."

I smiled, but it was every bit as cool as his expression. "As long as your prices are not exorbitant, we are more than willing to pay for what we need."

Jackson shot me a look that suggested he wasn't exactly on board with *that* sentiment, but he didn't dispute my statement.

"Fine. If you'll follow me, I'll take you upstairs to see the doctor; then we can discuss terms."

"If we follow you," Jackson growled, "will you guarantee our safety?"

"It's a bit late to be worrying about that now." Though Baker's voice was still cool, a hint of amusement creased the corners of his eyes. It didn't really soften the fierceness of his expression. "However, no further harm will come to you in this place."

With that, Baker spun on his heels and headed for the elevators.

Jackson rose and offered me a hand. I pressed one hand against my side in an effort to give it some support, then placed my other hand in his and nodded.

"Ready?" he said softly.

I nodded. Though Jackson was as gentle as he could be, getting up was every bit as bad as I'd thought. For several seconds I did nothing more than stand there, swallowing bile as I waited for the red mist to leave my vision once more. More blood trickled down the side of my face, but this time I didn't swipe at it. My head wasn't hurting anywhere near as much as the rest of me, and besides, I didn't have a free hand.

I moved forward tentatively. It hurt, but the mere fact that everything seemed to be working suggested the only thing I might have broken was my head. And even then, the amount of blood suggested the wound wasn't that deep. Jackson kept hold of my hand, his body humming with a tension that was part readiness to catch me and part the need to hit someone. I was damn glad he was resisting the latter—we had enough enemies. We didn't need to add the wolves to that list.

But he'd obviously done some damage to Hunt, because there was a whole lot of blood and gore splattered across the wall Hunt had hit. With any sort of luck, it'd be enough to at least stop him for a while. Of course, it would undoubtedly have made him even *more* determined to get us.

Baker and two security guards were waiting for us at the elevator. He waved us in, and then all three of them followed. The two guards faced us, both of them exuding a fury that suggested they'd rather be beating us to a bloody pulp than escorting us up to medical services. I wasn't sure if their restraint was due to Baker's presence, or because he'd informed them they'd be burned to crisps the minute they tried. Baker might or might not know I was a phoenix, but he'd know from Hunt that both Jackson and I could produce and control fire at will.

The elevator came to a bouncy stop on the sixth floor. I winced but otherwise didn't say anything. While I couldn't heal my body with a simple shift of shape like werewolves—the burn scars decorating my back were evidence enough of that—I certainly *did* heal faster than most humans. If I hadn't actually broken something, then a hot bath and a good night's sleep would probably take care of most of the aches and pains.

Baker led the way down a long, wide corridor. The two guards fell in step behind us. My skin crawled at their closeness, and sparks flickered briefly across my fingertips. I'd never had much to do with wolves, but I'd certainly been in situations similar to this—situations where I'd been guaranteed safety only to find my trust had been badly misplaced. I didn't think that would be the case here, but I couldn't help the unease and the memories that rose every time something like this happened.

I took a somewhat shuddery breath and studied our surroundings. This place wasn't what I'd been expecting. The thick carpet that swallowed the sounds of our footsteps was a soft gray, as were the walls. The corridor was empty of all adornment, and there were no windows to add a much-needed feeling of space. It reminded me of something you'd see in a military ship rather than the main headquarters of a large wolf pack. It was also very quiet, but I guess that wasn't surprising given it was barely morning. Most sensible souls would still be in bed.

At the far end of the corridor was a metal door, but this one was open. Above it was a red cross. The medical center, obviously. Standing in the middle of the doorway with his arms crossed was a big man with more hair around his chin than on his head.

"This the patient?" Even though his expression gave little away, it wasn't hard to imagine he was less than pleased about having to treat someone at this early hour of the morning.

Or maybe he just wasn't happy about treating *me*.

"Yes." Baker stopped and glanced at me. "We'll wait out here while the doctor examines you."

I sent Jackson a silent warning to behave—though whether he'd hear it or not was anyone's guess given the somewhat hit-and-miss nature of our link—then followed the doctor into the room. It was not only big, but also fully equipped and—given who the wolves dealt with on a daily basis—probably well used. I was betting the staff here saw more than their fair share of cut and broken bodies.

The doctor motioned me across to the examination table then walked over to the sink and sterilized his hands.

"I believe you're the one who downed Theodore Hunt," he said.

"Not this time, I'm afraid. I was too busy bouncing off the wall to even know what had hit me."

"Most people who are hit by Hunt stay down." His gaze swept me briefly. "I suspect you're more resilient than you look, young lady."

"Young I'm not, and I'm afraid most wouldn't call me a lady, either."

He didn't smile. Maybe it had been a very long night. Or maybe he simply had no sense of humor. "Take off your sweater and shirt, please."

I did so. He pulled on some gloves, then began examining my head. "No headache or feeling of pressure?"

I winced. Though his touch was light, it still damn well hurt. "Nope."

"Did you lose consciousness, feel nauseous or dizzy?"

"I saw plenty of stars when I hit that wall, but I didn't black out or anything."

He grunted, changed gloves, and then checked my pupils. Another grunt followed, after which he began prodding my upper body. More winces followed.

After thoroughly examining the rest of me, he stepped back and said, "You've a rather nasty lump on your head, but the cut isn't too bad. I'll clean it up and stick a butterfly bandage on it. There's nothing broken anywhere else. You're just bruised." His gaze met mine as he pulled off his gloves. "As I said, a surprisingly resilient young woman."

"Which is just polite way of saying I've a hard head, isn't it?"

A brief smile touched his lips, but he didn't otherwise acknowledge the comment. "I'll give you some pain relief that'll help ease the aches, and try not to do anything too energetic for a few days."

Which would be easier said than done, given all the shit going on in my life at the moment. "Thanks, Doc."

He nodded and moved across the room to a locked cabinet. "I also feel obliged to warn you that Hunt has a dangerously obsessive nature that's gotten much worse over the years. The wise would avoid him."

"Believe me, I have no desire to be either in his face *or* his path. Unfortunately, fate seems to have other ideas." I pulled my shirt and sweater back on, and tried to ignore the pain and the instinct to breathe shallowly. No matter how much breathing normally might hurt, it supposedly kept the chest clear from mucus and infections. Or so past doctors had informed me. "And if you're aware of the fact he's becoming unstable, why is he even allowed out on the street?"

"Because he is still very good at what he does, and he hasn't stepped over the edge." He paused and grimaced. "Yet."

If Hunt *did* step over the edge, would they deal with him then? And what would he have to do before they considered it "stepping over the edge"? I'd seen what he and his vampire mate had done to Amanda Wilson, and that certainly went beyond anything I would have called reasonable behavior, even for someone who'd taken the contract to kill her.

And the thought that he'd do something even worse to me . . . I shivered and silently cursed the luck that had thrown him in our path. Although I guess if our paths *hadn't* crossed, Amanda Wilson would now be dead and we wouldn't have gotten hold of her USBs. And while we now had only one of them, her notes had at least thrown some light on the sindicati and their operations.

Of course, she could *actually* be dead now, for all I knew. The last time I'd seen her was in the passenger seat of Jackson's truck just after the sindicati goons had rammed us, and she hadn't exactly looked well at that point. And I had only De Luca's word that she'd survived the crash.

But he'd also said that his "colleague" had decided he could use her talents, and that, I suddenly realized, could be another possible explanation for the leak at PIT. Because Amanda was a powerful telepath, and it was a pretty good bet that De Luca's colleague—and the other man who'd been in that room that day—had been none other than Luke himself.

I carefully eased off the table. "Trust me, Doc, I'll avoid him if I can."

"Good." He gave me two painkillers and a plastic cup of water. "Take these now, and I'll write you a prescription for some more. And if you get any of the symptoms I mentioned earlier, get yourself to a doctor."

I nodded and took the pills. He quickly wrote out the prescription then handed it to me. I shoved it into my pocket. "Thanks, Doc."

He nodded. "Good luck."

I grimaced. "I'm probably going to need it."

"Probably." Once again his smile held little in the way of humor. "But if you can't avoid Hunt, then keep to his left side."

I raised my eyebrows as the doctor reached for the door handle. "Why?"

"Because he has little vision left in that eye, and he's broken his nose too many times to have good olfactory input."

Surprise rippled through me. I obviously didn't do a good job at hiding it, because he added, "Some of us would not be to saddened to see him put down—especially by a snippet of a woman. It would be an odd kind of justice, given the many he's abused over the years."

And with that, he opened the door and ushered me out. Baker's gaze swept me. "Better?"

"Cut head and bruised all over, so no," I replied. "But thank you for allowing the doc to see me."

He nodded then spun on his heels and led the way

back down the corridor. After another short trip in the elevator, we were led into a wide office lined with windows that offered views not over Melbourne but directly into treetops. It gave the room a "foresty" feel, and the soft green walls and the many planters added to that. But that greenness was juxtaposed against bright splashes of color in the form of modernist artwork, both in paintings and freestanding sculptures. It was an odd combination that hinted there was more to this wolf than first appeared.

Hunt dismissed the two guards then moved around the huge mahogany desk and sat down. "So," he said, steepling his fingers. "What is it you wish?"

"Information, as I said." He didn't offer us a seat. I walked across the room and took one anyway. But sitting was just as uncomfortable as standing; hopefully the damn painkillers would kick in sooner rather than later.

"On whom?"

"This man." Jackson showed him Rinaldo's business card.

Baker raised an eyebrow. "And what is your involvement with this man?"

"He's blackmailing us," I said. "We send in a report on our progress daily, or people die."

"From what I know of him, that is very much his style." Baker leaned back in his chair and contemplated us for several seconds. His expression gave very little away. "What information does he wish?"

"Meaning you will help us?" I countered.

"Perhaps. For a fee, of course, as I have already mentioned."

"Of course." Jackson's voice was dry. "I take it, then, that he's not currently doing business with the city pack?"

"No, but he has certainly approached us. We have something of a standoff currently happening." His smile barely touched the fierceness in his brown eyes. "I do not expect it to last."

Meaning, no doubt, blood *would* be shed. Blackmail might have worked on us, but I doubted Baker and his pack would put up with any such threat—not when they saw the city as theirs to rule.

But would Rinaldo be foolish enough to even do that? So far, he'd played his cards very cleverly, and I wouldn't have thought making an enemy of the wolves to be a wise move. Especially if he was planning to take over both sindicati territory *and* operations.

"Then maybe we should wait," I said. "If you wipe him out, our problem would be solved."

Baker smiled. "The fact that you are here seeking information suggests you cannot or will not wait for such an event to occur."

"Very true." Especially given it wasn't either my life or Jackson's that the bastard had threatened. "What's your fee?"

"Our general fee for information is a grand, but given the subject, we'll quarter it."

"Why?" I asked bluntly. "The city pack hasn't a reputation for generosity."

"No, we do not—and with good reason." His smile held the first real touches of warmth and it lifted the coldness from his features. He was never going to win any awards for looks, but that smile at least made his sharp profile more interesting. "In this case, it's simply an admission that we do not, as yet, know a whole lot about Rinaldo."

"Then tell us what *do* you know," Jackson asked.

Baker merely raised an eyebrow. "The fee is agreed?"

Jackson got out his wallet, peeled out the appropriate number of bills, and put them on the table. "Now talk."

Baker swept the bills into the top drawer of his desk. "Rinaldo appeared in Melbourne just over nine months ago and has very swiftly gathered a large following among those vampires disenchanted with the current sindicati split. We believe he's from interstate, but have not as yet tracked down from where."

I frowned. "Why not? Surely the Australian Vampire Council would have some record of him?"

They were, after all, legally obliged to keep a record of not only all those who'd turned, but also those who'd undergone the ceremony—in which a human swore allegiance to a master vamp and shared his blood—so that both coroners and undertakers were not caught unawares by the dead rising.

"You would think so, would you not?" Baker agreed. "That they haven't suggests he is using an alias, or we are dealing with someone from overseas."

"Immigration would have some form of record if it was the latter," Jackson said. "And I'd imagine you'd be able to get your hands on that easily enough."

"Having access does not help if you do not know the target's actual name."

Suggesting Rinaldo was yet another alias. Either that, or he'd come into the country subversively. It didn't happen very often these days, as border security had become quite adept at stopping vamps and weres trying to sneak into the country illegally, but it certainly *had* been a problem in the days before radar screening and sniffer dogs. And Rinaldo was old enough to have been here a very long time.

"What else do you know about him? Because we certainly haven't gotten our money's worth yet."

"I did warn you we do not know much." He held up a hand, stopping my annoyed response before I had the chance to make it. Which was probably just as well, because it's never wise to annoy wolves when you're on their turf. "The sindicati are aware of Rinaldo's presence but do not currently deem him a threat. They are, of course, fools, but that is neither here nor there."

"If they know about him," Jackson said, "surely they must be aware of his past, or where he came from?"

"If they do, they are not saying."

"But they're aware Rinaldo approached you?"

Again Baker's smile flashed. "No. That is pack business. We would inform the sindicati of the event only if we decided to alter or even annul current contracts."

Given what he'd said about the standoff between the pack and Rinaldo, *that* seemed unlikely. "Do you have any idea why the sindicati deem him such a low threat?"

"Because so far he has concentrated his efforts on taking over the businesses that are traditionally rat controlled."

"Meaning minor black market trading, gambling

and the like?" I said. "I can't imagine the rats taking that lying down."

"Oh, they are less than pleased. There have been several skirmishes already, and I would expect more, especially if the rumors are true and he has executed a bloody raid on one of Radcliffe's main gaming venues."

"When did this happen?" Jackson asked, frowning. "There's been no mention of it on the news."

"It happened an hour ago, and it won't hit the news because PIT has placed a embargo on the event."

"But it was definitely Rinaldo's men?"

"Not just his men—he was seen there."

Jackson and I shared a glance. "Impossible. An hour ago he was threatening us at Rosen's apartment."

"Then perhaps we are not talking about the same man."

I got out my phone, brought up Rinaldo's picture, and showed Baker. "This was taken at Chase Medical Research Institute a few weeks ago. He was going under the name of Professor Heaton at the time and was supposedly there to replace Professor Baltimore."

"I'm gathering you and he had something of an disagreement over you continuing as his assistant?"

"No. I did the sensible thing and ran."

This time Baker's smile was full-fledged. It briefly warmed the fierceness from his eyes. "Possibly a wise move."

"I'm thinking so." I put my phone away. "I believe PIT knows him as Heaton."

"And yet, that is *definitely* the man I know as Rinaldo." Baker leaned back in his chair, expression thoughtful.

"It is impossible for someone to be in two places at once, so perhaps my source was mistaken about seeing him at the gaming venue."

"If your source happened to be working at the venue when it was hit," Jackson commented, "it would be understandable if he *did* make a mistake."

"Yes. But he said the gentleman in charge identified himself as Rinaldo, and that all the men accompanying him were vampires."

"Could it have been one of the sindicati factions?" After all, what better way to get rid of a possible rival than to commit a crime in his name, and have half the rat world after him?

"That is also very possible, although it would be at odds with what the vampires have said to me."

"And it's not like vampires to be dishonest about things like that," Jackson said, voice dry.

Baker acknowledged the point with a somewhat regal nod. "I'll question my source and some of the other survivors when PIT has finished with them. Something very odd would appear to be going down right now."

That right there had to be the understatement of the century. "What sort of deal did Rinaldo offer the wolves?"

"What sort of information is he blackmailing you for?" Baker countered. "I believe a fair exchange is warranted on this point."

"It's hardly a fair exchange when we're paying you for information," Jackson noted.

"You paid me for information on Rinaldo. At no point was his approach to us included in that price."

Jackson snorted. "And they say rats are thieves."

"Rats are. Just try to get information if you do not believe me. Our prices are modest by comparison."

Having never dealt with the rats in a business sense, I had no idea whether that was true or not. I briefly glanced at Jackson. He half shrugged in response.

"Okay," I said, returning my gaze to Baker. "A fair exchange. Rinaldo or Heaton or whoever the fucking hell he is wants any and all information regarding the missing research files."

"Which ones?" Baker countered. "The ones supposedly hidden by Wilson or the ones De Luca stole from Parella's crew?"

Jackson raised his eyebrows. "You're very up-to-date with recent events."

"We're dealing with vampires. It pays to keep up-to-date."

One again his tone was dry, and I couldn't help smiling. Baker might be every bit as cool and ruthless as the vamps, but that certainly wasn't the sum of him. You had only to look at the artwork in his office to guess that.

"What did he want from you?"

"He stated his intentions on taking over sindacati operations, and desired to know if we would be agreeable to continuing joint operations with him in control."

"I can't see the problem in that," I said, frowning. "Especially given you're already working with the sindicati."

"We have no problems with working with him per se," he said. "It's the 'him in control' bit we objected to."

"Meaning he didn't actually want a working

relationship," Jackson said. "I'm liking this vampire less and less."

"Quite." Baker's tone was heavy. "As I said, we have something of a standoff. He was less than pleased with our response, but has not yet the backing or the power to do anything about it."

"I'm surprised you're sitting back waiting for him to gain such power," I commented. "I would have thought dealing with the situation before it escalates would be your next move."

"It would be, if we could find him. He is something of a ghost."

"He's not too much of a ghost," Jackson commented. "Not if the amount of times we've spotted him is any indication."

"Then perhaps we could come to an arrangement," Baker said. "You give us a call whenever you see him, or whenever you uncover anything about him, and we will offer protection to those he's threatened."

Jackson's eyebrows rose. "That's a generous offer."

"Yes, but we really *would* like to deal with him before the situation escalates." He paused and grimaced. "This city has enough problems right now. It doesn't need a war between us and the vampires."

"Okay, deal," Jackson said, and offered Baker his hand.

Baker shook it then slid a pen and paper across the desk. "If you jot the names and addresses, we'll do our best to keep those people safe."

As Jackson began writing, I said, "Have you talked to the rats about the situation?"

After all, Rinaldo, for all his air of sophistication,

had to be hiding somewhere very unusual; otherwise the wolves would have found him by now. And when it came to unusual—to places dark and dank—then the rats were the kings.

"Yes. I suspect they might be more willing to chat after this current episode, however." Baker reached into his top shirt pocket and pulled out a business card. "You can contact me anytime on this number. Unlike the one Rinaldo has given you, it is a direct line."

"Meaning Rinaldo's isn't?"

"No. It's a call center. Rinaldo contacts them once a day for his messages."

Given the time frame he'd allotted us, what was the betting he collected them all right after eight? "Any chance of tapping the call center's lines and tracing where he calls from?"

"Unfortunately, no. And if I were him, I'd be calling from a public phone, not a private one."

So would I. I blew out a frustrated breath, then shoved Baker's business card into my purse and rose. "Thanks for the help."

He inclined his head somewhat regally. "I would suggest you call ahead next time you wish to enter this place. It will avoid future problems with Hunt."

"Or you could simply keep him on a leash."

"I could, but I won't." His sudden grin was anticipatory and very much a reminder of the savagery that lurked beneath the cloak of civility. "You created the problem, so it's up to you to deal with it. I have warned the pack not to interfere or retaliate in any way, no matter what the result. Doing anything more would be bad for pack politics."

Which basically meant he'd banned retaliations if we did kill Hunt. He *had* said he'd do that when we'd saved his ass, of course, but I wasn't entirely sure he'd meant it.

"We'll be in contact," I said.

He smiled again. "I'll look forward to it."

I glanced at Jackson, then led the way out the room. Our two guards were waiting for us in the corridor and escorted us down the elevator and through the foyer. I wasn't entirely sure if it was for our safety or to make sure we actually left.

"Well," Jackson said as we headed down the front steps. "That was all very illuminating."

"I'm not sure 'illuminating' is the right word," I said. "But it might be worthwhile trying to talk to Radcliffe again."

Jackson snorted. "After what we did to the bastard, I'm betting the only meeting he'd agree to is one where we're incapacitated and he's armed with a fucking big gun."

I grinned. "True. Except for one thing—we now have a common enemy."

Jackson's expression became thoughtful. "We do. And he certainly might consider us the lesser of two evils."

"Especially if we offer him the same sort of deal we gave Baker."

"There's only one problem with that." He lightly pressed a hand against my spine and guided me to the right. "As of this moment, the only information we have on Rinaldo is what Baker told us, and you can bet Radcliffe already knows all that. Remember, the raid on his gaming venue wasn't the first. It was just the bloodiest."

"It's still worth a . . ." I stopped as I spotted a familiar blond-haired figure just ahead.

"What?" Jackson said immediately.

I pointed at the woman. "Is that Amanda Wilson, by any chance?"

He followed the line of my finger and, after a moment, said, "It sure as hell looks like her. Let's find out."

Without warning, he bellowed her name, just about blowing my eardrums in the process. The blonde turned her head and stared directly at us.

Just for an instant, there was no life, no emotion, in her face.

Unease crawled through me, but before I could say anything, before either of us had even taken more than a few steps toward her, recognition flared and she turned and ran.

Chapter 5

"Well, I guess that's confirmation it *is* her, if nothing else," Jackson said. "Shall we give chase?"

He didn't wait for my answer, just bolted after the fleeing woman. I followed, but running woke all the bruised bits and hurt like hell, and it was all I could do to ignore the pain and keep on going. But it was pretty much a pointless exercise; within half a dozen strides I was already well behind.

Amanda hit Spencer Street and bolted across it against the lights. Car horns blared, but she didn't acknowledge them, looking neither right nor left as she ran for Southern Cross Station. I cursed. Even though it wasn't peak hour yet, there were still enough people about that we could easily lose sight of her.

But, rather surprisingly, she didn't head inside. Instead, she stayed on the footpath and raced toward Bourke Street.

Jackson hit Spencer Street, checked his speed slightly, and then flung out a hand to stop the traffic as he raced across. More car horns blared, and abuse flew. He ignored them and ran on.

I was too far back to follow, so I swung left and followed their progress from the opposite side of the street. But the pain was building, and my head was pounding. So much for following doctor's orders . . .

At least Jackson had gained on her . . . but even as that thought crossed my mind, she swung left and raced up the steps toward the Outlet Centre. Jackson followed several heartbeats later, and the two of them disappeared into the concourse between the rail station and the Outlet Centre. I cursed and stopped, one hand against my side and my breath ragged gasps of agony as I waited impatiently for a break in the traffic before running across. I took the steps as fast as I could then paused at the top and looked around for any clue as to where they'd gone. After a moment, I caught a brief glimpse of auburn hair far ahead and bolted after them again.

But by the time I reached that point, Jackson was already walking back toward me.

I frowned and stopped. "What happened?"

"The bitch knocked an old woman into my path." He thrust a hand through his hair, the movement quick and filled with repressed anger. "By the time I'd helped the old girl, Amanda had disappeared."

"Well, fuck." It came out as little more than a wheeze. My lungs burned, but breathing properly hurt like hell. Logically, I knew that it was better to breathe deep than more shallowly, but knowing and doing were two very different things when pain was involved.

Rather annoyingly, *he* didn't even seem to be winded. And I very much suspected it had nothing to do with a lack of bruised ribs and a whole lot to do with the fact he was superfit and I wasn't.

"Wonder why she ran?"

Jackson shrugged and caught my arm, leading me at a far gentler pace back the way we'd come. "Given the last time you and she had a conversation, she ended up smashed against a tree and in the hands of the sindicati, you can't actually blame her."

That was certainly true. And yet, the suspicion that something was off lingered. "There seemed to be this weird delay between her seeing, and then recognizing, us. Don't you find that odd?"

"Not when we're dealing with a someone who has spent a good part of her life sleeping with men to steal their secrets, and then either killing them or setting them up to take the fall."

"The strength of her telepathic skills only make the whole situation even weirder. She should have sensed us long before we spotted her." I wasn't telepathic, despite the connection Jackson and I were developing, but I'd certainly known them in the past. And for those involved in crime, skimming the thoughts of everyone around them to avoid trouble before it actually hit was almost second nature.

"Remember we're dealing with a telepath whose skills seemed to be intimacy based." He guided me back down the steps then swung left and headed for Hungry Jack's.

"A burger?" I said, with a trace of disbelief. "At this hour of the morning?"

"There is no right or wrong time for a burger." His grin flashed, and my hormones jolted to life. Everything might hurt right now, but there were small sections of me that weren't bruised and decidedly *un*satisfied. "And there is nothing quite like it for an energy hit."

I raised my eyebrows at that, and his grin grew. "Well, there is *one* thing, but given you're all bruised and battered, that's off the table."

"I appreciate the consideration."

"I'll appreciate your appreciation as soon as you're up and able, let me tell you. What do you want to eat?"

I scanned the menu board for a second then said, "I'll go for the Aussie, with a cup of tea."

He shuddered. "A hamburger with beetroot is just plain wrong, you know that, don't you?"

"It's an Australian tradition."

"And one we can do without."

"Says the man who slathers Vegemite on his toast as thickly as butter. You buying or am I?"

"My treat. You can return in kind later, if you like."

The twinkle in his eyes was decidedly wicked and had me imagining all sorts of things—most of them involving his tongue, for some strange reason. Not that I was against oral in any way, shape, or form—far from it, in fact—but it was something he and I hadn't overly pursued.

"Perhaps that," he murmured, "should change."

Which totally explained those damn images—I was catching them from him. I snorted softly. "Feed me, and I might just consider it."

His sigh was somewhat sorrowful. "Your priorities are not what they should be."

"My priorities," I replied drily, "are *exactly* what they should be, given where we are."

"No sense of adventure, either," he said as he joined the nearest queue.

I snorted again and moved across to the window to grab a table. He returned a short while later with not only four burgers, but also our hot drinks and a bag of fries. The latter was placed in the middle of the table so that we could share more easily. And while burgers and fries definitely weren't on anyone's list of recommended breakfast foods, right then I couldn't have damn well cared.

"So," I said around a mouthful of food, "what do we do next?"

He shrugged. "Depends how tired you are. You could get some sleep while I check out the file we stole, or we could go search Wilson's place."

I took another bite of the hamburger and considered the two options. Other than the bruises and the lingering pain that was a natural result of being smashed into a wall, I felt surprisingly okay, but that wasn't to say I wouldn't crash a couple of hours from now. Or that I wouldn't go out like a light once I closed my eyes.

"I think it'd be better to check out the file while we can. With the way our luck is running, someone will soon steal the damn thing."

"Totally true." He frowned as he opened his second burger. "I'll have to go back to the office at some stage, too. I need to commune with fire."

Jackson, like most of the dark fae, had to be near his element regularly; otherwise he risked fading and, eventually, death. Which is why our office was situated close to both Queen Victoria Market and Flagstaff Gardens.

The rent was hideously high, but it had one thing cheaper places didn't—it was right next to a blacksmith's. Jackson had an ongoing agreement with the owner for twenty-four-hour, no-questions-asked access, even though Jackson tended to only go there at night.

I finished the last bit of my burger then licked my fingers. Jackson's gaze followed the movement and the air grew heated. I flared my nostrils and drew in the sweet scent. "We could kill two birds—I'll catch some Zs at the office while you go next door and commune. We can check out the file when you get back."

"You're testing my strength, aren't you?" His voice was deliciously gravelly. "You know what fire does to me."

"I know." I picked up a fry and lightly licked the salt off it. His gaze darkened delightfully. "And maybe, after I rest, we could do something about it. But only if it's quid pro quo."

"That," he said heavily, "would be my pleasure."

"And mine, I would hope."

"Oh, you can be assured of *that*."

My sudden grin was one of anticipation. We finished the rest of our breakfast in silence, then headed back to the car and drove to the office. Hellfire Investigations was located on Stanley Street, which contained not only an eclectic mix of light industrial and old Victorian buildings but was also filled with early blooming blossoms and wattles that scented the air with their sweetness.

Jackson didn't head directly there, however. He drove past our street and parked in the market's parking area.

"They may be watching our place," he said, handing me the ticket. "Safer to park here and walk there."

"Good thinking, Agent Ninety-nine." I tucked the ticket away safely.

"See, my brain isn't entirely consumed by the need for sex."

I thought it safer *not* to reply to that. He took my hand and we strolled back lazily. To anyone else we would have looked like just another couple out for a morning stroll. But my gaze was never still, studying and assessing everyone I saw even as I kept an eye out for those who might be watching from afar. I had no doubt he was doing the same. But, as far as I could see, no one was taking the slightest bit of notice of us.

"It's the ones we *can't* see that I'm worried about," Jackson said.

"Then perhaps this is a bad idea."

"No. I need fire."

And sex. He didn't say it, but the words hung in the air, hot and heavy.

"Then you go there now, and I'll continue on to the office alone. It's better that they don't realize we have private access to the blacksmith's." Heaven only knew, we might well need another place to hide in the near future.

He nodded, then raised my hand and kissed my fingers. "Be careful. And lock the door."

"I will."

He walked away quickly. It only took me a few more minutes to reach our office. It was a pretty blue-painted double-story Victorian building and it looked no different now from when we'd left it a few days or so ago. There was no sign of a break-in, no sign of police tape, and the door appeared locked. Hoping there was nothing—or no one—nasty waiting inside, I grabbed the mail out of the letterbox then opened the old wrought iron front gate and bounded up the steps.

Once I'd unlocked the door, I pushed it all the way open but didn't immediately step inside. The place was very much as I'd left it, except that Rosen no longer lay spread-eagle and very dead in the middle of it.

The place was still a mess, with files that had been emptied out of the filing cabinets or knocked off the desks still strewn everywhere. The hours I'd spent cleaning it up really hadn't made a dent in the paper storm. My gaze ran to the end of the room, where a sitting area and Jackson's industrial-sized coffee unit were. Nothing had changed there, either, and no new cups had been added to the trash can. If someone had been here, then they'd left no immediate evidence—unlike the vamps who'd originally trashed this place.

My gaze drifted to the circular staircase that led up to the next floor and Jackson's living area. I could hear no sound and feel no heat, but that didn't mean no one was up there waiting to jump out at me. Besides, it might not be a flesh-and-blood trap; too many people now knew magic could restrict me, so that was also a very real possibility. I took a tentative step inside. Nothing happened. I took another, my heart hammering and fire flickering across my skin. The latter I toned down immediately; the last thing we needed right now was me accidentally setting this place alight.

Still nothing. I locked the door then carefully made my way to the base of the stairs and looked up. Only golden shafts of sunshine greeted my gaze. I was pretty sure I was the only person in this place, but that didn't stop me from climbing those stairs warily. The sunlight streaming in through the windows to my right lent a warmth to the lingering shadows of night and left absolutely nowhere for anyone to hide. I could neither see nor feel anything out of place, and something within me relaxed. Even so, I walked across the room to check the toilet—which was the only separate room on this entire floor—just to be doubly safe. It was, as expected, empty.

I swung around. While the upstairs area had escaped the paper storm of the floor below, the vampires had nevertheless searched the area. They'd stripped the bed, pulled the mattress away from the base, emptied out cupboards, and upended the couches. It was a freaking mess, but right then, I didn't care. What I needed was sleep and a bath, and not necessarily in that order. I spun around and walked over to the designated bathroom area to fill the large claw-foot bath. Fae, I'd learned, weren't into the whole privacy thing, and, from what Jackson had said, I should consider myself lucky he at least had a separate toilet.

Once the tub was full, I stripped off and stepped in. Heat shivered through me and the water steamed slightly as I slipped into it. And that's where I stayed until the aches in my body began to ease and I started feeling a whole lot better.

Jackson still wasn't back by the time I was done, so I dried myself off and headed over to the bed. I didn't want to risk starting up the aches again by righting the heavy mattress myself, so I simply tugged it the rest of the way onto the floor then threw on the sheets and comforter and climbed inside. I was asleep in seconds.

Heat kissed my skin. It brushed sweetly across my shoulders then moved ever so slowly down my spine. It was a caress of flame that never lingered long enough for me to identify its source, but, oh, it felt good. I stirred, torn between the need for sleep and the desire to find the source of fire.

The teasing continued down my back, lingering briefly near my spine, warming my skin and stirring deeper desires to life. The scent of warmed lavender hung in the air, but it was almost overwhelmed by the musky aroma of man.

I knew that scent. Jackson was back.

The realization had me tumbling toward full wakefulness. But I didn't move, content to remain on my belly, enjoying the featherlight caresses as they moved over my butt, down my left leg, then back up my right.

The mattress dipped as he straddled my legs. His calves pressed lightly against mine, his skin so hot that he felt like a being of fire, not a flesh-confined fae.

Then his hands swept up my legs, his thumbs teasingly skimming my inner thighs, and I forgot all thought. His caresses were gentle, interspersed with kisses, as they swept over my butt and up my spine again. His fingers brushed the sides of my breasts but didn't go any farther, and I couldn't help the groan that escaped. He chuckled softly but continued on, massaging the lavender oil over my entire body but not touching any of the places that were truly beginning to ache.

Then his touch left me altogether. I growled softly, and he chuckled again.

"My, my," he said, and lightly slapped my butt. "You do get grouchy when woken from a deep sleep. Turn around."

I did so carefully. Pain stirred, but it was nowhere as bad as I'd half expected. I glanced at the clock on the far wall. It was just after midday, so I'd actually had close to six hours' sleep. No wonder I felt a whole lot better.

And a whole lot hornier.

Jackson was buck naked, and his glorious body burned with a heat that was both desire and the afterglow of merging with his element.

And the devil was bright in his eyes. Anticipation shot through me.

"Good afternoon, sleepyhead," he drawled, his voice low and sexy. "About time you awoke."

"Thanks for letting me sleep. Were you next door all that time?" I reached out to run my fingers down his cock, but he lightly slapped my hand away.

"No. And no touching the goods just yet, young lady."

I raised an eyebrow, a smile teasing my lips. "I'm hardly young, and I thought you'd be ready to explode."

"Oh, I am. But I'm also capable of a little finesse occasionally, especially when the woman in question has recently copped something of a beating."

"The woman in question appreciates the concern, but really wishes you'd just shut the fuck up and finish what you started."

He chuckled softly. "Your wish is my command."

But he didn't, as I'd half expected, immediately thrust into me. Instead, he took me at my word and continued what he'd started. Only this time he used his mouth and tongue rather than oil and hands, and he left no part of my upper body untouched or unexplored. He discovered erogenous zones I'd forgotten existed, and exploited them to the fullest, nipping and licking and kissing until sweat sheened my body and every inch of me vibrated with pleasure.

Then he moved down.

When his tongue flicked lightly over my clitoris, I jumped and whimpered, needing—wanting—so much more. He chuckled softly, his breath so cool against my heated skin, then got to work, suckling and licking me, until I was all but screaming. Then my orgasm hit and I *did* scream, twisting and moaning and shaking as he continued to suckle me.

And *still* he didn't enter me.

"You, Jackson Miller," I said when I was able, "are the devil incarnate."

He chuckled again. It was definitely an evil if delighted sound. "I cannot comply with your wishes, as I do believe quid pro quo was promised earlier."

"Then we had best reverse positions, had we not?"

His grin grew. "Whatever the lady wishes."

I scrambled out of his way, then straddled his legs and squirted some oil on my palm. I began by massaging his shoulders and back, enjoying the tension and heat that rose from his golden skin. That heat grew as my touch moved down his well-defined body, until it felt like I was sitting astride a furnace. And, lord, it felt *good*.

My touched lingered on his rump, then slipped down his legs. My fingers brushed the insides of his thighs but went no farther, and he groaned.

"What the man gives, he shall receive," I murmured.

"In which case, I look forward to turning over."

"I'm not finished with this side yet."

"Damn."

I grinned and kept on working my way down his legs. I massaged his feet for a while, then slowly worked my way up his body. Then I shifted and slapped his rump, just as he had mine. "Time to turn."

"Finally," he grumbled.

He turned; his cock was hard and begging for attention. I didn't give it any, but instead straddled his thighs and leaned forward on my hands.

He groaned and brushed my hair from my face. "Seriously? I'm needing more than another massage right now."

"So did I. All I got was an evil laugh."

"Yeah, but at least I *did* make you come."

"And so will you." I paused. "Eventually."

With that, I kissed him. It was a long, slow, and sensual exploration, and he returned it in kind. By the time my mouth left his, neither of us was breathing very steadily. But there was still work to be done, pleasure to be had.

I kissed his neck, his shoulders, and then moved down to his chest, lingering there to nip and tease. He shifted, his breath hard and fast, his cock nudging my stomach, desperate for attention. I smiled and trailed kisses down his stomach, following the smattering of reddish-brown hair. When my tongue swept over the moist tip of his penis, he groaned and his hips jerked reflexively. But I didn't immediately give him the completeness he desired and instead shifted, letting my fingers drift inside his thighs, lightly caressing all around his balls but never actually touching them.

"Damn it, woman," he growled, his eyes ablaze with a mix of desperation and amusement. "Stop teasing!"

I laughed, then ended his agony and took him in my mouth. His sharp intake of breath was all the encouragement I needed. I worked him as thoroughly as he'd worked me, alternating between running my tongue all over his impressive length and taking him in my mouth. His movements quickly became urgent, his hips thrusting harder, faster, as the taste of precum grew stronger. But just as he was on the brink of release, I pulled back, threw my leg over his hips, and claimed him in the most basic way possible. He hissed and pressed his hands against the tops of my thighs, but instead of forcing me down harder on him, he held me still. For several seconds, neither of us moved. His eyes were ablaze and his skin burned with so much heat it fueled the air and caressed my skin. *That* heat wasn't normal for a fire fae, but any concern I might have had was lost to sensation as he thrust the rest of the way into me.

From there on in, there was no talking. No thinking. There was just heat, and desire, and rising need. There was nothing slow or sensual about this now; it was hard and fast, and it wound me up tight and then spat me out, leaving me a quivering, groaning mess as he came so very deep inside of me.

For several minutes, neither of us moved. Hell, I

was struggling to even breathe, and Jackson certainly didn't seem to be any better off.

Eventually, he took my face between his hands and kissed me softly. "That," he said, his voice filled with wonder, "was an amazing entrée."

I laughed and rested my forehead against his. His cock was already giving off recovery signals deep within. Communing with his element really *did* have an amazing effect on him. "I'm not sure it's safe to be wasting any more time than we have. We have people after us, files to find, stuff like that."

"All of which will be waiting when we're done." He wrapped his arms around me and reversed our position in one surprisingly smooth move. "All the doors and windows are bolted and the downstairs alarm is on. We're as safe here as we're ever going to be."

"Yeah, but—"

"I need you, Emberly," he said as he began to rock ever so slowly. "You have no idea how badly."

"Oh," I murmured, wrapping my legs around him. "I think I do."

"Good. Besides, I have this odd feeling I should enjoy your glorious body while I can."

"Meaning you think I'm going somewhere?" And that the ability to raise fire might not have been the only thing he'd gained when we'd merged? It was certainly possible, but at least *this* development wasn't as dangerous and as worrying as the other.

"No. I think you and I will have a very long and profitable partnership. I just don't think it's destined to be a sexual one."

"And why would you think that? I tend not to play

the field, Jackson, and there's no one other than Rory on the horizon. And he *has* to be there."

No one other than Sam, I supposed, but he was this lifetime's lost cause. I doubted fate was going to have a sudden change of heart and allow me a second chance at love.

"I know. It's just . . ." Jackson paused and half shrugged. "I can't explain it. I've just got this feeling we're short-term. Believe me, it is a thought that upsets me greatly."

"Yeah," I said, grinning. "I can see just how woebegone you are."

"I know. I'm all tears." His grin flashed again. "Which is why I now insist we cut the talking and just get down to business. After all, it may be the last time we get to share the delight of making love."

And, over the next four hours, we certainly did share.

Jackson placed a large mug of green tea on the coffee table in front of me then snagged the nearby box of donuts and offered me one.

"Thanks." I grabbed the last caramel donut and took a bite as I flipped open the file we'd snatched from Rosen's. "I'm gathering you've already been through this."

He nodded. "I flagged the interesting bits with a Post-it."

I flipped to the first marked page and quickly scanned it. My gaze shot to his. "Rosen's company is developing a device that makes the wearer immune to telepathic intrusion via an inversion process? Holy fuck!"

"If those notes are to be believed, holy fuck indeed." He took a sip of coffee. "Which makes me wonder why he was killed. A development like that could make billions."

I snorted. "I can't imagine the government releasing that sort of device to the wider market. Not before the military, police, and all government officials were given one, anyway."

"Agreed. So would why PIT allow him to continue with his gambling?" He leaned back against the sofa, his shoulder lightly brushing mine. "Surely to god that was a risk—"

"Not really," I cut in. "Sam mentioned them ensuring Rosen couldn't leak any vital information to the sindicati. I'm betting this device would have been on that list."

"Maybe. Doesn't explain how Heaton got wind of it, though."

I frowned and glanced back at the notes. Heaton had apparently approached Rosen a few months after his arrival here in Melbourne, and he'd offered a very large amount of money for information and prototypes. Rosen had refused.

"I can imagine how well *that* went down." I finished the last bit of donut and licked my fingers clean. That had been my fourth, but my belly still wasn't satisfied. A serious lovemaking session tended to do that to me, though.

"It didn't," Jackson said. "Read on."

I did. Rosen continued with *The arrogant bastard got violent at that point, but I had the boys grab him by the scruff of the neck and toss him out on his ass.*

I raised my eyebrows and met Jackson's similarly disbelieving gaze. "No way."

"My thought exactly." He leaned forward and snagged the last donut, tearing it in half before offering me one piece. It was gone in seconds. "Heaton is a vampire, and while sheer weight of numbers *could* take him down, he's also a powerful telepath. He could take out the cavalry with a simple thought."

"Unless, of course, Rosen's device isn't in the planning stages, but rather an up and running prototype." I frowned and took a sip of tea. "But that still doesn't explain how they overpowered Heaton. Even if Rosen *had* called for backup, he would have heard them coming." Vamps were attuned to the beat of blood through the body, after all, and could hear its call as sharply as any dog did a whistle.

"Unless he allowed it to happen. And remember who's making the notes—I would imagine there's a fair bit of embellishment happening."

"Probably." And Rosen had had a very inflated opinion of himself. I flipped the pages to the next Post-it. This was a brief note about Rosen hiring one Jake Barrett—another private investigator—to seek out information on Heaton. Scrawled on the bottom of this was update: *Paid the bastard a good deposit, but the prick has done a runner. No info. Might have to go elsewhere.*

I glanced at Jackson. "I'm gathering he never asked you to check on Heaton?"

"No. This was months before I was employed to find Wilson. For whatever reason, he'd obviously forgotten about Heaton by then."

"I can't imagine Heaton letting the matter go so

easily." I drank some more tea and checked out the rest of the file. It was just more notes on random people, none of which seemed related to anything we were investigating.

"No, which doesn't mean he wasn't employing other methods to get what he wanted."

I frowned. "But surely PIT—"

"PIT has trouble aplenty and not enough people. While they might be aware of Heaton, they could be unaware of his interest in the inversion device."

I guess that was possible. I closed the file and dumped it on the coffee table. "Do you know Jake Barrett? Can we go talk to him?"

"I know *of* him, but we can't go talk to him." His voice was grim. "He's dead."

"I'm gathering it wasn't from natural causes."

"No. He was found floating in the river about a month after Rosen made that comment." He grimaced. "I had my source check the autopsy results. He was knifed the same day as Rosen hired him."

My eyes widened. "There's a mole in Rosen's company."

"It would seem like it. And it would surely have to be the secretary. She's the one who made the initial contact with me. I don't doubt it was the same for Barrett."

"Then maybe the secretary is someone we need to talk to."

"Yes." He glanced at his watch. "But she would have more than likely left work by now. We'll have to catch her tomorrow."

"But not at work," I said. "If she isn't the leak, then maybe the place is bugged."

Rosen's building would undoubtedly be regularly swept for such devices—all government places and most nongovernment ones dealing with anything high-level and supersecret were these days—but that didn't mean bugs couldn't exist. Or that there wasn't someone in the building—someone capable of telepathy—doing regular mind raids.

I drank some more tea then said, "I wonder why Rosen kept a file like this."

"The mind of an egomaniac is sometimes hard to understand." Jackson shrugged. "Maybe he simply liked reading about his perceived conquest over the fuckwits."

I snorted. Once again, *that* was totally possible. "So what do we do next?"

"We hide the file in case we need it later. Then I suggest we return to our apartment, before Rory starts getting antsy."

"Good point." Especially considering that as far as Rory was aware, we'd been doing nothing more than a simple raid on Rosen's place—over twelve hours ago.

He drained his coffee then picked up the file and walked over to the coffee machine. He pulled it away from the wall slightly, shoved the file behind it, then slid it back into place. I guessed it was as safe there as it was anywhere else in this place—and it was certainly a spot few would think to look.

I finished the last of my tea, then put the cup in the sink and collected my bag. Twenty minutes later we were in the car and cruising back to the apartment.

Rory glanced up as we walked in the door, and the relief that swept his face had guilt slithering through me.

"We need a means of contacting each other," he said. "Because the last few hours have been the worst."

"I know, and I'm sorry." I waved a hand inanely. "But lots of things happened."

He leaned back in the chair and raised an eyebrow. "Like what?"

I put the Chinese we'd bought on the way back here on the table then sat down beside him and gave him a quick update. Jackson collected some plates and cutlery from the kitchen then dumped them on the table and began opening the various tubs of food.

"Do you trust the wolves to carry through with their promise and protect both the guard and your friend?" Rory reached for a plate and the nearest tub of chicken and cashews. "They don't usually do that sort of thing for free."

"It's not free," I said. "They expect any and all information we get about Rinaldo in return."

"And are you including Rinaldo's visit to Rosen in that? Because I'm thinking PIT wouldn't be pleased if you did."

"No, but if Rinaldo knows about the device, you can bet the sindicati and the rats do." Jackson scooped half the contents of the black bean steak onto his plate then handed the container to me. "And yes, I believe the pack will protect the guard and Shona. As well as anyone could, given who we're dealing with, anyway."

Rory grunted and began eating. "So your first report has to be made in less than an hour?"

I glanced at the clock. I hadn't realized it was that late. "Yes. Not that we've much to report. Why?"

"Because a couple of hours ago, I had another of those interesting conversations with Lan."

Lan was the old Filipino shaman who'd helped us stop an Aswang's recent killing spree. But he'd left us with a rather dire warning—that a time of metaphysical darkness was approaching this city, and it was a darkness that would draw dire creatures and black events to this place. The Aswang, and the virus, was just the beginning of our troubles, apparently.

"So what did he come for this time?" Jackson asked.

Rory grabbed one of the containers of special fried rice and added most of that to the pile on his plate. "He wants us to help out a friend."

Jackson grimaced. "We really don't need to be dealing with another problem right now."

"No, we don't," I agreed. "But if weren't for him, who knows how many more people that Aswang would have killed. We owe him."

"I guess." Jackson didn't exactly look convinced. "Did he say what sort of trouble his friend was in?"

"No," Rory said, "but he was very insistent that you and Jackson go see said friend tonight."

I couldn't help smiling. If there was one thing all true shaman had in common, it was that if they wanted something done, it had to be done *now*.

But it was an urgency I could understand. My dreams didn't have anywhere near the power or scope of a shaman's, but when they struck, I generally didn't have the luxury of sitting back to contemplate them. "I'm gathering he left a name and address?"

Rory nodded and pushed a business card toward

me. "Lan also said she could help us with our current problem."

"Did he also happen to mention which of our many problems he was actually referring to?" Jackson's tone was amused.

"I'm betting the answer to *that* would be no." I picked up the business card. It was a pretty pink color, and a cute black graphic of a cat sitting in front of an old-fashioned straw broom dominated the right side of the page. On the left, it simply said, *Grace Harkwell, Consulting Witch*. Underneath that was an address and phone number. Unsurprisingly, she lived—or maybe just worked—in Sassafras, which had become something of a witch and psychic haven over recent years.

"I'm thinking she's a fairly high-ranking member of the local coven," Rory said. "Because very few witches can legally advertise themselves like that."

"That's because most of the so-called witches are either psychics or charlatans," Jackson said. "There aren't many around these days who are truly gifted."

"How old are you again?" Rory said. "Because *that* sounds like something a cynical old soul would say."

Jackson grinned and acknowledged the point with a wave of his fork. "No, *that* was spoken like someone who has come across far too many of the latter in his brief time on this planet."

I finished the rest of the food on my plate, then rose and put it in the sink. "Did Lan say what time she was expecting us?"

"Eight o'clock." He paused. "And I contacted work today. They need me in tonight. A couple of the boys have called in sick."

I frowned. "I don't know if that's wise—"

"Em," he said patiently, "I'll be fine. Nothing will happen at the station house, because there are far too many witnesses. Besides, the wrong sort of people might start putting two and two together if I completely disappear."

"They've already done *that*," I muttered. "Luke made a direct threat against you, remember, and he has the manpower to carry it out."

"And between my fire and the mother's, he hasn't a hope of pulling anything off." He smiled, but his eyes were serious. "I can't sit around here all day and night, Em. I'll go stir-crazy."

"And," Jackson said, "if Rory is out and about, then at least he's taking some of the heat from us."

I crossed my arms and glared at him. I *could* see the sense in Rory going back to work, but that slither of unease was back. Intuition, once again murmuring rather unhelpfully that something was going to go very wrong in our near future, something that might involve Rory. I really wished intuition would either give it a rest or become a full-blown dream and give me something concrete to work with.

"I promise, I'll be careful, and I'll come back here after each shift," he continued, "but I need to do something—something apart from helping you two out. As I said, it's better I'm only involved in direct attacks."

"Fine," I muttered. "Just . . ."

My voice faded, and he smiled. "We made a pact to live out this lifetime, remember? I have no intention of being the one who breaks it."

Goose bumps fled across my skin, and I rubbed my

arms. Fate, I suspected, had just been tempted. But I didn't say anything because, in truth, I would have hated being cooped up here just as much as he did.

"You might as well source some alternate form of communication while you're out," I said. "I know we can use Wi-Fi to remain in contact, but that's not practical in most situations. Maybe you could ask Mike about acquiring some black market phones?"

Mike was a street kid who'd started coming to Rory's kung fu classes when he was barely a teen. He and Rory had become friends, mainly because Rory didn't judge him. Over the years, Mike had moved from selling his body to selling drugs and whatever else he could get his hands on. These days, he was an extremely successful black market "tracker." If it was illegal and it could be bought or stolen, he'd find it. For a price, of course. Why the rats let him do business in their territory I had no idea, but maybe it was simply a matter of the stuff he was moving not being of a high enough volume to worry them.

"New cell phones will only be useful if someone else buys and activates the SIM cards for us," Jackson said. "Otherwise, we might as well start using our own phones again."

"Trust me, Mike *can* arrange that." Rory pushed up from his chair. "I'll ring him tonight."

"Not from the work phone," I said. "It might be bugged."

"I'm not that dumb, Em."

I grinned. "Well, good, because one of us really does need to be sensible in this outfit."

He snorted softly, then gave us a wave and headed

upstairs. A few seconds later, the water pipes rattled as he turned on the shower. I glanced at Jackson. "We might as well get our phone call over with, then go see Lan's friend."

"Agreed." He rose, dumped the empty containers in the nearby bin, then ushered me out. We found a public phone on the way to Grace's, and I jumped out and made the required check-in—which didn't take long because we really had nothing to report. There was a bakery nearby, so I grabbed some pastries and returned to the car.

"I do have to wonder," Jackson said as he pulled back out into the traffic, "how the hell Rinaldo is ever going to know if we're holding something back?"

"Maybe he's trusting the fact that his threat will be enough to keep us honest." Because in truth, it was.

Jackson took one the pastries from the bag then said, "Possibly, but he doesn't seem the type to trust a person's honesty. I suspect he's probably got something else planned to keep us in line."

I frowned. "Like what? We're not being followed, are we?"

"Not that I can see. Doesn't stop the uneasy feeling, though."

"Great," I muttered. "Just what we need—another person in this outfit getting bad feelings."

"Well, you have no one to blame but yourself. If you'd kept your premonition and fire abilities to yourself when we shared energy—"

I grinned and lightly punched his arm. "Idiot."

He chuckled. "Are we going to charge the witches for whatever favor they want?"

My smile faded. "I'm thinking it's probably not wise. We may in the future need their help, and it'd be good to have a favor owed."

"My thinking exactly." He paused and made a right-hand turn. "Which is why I offered you the partnership. Our thought trains are very alike."

"And here I was thinking I was offered the partnership because you were hoping it meant sex on tap."

"Never tried sex on a tap," he mused. "I'd imagine it would be very painful."

I laughed and decided to concentrate on the serious business of eating my pastry. It was far safer than replying to a comment like *that*.

The address on Grace's business card did indeed turn out to be a shop rather than a residence. It was a wide, glass-fronted, purple building in a long row of shops, and even from the street, it looked magical.

Once Jackson found parking, I grabbed my jacket and climbed out. The night air was crisp and filled with the scent of eucalyptus.

Jackson breathed deep, and delight touched his expression. "Ah, I do so love trees."

"Which totally explains why you live in a major city."

He smiled, caught my hand, and tugged me across the road. "Trees have no hope against lust. And, as I've said, the city holds the lure of a female fae who will come into season sooner rather than later."

He was referring to Rochelle, but it was a liaison fraught with danger—and not only because she was currently in a relationship with Sam. "*That* fae is also infected with the red plague and totally off-limits until they find a cure or at least develop a vaccine. Or have you conveniently forgotten about that?"

"I forget very little when it pertains to sex." He released my hand and pushed the shop's door open. A small bell chimed softly, the sound as sweet as the scents in the air. "There's always hope a cure will be found before she comes into season."

"Yeah, because luck has totally been running our way up until now."

"Well, at least it can't get any worse."

I snorted and stepped through the door. It was as if I'd entered wonderland. Books, stones, incense, herbs, crystals . . . everything a witch might need was here. There were also gifts, artwork, and jewelry, as well as tarot reading for those seeking advice from the other side, and meditation for those who simply sought peace. All manner of mobiles, scarves, and flowers trailed from the ceiling, many strung with cobwebs that only added to the charm. And the smell of the place . . . "Divine" was the only way to truly describe it, though I daresay a werewolf might have found it more than a little overwhelming.

"Something has to go our way eventually," he said. "Even fate isn't that big a bitch."

"I wouldn't bet on it." And considering we were still alive after all we'd been through, it was totally possible we were getting as much help from fate as we were ever likely to get.

We began to wind our way through the crowded but totally wonderful shop, but had barely taken more than half a dozen steps when a gorgeously Rubenesque woman in a multicolored gypsy skirt and white shirt stepped through the silk curtains at the far end of the room. An equally colorful shawl lay loosely draped across her shoulders; its vivid colors were a stark contrast to the flat gray of her hair.

"Welcome to my haven. How may I . . ." She paused, her blue eyes narrowing fractionally. "Lan sent you here, didn't he?"

I exchanged a brief, somewhat surprised glance with Jackson. If she could tell who we were within a few seconds of us entering her shop, then she really *was* powerful.

So why on earth did she need our help?

"Yes, I'm afraid he did. I'm Jackson Miller, and this is Emberly Pearson."

"Grace Harkwell," she said. "It is a pleasure to meet you both. I only wish it could have been under different circumstances."

"Lan didn't explain the circumstances," I said. "And I have to say, we're a little perplexed as to what we can do that someone of your power cannot."

"That's easily explained. But not here." She caught the curtains with one hand and swept them aside. "Please, come into my workspace."

I followed Jackson across the room, my nostrils flaring as I neared her. Not because of her scent—which was as sweet and as warm as her shop—but because of the sheer amount of power emanating from her. It was almost furnace hot, and its source was *very* familiar; this woman was locked into the energy of the earth, the energy of the mother herself. And it was very, *very* rare to find a human capable of such a feat.

The small room beyond the curtains was as plain

and understated as the main room was over-the-top. There was a large pentagram etched onto the floor, and though there were no candles sitting on each of the points—meaning it wasn't currently active—the droplets of white wax that surrounded each were evidence enough that it recently had been. There were also candles and a small collection of what I presumed would be spell stones in each corner of the room. This place was well and truly protected from evil.

She waved us toward the small sofa to one side of the pentagram then perched on the red velvet chair opposite.

"Two and a half weeks ago," she said without preamble, "three of my kin went missing. No matter what any of us have done, we cannot find any trace of them."

"By 'kin,'" I asked, "are we talking blood relatives, or coven sisters and brothers?"

"The latter." She caught the ends of her colorful shawl and wrapped it tighter around her shoulders. Fighting off a chill, or fear—I wasn't sure which.

"And there was no warning, no strange events or portents, nothing that made you suspect anything might be wrong beforehand?" Jackson asked.

She shook her head. "Nothing at all. There *is* an element up here now that are less than pleased about the small werewolf pack that has claimed a large swath of the Olinda State Forest as their own, but witches have been a part of this community for as long as anyone can remember. I do not believe a local could be responsible."

"Is it possible that the three of them are dead?" It

would certainly explain why no one had been able to find them. When a soul moved on, it left nothing behind but inert flesh, and even magic found *that* difficult to trace. Certain psychics could, of course, but the ability to find a body and touch whatever memories might linger within was a dangerous gift, and one that often resulted in madness.

Grace waved a hand. "It's certainly possible, but I know in my heart that is not what has happened."

"Tell us what you do know, then." Jackson got out his phone then paused. "You don't mind if I record this conversation, do you?"

She shook her head. "All three were booked to appear at an alternative lifestyle expo in the city. We know they appeared on the Saturday, but not the Sunday."

"Meaning they disappeared Saturday night?"

"Yes. The police have told us they have footage of them leaving the hotel together at eight forty-five, but they never returned. Nor did they check out."

"And their luggage?" Jackson asked.

"Was still in their rooms. The police have passed it back to their families, as there's no evidence of a crime having been committed within the room."

"They would have search the CCTV footage near the hotel," Jackson said, glancing at me. "If anything had happened to them, they would have caught it."

"Except if it happened in a black spot. There are still a few of them in Melbourne, apparently." I glanced back at Grace. "I still can't see where we'd be able to achieve what you cannot. We're private investigators, and simply don't have access to the resources a case like this needs. And we certainly haven't the metaphysical power at our disposal that you have."

"Under normal circumstances, that would be true, but I suspect their disappearance is actually linked to whatever it is you're currently investigating."

My eyebrows rose, even as my stomach sank. More shit, I suspected, was about to be piled on.

"How so?" Jackson asked. The tension in him was so fierce sparks danced sharply across his fingertips.

I frowned at him. He followed the direction of my gaze and instantly curled his fingers into a fist. But it was a worrying sign that he was doing it without thinking. Phoenixes learned control from a very early age, and even then, our fires could sometimes get away from us. And while Jackson was a fire fae and should certainly have no problem controlling *any* sort of fire, he'd obviously become something more than a fae but less than a phoenix when he'd merged with me. Which meant his inner fire might just grow faster—stronger—than his ability to contain it.

It was certainly something we'd better talk about sometime in the very near future.

If Grace noticed the sparks, she made no mention of it. But then, she obviously knew exactly what we both were. Which was, I thought grimly, a worrying trend.

"The reason I believe their disappearance holds a connection to your current investigation is simple," Grace said, her voice solemn. "The week before that happened, three very different men made an appointment with me, and all of them were seeking the same thing."

That bad feeling grew. I swallowed heavily and said, "And what was that, exactly?"

But even as I said it, I knew. God help me, I knew.

She took a deep breath and slowly released it. Her gaze, when it met mine, was filled with sympathy.

"They were after the means to restrict—and preferably kill—a phoenix."

Chapter 6

"Fuck." Jackson scrubbed a hand through his short hair. "You didn't give it to them, did you?"

"No, of course not. Killing another soul goes against everything we believe in."

"What about restricting them?" I asked. After all, more than one person *had* been using spell stones against me of late, and they had to be coming from somewhere. None of those who'd used them had the capacity to make them, of that much I was sure.

"That, too, would not be something we'd do, unless the soul in question was in league with the dark forces of this world. You, clearly, are not."

"You couldn't have known that," I said. "You've only just met me."

She smiled. "True, but sometimes one does not have to meet a person to know their heart. Especially when both are connected to the mother herself."

Finding another soul through the mother was not something I'd ever attempted to do—and probably couldn't, to be honest. That was not the way I connected to her.

"So you think your coven kin were kidnapped to do what you would not?" Jackson asked.

"I believe that was the original idea, yes." Worry

creased her features. "But the fact that we can no longer sense them is not a good sign. We should be able to, you see."

"Well, I *can* tell you that in the last couple of weeks, spell stones have been used against me on several occasions. So if your missing witches are *not* the source, then there's someone else in this city capable of creating them."

"No, there isn't." Her gaze met mine squarely. "If a dark sorcerer or witch had taken up residence here, we would have felt his or her stain."

"Meaning," Jackson said, "we've at least found the source of those damn spell stones."

But even as he said it, Grace was shaking her head. "They wouldn't do it. They couldn't. It would be a knife to the heart of everything they believe in. They would die first."

"And yet," I said as gently as I could, "if there is no one else in this city capable of creating that sort of spell, then at least one of them is working with their kidnappers."

She didn't look happy with that statement, but she didn't dispute it, either.

"Have you talked to their partners or families?" Jackson asked. "Is it possible that they're being used as a means of leverage?"

"All three are unattached." Grace frowned. "Two do have well-off families, though, so I guess that *is* possible."

"But you doubt it," I said. "Why?"

She waved a hand. "Intuition. A gut feeling."

I wasn't about to disbelieve her instincts—especially

when I tended to rely heavily on the damn things myself.

I crossed my legs and leaned on one knee. "The men who came to see you about the spells—can you describe them?"

She immediately rose and moved across to the corner of the room, collecting what looked like several sheets of art paper before returning to her chair.

"I did a sketch of the men after each of the visits," she said, offering them to me. "I haven't got security cams in the shop, but the mother whispered the need of a record."

Then her experience with the mother really *was* different from mine. Which, given she was human and I was not, was to be expected.

I studied the first sketch. He had thick sideburns that covered half his cheeks and were as black as the monotone brow that dominated the upper portion of his face. His nose was bulbous and his eyes somewhat beady. *Rat,* I thought instinctively, though I'd never seen the man before. But it would hardly be surprising if the rats were seeking some means of restricting my fire, given what Jackson and I had done to both Radcliffe and his men.

The next two men she'd sketched were, unfortunately, all too familiar—Theodore Hunt and Luke. The *last* thing I needed was for either of *them* to get their hands on a means of restricting me.

Although Luke *had* used magic to protect himself when I'd confronted him in that laneway. Had that spell come from the missing witches? I really hoped not—for their sakes. Because if he had them, they *would* be infected. It certainly would explain why Grace felt they were alive, and yet had no sense of them. The red cloaks—the mad ones at least—didn't seem to have any life in them. They were alive, they functioned, but all that they were, all that they thought and did, came from the hive mind rather than individual consciousness. What that did to their actual souls I have no idea. Maybe they were simply locked deep within their bodies, or maybe becoming one of the red cloaks meant a long, slow slide into death for body *and* soul.

It would certainly explain why Luke wasn't at all concerned by his losses. He probably figured that if they were going to die, then they might as well go down trying to achieve *his* desires.

"I'm gathering from your expression that you do indeed know them?" Grace said.

I nodded and handed the sketches to Jackson. He looked no happier than I felt.

"One has sworn vengeance on me because I've interfered with several of his missions," I said. "And the other—"

"Is the source of the darkness that now holds Brooklyn hostage," Grace finished for me.

I shared another glance with Jackson. Sassafras might be at the far end of Melbourne's outskirts and a long way from Brooklyn, but this witch didn't miss much.

"How much do you know about the troubles there?" Jackson said.

She shrugged. "Not a great deal. I have felt the darkness descending on this city for a while, of course, and have spoken of my fears with Lan many a time. Brooklyn itself is but the beginning."

"Yeah, he's told us that." I scrubbed a hand across my eyes. How much should I tell her? Sam had warned us—under the threat of incarceration—not to tell anyone about the virus, but Grace deserved to know what might have happened to her friends.

Because if they *had* been infected, then finding them was just the first part of the problem.

"It is possible," I said carefully, "that your missing friends have been infected by the darkness that now holds Brooklyn. And if that is the case—"

I hesitated, and Jackson stepped in, saying what I didn't want to. "If that *is* the case, then they are lost to both you and us. If we do find them, we may have no choice but to kill them."

Grace's eyes went wide, and her cheeks lost color. For several minutes, she didn't say or do anything, and yet I had a feeling a whole lot was going on at a deeper level. Power stabbed the air, its touch so rich and heated and familiar that my skin tingled in response and the spirit within wanted to reach out and take.

Because that power was the mother.

Whatever Grace was doing, whomever she was contacting, she was doing it through the energy of the earth.

After a few minutes, tears shone in her eyes, and she blinked. "So be it," she said, voice soft. Then her gaze refocused and swept between the two of us. "You must try to find them for us. And if they *are* affected by this darkness, you have to kill them. We cannot allow the earth mother to be tainted by this darkness via them. Not when we have deeper problems coming."

"I'm not entirely sure there can be anything worse than what's currently happening in Brooklyn," Jackson muttered. "And if there *is*, I don't want to know about it."

Grace's sudden smile was almost sad. "That choice, I'm afraid, has long since departed. Like it or not, your fate is connected to hers"—she nodded at me—"and *hers* is connected to this city."

Humans with power, it seemed, liked their prophecies filled with ominous warning that didn't really give you a whole lot of information to run with.

But then, if she and Lan were right, we'd understand it all too soon.

"I still don't know why you expect us to find them when neither you nor the police can," I said.

"We do so because of this." She rose once more and walked over to the desk. This time she picked up what looked to be a yellow Post-it note and handed it to Jackson. "It was written by Angie, one of those missing."

"'The Vic is the key, and fire is our savior,'" he read. "'She must follow the ghost seen from room two nineteen at midnight on the tenth.'"

The tenth was tomorrow night, but the rest of it made little sense. "Where did you find it?"

"At her place yesterday. She obviously had a premonition something might happen."

"And yet she didn't contact you or anyone else about her fears?"

Grace shook her head. "Premonitions are events that *may* happen, not must. We cannot go through life fearing to take a step out because of what *might* eventuate."

True. And it wasn't like I spared much thought for

the consequences—or, at least, what it might mean for me—when I had a premonition.

"I'm gathering we're the fire reference," I said. "But I'm not clear on the rest of it."

"Neither are we. We Googled the name, of course, and there is both a Vic Bar and a Victoria Hotel in Melbourne. I suspect Angie meant the latter, as it is the only place with accommodation."

"If it *is* the hotel, then surely you could deal with whatever it is—"

"No," Grace said. "She would not have mentioned fire if you were not their best hope."

The mention of fire didn't necessarily mean us, but I guess it was highly unlikely that it was a coincidence.

"Have you got a photo of the three of them?"

She pulled a small photograph from her pocket and handed it to me. There were five women in the picture—Grace and four others.

"Angie is the tall black woman to my right. On my left is Meredith, who is safe and well. The other two are Rennie and Neriana."

Rennie was about five six, with frizzy brown hair and a well-lined, happy face. Neriana was small, blond, and cute.

I handed the photo to Jackson. He looked at it for a moment then put it and the note into his pocket.

"We'll do our best to find them alive and hopefully well," he said, "but I wouldn't put a whole lot of hope—"

"You are their *only* hope," Grace cut in again. "Angie believed that. I believe that. If you cannot achieve this, then I fear for their souls."

And wasn't *that* just what we needed—the weight of souls on our consciences.

"We do not have the cash to pay you for your time," Grace continued. "But we can perhaps offer something far more valuable."

Jackson raised an eyebrow. "We weren't going to ask for payment, but I'm nevertheless intrigued."

Grace smiled and for the first time since we'd entered the shop, it warmed the sadness from her eyes. "What we can offer is a means of protection against any spell that attempts to block your fire or restrict your access to the mother."

I stared at her for a moment then somehow said, "God, if we could get something like *that*, it would be a huge help."

She nodded. "It will not protect you from anything *other* than that particular type of spell, of course, but Lan tells me there *is* no protection for what comes at you in the nearest future."

"And isn't *that* nice to know," I muttered grimly.

Her smile faded. "You know in your heart things will grow worse. You feel it, as we do. All of us will be tested by what the future brings, but you three are certainly at the forefront of that battle."

Three. That surely meant Rory as well. *Fuck*.

I batted away the fear that rose with the thought and said, "When will we be able to get hold of these charms?"

"We will start work on them tonight. Lan will contact you when they are ready."

"And if we find your missing kin?" *And are forced to*

kill them? I didn't say those words, but they seemed to hang in the air regardless.

"We will know. We will feel the release of their souls if they move on."

"Even if they are infected by the darkness?"

"Even if. Death frees the spirit from whatever assails it, be it physical, mental, or metaphysical."

"Let's hope it's not the latter, for their sake, at least." I held out the sketches then hesitated as my gaze fell on Hunt's image. "Neither you nor any of your coven kin has given this man a means of restricting my fire, have you?"

She frowned. "No, but that is not to say he can't find such a means. I do not believe it was chance that brought all three here, and I suspect—given the timing—that at least one witnessed the other's departure."

Tension wound through me again. "Which one?"

She pointed instantly to Hunt. "That one would have seen the rat leave."

I relaxed, but only a little. Hunt was already acquainted with the rats; it was Luke I didn't want him knowing, if only because Luke could very easily twist an already twisted mind. But if Hunt had seen the rat's representative leave, it was also possible he'd seen Luke, given what Grace had said about their arrival times.

Luke and Hunt working together was a very, *very* scary thought.

"Please call me if you do find them," Grace said. "It matters not the time. When I'm not here, I divert calls to my private number."

"We will."

And with that, we left. We collected a coffee—or tea, in my case—from a nearby café, then climbed into the car and headed home. It was after midnight by the time we got back and, despite the sleep I'd had earlier, I was bone tired. Jackson must have felt the same, because he kissed me good night then climbed into his own bed. He was asleep within minutes.

My sleep, however, was slower in coming, and even when it did hit, it was filled with a turbulent mix of warnings that involved not only fire, but death and destruction. And yet—unusually for my dreams—none of it was clear.

Which meant I woke at dawn, feeling less than rested and a whole lot more troubled.

Jackson was still snoring away, and Rory wasn't yet back from his shift, so I silently pulled on a sweater and padded downstairs. After making myself a pot of tea and several slices of toast, I sat down at the table and booted up the laptop.

A Google search for "The Vic" revealed the results Grace had mentioned—the Victoria Hotel and a bar. I clicked on the hotel link and read through the various bits about its history, and discovered it had once been more commonly referred to as "The Vic." I made a reservation for the following night and requested the room the note had mentioned. I had no idea what we were going to do if it wasn't available, but I guessed we could worry about that when the time came.

For the next hour or so, I checked out various news and social media sites to catch up on what was happening in the rest of the world. Rory came in just as I'd started answering work e-mails. He smelled of smoke, fire, and happiness, the latter reflected in the huge grin that split his features when he saw me.

"I'm gathering it was a very good night," I said, voice dry. His whole body vibrated with the force of the flames he'd drawn in, and his skin was practically glowed.

"We had to attend a massive factory fire that took all night to get under control. It was glorious." He caught my hands, tugged me into his arms, and kissed me soundly. Only it was more than just a kiss; energy flowed from him to me, and, oh, it felt *fine*.

"Seriously, you two," Jackson said behind us. "This place is about three seconds away from combusting. How about we tone it down several notches?"

Rory laughed, the sound vibrating briefly against my lips as he pulled away. "Sorry, but I just had to share the joy."

"Hey, if I were *that* way inclined, I'd be standing in line for the sharing, trust me." He moved across to the kettle and flicked it on. "However, doing so here is not a good idea, as evidenced by the wall."

I twisted around. There were scorch marks running up the wall, some of them bad enough that the paint had browned and begun peeling away. Any longer and we *would* have set this place alight.

"Oops," I said, even as Rory added, somewhat sheepishly, "And we were discussing just how inflammable this place is only a day ago."

"You might have to start using the blacksmith's place," Jackson said. "At least *that* has some protection against flames."

"True, but it wouldn't be wise." I picked up my

empty plate, walked into the kitchen, and dumped it in the sink. "You need it to commune with your element. If we start using it, too, we risk someone finding out about it. Besides, we can simply take a drive into the country."

"Which is also not without its problems."

"Right now, nothing is." I glanced at Rory. "Do you want something to eat?"

"Nah, I had something at the station before I left. What are you two up to today?"

I shrugged. "We'll probably search Wilson's place."

Jackson nodded as he picked up the whistling kettle and poured some water into his mug. "Right now, there's nothing much else we can do."

"What about Radcliffe's phone?" Rory asked. "You hacked into that yet?"

"The program broke through five minutes ago," Jackson said. "It's what actually woke me. But I haven't had a chance to look at it yet. Why?"

Rory hesitated. "There were a couple of occasions last night when I had an odd feeling I was being watched. Which, given the enormity of the fire, we definitely were, but this just felt more personal."

I frowned, that slight knot of unease sharpening in my chest again. But I resisted the urge to tell him yet again to be careful. Or, better yet, to stay here. I'd done enough of that already; besides, I could hardly beg him to be safe when what I was doing was an even bigger risk. "Did you feel it when you were at the station?"

"No, but that doesn't mean they weren't there—especially if it's the rats. They're harder to sense when they're in animal form."

"What makes you think it is the rats?" Jackson raised his mug, silently offering Rory one.

Rory shook his head. "Just a feeling. But if *was* the rats, why watch me? Radcliffe must suspect we have his phone, so why hasn't he activated the search program and come here to retrieve it?"

Jackson swore loudly. "Fuck, I didn't even *think* of that possibility. Which is dumb, given we got rid of our SIM cards for that same reason."

"Yeah, I felt like an idiot last night when I thought about it." Rory's voice was wry.

"Maybe he thinks we gave the phone to his ex," I said. "We did tell him she had his wallet, remember."

"True," Jackson mused. "And I suspect Radcliffe didn't fancy tackling her in any way, shape, or form."

That's because Mary Johnson—Radcliffe's ex, and the mother of his son—was a straight-talking and, I suspected, straight-shooting woman. She certainly wasn't someone I'd want to get on the wrong side of.

"Either way, we'd better get that damn phone out of here, just in case."

Jackson nodded. "Once we retrieve any information from it, we can basically dump it." He hesitated, and the smile that touched his lips had a decidedly devilish edge. "Perhaps Mary Johnson might like to see it."

"I'm sure she would. Imagine the havoc she could wreak." I glanced at Rory. "Are you working again tonight? Because we have to go chase a ghost at a hotel in the city."

He raised an eyebrow. "And how did ghost busting suddenly become part of this mission?"

I gave him a quick rundown of both what Grace

had wanted and what she'd said about us. He grunted and shook his head. "I'm liking the sound of the future less and less."

"We've been through dark times before." My tone was philosophical, even though I totally agreed with him. "We'll get through this one, too."

"So what were the Dark Ages like?" Jackson asked. "As bad as history would have us believe?"

"And what makes you think we're old enough to have lived through the Dark Ages?" I raised an eyebrow. "Or that we'd even answer that particular question?"

He grinned. "Oh, come on, you can tell me. I won't share with anyone else. Scout's honor."

"And were you actually ever a scout?" Rory asked.

"No, but that's not the point."

Rory snorted and pushed away from the table. "I'm heading upstairs for a much-needed shower. Make sure you lock up tight if you leave before I'm out."

"Will do." I hesitated. "Did you manage to ask Mike about getting some clean phones?"

"Oh yeah." He dug into his jacket pocket and pulled out what looked like a brand-new Sony. "One is the best he could do on short notice, but he's going to see if he can acquire a couple more tonight. He'll get back to me tomorrow."

I accepted the phone and hit the POWER button. The little Optus signal came up in the corner. "Who is it registered to?"

"He didn't say, but it's got six months of calls and data paid up front."

I raised an eyebrow. "Is it likely to be reported stolen?"

"Nope. Don't ask why, because I don't know." He motioned to the old phone on the wall. "Take note of the number, and leave me a message if necessary."

"I will.

"Good. And now I'm off for that shower." He gave us a half wave and disappeared up the stairs.

I returned my gaze to Jackson. "So, Wilson's?"

"Yes. We'd better pack some clothes for tonight, though, just in case we don't get back here."

"And Radcliffe's phone?"

"I'll copy everything across to our new phone. Then we can either dump Radcliffe's on the way to Wilson's or after."

"After would be easier. We'll be hitting peak-hour traffic if we try to cut across to Mary's now."

"Good point. After, it is."

I tossed him the new phone then headed upstairs to grab some clothes. Half an hour later, with the data transfer finished, we were in the car and heading toward Wilson's place. This time, instead of parking out on the road, he pulled straight into the driveway.

"Might as well pretend we're meant to be here," he said. "It'll stop the neighbors reporting us."

"If the neighbors didn't bother reporting a ruckus when Hunt and his vampire mate attacked us, I doubt they'd even look twice at us today."

"Yeah, but word would have gotten out by now that Wilson was murdered and Amanda is missing. Neighborhoods like this exist for that sort of gossip."

"They used to, but these days it seemed that most people don't even know their neighbors, let alone look out for them." I climbed out of the car and studied the house. It was a double-fronted brown brick home that looked no different from any of the other houses that lined the street. It certainly didn't reflect the money Wilson would have earned over the years, but maybe he didn't care about all that sort of stuff. Not everyone flaunted their wealth.

Jackson strode over to the front door; in matter of seconds, he had the thing open.

"Just where did you learn that trick?" I asked as he tucked the lockpick back into his wallet.

"A friend of a friend." He cautiously took several steps inside then stopped, his body tense, ready for action. Heat emanated from his skin, but at least this time there weren't sparks.

"I'm gathering said friend was something of a thief." I stopped beside him. The house was still and the air was cold and stale. I couldn't sense any sort of body heat, but then, I hadn't last time, either, and that had almost resulted in Hunt killing me.

Neither of us was about to make that sort of mistake again. Jackson went right, into the bedroom where we'd found a barely alive Amanda, and I went left, into the living room. I checked every possible hiding spot, moving from there into the kitchen then the laundry.

"Nothing here," I said, meeting Jackson back in the hall.

"No." The tension might have left him, but heat still rolled off him.

I frowned. "Is that normal?"

Confusion flitted across his features. "Is what normal?"

"The heat you're emitting."

"I'm not . . ." He stopped and raised his fingers. They weren't glowing red, but I could nevertheless feel the waves of warmth coming off them. He stared at them intently for several seconds, and the heat abated. "It's obviously happening on a subconscious level."

"Meaning you and I might have to start having some training sessions."

He grinned. "Do they involve nakedness?"

"No, they do not."

"Well, damn." He lowered his hands, his grin fading. "While it sounds rather ludicrous that a fire fae would need lessons on controlling flame, I'm thinking they might be a good idea."

"Especially if Rory is right, and that in combining our spirits, you've somehow gained phoenix DNA."

He frowned. "I really can't see how that's *remotely* possible."

"I'm not flesh and blood. I'm spirit." I shrugged. "How we can say what is and isn't possible when, as far as I know, nothing like that has ever been tried before?"

"Nothing like being a pioneer, is there?" He shook his head and motioned toward the nearest doorway. "Let's start searching."

We did. And it took hours. We pulled every room apart, and we found precisely what I'd expected to find—nothing. If Wilson had been keeping a copy of his notes, then he certainly wasn't keeping them here. Even Jackson's handy little image radar device didn't reveal any hidden spaces or safes.

"Well, that was a big fucking waste of time, wasn't

it?" I crossed my arms and leaned one hip against the kitchen counter.

"The whole search might be," Jackson said. "The truth of the matter is, no one is *actually* sure if Wilson had a secret stash of notes. Everyone is just presuming he did."

"Well, Baltimore did, so I guess it's a fair enough assumption." I stared moodily out the window. The backyard was overgrown and unkempt, and the two sheds that lined the rear fence looked about ready to fall down. I motioned toward them with one hand. "Neither of those outbuildings looks like the type of place you'd want to store important information."

"Which is all the more reason to check them."

"Totally, but I really don't think—" A flicker of movement near the edge of one of the sheds caught my eye, and I stopped.

"What?" Jackson said, instantly alert.

"I'm not sure." I frowned. The movement wasn't repeated and yet goose bumps were crawling across my skin. I might not be able to see anything, but that instinctive part of me sure as hell could *sense* something. "It might be just the wind, but—"

The words died as my heart leapt up into my throat. It wasn't the wind.

It was a man, and he was aiming a gun straight at my face.

Chapter 7

"Gun!" I yelled, and threw myself sideways.

I hit the floor with a grunt and covered my head with my hands as bullets sprayed through the kitchen. Glass, china, plaster, and wood rained all around me, filling the air with dust and deadly missiles.

"Fucking *hell,*" Jackson said from where he'd hunkered down in the hallway. Bullets cut through the plasterwork on either side of the doorway, but the hall itself remained relatively untouched. "Whoever these bastards are, they certainly mean business."

"Which means the assault force at the back may not be the only one." I winced as a shard of glass stabbed into my arm. "Do you want to check the front?"

"Good idea." He disappeared, the sound of his footsteps swallowed by the continuing storm of metal in the kitchen.

I plucked the glass from my arm, tossed it one side, and then crab-crawled toward the doorway Jackson had just vacated. The deadly rain of plaster and wood eased as I hit the hall, but I'd barely had a chance to drag in a relieved breath when the rear door flew open and a thickset man bearing the biggest fucking gun I'd ever seen stepped inside. His gaze hit mine, and a delighted grin stretched his thin lips.

"I do so like an easy tar—"

He didn't get the rest of the sentence out, because I hit him with fire and sent him tumbling backward. He screamed as he fell down the steps, even though my flames weren't burning him. It was a sound that abruptly cut off.

Hurt, I thought. *Or dead.*

Either way, it didn't stop more bullets spraying through the open door. They splinted the floorboards and threw needle-sharp daggers of wood into my face. Machine-gun guy had a friend.

I cursed and became fire. As my flesh form disappeared, a second man stepped through the doorway, raised his gun, and fired. The bullets cut through me but, in this form, caused no harm. I ignored them and surged forward. The man kept firing even as he backpedaled; the intensity of my flames—fueled now by anger—had the bullets exploding, sending shards of metal spinning through the air. He cursed, spun, and ran—but not fast enough. I grabbed him by the back of the neck with one hand then spun a fiery rope around his body and pinned him in place. He screamed and fought my hold on him, with little effect. I lassoed him to a nearby porch post—ensuring the flames didn't set the house on fire—and did a quick search around the backyard. There was no one else here.

The man I'd pushed out the door hadn't moved. I suspected—given the odd angle of his neck—that he'd broken it, but he was, at least, still breathing. Which was good, as I hadn't actually meant to kill him. Dead men can tell no tales, after all, and we needed to know who'd sent these bastards.

Although I very much suspected the "who" was Radcliffe.

I relieved my captive of his gun then made my way back into the house—and had to do a quick sidestep to avoid crashing into Jackson as he belted down the hall.

I regained flesh form and quickly scanned him. Aside from the beginnings of a bruise on his left cheek, he looked unscathed. "How many more were there?"

"Two. The bastards were obviously intending to finish us while the rats at the back had us pinned down. Both are currently unconscious." He paused, and glanced out the back door. "I'm gathering from all that screaming you've got one tied up?"

"Yes. I think other one broke his neck falling down the stairs."

"Dead?"

I shook my head. "But we'd better call the ambulance. I imagine the cops will already be on the way—I doubt even Wilson's neighbors will ignore all that gunfire." I hesitated. "Maybe we should just leave. At the very least, we're going to end up in police custody for a few hours, and we can't afford to take the chance of being charged. Not when we've got to be at the Vic tonight."

Jackson was shaking his head even before I'd finished speaking. "Someone will have taken note of our car."

"It's a rental—"

"With our names on the agreement. We don't need the cops putting a BOLO on us." He paused. "It might be worth putting a call into PIT, though."

I snorted. "Like *they're* going to help us out of this mess."

"Actually, I think they will. Especially if they *are* using us to do some of their legwork."

"That's a mighty big 'if.'"

"Yes, but what have we got to lose?"

"Nothing, I guess." I dragged out our new phone to make the call then paused. The last thing we needed was PIT getting ahold of our new number and running a trace on us. I peered around the kitchen door. The landline on the wall appeared in one piece. "I'll leave Sam a message; whether he'll pass it on or not is anyone's guess. Why don't you bring in the screamer? We can at least question our captives before the cops arrive."

"Twenty bucks on Radcliffe being behind the attack," he said as he strode outside.

"The odds on that are so short not even the biggest gambler would risk a bet."

I headed into the kitchen and made the call. I guessed we'd find out soon enough whether Jackson's theory about PIT using us was right or not.

Jackson reappeared, my captive slung over his shoulder. The man had finally stopped screaming, but his gaze, when it met mine, promised murder. It was an expression I'd seen many times before, and on far scarier individuals than this particular rat.

I followed them into the living room. The other two men were sitting on the sofa and, like my captive, had been tied by a fiery rope, though their bonds had burned through their clothes and were beginning to blister their skin. I had no idea if it was intentional or not, given the recent incidents.

"Oh, it's very intentional," Jackson said. "They deserve a lasting memento after trying to shred us to fucking pieces."

With that I could only agree.

He none-too-gently dumped my captive beside the other two, then pulled a chair across to the front of the sofa and sat down. "So, gentlemen, kindly tell me who sent you here to kill us."

The men remained mute. Stupid move.

Jackson flicked a finger, and the flames binding them briefly caressed their chins. Two men jumped back, but made no sound, while the third hawked and spat. Flame leapt from Jackson's fingers, quickly sizzling the offending globule.

"That," he said, letting the flames die down again, "was not polite. Do it again and I'll burn your face off."

Jackson, it seemed, was a whole lot more pissed off about being shot at than me.

Three sets of eyes glared at him. Jackson sighed. "Gentlemen, PIT has been called in, and we all know that they have no love for rats. They certainly won't treat your actions here kindly."

One of the men—a black-haired, sallow-skinned fellow with pockmarked cheeks—snorted. "I'm thinking they're not going to be too pleased about *your* actions, either."

"Ah, but here's the rub," I said. "They gave us tacit agreement to be here. I'm guessing you can't say the same."

Which wasn't exactly a lie. They might not have given us permission to break into Wilson's place, but they certainly hadn't told us *not* to.

The sallow-skinned fellow looked from me to Jackson and back again. "You obviously know why we're here, given you know we're rats."

"Maybe we do and maybe we don't." Jackson was still being ultrapolite, despite the annoyance that practically radiated from his skin. "Either way, you *will* answer our question."

Sallow Skin glanced at the other two men. My captive shrugged, and Sallow Skin sniffed. "We've been watching the place for weeks. When we saw you enter, we contacted the boss—"

"'The boss' being Radcliffe?" I cut in.

He nodded. "He's got something of a hard-on for you two. Needs revenge *real* bad for what you did both at his café and in the casino's parking lot." He paused and shook his head. "It never pays to make a rat king look bad."

I snorted. "From what we've been told, he doesn't hold the throne, his grandmother does."

"She's the figurehead, not the true power."

"Wonder if the grandmother is aware of that?" Jackson glanced briefly at me. "Maybe we should ask her."

"She don't see no one," Sallow Skin sneered. "Only her direct line has that honor."

"Yeah, well, that might all change after Rinaldo hit on one of your boss's main gaming venues this morning."

The look the three exchanged spoke of confusion. Obviously, they weren't up-to-date on the latest events, which was interesting. Although maybe it was simply a matter of Radcliffe forgetting he had these four out here.

"Look," I said as the wail of sirens began to cut through the air. "We need to speak to your boss—"

Sallow Skin snorted. "*That* is never going to happen."

"I think it will when you tell him we now have an enemy in common," I said. "And it will certainly be in both our interests to share information about Rinaldo."

"I don't know who that fucking is, and I don't think—"

"If you were paid to think," Jackson cut in, "you wouldn't be sitting outside an empty house for weeks on end."

The rat scowled. "I should have shot you when I first saw you, instead of checking with the boss."

"Then it's lucky for your boss you didn't." Jackson reached into his pocket and took out Radcliffe's phone. "One of you has the chance to leave right now and avoid both the cops and PIT. But only if you give this to Radcliffe, and tell him to leave a message on our office's phone if he's at all interested in discussing Rinaldo's demise."

The three men glanced at one another. Trying to decide if it was a trick or not.

"I suggest you decide quickly," Jackson said. "Because those sirens are getting closer, and that means we're running out of time."

"I'll go," Sallow Skin said. "And I'll give him the fucking message. Just don't expect a response."

Jackson released the flames around the rat, allowing Sallow Skin to take the phone. "You might want to also tell him that if he *doesn't* talk to us, we'll go over his head to his grandmother. And I'm thinking that won't help his standing in the rat community."

"And," I added, "you can tell him that if he orders any more attacks on us, he's toast. Literally."

The rat glanced at me, a half snarl tugging at his lips. But he didn't say anything, just rose and walked out.

"What about us?" one of the other men said.

"You," Jackson said, "have the pleasure of talking to the cops, and possibly PIT."

The men swore. The sharp sound of the siren abruptly cut off as the ambulance pulled into the drive and stopped behind Jackson's car.

He rose abruptly. "I'll go find something more conventional to tie our captives with. You direct the paramedics around to the back."

I nodded and headed for the front door. The cops arrived as I was leading the medics through the rear gate. There was, unfortunately, no sign of anyone from PIT.

To say the cops were less than impressed by the events would be something of an understatement. After taking initial statements from us all, we were hauled down to the local police station and thrown into separate interview rooms.

I paced the small room in annoyance. It was little more than a white box, with a two-way mirror on one wall, three chairs and a table against the other, and monitoring equipment above the door. Which meant they were undoubtedly watching, but I didn't really care. I couldn't just sit still and wait. Not when there was so damn much we needed to do. Hell, we hadn't even finished searching Wilson's place.

The minutes ticked by. Tension gnawed at my insides, and I couldn't help wondering what the fuck was going on. I'd been a cop myself in previous lifetimes and, unless things had changed a whole lot since then, leaving me in here alone went against all manner of protocol. Especially since they hadn't even searched me.

The door finally opened, and I spun around. It wasn't a cop who entered. It was Sam.

"What the fuck are *you* doing here?"

He raised an eyebrow as he closed the door. "You did call for help, did you not?"

"Well, yeah." I crossed my arms. "But I didn't expect a response, and I certainly didn't expect to see you. Aren't you under house arrest?"

"Yes." He motioned me to the nearest chair, then moved across to the other side of the table and sat down.

I didn't. Sitting would bring me entirely too close to the damn man. "Then why are you here?"

"Because, as I mentioned earlier, PIT is stretched for staff at the moment and this task is one we can perform without risking other operations."

"Meaning Rochelle's here as well?"

"Yes." He paused, his gaze narrowing slightly. "Do you have a problem with that?"

Only if she's the source of the leak. Because if she was connected to Luke, however unintentionally, then there was always the prospect that he'd use her to reinfect Jackson . . .

I went cold. Maybe *that* was the source of the leak. Maybe she'd already infected someone.

Or maybe *he* had.

No, that was stupid. If either Sam or Rochelle *could* infect others, PIT wouldn't have put them in the field. "I don't have a problem with her, but I'm betting she's a little pissed about you continually being thrown into the path of your ex."

"'Ex' being the operative word," he said, voice flat. "She has no reason to be annoyed. She knows the state of play between us. Besides, she's fae."

And fae didn't do commitment. But Luke believed Sam still cared for me, and if he wasn't getting that information from his brother, then Rochelle was the next logical choice. Even if that *didn't* make sense.

"But why send both of you? Isn't that risky?"

Especially if she *was* Luke's source. But if she was, at least neither she nor Luke would learn much from this event, as we'd achieved nothing more than pissing off a couple of rats.

"Everything is a risk at the moment, but on the scale of such things, interviewing the two of you is at the lower end." He tapped the table. "Sit down, Em. I have no desire to strain my neck looking up at you."

It was politely said, but annoyance wasn't far away. I pulled the chair away from the table and sat down.

"Did you find anything at Wilson's?"

"Not in the house. The rats interrupted us before we could check the outbuildings." I hesitated, my gaze scanning him. The darkness that was the virus seemed to be little more than a vague stain around the edges of his energy output, and his skin seemed warmer than it had in the cemetery. I frowned. "What have you done?"

He blinked. "What?"

"There's something different about you."

His expression closed over. "We're not here to discuss me."

"I know, but—"

"I can very easily hand you back to the cops, Emberly," he said, voice cool. "Just answer my questions and don't deviate."

Because you never know who is watching or listening. He didn't say the words, but they nevertheless seemed to hang in the air. And it was a good point, because if neither he nor Rochelle was the leak at PIT, someone else was. And if Luke could get his people in PIT, he could get them anywhere.

"Fine," I muttered. "What else do you want to know?"

Amusement briefly flirted with the corners of his mouth and eyes, and my heart did its usual happy dance. I ignored it.

But he *didn't*.

His pupils dilated fractionally and, just for an instant, hunger flared bright in his gaze.

And suddenly the puzzle pieces fell into place. He'd told me, when I'd commented about the retreat of the darkness earlier, that he'd given in to the inevitable. He'd refused to explain what that meant, but given his reaction to the rise in my heart rate, it wasn't hard to guess. The virus turned humanity into pseudo vampires. Sam was drinking blood to control it.

I swallowed heavily, not sure whether the sinking in my gut was sorrow or anger.

But before I could say anything, he said, "Don't. Not here."

His voice was grim, cold, and his face set. But something flared briefly in his eyes. Something that wasn't the darkness or any sort of bloodlust. Something I'd glimpsed on several occasions now, and, each time, it had chilled me to the core.

That something was utter desolation.

He saw no hope for himself. He was just doing whatever it took to keep on surviving so that he could find and kill his brother before the virus took him over.

Without thinking, I reached across the table and wrapped my hand around his. "Sam—"

His muscles twitched, as if he was tempted to turn his hand around and twine his fingers through mine. But he didn't. Instead, he pulled away and leaned back in the chair. "What did you hope to achieve at Wilson's place? You know we've already searched it."

I curled my fingers, trying to hang on to the heat of his skin that lingered on my hand, even if only for a few seconds more. "Nothing. But Rosen's company is paying us to be thorough, and that, by necessity, meant double-checking Rosen's place."

"So they're still keeping you on the case even though Rosen is dead?"

"Well, they haven't told us not to search, so we'll keep doing it until otherwise informed." I paused. "Are you sure he's actually dead?"

Sam hesitated. "We're running blood tests, but there was no sign of anything to suggest he'd turn."

Yeah, but they'd thought that about Baltimore, too. "You're keeping an eye on his body, just in case?"

"Yes. We do not make a mistake more than once, trust me."

I raised an eyebrow, amusement lurking around my lips. "Is that an admission that PIT actually does make mistakes?"

He half smiled. Though it didn't quite touch his eyes, it nevertheless warmed my heart. "Of course. No one is perfect."

"And yet you expected me to be." It came before I could stop it, and I silently cursed. It was a stupid thing to say when we were over and done, but moving on was damnably hard when fate kept throwing this man in my path.

He didn't say anything. He didn't need to. We both knew it was honesty, not perfection, that had been the problem.

"Sorry," I said quietly. "That was uncalled-for."

He didn't acknowledge that, either. "Tell me what happened with the rats."

I shrugged. "We'd just finished searching the house when the bastards started shooting at us. While one of them kept us pinned down, the others busted through the doors to finish us off. Unluckily for them, we were quite unimpressed with that idea."

"The neighbors reported seeing a man leaving just before the ambulance arrived. Did you let one go?"

I nodded. "We don't need Radcliffe sending more men after us."

"You should have thought of that before you busted up his café and his men."

"Yeah, well, they did attack first."

"That seems to be something of a theme with you two."

"And it's one I can do without." It wasn't as if I liked being beaten up and shot at. It just seemed to be my lot in this lifetime—recently, at least. "There's really not much more I can add. You must have known that coming in."

"We did."

"Then, to repeat an earlier question, why are you here? Couldn't you have just rung the police and gotten them to release us?"

"We could have."

There was something in the way he said that that had the hair at the back of my neck rising. "So why didn't you?"

"Because my boss wanted me to put a proposition to you."

"And I'm guessing it's something we're not going to like."

He smiled, but it certainly didn't warm his expression or wipe the coolness from his eyes. "If you're going to use PIT as an escape clause, then you will do so legally."

"*That* statement makes no sense," I said, even as my stomach sank. I wasn't stupid. I knew what was coming.

"You have two options," he said, with very little emotion in his voice. And yet I had the sudden impression that he didn't agree with what he'd been sent here to do. "You can quit the case now—"

"We can't do that," I cut in. "And you know it. Besides,

neither the vamps nor Luke would leave us alone even if we did."

"Or," he continued, ignoring me, "you work for us on an associate level."

Chills raced across my skin, even though the room was far from cold. A recognition of fate, perhaps? Or just fear? "No."

He raised an eyebrow. "No, you won't work with us? No, you'd rather spend time in jail?"

"It's no, I don't want to be blackmailed again . . ."

I cut it off, but it was already too late.

He leaned forward abruptly. "Again?"

I took a deep breath and blew it out in frustration. In for a penny, in for a pound, I guessed. "The man I know as Heaton found me."

"Indeed? What did he want? Information?"

"He wants Wilson's notes, just like everyone damn else." I paused. "You know he met with Rosen before all this went down, don't you? He wanted the inversion device Rosen's company is working on."

Sam frowned. "How the hell did he find out about that? That's top level and very secure."

I snorted. "Obviously not. Rosen apparently rejected the offer, and Heaton was very displeased."

"Rosen walked away from the meeting, so Heaton couldn't have been *that* displeased." He paused. "Although Rosen is now dead, so it's always—"

"Heaton didn't kill Rosen."

His gaze sharpened. "Why would you think that?"

"Because he came in *after* Rosen was dumped in our office and examined him. He didn't look all that happy."

"Is that what you erased off the tape?"

"Yes." And that wasn't all—we'd also erased both us and Heaton or Rinaldo or whatever the fuck his real name was reading the note that had been left in Rosen's hand.

"Why?" Sam asked. "Was he already blackmailing you then?"

I hesitated, Rinaldo's warning ringing in the back of my mind. But I guessed it was too late to stop. All I could hope was that he hadn't been in the state long enough to have cultivated a source in the police department—though I'm sure the sindicati probably had them.

"No, not then. He confronted us later."

"When you were searching Rosen's place?"

"So we *are* being tailed."

He snorted softly. "No. We saw you on the floor's security cams. I'm gathering, given the foyer systems went down for fifteen minutes, that that's when it happened?"

I nodded and told him what Rinaldo had wanted, and what he'd threatened. "Is there anything PIT can do about him?"

"Legally, no. He hasn't done anything to warrant action from us as yet."

I raised my eyebrows. "What about the raids on Radcliffe's gaming venues?"

"You are better informed than we thought."

Which *wasn't* a compliment, if his expression was anything to go by. "It pays to be in our current situation. And you didn't answer the question."

"The raids have no direct link back to Heaton—"

"How can you say that when Rinaldo was apparently seen at the crime?"

"Says what source? Because we certainly get that information out of the rats."

I guessed *that* wasn't surprising. The rats had never been overly keen on cops no matter what division they belonged to. "The wolves told us."

"Indeed?" He sounded more than a little peeved by that, but I guess being behind on the information train would be annoying. "Heaton's done nothing so far to warrant PIT intervention; until we get someone to tell us otherwise or catch him in the act, there is little we can do."

"So you know where he's staying?"

"No, we do not. And *you* didn't actually answer the question on the table."

"I'm not becoming a PIT employee."

"I'm not asking you to."

And didn't want me to, I suspected. "Then what are you asking?"

"As I said, you become associates—you get the security of PIT's name at a legal level, and we get all information you find relating to Wilson and Baltimore's research."

Exactly what Rinaldo wanted, in other words. And while I doubted PIT would use the threat to kill someone if I didn't comply with their wishes, there'd still be a nasty sting in the tail somewhere.

"How do you know you can trust us to hand over any information?"

"We don't."

"Then why even bother placing the offer on the table?"

"Because," he said heavily, "if you and Jackson continue down your current path, you'll end up either imprisoned or dead. And no matter what I might think of your actions in the past, or how little I actually want you working with us at *any* level, I also have no desire to find your broken body somewhere."

He wouldn't, because my body reverted to energy on death. But it was nice to know that no matter how much he might hate what I'd done to our relationship, he still wanted me alive just as much as I did him.

"How long have you and PIT been planning this all of this?"

He glanced at his watch, a trace of amusement touching his lips. "A couple of hours, if that."

"So it was my phone call that gave you lot this whole associate idea in the first place?"

"My boss had broached the subject previously, but your call reaffirmed the idea."

"Why don't you agree with the idea?"

"Because while we do have other associates currently working with us, I can't see any continuing value in having you on the team."

"And the fact you and I had a broken relationship in our past has very little to do with it."

"Very little."

Anyone else might have believed that statement. I didn't. "What happens if we decline the offer?"

"You quit the investigation, as I said."

"You can't force us to do that."

"Oh," he said softly. "Yes, we can."

I stared at him for several seconds, chills running down my spine. It wasn't so much what he said, or even the way he said it, but rather the rise of the darkness. It wrapped around him like a cloak, staining his blood-borrowed warmth and briefly making him appear as cold and as alien as some of the very ancient vampires.

He'd only been infected for a year, and it had changed him so much already. What the hell would it do to him with more time?

I rubbed my arms lightly. "Even PIT can't lock us up and throw away the key, Sam. There's laws against—"

"PIT isn't bound to the laws of the land when it comes to national security. This investigation falls into that sphere." He leaned forward, his arms crossed and something close to pity briefly gleaming in his bright eyes. His scent wrapped around me and would have been enticing had it not been so thick with darkness. "There is only one choice here, Em. And if you don't abide by the rules that come with that choice, then you face the consequences."

I leaned back in the chair and dragged in a shuddery breath. "Damn it, this is unfair *and* unjust—"

"Life is unfair. Deal with it."

"Life has nothing to do with it," I bit back. "This is simply an organization being overly heavy-handed."

"This is *not* heavy-handed. But that might yet come, never fear."

My eyes widened at *that* particular threat. "Meaning what? Incarceration? More obedience drugs? It's not like the first lot worked overly well."

"No." His voice was grim. "But you can rest assured the next lot will."

"Oh, this just gets better and better—"

"Damn it, Red," he all but growled. "Have you forgotten what we're up against? Have you considered what would happen if this situation gets out of control? Even people like you won't be safe in a world gone mad."

Actually, Rory and I *would* be safe, as long as at least one of us remained alive. The real question was, would we want to live in a world where the virus-infected reigned supreme?

The answer was a definite no.

"Understanding the reason for your actions doesn't make acceptance of them any easier, Sam."

"I warned you at the start of all this to walk away. You didn't, so you have no one to blame for the consequences but yourself."

As he spoke, the air became thick with a menace that was both frightening and alluring. It was all I could do to remain seated, to not scramble out of the chair and back away. I'd witnessed many a vampire over the centuries lure unwilling targets into their arms, and what Sam was now unleashing was something very similar. He may not be doing it consciously, but that didn't alter the fact that it was happening. And it didn't make it any less dangerous—especially if he *was* drinking blood.

"Your answer, Emberly."

"I don't even know why you bothered offering it as a choice, because we both know it's not." I crossed my arms against not so much the chill crawling through my body, but rather the sense of foreboding—one that told me this was but the first step down a very unintended and definitely unwanted path. "What happens when the current situation is over?"

"Nothing. Life goes back to the way it was."

Or not, my inner voice whispered.

"So we report to you whenever you find anything useful? And how does PIT define 'useful'?"

"You don't report to me or Rochelle." He leaned back and dug into his pocket. The darkness within him retreated once again; it made it easier for me to breathe but it didn't negate my chills. They seemed to have lodged somewhere deep inside me, and I wasn't sure even flame could chase them away. He took a card out of his wallet, scrawled a number on it, and then slid it across the table. "You report to my boss, and no one else."

I reluctantly picked it up. "And your boss's name?"

"Chief Inspector Henrietta Richmond," he said. "That's a direct, secure line. Jackson aside, you're not to give it to anyone else."

I nodded and slipped the card into my pocket. "Is that it?"

Because if it was, then this so-called offer sucked.

A small smile teased his lips, but there was little reaction from my hormones. Obviously, they were just as pissed off with this situation as the rest of me.

"No, it's not."

He produced two small wallets. I opened one. Inside was an oval-shaped badge that bore the inscription PIT ASSOCIATE INVESTIGATOR NUMBER 05. On the other side of was a very recent photo with my name underneath.

"There's no way these could have been done in a couple of hours, Sam."

"No. As I said, the idea of inviting you onto the team had been discussed previously."

I snorted and picked up the second wallet. It was Jackson's. I very much suspected he wouldn't object to having legal ID from PIT, given it would undoubtedly make it easier to question people.

I shoved them both into my purse then said, "I'm gathering you've got no objections to us going back to Wilson's and finishing the search?"

"None at all."

"And what about the rats?"

He shrugged. "The cops will deal with them."

"Good." I hesitated, my gaze sweeping him. "You're back to isolation now?"

Again that smile teased his lips. "It's hardly isolation when I'm not alone."

"I know, but . . ." I hesitated. "Just be careful. If she is unknowingly connected—"

"Enough." He thrust to his feet and walked to the door. "I probably won't see you again, so be careful, Em."

With that, he opened the door and waved me through. I hesitated then left. There was no point in saying anything, no point in warning him to watch his back. He knew the dangers of the situation as well as I, and I couldn't afford to antagonize him any further.

A cop was waiting for me outside the interview room. As he silently escorted me down the hall, I glanced over my shoulder. Sam wasn't watching me. He was walking in the opposite direction, toward the waiting Rochelle.

Only *she* wasn't looking at him. She was looking at me. And even though her expression was void of any sort of emotion, I couldn't escape the feeling that something was going on with her.

The question was, was that something virus based, or simple—if well-concealed—annoyance?

Jackson was waiting on the steps outside. I stopped beside him. "How did question time go with Rochelle?"

"Well," he said. "It certainly was an interesting experience."

"I'm gathering they made you an offer you couldn't refuse?"

"Yeah," he said. "And Rochelle is not a happy woman."

"Sam wasn't exactly ecstatic about having us on the team, either." I headed down the stairs then turned left. I didn't know this area all that well, but I'd seen a railway station coming here, and that was probably the best place to grab a taxi.

"Undoubtedly, but I think Rochelle was more pissed at you than the situation."

I frowned. "Why would you think that?"

"Because the first thing she said when she walked into the interview room was 'I'm totally over him running after that bitch and you.'"

"Which does imply annoyance, but at Sam more than me."

"I initially thought that, too, but she made a couple of other comments that made me think it was you rather than him."

I frowned. "But why? It's not like I'm a threat to her

position in his life. Besides, she's fae. You lot don't do emotion."

"Which doesn't imply we can't feel propriety on certain occasions."

I squinted up at him. "Have you ever felt that way?"

"Hell no. But you can't tar an entire race with the same brush. There are always outliers who prefer something a little different."

"So there's a definite change in her since the last time she interviewed you?"

"Yes. There's a definite coldness in her now." He hesitated. "But it's always possible it stems from her being annoyed."

"But you don't think so?"

"But I don't think so," he agreed heavily. "Fae flirt. You know that. And despite the seriousness of the situation, there was definite byplay between us last time. Today, there was nothing. She was distant and professional, and it just didn't feel right. I didn't like the change, nor did I trust it. Or her."

"And yet Sam does."

"Yeah, well, he's fucking her. It's a long-known fact that men tend to think with their little heads more than the big in situations like this."

I grinned. A more true statement I had never heard.

"I will also say," he added, "that there were moments when she felt more like a vampire than a fae."

"Yeah, so did Sam." I briefly caught my bottom lip between my teeth. It was natural that they'd both be gaining more vampire qualities, given that was what this virus was all about—making people pseudo vampires.

But did that necessarily mean the link to Luke was getting stronger? Or that I had every reason to *not* trust her when I *did* trust Sam?

No, it did not.

And that instinctive part of me that kept whispering doubts about her might well be based on annoyance and jealousy rather than anything rational.

We headed down to the railway station and didn't have to wait long for a cab to turn up. Jackson opened the door, ushered me inside, and then gave the driver Wilson's address.

"Sam gave me these." I dug his new ID out of my purse and handed it to him. "I'm guessing Rochelle told you what their protection is going to cost us?"

He nodded as he opened the badge and examined it. "I can't say I'm overly concerned about it at the moment, though. I've a feeling we're going to need the use of these things in the near future."

"It's not the near future that worries me."

He tucked the badge away in his pocket and glanced at me. "I doubt they'll want—or even need—to keep us on at *any* level once this shit is sorted out."

"Maybe." And maybe not, if the little voice inside was right. "Did Rochelle say anything else?"

"Nope. She basically told me we were now officially PIT associates, read me the riot act on what would happen if we didn't feed them all appropriate information, then sat in the chair and ignored me. It was, as I said, a very weird situation."

"We seem to be attracting a lot of that."

"Must be you, because my life was completely sane and normal before you came along." He paused and his grin flashed. "Of course, it was also rather boring. And we both know I hate boring."

I snorted softly. "Right now, boring is something I'd actually settle for."

After all, I'd come into this lifetime planning just that. Trust fate to throw a damn wrench in the works.

It didn't take us long to get back to Wilson's. The cops had already departed, and there was now yellow-and-black tape across both the front and back doors. Why they still considered it a crime scene I have no idea; maybe they simply hadn't yet collected all the spent bullets yet. The rats had certainly blasted enough of them through the house.

We made our way around to the rear of the premises and headed for the sheds. The first one was small and didn't really hold anything more than dust, spiders, and gardening tools. The second one was double the size—more a garage than a shed—and filled with an odd assortment of cabinets, woodworking tools, and machines, along with a couple of half-finished projects, and both a fridge and a freezer.

"You want to start on the left or the right?" Jackson asked.

I shrugged. "Left, I suppose."

"Meet you in the middle, then." He headed right and opened the freezer. It was doubtful anything other than perishables was stored there, but it still had to be checked.

I opened the nearest filing cabinet, which contained little more than a collection of old tools. It was pretty much the same story in the rest of them. By the time I reached the last one, I was almost certain Sam was right—there was nothing here to be found.

The final drawer revealed a collection of old tins. I checked each one, and in seven of them found nothing more than screws and nails.

In the eighth, I found three keys.

CHAPTER 8

"Found something," I said as I picked up the keys and examined them. Two looked brand-new and bore letters and numbers on them—C34 and N85 respectively—while the older one was larger and looked more like a house key.

Jackson closed the door of the cabinet he'd been examining then wandered across and plucked them from my hand, turning them over in his. "The locker keys are newer, suggesting they haven't been in that tin long. Wonder if the third is a spare house key?"

"Possibly. Wait a sec while I check."

I retrieved that key and headed out of the shed. It didn't open the back door, but it fit perfectly in the front door lock.

"Neither of these two keys fits any of the filing cabinets here," Jackson said as I returned. "But I'm gathering you were more successful?"

I nodded and tossed the key back into the tin. "Which means the other two belong somewhere else. The question is, where?"

"The only person who knows the answer to that particular question is dead." He lightly tossed the keys into the air and caught them again. "Might pay to go to a locksmith, though. They should at least be able to give us some idea what to look for."

"Worth a shot." And we had nothing but time to lose. I glanced at my watch and saw it was closing in on five o'clock. "We'd better get a move on if we want an answer today, though. The shops will be shutting soon."

"After you, my dear," he said, with a grand sweep of his hand.

I smiled and led the way out to our car. As Jackson reversed out of the driveway, I Googled "locksmiths." There was one fairly close by, but parking was impossible to find. Jackson double-parked long enough for me to get out then continued on around the block.

A small bell chimed as I entered the shop, and an old man looked up from the shoe he was repairing. "How can I help you, lass?"

I dug out my new badge and flashed it. "I've got a couple of keys I need to find a home for, and I was wondering if you could give me a heads-up on what sort of cabinet or storage unit they might belong to."

"Looking for a needle in a haystack, in other words." Amusement creased his leathery features. "But I'm more than happy to take a look."

He held out a hand and I dropped the two keys into it. After he'd examined them for several seconds, he said, "Well, you've got two different keys here, and they belong to lockers rather than a filing cabinet."

"How can you tell?"

"The numbers stamped on them. There's no real difference in the size and shape of keys belonging to filing cabinets, lockers, desks, and whatnot, but they used to be coded differently to make identification easier for the end user." He handed them back. "Keys like that are rather old-school these days, unfortunately. Most places providing lockers for the public are using electronic locks."

"So what sort of venues might still be using the older-style lockers?"

"That's presuming they *do* actually belong to a venue and are not privately owned. Secondhand cabinets and lockers can be found in many a shed these days."

"Which is were we found the keys. They don't fit anything there, however."

"Ah." He hesitated. "Maybe check out gyms near where you found them. A lot of the older places are still using keyed lockers. Train stations might also be worth checking, as it's cheaper to replace old-school locks when they get vandalized than it is the electronic."

The train station is where Amanda had been heading yesterday before we'd spotted her and given chase. Coincidence? Unlikely. Especially if Wilson *had* been infected and turned rather than simply murdered by the red cloaks, because he would have had his keys on him when they'd assaulted him. Although if he'd become part of the hive mind, they'd also have the location of the lockers, which might well mean any useful information would be gone by the time we got there.

"Anywhere else?"

He shook his head. "I'm sure there is, but it's not like I keep track of them. I haven't dealt with that sort of key for several years now."

"Well, I guess it was always a long shot. But thanks for your help."

"It's not like I actually helped," he said, with a half shrug.

I smiled and headed out. Our rental car reappeared a few minutes later, and I quickly climbed in.

"Anything?" Jackson said as he accelerated away again.

I quickly updated him then said, "It's probably worth checking the lockers at the Southern Cross railway station. Maybe Amanda wasn't the only one keeping stuff there."

Jackson's expression was doubtful. "Wilson didn't catch public transport—he drove to work. He'd have to go out of his way to store stuff there."

"Maybe that's why no one can find his backups—he did the unexpected."

"And maybe there simply *aren't* any."

"De Luca believed there were. Luke still believes it."

"Luke more than likely has Wilson. If there were notes to be had, he'd have them by now."

"Not if the virus is working more slowly on Wilson than it does others."

"But didn't De Luca imply both scientists were now not only active but working for Luke?"

"Just because he implied it doesn't mean it's true."

"True. And Amanda *was* there yesterday—maybe she'd been sent to retrieve something."

I couldn't imagine any other reason for her being there. Amanda hadn't seemed the public transport type. "If there's nothing at the station, then I have no idea where else to look. Was he a member of a gym or some other sporting club?"

We hadn't uncovered any obvious gym gear at his

house, but most guys just tended to wear either regular shorts or track pants, and T-shirts. We certainly hadn't found anything suggesting he'd been into any sport, like tennis or golf.

"It's not something that came up in my background research, but that doesn't mean anything," Jackson commented. "I don't have access to his financial records, so there's no way to check if there were regular debits coming out."

"PIT might be able to check for us," I mused. "After all, we're now associates."

Jackson snorted. "I have a feeling that particular street is all one-way."

He was probably right, but I guess it wouldn't hurt to ask if our search at the rail station came up a blank.

"Besides," Jackson added, "I did ask Amanda if Wilson was a member of any sort of club when I first accepted this assignment, and she said no."

"Yeah, but can we believe anything that comes out of her mouth? She married the man purely to siphon information out of him. Besides, Wilson wouldn't be the first person to pay for a membership and not actually use it."

"Like me," Jackson said with a grin.

I laughed. I couldn't help it. The thought of Jackson sweating it out in the gym was just too ludicrous to contemplate. Hell, the only time he did *anything* remotely resembling serious cardio was when he was either chasing someone or making love.

"*That* is not a polite reaction."

"But an understandable one, you have to admit. I'm gathering there was a girl involved?"

"Two, actually. And one has a very private office."

"You are incredible."

"So I keep getting told." Amusement played about his mouth. "If Wilson *had* joined a gym, any information hidden there would be long gone."

"Unless, of course, she didn't know where the locker keys were hidden and couldn't snag that information from Wilson's mind." I stared unseeingly out of the windscreen for a few seconds then said, "If Wilson drove to work every day, how come he was murdered in the middle of the street at night? He couldn't have been walking home from Rosen Pharmaceuticals—it's too damn far."

"Good point. Maybe you should put Mr. Google to work again, and see what sort of clubs might be around that area."

I dug out our new phone and began the search as he drove on into the city.

"There's two within reasonable walking distance," I said as he pulled into the parking area near the Spencer Street Outlet Centre.

"We'll check them both out when we finish here, then."

Once we'd found a parking spot, I climbed out of the car and followed Jackson up the stairs to the main concourse.

"Amanda was headed for the bus interchange area when I stopped her the first time," I said as he opened the stairwell door and ushered me through. "It might be worth checking if our keys fit any of the lockers there before we move on to the rail station."

"It's on the way, so we might as . . ." He stopped abruptly. "Well, fuck me."

"What?" I immediately scanned the area, but a Sky-Bus had just arrived from the airport and there were people everywhere.

"It would appear our black widow has returned to the scene of the crime." He motioned to the left with his chin. "She's over near the exit."

I stood on tippy-toes and scanned the crowd. After a moment, I spotted her. She was pushing her way through the throng of people, moving with intent toward the exit and not seeming to care about the abuse that was being flung after her.

And she was carrying a leather satchel under her arm.

"I think we need to see what is in that bag."

"I agree. Let's go."

He strode forward, moving swiftly but nimbly through the crowd. I followed in his wake and wished I were half as graceful.

Amanda moved out of the interchange area then up some steps, heading once again for the concourse and the wide bridge that stretched across the rail yards. But at the top of the steps she hesitated and looked down. Once again, her expression was initially blank. When recognition *did* arrive, it was accompanied by a flash of both frustration and anger. The unease I'd felt before became full-blown fear.

Not of her, but at what had been done to her. Because I'd seen this sort of emotional delay before.

Someone had rolled her mind.

This might outwardly be Amanda, but someone else now resided inside her brain, controlling her every move. And given the strength of *her* psychic gifts, that meant a master vampire with *very* strong telepathic skills was behind it.

And while I couldn't exactly feel sorry for Amanda given her long history of destroying the lives of her victims after she'd stolen whatever she'd needed from them, having your mind rolled and being totally under the control of your attacker was not a fate I'd wish on anyone. Because somewhere deep inside of her, there *would* be an awareness of what had happened—an awareness that her life and her body would never again be hers to control.

The question was, who now controlled her? Was it Parella and his people, or whoever had taken control of the vampire faction working with Luke? Was Luke capable of such a thing now that he'd become something more than human?

Hell, it might even be Rinaldo, for all I knew. Except that the last time I'd seen Amanda, she'd been in sindicati hands, not his. And I doubted the sindicati would allow such a valuable commodity to walk free, let alone start working for the opposition.

Whoever *did* control her, they couldn't have wanted a better weapon. Not with the strength of her telepathy skills.

She turned and ran. Jackson swore and quickly followed, taking the steps two at a time. I wasn't far behind. I might still bear the bruises of my brief encounter with Hunt, but the pain had retreated to an occasional niggle—one I could certainly ignore in situations like this.

The three of us bolted through the concourse. Jackson was rapidly gaining on her, taking one stride for every two of hers, and was almost within grabbing distance. She didn't look over her shoulder but must have sensed his closeness, because she suddenly made a beeline for the bridge railing. Without breaking her stride, she tossed the satchel over the edge and ran on.

Jackson didn't give chase. Instead, he followed the satchel right over the railing and disappeared from sight.

Chapter 9

The high-pitched scream of a train whistle blasted, accompanied by the screeching of metal against metal as it tried to stop.

"Jackson!" I screamed, and dove for the railing.

All I could see was train. I had no idea whether Jackson was under it or not. I ran to left and leaned over the railing farther, desperately scanning the track for any sign of life or blood or—god help me—body parts. There was nothing. Just sparks that danced like giddy fireflies as the train came to a shuddering halt.

Then a flash of movement caught my eye to the right of the train. Jackson, striding across the tracks, his jeans torn, shirt filthy, but very much alive and unhurt. And he had the satchel in his hand.

Tension fled, and I took a deep shuddering breath. I hadn't realized until that moment just how much I'd actually come to care for the damn man.

He looked up and gave me a wave, his grin wide as he motioned to the nearest platform. I gave him a thumbs-up then ran back through the concourse to meet him. There was little point in even trying to find Amanda—she'd long disappeared into the crowd.

Jackson met me near the exit gates.

"You," I said, grabbing his shirt and dragging him

close, "just about gave me a heart attack. Don't ever do something like that again."

"Like you wouldn't have done the exact same thing had our positions been reversed." He dropped a quick kiss on my lips. "And Superman is not the only one who's faster than a speeding bullet—or fast-braking train, as was the case."

I snorted then glanced past him. Security guards were heading our way. "Unless you want to spend some more time twiddling your thumbs at a police station, we'd better get out of here."

After a quick look over his shoulder, he caught my arm and guided me quickly but efficiently through the crowd. It didn't take much time to lose the guards, and once we had, we headed back to the car. Jackson shoved the key into the ignition then opened the satchel. It had two compartments, and both were stuffed full with paper.

He pulled out one lot and handed them to me. "You check those; I'll check the rest."

I quickly flicked through the paperwork. It was mostly handwritten stuff and reminded me somewhat of the notebooks Baltimore had given me to translate into readable English when I'd been his research assistant. I couldn't see any mention of the virus in any of it, though, just a whole lot of mumbo jumbo about DNA strands and misshapen molecules.

"Anything?" I said, glancing at Jackson.

He shook his head. "Nothing that jumps up and screams *red plague virus*. But you're the research assistant. You tell me."

He handed over the notes, and I scanned them

quickly. They were much the same as mine. "I think what we might have is pre-virus notes. They're talking about vampire DNA and misshapen molecules, from what I can gather."

"No mention of the virus?"

"Not that I can see."

"So, useful, but not what we're looking for." He paused, expression thoughtful. "Do you think it's worth taking a copy of them? Or shall we just hand them over to PIT and move on?"

"PIT will undoubtedly want them, but so will Rinaldo and the sindicati."

"If the wolves are doing as they promised, Rinaldo isn't our biggest problem right now."

"Yeah, but are you willing to risk Shona's safety to something as fragile as a promise to keep them safe?"

"No." He scraped a hand across his jaw. "I think there's an office supplies place just up the road. Why don't we go there and get some photocopies?"

"I think that's the best option, but we both know PIT isn't going to be too impressed if we give this information to Rinaldo." I hesitated, glancing down at the notes. "What about if we give both him and Parella a selection of pages rather than the entire lot? Neither of them are going to know any different."

Unless, of course, one or the other had people within PIT, and that was an option I didn't want to contemplate.

"*That* sounds very sensible."

"See, I can do sensible. Sometimes."

His quick grin suggested disbelief, but he didn't say anything, just handed me the satchel then started the car and drove out of the parking lot. Forty minutes later, we had our copies—two were a direct paper copy of only a select portion of the notes, and the other a full copy that had been scanned and stored as JPGs on a USB. The latter might have been overkill, but given how often we'd been accosted for information of late, it was better to be safe than sorry.

It was raining by the time we left. We made a mad dash for the car but still managed to get soaked through to the skin.

Jackson dumped the wet satchel with a partial copy of the notes onto the backseat then tucked the other copy under his seat. I pulled the originals from my sweater; the first couple of pages were damp, but they were still readable. I stuffed the lot of them into the glove compartment then shoved my hands in front of the warm air blasting out of the vents. I could have used my own internal heat to warm them, but sometimes it was nice to use old-fashioned methods.

"It might be best to ring Rinaldo now," I said, noting it was close to six thirty. "That way, it won't matter if we get sidetracked tonight."

"You might as well make a call to PIT, too." He pulled back out into the traffic. "And we should probably check out the two gyms near where Wilson was attacked while we're out. You never know, we might get lucky."

"I think you used today's allotment of luck when you jumped in front of that damn train." My voice was dry. "And probably tomorrow's."

He laughed. It was a sound so infectious a smile tugged at my lips.

"What fun is life if there isn't a bit of risk occasionally?" He glanced at me briefly, one eyebrow raised. "Don't try to tell me you're not enjoying the adrenaline rush of this whole situation, because I can't and won't believe it."

"I'm not denying I enjoy taking the occasional chance, but this lifetime was *supposed* to be a staid one. My 'sit back and chill' time."

"No chance of that with me around." Amusement crinkled the corners of his bright eyes.

"No chance at all," I agreed sagely. "But I'm seriously hoping that once all this virus shit is sorted out, we can drop back to a more demure pace."

"And I'm betting chasing wayward husbands or spying on welfare cheats . . ." He chopped the sentence off and slammed on the brakes as the car in front suddenly stopped.

Even though we weren't going fast, our car slewed sideways on the wet road. I swore, bracing myself for impact as the rear end of the vehicle loomed way too fast for my liking.

Somehow, Jackson managed to stop inches from the other car. But I'd barely released the breath I'd been holding when two men jumped out of the vehicle and ran toward ours—but not with any intention of checking that we were okay. Quite the opposite, if the guns they held by their sides were any indication.

I swore and undid my seat belt, but I was too close to the other car to get the door open even a fraction. Jackson was slightly faster than me—he had one foot out of the car when the one of the gunmen shouted, "Move, and she dies."

Jackson's gaze met mine, one eyebrow raised in query and sparks flying across his fingertips. I shook my head minutely. If the gunmen had intended any immediate harm, they would have simply shot us. They'd had time enough in that brief moment of disorientation as our car had slithered to a stop.

He extinguished the sparks and held his hands up. "And who would you gentlemen be representing? The rats, the sindicati, Rinaldo, or the city pack?"

"City pack?" I muttered. Why the hell would he ask that given the agreement we had with them . . . then I realized why. At least one of these two men was a werewolf.

A look of intense concentration crossed his features. Then a heartbeat later, his voice whispered into my mind. It was distant, fuzzy, with some of the words dropping out. But I could nevertheless understand him.

Not sure other. Don't think city.

Surprise flitted through me, but with it came relief. If this link between us was two-way, it could be damnably handy in situations just like this.

I frowned, concentrating on mentally replying as succinctly and clearly as I could. *No, because they have no reason for this sort of action.*

Then I crossed mental fingers and hoped he *did* hear me. Because if this link between us *was* telepathy, then it was a different form of it—at least if what telepaths had told me about the ability was true, anyway.

A second later, surprise and delight flitted across his expression. He'd heard me.

Outliers, came his response. *This hard.*

Yes. I'd barely said anything, and yet a slight ache

was beginning to appear at the back of my brain. But maybe this skill, like any other skill, needed time and effort spent on it for it to get stronger and easier.

"Parella contracted us," the wolf closest to Jackson said. "He wants the notes."

I raised an eyebrow. The sindicati boss was keeping an even closer eye on us than we'd presumed if he knew about notes we'd only just gotten. And I hadn't seen either of these two in the station's concourse, which meant they were damn good at their job.

"If Parella wants the fucking notes," Jackson replied, voice mild, "then he can come and get them himself."

"That is not accept—"

"I don't care what is and isn't acceptable," Jackson cut in. "I'm simply telling you how it's going to be. You might also want to know I've had my quota of being shot at for today, so get that damn gun out of my face."

"Or what?" the idiot sneered. "You're not close enough to grab me, and I can shoot faster than—"

He didn't finish the sentence because Jackson unleashed his fire. It shot out with an audible *whoosh* and wrapped around the gunman's hand, melting both the metal *and* his flesh.

The thug screamed—a high-pitched sound of agony that almost drowned out the other gunman's "What the fuck?"

"Jackson . . ." I warned, even as he cursed and withdrew his fiery lasso.

The other man kept screaming. I can't say I blamed him—his hand was a mess.

Jackson glanced at the other thug. "Take your friend

to the hospital, then give Parella the message. And if we catch you following us again, the results will *not* be pretty."

The second man didn't argue. He simply grabbed his companion and shoved him toward the car. No sympathy happening there, obviously.

I took a deep breath and looked around. While a few people had gathered on the sidewalk, expressions curious, everything had happened so fast—and was over so quickly—that I doubted they'd witnessed too much.

Jackson climbed back into the car then slammed the door shut and punched the steering wheel violently, making me jump.

"I didn't mean to do that." His voice was soft, but anger vibrated through it—through him. "I simply meant to melt the trigger mechanism so he couldn't fire the damn thing."

"So what happened?" I knew well enough what had happened—he'd lost control.

"I don't know." He scrubbed a hand across his eyes. "It was weird. It was almost as if, just for an instant, the fire within me gained a life and a mind of its own."

"Or, more likely, it was simply reacting to your anger."

It sometimes happened with young phoenixes who'd yet to gain full control over the flames that were theirs by nature. The minute they got overemotional, they reacted instinctively, spewing forth fire at whatever—whoever—had threatened or upset them. Which was why, whenever I'd gotten pregnant, Rory and I had retreated to somewhere nice and secluded. It was easier than explaining a six-month-old setting his surroundings alight.

"But what just happened was inexcusable," he bit back. "I'm a damn fire fae . . ."

I reached across and placed my hand on his thigh. His muscles twitched in response, but he didn't reject my touch, as I half expected him to. "Who merged his life force with phoenix, with who knows what consequences?"

"That still doesn't—"

"Jackson," I cut in, tone holding just a hint of steel. "Young phoenixes do not come out of the womb in full control of themselves, let alone their fires."

"But I'm not—"

"For all intents and purposes, you might as well be. Maybe everything you learned as a fae will have to be relearned now that you're far more. Phoenixes are spirits with an intimate—and very dangerous—connection to the energy of the world itself. Even *you* can't be expected to control such a force without at least some tuition and practice."

He glanced at me. His expression gave little away, and anger still radiated from every inch of his body. But it was now accompanied by the faintest hint of fear.

"What if it's the virus? What if this is just the first sign that our merging *didn't* work, and that I'm becoming one of them?"

I hesitated. It was possible—I had to admit that. Just because I burned off all human toxins and diseases when I took spirit form didn't mean the same had happened to him when we'd merged and he had—for the briefest of moments—become what I was.

"There's one way we can find out," I said. "We can get PIT to do a blood test."

"And if I'm fucking positive? Then what? We both know that will be the end of life as I know it. They're not about to let me run about the general population willy-nilly."

"Sam and Rochelle were, at least until recently. That wouldn't have happened if they were, in any way, infectious."

"And now they're locked up, because they might just be telepathically linked to Sam's bastard brother. What if I am?" His tone was grim. "What if the reason everything keeps falling apart for us is because Luke is reading my brain and keeping one step ahead of us?"

"You're not telepathically linked to the sindicati or Heaton, and they've caused more problems for us than Luke at this point."

"You know what I—"

"Yes," I cut in. "And there's only one thing we can do if we want to know for sure, and that's to get the damn test done. We can deal with the fallout once we know one way or the other." I squeezed his knee, though I doubted he was taking much comfort from my words or my actions. "Besides, if Luke was reading your thoughts, don't you think he would have attacked us at the hostel by now?

"Probably." He scrubbed a hand across his eyes again. "You *can* teach me control, can't you?"

"Jackson, you're a fire fae. Teaching you will be a walk in the park compared to a screaming toddler who will neither see reason nor be pacified."

He snorted softly and placed his hand over mine.

His fingers still contained way too much heat, even for a fire fae. Worry gnawed at my insides, but there wasn't a whole lot I could do about the situation right now.

"When you ring PIT to tell them about the notes, ask about the tests. We need to at least find out if I'm infected or not." He squeezed my hand then released me.

"I will." I did my seat belt back up as Jackson straightened the car and sped off. Neither of us said much after that. I just stared out the window, going over and over what had happened at Hanging Rock, wondering if we could or should have done anything different. But the answer was simply no. He'd been attacked—and scratched—by the red cloaks. If he hadn't taken my fire, then he would now be one of them. If nothing else, merging with me had at least given him time.

And if it wasn't the virus, but simply an aftereffect of the merging? I could reteach him control, but would it do any good? We had no idea how far—or even what changes might yet emerge.

I wished there were someone I could talk to—an elder who might have seen or heard of something like this happening before. But, as I'd once told Jackson, phoenix families didn't tend to keep in close contact once adulthood had been reached and a life mate chosen. I had parents and grandparents somewhere out there in the wider world, but I had no idea where or even how to contact them.

For the first time in my long life, I really wished that we, as a race, had a far closer bond. Maybe then Jackson could have gotten the help he so obviously needed.

Jackson must have caught that particular thought, because he reached across and squeezed my leg, in much the same manner as I had his. "I'm alive today because of what you did in that forest," he said softly. "No matter what happens, I don't regret it."

Good, because it wasn't like we could change anything now. "What makes you think those wolves were outliers rather than the city pack?"

"Logic. We've an agreement in place with Baker, and I doubt either he or his pack would break it without reason."

"Could they be members of a different pack?"

"Possibly. True outliers are actually rare."

"Do you think it's worth mentioning to Baker? I doubt he'd be happy to learn there's another pack operating in his territory."

"It can't hurt." He paused and grimaced. "Although I'm guessing he won't be too pleased when he discovers what we did. Especially if that wolf *is* one of his."

"Yeah, well, maybe it'll warn him and others not to stick fucking guns in our faces." I glanced around and realized we were close to the street where Wilson had been attacked and abducted.

"The gym is just up the road," Jackson said, "but I'll have to do a U-turn and park in the lot we just passed if there's no free spaces."

As it turned out, there weren't. Jackson did the U-turn but found some street parking not far away from the gym. Once he stopped the car, I grabbed my purse and climbed out. "How do you want to play this?"

"I'll go check if either of our keys fit their lockers.

You might want to find a pay phone and make that call to PIT."

"What about Baker?"

"Definitely. If they were his men, we need to confront him about it immediately, otherwise the shit will fly."

He walked away. I glanced around to get my bearings. Most pay phones these days were restricted to places like bus shelters, rail stations, and, for some weird reason, supermarkets. There was no sign of the first two, but there was a large Woolworths on the far side of the gym.

I headed that way. Jackson had already reached the gym, and I crossed my fingers and hoped like hell that we'd finally catch a break. Because, honestly, how many more things could go wrong for us?

Don't ask, that inner voice warned, *because you really do not want to know.*

Sometimes I hated that inner voice.

I walked into Woolworths and found the pay phone at the other end of the store. I fished out the business card Sam had given me, then swiped my credit card through the slot and dialed the number. The phone rang a couple of times, and then a somewhat plummy and decidedly unfeminine voice said, "Chief Inspector Henrietta Richmond speaking."

"Inspector," I said, imagining a tall woman with thick black glasses and a stern, ungiving expression. Which probably meant she was a petite blonde with a face and body to die for. "It's Emberly Pearson."

"Ms. Pearson," she said, a slight hint of surprise in

her tone. "I certainly wasn't expecting a call from you so soon."

"Yeah, well, we were told to report everything, so 'everything' is exactly what you're getting."

She made a sound that sounded suspiciously like a smothered laugh. "Indeed? What have you got for us, then?"

"Notes."

"What kind of notes?" The amusement, if indeed it had been that, had faded from her tone. "The missing kind?"

"I don't think so. It talks about vampire DNA, a malfunctioning chromosome, and misshapen molecules, but whether that all relates to past research or current I couldn't say. There's no dates on any of the notes."

"And they're Wilson's?"

"I presume so. We got them from Amanda Wilson."

"She's alive?" Surprise registered in her voice. "From what we'd been able to glean, even if she *had* survived that crash she wasn't going to be of much use to anyone."

I hesitated, remembering again the blankness in Amanda's expression. "She's alive, but whether she's actually the same person she was before the crash is debatable."

"Ah." The inspector paused. "When and where can we collect the notes?"

"We'll be working another case and staying at the Victoria Hotel tonight. You can collect them there."

"I'll send someone. Thank you."

"Don't thank me, Inspector. Just keep your end of the deal and release us when all this shit is over."

"If this shit is ever over, I will."

Her words had foreboding pulsing through me again. The future I didn't want was creeping ever closer . . .

I shoved the thought away and said, "There's one other thing."

"What?"

"Can you arrange a blood test as a matter of urgency?"

"Whom for? You?"

"No. Jackson was attacked by the cloaks, and while we believe we've burned the virus from his system—"

"You *what*?"

I hesitated, but there really wasn't much use in keeping anything back. Especially not when Jackson's life might well depend on PIT knowing everything. "We merged our fires and burned the virus from his body—or, at least, we think we did."

"And he's shown no sign of infection since then?"

"Given I'm not entirely sure what the signs are beyond the madness that seems to affect all but a few, I really couldn't say."

"You've seen Sam often enough lately," she said. "And he is the perfect example of what we call a 'non-rampant' virus recipient—no appetite, loss of all excess body fat, development of vampiric capabilities."

"He's shown none of those, but that doesn't mean he won't. We need to be sure."

"That you do." Her voice was absent. "We hadn't thought of using heat to eradicate—"

"It's not like it would work on everyone," I cut in bluntly. "He flooded his entire body with my fire, and

I burn far hotter than anything here on Earth when I'm in my true form. Jackson's a fire fae and barely survived the experience."

"Even so, if there's no sign of the virus in his system, then that means this thing *can* be destroyed by extreme heat. And that gives us something to work with—something we hadn't had before now."

Then it was worth mentioning it. "So you'll arrange a test?"

"Straightaway. I'll get someone to you at the hotel tonight, if possible."

PIT certainly didn't muck about. But then, we already knew that about them. "Thanks."

"Keep in contact," she said, and hung up.

I replaced the receiver and wasn't entirely sure whether I should be relieved or worried. PIT might be the only ones who could tell us whether or not Jackson was still infected, but that instinctive part of me couldn't help but wonder if we were just digging our own graves when it came to them. That the more we worked with them, the harder it would be to escape their net.

But—as I kept repeatedly saying—it wasn't like we could do much about it now.

I fished Baker's card out of my purse and gave him a call. He answered on the second ring.

"It's Emberly Pearson," I said, without preamble. "And we need to talk."

"Indeed?" There was a touch of mild curiosity in his voice, but little else. Which was somewhat comforting. "Does this mean you have information on Rinaldo already?"

"No, but we were attacked by two wolves who said they were working for Parella. We suspect they're either a rival pack or outliers working your patch, and we thought you'd like to know."

"You thought right." The curiosity had given away to anger. "Can you describe them?"

I did, and he growled softly. "I know them both, and they are, I'm afraid, members of my own pack. I'll deal with them."

"Jackson's already dealt with one. I'm afraid his gun was melted into his hand."

"That will be the *least* of his problems, I assure you. Not only have they gone against direct orders, but they are freelancing for the vampires."

And that was *not* something the sensible did, if his tone was anything to go by.

"Accept my apologies on behalf of the pack, Emberly. I assure you it will not happen again."

"Thanks, Mr.—"

"Please, call me Scott," he cut in, tone amused. "Only my father insists on being called Mr. Baker."

I smiled. "Thanks, Scott."

"No problem. I'll talk to you soon."

With that, he hung up. I spun around and headed back to the car. Jackson wasn't there, so I crossed my arms and leaned back against the car to wait. He appeared ten minutes later, and he didn't look happy.

"No luck?" I pushed away from the back of the car and moved around to the passenger side.

"He's not a member there. I checked the lockers anyway, but neither of the keys fit anything."

"Well, damn."

"Yeah." He started the car, then checked the mirrors and pulled out into the traffic. "On to the next one. What did PIT say?"

"They're sending someone around to the hotel to collect both the notes and your blood."

"Huh." He paused. "I wonder why Amanda dumped that satchel. Neither she nor whoever is controlling her could have known if they were virus related or not."

I shrugged. "Maybe they considered Amanda more of an asset than whatever was on those notes."

"Given how desperately everyone wants the missing fucking notes, I very much doubt that."

True. So why *had* Amanda chucked the notes rather than try to lose us? Even if her mind had been rolled by one of the sindicati factions, they couldn't have known whether or not the notes were virus related until they visibly sighted them. Hell, even *I* wasn't entirely sure, and I'd worked as Baltimore's research assistant.

And even if she *was* now infected—and under Luke's control—he'd still have to sight . . .

The thought trailed off, and I blinked. No, he didn't, because those who were infected became part of the hive mind—a collective consciousness that Luke controlled—and *that* meant it would be very easy to check whether the notes were related or not. Especially if he *did* have both scientists—all he had to do was bring them "online" and get them to see through Amanda's eyes.

Presuming, of course, the hive mind was that powerful—and I very much suspected it was.

And if her mind *had* been rolled? Then whoever was staring out through her eyes might know enough about research to understand the notes weren't directly related to the virus.

"I vote the latter option," Jackson said. "You're right—she's exhibiting the classic signs of being mind rolled."

"Yes." I paused. "But is it possible she could be both?"

"Anything is possible these days, but really, there'd be no point in doing both."

"Unless the vamp who rolled her mind was aware that she's working with Luke, and is using her to keep an eye on him."

"Maybe." His expression suggested he wasn't buying it. "Besides, Luke couldn't have guaranteed she'd end up one of the sane cloaks."

"According to PIT, what you become very much depends on who you're infected by, so maybe that isn't such a problem anymore."

Although *that* theory wasn't exactly watertight, given the original source of all this was a scientist made crazy after he'd tested the virus on himself.

"Meaning he wanted me to become one of the insane?" His voice was flat. "I really *am* going to enjoy killing that bastard if I ever get my hands on him."

"You and me both." Though I wasn't entirely sure either of us stood much chance. Not when Sam had every intention of getting there first. "I also rang Baker. They were his wolves, but they weren't there on his orders. He assured me it wouldn't happen again."

"Good. I hope he's going to teach the bastards a lesson."

"Oh, I think he will. And I very much doubt anyone else from the pack will be tempted to take contract work from the vamps without his permission." I spotted the second gym up ahead. "Do you want me to go in this time?"

He hesitated and glanced around. "Yeah. Why they build these fucking things so near small shopping strips where parking is at a premium, I have no idea."

I grinned. "Maybe it's all part of an evil plan to get people out of their damn cars and use their legs occasionally."

He gave me a shocked look, though the amusement crinkling the corners of his eyes somewhat spoiled the effect. "You mean they want people to exercise for real? Not just go to the gym and sweat for an hour, but actually do real stuff in the day as well? That is outrageous!"

I laughed then undid my belt and leaned across, dropping a quick kiss on his cheek. "Glad you've still got your sense of humor."

"It's the only way to get through life's shit sometimes." Despite the lingering amusement, his tone was sober. He fished the keys out of his pocket and dropped them into my hand. "I'll drive around the block until you come out."

"Okay."

The rain was once again pelting down, so I jumped out and bolted into the gym's entrance to avoid getting any wetter than necessary. A slim, ponytailed teenager glanced up from her computer and gave me a welcoming smile. "And how can we help you today?"

I flashed my new badge and said, "Could you tell

me if you're using the old-fashioned key lockers or the electronic ones here?"

She frowned. "The older type—why?"

"Because we're investigating a murder and have a couple of keys we need to find a home for." I grimaced. "I'm the newbie on the team, so I get the odious task of wandering around all the places likely to hold such lockers to find a match."

She laughed. "That doesn't sound like a fabulous job."

"It's not. Especially on miserably wet days like this." I paused. "Do your members have their own permanent lockers, or are they shared?"

"The former. We don't have a lot of casuals here, I'm afraid."

Which meant there was a slightly better chance that the keys belonged here than at some place where lockers were used on a first-come, first-served basis.

"Do you think it'll be okay if I have a quick look and see if any of your lockers match the keys we have?"

"I'll have to check with management, but I can't see that it'll be a problem."

She made a quick call then said, "They've said it's okay, although they don't want you to remove anything until management is present."

Technically, they should have also asked for a warrant, even if it wouldn't have done them any good given I was—at least temporarily—working for PIT, and they seemed to have official permission to ride roughshod over rules when it was appropriate.

"I won't. Thanks."

I headed into the gym. The main exercise room smelled vaguely of sweaty men and dust, but the equipment was new and there was plenty of it packed into the tight space. There were a couple of other rooms tucked off a long corridor—one containing speed bikes, the other a boxing ring and bags—and, down at the very end, two change and shower rooms.

I checked the women's change rooms first, just on the off chance that if Wilson *had* decided to be sneaky and hide something here, the women's rooms were less likely to be searched and therefore discovered.

Naturally, Wilson hadn't decided to be sneaky. I switched over to the men's and, after yelling a warning, headed in. Like everything else in this gym, the change rooms were small and slightly odorous. There were two rows of lockers dominating the middle of the room—double the number that was in the women's—and a further eight around the corner, near the toilets.

I began the search, reading each of the numbers, looking for a lock that matched the numbers on our keys. It was a task made harder by the fact that most of these lockers had seen better days, and the numbers on many of the locks had all but worn away.

I was three lockers away from the last of them when I finally saw a lock that matched the number on one of our keys. I was so surprised that I actually took it out of my pocket and double-checked. It definitely was a match. Luck, it seemed, hadn't totally abandoned us.

I shoved the key in and opened it up. The locker was one of those long, thin ones that had hanging room on one side and a couple of shelves on the other.

It was also empty. I swore and stepped back to close the door again, but caught the faintest glimmer of metal right at the back of the top shelf.

Frowning, I rose on tippy-toes and swept my hand across the shelf. At the very back, tucked right in a corner, was a USB. I plucked it free from its bed of dust then—after casually checking there were no watching cameras—shoved it into my pocket. I may have agreed not to remove anything, but that didn't mean I actually had to abide by it. Besides, the fewer people who knew we'd found something, the more chance we had of checking it out before someone arrived to take it out of our hands. And while I doubted the teenager at the front desk was in any way connected to any of the people after us, caution would nevertheless be wise.

I checked the remaining lockers, but the second key didn't fit any of them. Which wasn't surprising given it would have been a daft move to have two hiding places in such close proximity. I spun around and headed out.

"Any luck?" the receptionist said as I reappeared.

I shook my head. "Nope. It's on to the next one, I'm afraid."

"Hope you have more luck there," she said.

"Me too." I flashed her a smile then headed out into the rain. Jackson appeared a few seconds later, so I didn't get that much wetter than I already was.

He took off again the minute I jumped in then said, "No luck?"

"Plenty of luck." I dug out the USB and showed it to him. "Unfortunately, we haven't a laptop with us at the moment."

"Then maybe we need to find another office supplies place and buy one. Besides, with the way we keep getting intercepted, it'd pay to keep a backup of everything."

Especially given we now had both PIT and Rinaldo expecting information out of us. I got out our new phone and Googled "office supplies." "There's an Officeworks on Bridge Road."

"That'll do."

We drove there, picked up a new laptop as well as a couple of extra USBs, and I got the computer up and running and transferred all the information over while Jackson headed back into the city.

The Victoria Hotel was on Little Collins Street, right next to Melbourne's town hall. It was an old building that showed hints of grandeur in its grimy façade, and was dwarfed by the other, newer buildings that now surrounded it. Jackson parked in the lot just across the road, and then we grabbed our things and headed into the hotel.

The receptionist smiled as we approached. "How may I help you?"

"We have a booking under the name of Pearson," I said.

Her fingers flew across the computer's keyboard. "We've been able to give you the room you requested. You're lucky, though—the previous booking had to cancel at the last moment."

Meaning fate—with a little prompting from some witchy power, perhaps—had intervened on our behalf. Maybe it was a sign that things were beginning to swing our way. I mean, they had to sometime, didn't they?

Once they'd taken our credit card details—there was little point in concealing our presence given PIT were well aware we'd be here—we collected our key and head up to the room. It was small, basic, and a whole lot fresher than our other accommodation. Jackson dumped our bags on the bed while I moved over to the window. Little Collins Street lay below us, currently filled with people and cars making their way home for the evening. We could see a good portion of the street from Swanston back up toward Russell Street, so maybe that was why we'd been told to get this room. It'd be interesting to uncover what we were actually meant to see here.

Jackson's arms slid around my waist as he pressed a kiss against my lips. "I'd really like to waste some time making love to you right now, but that might not be a wise move until we discover whether I'm infected or not."

"We've made love a few times since that day in Hanging Rock. Besides, you'd have to break my skin with a bite or a scratch to actually infect me."

"As far as anyone is aware. There could be other means of passing this thing that they don't know about."

PIT had been on this case for a while now, and if there had been any other way, surely Sam would have mentioned it. He was well aware that Luke kept flinging the bastards at us, after all.

Still, I could understand Jackson's concern. "If

you're at all worried about the possibility of infecting me, I'll simply shift form for a few seconds and burn any possible residue from my system."

"Good."

He dropped a kiss on my neck then swung me around to kiss me more thoroughly. We took our time, exploring each other thoroughly, kissing and teasing and caressing, until heat burned the air and need was so high that I could barely breathe, let alone think. And yet, through it all, there was an odd sort of . . . not desperation, but something close to it, in all his actions. It was almost as if he was savoring every moment, every touch, every sensation, just in case he never experienced them again.

When he finally entered me, my groan of pleasure echoed his. But he didn't immediately move, simply held himself still deep inside me and wrapped his arms around my body, holding me tight.

I gently ran my fingers down his warm, muscular back. "If there's one thing I've learned over the centuries, it's that it's useless to worry about things you cannot change."

A smile tugged his lips, but didn't stretch as far as his eyes. "I bet that never stopped you doing so."

"Well, yeah, but I was born a worrier. It's not an emotion that suits you." I paused, then grinned and added, "And, hey, look on the bright side—if you *are* infected, then the lovely Rochelle is once more on your radar."

He laughed, a booming sound that vibrated through every inch of me. "There is that."

And with that, he began to move. The fires that had

been banked so very briefly flared to life, and in no time at all, I came. He followed me over that edge a few seconds later then rested his forehead on mine and closed his eyes for several seconds.

"Are you okay?" I asked softly.

"Yes. And I'm seriously going to miss these moments with you when it's over."

"As I said before, that's not likely to happen in the near future."

Unless, of course, Luke succeeded in killing me. Because once Rory called my spirit back into being, I would be free of Sam and therefore free to love again. And if Rory was right—if it *was* all about honesty—then Jackson and I would also be finished. Or, at least, finished sexually. I couldn't imagine finding someone new to break my heart when I was already involved in a hot and heady relationship with Jackson, and—Rory aside—I really *did* prefer a one-on-one relationship over playing the field.

But leaving this lifetime behind was a thought that left me unmoved. While the prospect of being free to love again was exciting, it oddly felt as if *this* lifetime was unfinished. That there was still much to be achieved.

But when didn't a lifetime feel unfinished? It wasn't like Rory and I had made old bones very often in the past.

Jackson kissed me then rolled to one side and snuggled into my back, one arm flung lightly over my hip. In very little time, he was asleep.

I must have dozed off as well, because the next thing I remember was being woken by the sound of someone thumping on the room's door.

"What the hell?" I muttered as I glanced at the clock on the bedside table. It was nearly eleven . . . which was way past the time I was supposed to call Rinaldo.

Panic hit me, and I threw myself out of bed.

"What?" Jackson muttered, his voice muffled by the blankets he'd thrown over his head.

"I forgot to call Rinaldo when I was making those other calls."

"Fuck." He sat up abruptly and scrubbed a hand across his eyes. "Did I hear someone knocking on the door or was that imagination?"

"It wasn't imagination. It's probably PIT." I found my clothes and hurriedly pulled them on.

"Fuck," he repeated, and began getting dressed.

I found my shoes then headed for the door and said, "Who is it?"

"PIT, ma'am. Sorry for our lateness, but I believe you *are* expecting us."

The voice was deep, male, and not one I'd heard before. Sam had said that Adam would be our liaison point until he was released, so either Adam was on another investigation or his boss had other ideas. "Hold your badges up to the peephole, please."

I rose on tippy-toes, checked both their credentials—or at least as much as it was possible through a tiny fish-eye window—then opened the door.

The man who'd spoken was tall, dark-haired, and a little on the chubby side. The other was thin, blond, and holding a medical bag.

"We're here to collect some notes," said the man, whose name was Brad Harvey, according to his badge. "And some blood."

I stepped to one side and waved them in. "Jackson can help you with both. I've got to go downstairs and make a phone call."

Brad frowned. "Your room hasn't a phone?"

"It has, but I don't want to risk the call being traced back to here. You guys knowing our position is dangerous enough."

"I can assure you—"

I held up my hand, cutting him off. "Save it for someone who cares. Jackson, you want coffee?"

"And food." He hadn't bothered putting his shirt on, and his skin glowed with inner heat. The minute he caught my look it was toned down, but the fact it was happening still worried me.

I didn't say anything, though, and simply headed for the elevators. I found a public phone in the 7-Eleven just down the road on Swanson Street, so I made the call to Rinaldo, apologizing for being late and giving him a rundown of all events. I did, however, omit the details of what was actually inside the satchel, instead saying it was illegible rubbish that he could view if he wanted. It was a dangerous ploy given there were lives at stake, but there was no way in hell I was going to give him anything that might be—in even the vaguest way—related to the virus research.

I just hoped there were no reprisals over our late check-in.

There wasn't much in the way of restaurants or takeouts open at this hour, but I eventually found a Vietnamese place and ordered some soup and a couple of beef and chicken dishes, then headed back to the hotel. Both men were gone by the time I returned.

"How did it go?" I asked as I dumped our food on the tiny excuse for a table.

He shrugged. "They're going to push the test through as a priority, so we should have an answer within a week."

I began peeling lids off containers. "Well, at least you don't have to worry *too* long."

"Actually, I do, because you didn't shift form after we'd made love."

"Jackson, the virus can only be transmitted through a cut or—"

"We made an agreement," he cut in gravely. "So kindly humor me and just shift form."

"I can't do it here—"

"You can. I'll stop the flames setting off the alarm."

I opened my mouth to protest, then caught the worry in his eyes, and simply shut up and became spirit—one second I was flesh, the next fire, and then I was flesh again.

Jackson blinked. "Wow. Fast."

"Yeah, because I'm hungry." I gripped the end of the chair and sat down before I fell down. Ripping through forms so quickly tended to make my head spin, but it was the safest approach given where we were. It was certainly safer than Jackson attempting to control my fire and shield the alarm.

I grabbed one of the soup dishes and a plastic spoon, and began tucking in. Jackson grabbed the combination fried noodle and moved across to the window. "Did you give them the USB we found at the gym?

He nodded. "There's little point in withholding

information from them now. Like it or not, we need to work with them for the time being."

For the time being, I was more than willing to do that. It was the suspicion that PIT had something longer term in mind that worried me. "What time were we supposed to spot this ghost?"

"Midnight."

I glanced at the clock. We had ten minutes to go.

Jackson leaned against the window frame, the streetlights casting a cool light across his skin. "So what do you think we're actually looking for? I'm guessing it won't be an actual ghost."

"It could be. There are some creatures who can take on ghostly form, remember." Hell, it was only a couple of days ago that we'd tracked down and killed a creature that could become little more than ash and shadow. And, if Lan was to be believed, things like that were about to become a whole lot more prevalent in Melbourne.

"Yeah, but Grace seemed to think their disappearances were linked to us—or rather, our investigations—and right now, that means the whole virus mess rather than some random creature."

"Grace may think that, but the message came from the missing woman." I exchanged the soup for the other noodle dish. "Grace has no more clue what she meant than we did. If she did, we wouldn't be here."

"I'm not so sure . . ." He cut off abruptly, glanced at the time, then said, "Well, I do believe the ghost in question just appeared."

I scrambled over to the window. Down on the street

below us, a solitary figure moved. He was dressed from head to foot in black and was almost one with the shadows and the night.

Only it wasn't a ghost, because ghosts didn't have death's scythe burned into their cheek.

It was a red cloak.

Chapter 10

"They generally hunt in packs, so why is one out on his lonesome?" I spun around and grabbed my coat.

"It's more than likely a trap." Jackson opened the door and waved me out. "If it *is*, I guess we're about to spring it."

I strode over to the elevator call button and pressed it. "I doubt it's a trap. They don't even know we're here."

"Unless, of course, I'm telepathically connected to the hive queen himself."

"Luke can't even read the thoughts of his own *brother*." I couldn't help the trace of impatience in my voice. His worry about being infected was understandable enough, but I was nevertheless pretty certain he *didn't* have any form of connection to Luke. Things might not be going our way right now, but our situation would be a whole lot worse had Luke been getting a constant location update from Jackson. "He's only catching some of Sam's emotions, even though well over a year has passed."

"And yet he has full mental control over the cloaks with the scar from the get-go."

"Which is yet another reason to believe you're not infected. You're as sane now as you've ever been."

A faint smile touched his lips. "I believe you just insulted me."

"It's not an insult if it's the truth."

He snorted softly and pressed a hand against my back, lightly guiding me inside the elevator as the doors opened. Once we reached the ground floor, I hurried through the foyer and stepped into the street. The night had become colder in the brief time I'd been indoors, and it had begun to drizzle again. I flipped the hood up over my head, which also had the benefit of hiding my fiery hair, and looked down the street. The red cloak was just crossing Russell Street.

"Let's walk down the other side," Jackson said. "It'll be less obvious that we're following him."

He tucked his arm through mine and we started after the cloak, though our pace was, by necessity, slow, simply because the cloak's was. And—though I hadn't noticed it earlier—there seemed to be some sort of hump across his back.

"I hope like hell that's *not* a body," I said, keeping my voice soft. These things might now be pseudo vampires, but we had no idea what he'd been before he turned. If he'd been a werewolf rather than a human, there was a chance he'd have better hearing than a human. Infection might make them mad, but I doubted it robbed them of their sensory capabilities.

"Whatever it is, it's in a sack of some kind." Jackson paused. "If it *is* a body, it's only a small one."

"One of the missing women was rather petite."

"Let's just hope it's not her." He paused. "Or anyone else, for that matter."

Amen to that. Besides, why would Luke have a red

cloak carrying a body through one of Melbourne's busiest streets? It might be midnight, and most of the theaters and many restaurants might now be closed, but that was still a hell of a risk.

"I think we can safely say we're not dealing with any sort of reasonable mind here." Jackson's voice was dry. "He probably thinks he and his army are all but invincible."

"He knows they're not. We've certainly proven that."

"But we have capabilities most normal folk do not. Besides, the cloak would undoubtedly attack if stopped, and that's just more fodder for Luke's army."

"True." I eyed the figure ahead. He'd crossed Exhibition Street and seemed to be going even slower. "Wonder why he's using the streets? Sewers seem to be their more usual mode of getting about."

"Might have something to do with the rain. Sewers can be a dangerous place to be when it's pouring."

It wasn't pouring now, but I guessed it had been. Either Luke was showing some consideration for his people—which I doubted—or it was, as Jackson said, simply another part of the trap.

"The cloaks *can* drive, so why not use a damn car to get about?"

Jackson shrugged again. "The only person who can answer those questions is the bastard who controls them. And I'm guessing he'd be more inclined to kill than enlighten."

Also true. The cloak turned right into a lane and disappeared. We quickened our pace, slowing again only once we'd reached the corner of the lane. Jackson peered round cautiously.

Halfway, came his somewhat broken comment. *In cage.*

Which didn't do a whole lot to enlighten me. I peered past him. The cloak had stopped just over halfway down the lane, just before a metal door that had a big, bold TWENTY-FOUR-HOUR ACCESS REQUIRED sign on it. To the right of this were two further doors, both a heavy steel mesh. The cloak opened the right one and disappeared inside.

I scanned the buildings on either side, but couldn't see any form of security or cameras. *Shall we follow?*

No choice.

He padded forward. I followed, keeping half an eye on the two Dumpsters positioned against the other building about a third of the way down the lane. Just because we couldn't see any guards didn't mean there weren't any. The cloaks certainly wouldn't have complained about being ordered into a Dumpster to keep watch, simply because they *couldn't.*

Jackson paused as we reached the first—unopened—mesh door. He cautiously looked inside. *Bins . . . black . . . no cloak.*

His voice was even softer and more fragmented than before. *As you said, we have no choice here.*

Pain slithered through my brain as I said that, and was yet another warning that while we might be able to communicate telepathically, it wasn't without cost. Whether that would change as—or rather, *if*—the link between us deepened, I couldn't say. But for now, it was at least better than risking actual speech—even if it had the capacity to create a mind-blinding headache.

Wish gun, Jackson said as he moved forward again.

If there's a pack of cloaks down there, a gun isn't going to be of much use.

I wasn't sure how much of that he heard, but he flashed me a smile. *Feel safer.*

Old habits die hard, it seems. Because he, like me, no longer needed to rely on guns. And while summoning fire to life *did* sap him of strength seriously fast, it would at least slow the cloaks. And I'd finish them.

The niggling ache in my brain got stronger. *We shouldn't use this method of communication anymore unless it's really needed.*

He nodded and disappeared into the darkness. I followed; the ink closed in around us, sucking away any sense of light or life. I lightly touched Jackson's back to ensure we didn't lose each other. It was tempting to flame, but that would only warn the cloak—or anyone else who might be watching—that we were near.

The deeper we moved into the ink, the more certain I became that it was unnatural. While it *was* a miserable, rainy night, that didn't explain this. There'd been a light in the lane, and another above the roller door that had required twenty-four-hour access, and that meant at least *some* light should have washed into this place.

That it didn't could only mean there were other forces at work here. Magical forces, perhaps. I couldn't sense anything untoward, but if it was little more than a concealing veil, then I probably wouldn't.

Jackson continued to move forward slowly. After a dozen more steps, the ink fell away and the night became normal again. What it revealed was a dead end.

"There's got to be a doorway here somewhere,"

Jackson said. "Even red cloaks can't disappear into thin air."

As he stepped forward and brushed his fingers along the wall, I turned around and studied the dark wall. It was so damn thick I couldn't see the lane, despite the fact it couldn't be more than twenty feet away.

"I'm betting if there's a doorway, it's concealed in that blackness somewhere." Though I kept my voice soft, I doubted anyone was near; they'd have attacked by now if they were.

"Probably. There's definitely some sort of spell at work, because I was fighting a flight response as I moved through it."

I glanced at him. "Really?"

He looked at me, eyebrow raised. "Interesting that you didn't. Maybe the spell was aimed solely at humans."

"You're not human. You're dark fae."

A smiled touched his lips. "You know what I mean."

"If it *is* aimed at humanity, then they obviously don't want anyone in here. And that means we could have found one of their lairs."

"Possible. Every good general knows it's never wise to keep your entire army in one place." And though I doubted Luke could, in any way, be labeled a good general, he certainly wasn't stupid.

I called fire to my fingertips and pressed my hand back into the ink. Rather disconcertingly, the ink swallowed both my hand and my flames whole; there wasn't even a flicker of light evident within the veil. I increased the heat and the height of my flames, and still there was nothing. I extinguished the fire and withdrew my hand.

"There's no secret entrance along this wall that I can find," Jackson said. "If there *is* a concealed doorway here, it's not in this area."

"Shame you don't have your radar thingie with you." I thrust my hands on my hips and glared at the wall. There'd been many a time over the centuries when I'd wished I'd had a working knowledge of magic, and this was fast becoming another on that list. "It might be the only thing that can see beyond whatever spell is being used."

"Possibly." He stopped beside me. "I guess there's only one thing we can do—dive in and search the area the spell is concealing. This place isn't vast—surely if we keep close to the walls it won't be difficult to find a door."

"Except we may not be looking for a door."

"One problem at a time, woman, please." He grabbed my hand, his fingers thankfully a little cooler this time around. Whatever was causing his body to randomly emit heat seemed to have subsided. "If we walk at arm's length, one of us is bound to find something."

"Probably a rubbish bin. Or a set of steps, which we'll fall down."

He grinned. "Hence the joined hands. This way, one can stop the other falling and possibly breaking something."

He tugged me sideways, placed his free hand against the wall for guidance. Then, as one, we stepped into the veil again. Given the darkness was temporarily robbing me of sight, I closed my eyes and tried to use my other senses. Our footsteps were light—cautious—and beyond the soft sound of our breathing, there was little other noise. We might be in the middle of a major city, but with this ink in place, we could have been out in the middle of the bush. Which meant that although I wasn't feeling the *get out of here* vibe that Jackson was, the magic behind it was still having some effect on my senses beyond just robbing me of sight.

As we slowly shuffled forward, I swept my free hand back and forth, trying to find anything in our way before we actually hit it. There were bins here somewhere—we'd seen them when we were standing in the lane—and despite the lack of anything that would give us some idea of how wide this hidden area was, it hadn't actually looked that large from the outside. Jackson stopped suddenly, forcing me to do the same.

"What?" I whispered.

"Bin." He edged around it carefully, but didn't immediately move on. Instead, I heard the sweep of his foot against the concrete. "And steps."

"Nice of them to put a bin in front of them."

"I doubt it was done out of niceness. Given the way it's positioned on the edge of the step, I'm thinking it was more an alarm."

"Makes sense." I stepped a bit closer and felt for the bin with my foot. It connected to hard plastic a second later, and just to the left of it was the step. "I'll lead the way, if you want."

"The gentleman in me wants to object, but the reality is, you're more dangerous than I am."

I snorted and edged forward. Once I'd found the wall on the side of the steps, I started down them. Jackson released my hand and touched my shoulder instead, keeping contact as we continued down. After a dozen or so steps, the inky veil gave way to regular darkness, but I still couldn't see that much. A breeze stirred lightly past my skin, suggesting there was an opening here somewhere, and the air was musty and slightly odorous.

I hit the bottom step—something I knew simply because a sweep of my foot revealed the floor had flattened out—and paused.

Have halted. Which would have been obvious given his hand on still my shoulder, but I didn't want to risk him running into me. *No body heat nearby. If the cloak did come down here, he's gone.*

Risk fire, came Jackson's reply. *Necessary.*

If we wanted to find out where the hell the cloak had gone, that was certainly true. The darkness here might not be magic enhanced, but it was still pitch-black.

I raised a hand. Fire flared around my fingers and light rippled across the darkness, lifting the shadows and revealing a long, thin room. There were several large wooden boxes to our right, but little else. I glanced up. Electrical wires dangled from the concrete ceiling above us, but that was about it. Certainly there were no rotting piles of rubbish, old damp patches, or even any evidence that the place had been flooded at some point that would account for the odd smell permeating the room.

Jackson stepped around me and studied the room for a second. "It's rather strange that this place is empty. You'd think it'd make a good storage area, at the very least."

"I guess it depends on whether the building above us has direct access."

"True." He frowned. "There's some sort of grating in the middle of the back wall. I'll check that, if you want to check those boxes."

He strode away without waiting for an answer. I molded my fire into a ball and threw it into the air so that it lit the entire room, then walked across to the boxes. They were actually large wooden crates—the type machinery was often shipped in. Right now they contained little more than some yellowed newspapers and a couple of dusty beer bottles.

I walked down to the end of the room. Jackson was squatting in front of the grate, which was about three foot square and very rusted. The odor of rot was much stronger here, and seemed to be coming from somewhere behind the grate.

I wrinkled my nose. "God, it smells like rotting meat."

"Let's hope it's just rats and rubbish, and not something larger."

Like maybe a human. Or three of them. I shivered. I might have seen plenty of the rotting dead over the centuries—especially during times of plagues—but that didn't mean I'd ever become used to either the sight or the smell.

Jackson pressed his fingers into a slight indentation on the left side of the grate and pulled it away from the wall. He leaned closer but stopped short of sticking his head inside the hole. Last time he'd done something like that, a fist had sent him flying. "It looks like an old drain."

"I guess that's no surprise, given the cloaks seem to be using sewer tunnels to get around." I shoved my fists into my pockets and tried not to breathe too deeply. If the damn smell was bad here, what was it going to be like in there? "But as you said earlier, it's not exactly the safest place to be on a rainy night."

"I can't hear any running water, and I surely would if it was connected to a major drain." He glanced up at me. "Shall we risk entering it?"

"Like we have any choice?" The witch's words had led us here for a reason. We couldn't walk away—not if we wanted any chance of rescuing those women or living with our conscience. "But I'm not going down there blind. We need light."

"Agreed. And it's not like they won't hear or sense us coming . . ." He stopped abruptly.

"What?" I immediately said.

"Footsteps, coming from the right."

"The cloak is coming back?"

"It's either him or someone else." He shoved the grate back into place then thrust to his feet. "At this point, I think retreat would be better than an attack."

"I totally agree."

I spun around and ran back to the boxes. Once we were well hidden behind the largest of them, I snuffed out my fiery orb and drew the energy back into my body.

Darkness once again claimed the cellar. I couldn't immediately hear anything beyond the thunder of my heart, but, after a couple of minutes, metal clattered against concrete then a slight grunt broke the silence. I peered past the edge of the box, trying to see who—or what—had climbed into the room, but couldn't see anything more than a shadow. It replaced the grate then straightened. If this was the cloak we'd been following, then it no longer carried the sack.

It padded forward, the slap of its footsteps light against the concrete. As it neared the boxes, it paused. I held my breath and hoped like hell these things weren't as sensitive to the pulse of blood through a body as true vampires were.

Tension wound through me, and with it came heat. But while I could keep my flame under control, I wasn't entirely sure that Jackson could. It was radiating off him in waves, not yet visible but damn close to it. And while I had no doubt he was fighting it, we couldn't afford another fire show—not if we wanted to keep our presence here a secret. I closed my eyes, reached for that heat, and drew it in. Under normal circumstances I might have enjoyed the pleasure that came from feeding on another's fire, but I was too aware of the precariousness of our position to do so right now. We simply couldn't afford to have Luke know—through his connection with the cloak—that we were here.

After what seemed like an eternity, the cloak moved on. It padded past the boxes and up the stairs, but neither Jackson nor I moved. After a few more minutes, there was a creak of metal followed by the sound of a bolt being thrown. We'd been locked in.

Which was a whole lot better than being discovered.

Jackson relaxed, and the heat radiating from his flesh eased. I stopped siphoning it and refrained from saying anything. There was little point; he was as aware of the problem as I, and there was nothing either of us could do about it right then.

I threw up another fiery ball and led the way back to the grate. Jackson pulled it free once more then conjured some fire to his fingertips and threw it into the void. It revealed a grimy, semicircular tunnel before fizzling out.

He glanced at me. "How do you want to do this?"

I hesitated. "It might be better for me to take fire form to investigate. If I spot the missing women, I'll come back for you."

"Luke's been using magic to both protect himself and attack you." His voice was grim. "This might well be another setup to capture you."

"Possibly." Especially if he did have the witches and *had* infected them. He'd know, via the hive connection, about the cryptic note Angie had left. Hell, for all we knew, she'd written that note under duress—at Luke's orders—*after* she'd gone missing. "If there is a trap, I'll shout for help—either physically or mentally."

"And if you can't do either?"

"Listen for noise. A whole lot of noise."

Because no matter what happened, I would *not* go down—or even be captured—without a fight.

He squeezed my arm then rose and stepped back. I called to my fire form. Energy swept through me, a fierce storm that melted away flesh and returned me to spirit in little more than an instant. I surged into the old drain then paused, looking left and right. Neither direction looked particularly inviting, but the footsteps had come from the right, so that was the most logical direction to take. I headed down. As old drains went, this one was pretty typical. Slime dripped off the filthy walls in long curtains and the trickle of water that ran down the middle of it was thick with refuse. There were also dead things here—not just mice or rats, but larger animals, such as cats or dogs. Only there were far too many of them; one or two I could perhaps put down to an adventurous stray falling into the system and dying because it was unable to get out, but there were more than that. Like hundreds.

But I guessed Luke had to feed his army somehow.

Was that what the cloak had been doing? Delivering a meal to some new conversions? It suspected it might be. And while I hoped the witches weren't among those being fed in such a way, the chances of that being the case were close to zero. The only way Luke could ever hope to control three powerful witches was to infect them.

The deeper I moved into the tunnel, the more the carcasses began to pile up. While those near the grate had been picked so clean the bones were basically white, the ones here were fleshier. Thankfully, my sense of smell wasn't overly acute in this form. If I'd been in human form, my stomach might have rebelled.

Ahead, shadows danced across the edges of the light cast by my fiery form. I paused and flared brighter, so that my flames pierced the greater darkness. It was only rats feasting on the carcass of what looked like a horse. Or, at least, a part of it.

But it appeared a whole lot fresher than the other kills I'd passed, and that suggested that I was drawing close to wherever the cloak had come from. I couldn't hear or sense anything in this infested hellhole, but maybe I wouldn't, particularly if Luke was using more magic to protect this place.

I muted the brightness of my flames and moved forward again. The darkness closed in once more, thick and heavy with tension, though I was pretty sure it was emanating from me rather than anyone ahead.

As the tunnel curved left, I moved across to the opposite wall. It might make me more visible from a distance, but that was preferable over running into something—or someone—unexpectedly.

Odd sounds began to crawl through the darkness. I frowned and, after a moment, realized what it was.

Someone was eating.

An image of the vampire who'd once torn my throat open and greedily drunk from the fountain of my blood slipped into mind. I shivered, sending sparks skittering through the darkness. I doubted it was a vampire up ahead, though, as most of them tended to avoid stinking holes like this. But a pseudo vampire? *That* was certainly possible.

I doused my flames even further, so that I was little more than a dull red glow that would—hopefully—be barely noticeable against the slimy red bricks, and inched forward.

Ahead, firelight began to flicker, and more shadows danced. Not rat shadows, but humanoid. They were hunched over a blob at their feet, tearing off bloody pieces then raising them to their mouths and sucking on them noisily.

It wasn't a cat or a dog or even a horse that they were eating. It was a body. A *human* body.

I gulped and stopped. Part of me didn't want to go any farther. But I really had no choice if I wanted to confirm my suspicions.

And if those suspicions were right . . .

I briefly closed my eyes. If they were right, then the figures up ahead would have to die. They would not want to live like this. No one would, but to do this to those who considered all life sacred . . .

Fury surged, but I squashed it down fiercely and moved up to the ceiling as I continued on. It was unlikely, though, that the women would look up from their feast let alone see me approaching. The way they were tearing at the body between them spoke of a desperate need to eat—the sort of desperation that came with starvation—and I doubted they were capable of concentrating on anything else right now.

Damn it, this *had* to end. Luke had to be stopped. Even if we couldn't find and kill all the cloaks, if we at least killed *him*, they would be left rudderless—brainless—and would be far easier to hunt down and destroy. They might well swarm, but surely PIT and the army could take care of that.

I edged closer. The tunnel widened out into some sort of junction. In the middle of this was the fire, which had been lit in what looked like some sort of metal barrel. It was witch fire rather than real, and it cast a weird orange-green glow across the darkness. Beyond it lay several other tunnels—a large one to the left, and two smaller ones on the right. These had been fitted with metal bars and appeared to be cells of some kind. One was open, the other closed. Though I couldn't see anything in the latter, something was in there. Something that didn't feel human.

I shivered and returned my gaze to the two women. I didn't actually have to see their faces to know that I'd found Rennie and Neriana, two of the three missing witches. The power radiating off them was evidence enough, though it had an odd, almost corrupted feel to it. Which wasn't surprising given what had been done to them.

As for what they were eating . . .

I closed my eyes again, suddenly glad I wasn't able to vomit in this form.

Because what they were dining on was Angie, the third missing witch. And beside her remains was the old sack she'd been carted there in.

Anger surged anew, and this time there was no controlling it. As the flames burst from me, the witches squawked and scuttled away from the body of their former companion, their eyes wide and empty of everything except cunning.

That cunning was Luke, watching through their eyes. Savoring his victory.

This *was* a trap.

But even as I spun around, he sprung it.

Chapter 11

Magic exploded through the intersection, covering the ceiling, walls, and the tunnel I'd used in an instant. It was a thick, unnatural force that blanketed my entire being, making it hard to breathe, to think.

This spell was different—stronger and dirtier—than the one he'd used in the cemetery. My flames began to flicker in and out of existence, as if torn between the need to stay in this form and the demand to attain another. Fear spun through me, and it was tempting—very tempting—to risk running into one of the other open tunnels in the hope of escape.

But that was undoubtedly what Luke wanted, and there was no way I was about to spring whatever secondary trap he had waiting for me in those tunnels.

The magic bit deeper, the threads of it pressing into my soul. The desire to change grew stronger, and my skin rippled and burned with its force. Maybe Luke figured I'd be more controllable in human form—especially if I was restricted from reaching for fire. Which meant maybe it would be better to shift shape before it was actually forced onto me. I had a bad feeling I didn't want the threads of this spell any deeper in my body than they already were.

I shifted form and landed in a half crouch on the

junction's floor. The threads within fell away, but the magic continued to sting and bite, flaying my skin and leaving dark welts. The fires that were mine by nature crawled away from the sensation, leaving me without my main weapon.

Which didn't mean I was powerless. Unlike the spell that had been used against me in the Highpoint parking lot, this one didn't appear to have any built-in restrictions when it came to using the mother's power. Maybe the sindicati had access to a better class of dark witch than Luke—or maybe they simply didn't know I could access the mother.

I reached for her fire, and she stormed into my body, making my skin briefly glow with the colors of all creation. I rose and turned. As I did, the witches ran—not toward me, as I'd half expected, but rather toward the biggest of the three other tunnels. Luke was either protecting his assets now that his trap had been activated or—more likely—he was trying to entice me into that damn tunnel and whatever other madness he had planned for me.

I remained where I was and simply flung out a hand. The mother's force—unhindered by the smothering weight of magic—streamed from my fingertips. She arced across the shadows and wrapped a fiery arm around each woman. In an instant, they were gone. I swung her flames around and burned the body of the third witch. When there was nothing left but cinders, I held out my other hand and called to them. The faintly glowing embers swirled upward and flowed toward me, three small streams of ash that had once been humanity. While I couldn't draw them into my body as I could with Rory's embers, I could still keep them close and safe. Whatever else happened, the remains of the witches would *not* be left in this place of evil. Not if I could help it.

I flicked my fingers, and the three streams of ash wove themselves around my neck, until they had formed a thick black rope. The fading heat of them warmed my skin, as did the echo of earthly power that still lingered within them. At least now Luke would have no access to that power.

Even as the thought crossed my mind, a scream ripped the air. Only it wasn't one voice, but many. Luke, venting his fury through the cloaks. But they didn't appear, and they certainly didn't attack.

The mother's energy spun back into me. My skin felt tight, heated, and my body ached with not only the ever-increasing weight of magic, but the force that now burned within me. I had no idea how long I could hold on to her without seriously compromising my strength and my life, but I'd do whatever it took to get out of this place. To get free.

I flexed my fingers. Sparks spun away from them, tiny stars that glowed brightly against the unnatural light of the witch fire . . . which should *not* be still alight now that the witches were dead.

Luke obviously had another one somewhere in his hive.

So what was he waiting for? Why didn't he attack? Or was the spell itself his main attack? Was he simply waiting for it to suck away my strength so that his cloaks could collect my unconscious body without threat or fear?

Were those things even capable of feeling fear? I'd certainly seen no sign of it in any of our previous encounters. Even when the force of my flames was melting their bodies, they showed little more than an inhuman determination to fulfill the orders they'd been given.

I had to get out of here. Had to escape before the fucking things had a chance to fulfill their current orders.

I spun around and walked toward the tunnel I'd come in through. The magic flared brighter as I approached it, and the stinging and biting got stronger. I hissed and tried to ignore it, but my steps got slower and my vision blurred, until I couldn't even see.

I swore and backed away. The stinging immediately eased. Whoever had designed this spell had done a damn good job. I thrust a hand through my hair, brushing the sweaty strands out of my eyes as I reached for Jackson.

I need help, I silently sent, *and fucking fast.*

I had no idea if he'd hear my call given the distance between us, but even if he didn't, he would have surely heard Luke's scream. All I had to do was hold out until he got here.

I scanned the rest of the junction warily. To get out of this rattrap, I'd have to break the damn spell. There were no spell stones in the immediate area, but I guess that wasn't surprising given events at the cemetery. Luke would have made sure I couldn't get at them this time, and that meant they were more than likely in each of the tunnels. But given that's where Luke obviously wanted me, it was the one place I wasn't about to go.

I returned my gaze to the original tunnel. I hadn't sensed any magic within it, but that wasn't entirely surprising given my attention had been on the fire and the two women. And while it was more than possible the spell would prevent Jackson entering the junction, he could at least search for the stone and break the spell by displacing it.

The creak of metal caught my attention. The door that had barred the entrance of the smallest tunnel was slowly opening. Nothing rushed out at me, but the hairs at the back of my neck nevertheless stood on end.

Because something was in there. Something *other* than cloaks.

The door clanged as it hit the slimy tunnel wall and the sound reverberated across the stillness. I clenched my hands, my fists translucent and glowing with the mother's fire. Deep within the tunnel, the darkness seemed to shift. Move.

I backed away. Fire bled from my fists and dripped onto the junction's floor, but rather than fizzing out, the globules slowly rolled toward the newly opened cage. As they neared it, something snarled, the sound eerie, otherworldly.

The mother's force pressed against my skin, burning to get out, to attack. I held her back, held my breath, and waited.

I didn't have to do so for long.

Three huge black forms bolted out of the tunnel, their teeth bared and their eyes glowing with a ruddy fire. I dove away from them and unleashed the mother. She streamed toward the creatures, her flames forming an incandescent wall between them and me. It should have cindered them.

It didn't.

The three of them simply dove through it as if it wasn't even there.

And *that* meant these things weren't ordinary dogs twisted by dark magic, but rather hellhounds. And hellhounds weren't from hell, despite what humans might believe, but rather were spirits born within the mother's fiery heart. The force that gave them life could not kill them.

The fact that they were here hunting me was confirmation that Luke *did* have another witch in his hive. Hellhounds tended to keep to the deep, wild places of this world, and only those well versed in the art of black magic could summon them. But it was a risky thing to do, as they were just as likely to kill the person who'd summoned them as those they were being sent against—and the longer the spell was in place, the more it drained the witch, and the more likely *that* became.

Of course, the summoning spell wasn't often held for long, because hellhounds were very efficient killing machines.

The presence of these creatures also explained why the magic had forced me into flesh form. Hellhounds tended not to hunt their own kind, but they couldn't actually tell us apart from humans when we were wearing this form.

If I could shift shape, they might halt their attack—depending on how strong the will of the witch who'd summoned them was, of course. But shifting shape was dependent on breaking the spell, and that was problematic at the moment.

The creatures skidded to a halt and twisted around. I scrambled to my feet and backed away, flames not only dripping from my fingertips now but also pulsating across my body. The hounds slowly followed, heads low, teeth bared.

They weren't here to hurt me. They were here to *herd* me.

Air brushed the back of my neck. I instinctively ducked, and the club that had been aimed at my head whistled over it instead. But I barely had time to suck in a breath when something smashed into my side and sent me sprawling. I hit the ground with a grunt and slid several feet farther, ending facedown in a puddle of foul water near the odd-colored fire. Pain flared down my barely healed side, but I ignored it and unleashed the mother's force. This time she *did* burn; the cloaks who were streaming out of the nearby tunnel barely had time to open their mouths, let alone scream.

As their cinders rained around me, I pushed upright. But weakness washed through my limbs and the world did a drunken dance around me. My knees hit the ground again, and the foul water splashed my arms and dribbled off my chin as I fought for breath.

It wasn't the spell. It was the mother, draining me to the point of exhaustion. I had to let her go or risk fading completely.

I released her then took a deep, shuddering breath. The air shimmered briefly as her heat bled from my body, and then she dissipated, bleeding down through the grime and the bricks, returning to the earth itself.

Leaving just the witch fire between the damn hellhounds and me.

I blinked and focused on the odd-colored flames. My own fire might be restricted thanks to the spell, but it obviously wasn't affecting *these* flames. I'd never attempted to use witch fire before—and had no idea if I could use it now—but if it *was* possible, then it at least gave me another means of defense. Hellhounds might be impervious to the force of the mother, but they could be controlled my magic. And a fire born of magic might just be enough to at least hold them at bay.

Em, here. Jackson's broken thoughts whispered into my brain, thick with fury and fear. *Can't enter. What do?*

We need to break the magic, I sent back. *You have to find the spell stone and force it out of alignment.*

Will do.

Hurry.

Try.

Try hard, I wanted to reply, but didn't. Jackson was a dark fae—he'd be familiar enough with the capabilities of hellhounds even if he'd never come across them before now. Dark fae had, in the past, been something of a favorite hunting toy for bored hounds. It was only when the human population and her cities had begun to claim much of the world's lands that the hounds had fully retreated to the deeper parts of the world.

I carefully pushed upright again. The junction did another mad dash around me, but the dizziness didn't last long. Yet it was warning enough that I had to get out of here. The mother had weakened me far too much and the spell was taking an even greater toll now. If I didn't break free soon, Luke might actually win this round.

And I doubted there'd be any further rounds if he did.

The hounds hadn't moved from their position. I took a careful step toward the fire, and the biggest of the three bared its teeth in warning. I slowly raised a hand and called to the witch fire. It shivered and danced away in response, as if attempting to deny my right to use it. The hound's growling got stronger. They might be more beast than most spirits, but they weren't stupid. They knew what I was attempting to do, even if they weren't aware of what I was just yet.

"My lord, you don't want to do this." Hellhounds, unlike most spirits, had something of a feudal hierarchy in place. I had no idea if the any of these were of royal bloodlines, but it never hurt to be polite. "I am what you are—spirit rather than flesh—and the mother will not be pleased if you attack one of your own."

Which was probably another reason why her flames hadn't hurt these creatures.

The growling grew stronger. Either he'd been called from the deepest recesses and had no understanding of modern English, or the spell was simply too strong for him to ignore.

I stepped closer to the flames and thrust my hand into the fire. The heat of it wrapped around my fist, its touch unpleasant and foul. My skin crawled at the sensation, but I ignored it and began winding the flames around my hand, until a large globe of molten green and gold had formed.

"Last chance, my lord." I met the hellhounds' gaze evenly. "Retreat now, or I will unleash this fire."

They didn't respond. They simply leapt.

I swore and threw myself sideways. One of the hounds twisted in midair and snapped at my leg. It didn't fully catch hold, but its teeth nevertheless tore through my jeans and bit deep into my flesh. I yelped and unleashed the ungodly fire. It shot from my fingers and hit the hound full in the face, melting his flesh and burning his eye sockets. He howled and shook his head from side to side, but the movement only succeeded in spreading the fire. All too soon, his entire body was alight and, oh god, the sound he made . . .

I hardened my heart against his agony and spun as the other two attacked, coming in from either side. I unleashed another stream of fire, but around me rather than at the hounds, forming a molten barrier between us. I couldn't face burning another hound, not when they were being forced into this action.

The two of them twisted in midair and landed short of my fiery cage. I took a deep, shuddery breath then glanced over my shoulder at the one I'd burned. It was making little noise now, but only, I suspected, because its larynx had been cindered along with half its face. I closed my eyes and recalled the fire. I couldn't undo the damage already done, but the hound would heal if it could get back to the mother's heart quickly enough.

"I'm sorry," I said. "You left me with no choice. Go while you still can."

The hound showed no sign of understanding, nor did it move. Whoever had leashed these things was obviously very strong. Anger ripped through me, but there was nothing I could do—no one I could attack—to help either these creatures or myself.

Not until the damn spell was broken.

I glanced at the tunnel, but all I could see was the glimmer of flame across its walls. Jackson, using his fire to lift the darkness. The urge to call out, to tell him to hurry, was so strong I had to bite my tongue against it. I had no doubt he was doing all he could, as fast as he could. I just had to keep standing, keep resisting.

But it was getting harder and harder. The force of magic was so strong now that my back was beginning to bow and my legs were quivering—although part of that was undoubtedly due to the wound on my calf. Blood was flowing freely from it, staining my shoe and pooling on the floor. The hound's teeth had slashed deep enough that I could see the glimmer of bone, but it apparently hadn't caught anything vital. I could put weight on the leg—even if it hurt like a bitch—and that meant I could run if my cage gave way.

Although where the hell I'd run given these things were faster than I'd ever be in *this* form . . .

I tore off a shirtsleeve and wrapped it tightly around the wound. It was pretty much stained red in an instant, but at least the wound wouldn't open any farther if I did have to run.

The other two creatures began prowling the outside of my fiery cage, their teeth bared and a low rumble coming from the depths of their chests. The witch fire flickered and danced, giving their velvet black fur an unhealthy glow and their eyes . . . I shivered. They might have been summoned here to herd and contain, but they now wanted death. If my fiery barrier gave way before Jackson could find the stone and dismantle the spell, I was in deep trouble.

The scratch of nails against concrete caught my attention. The third hound was limping toward the tunnel I'd come in through. The magic flared as it approached, meaning it had been directed at spirits in general rather than me specifically. It stopped and bared its teeth, although only one small section of them remained. One of the hounds circling me moved over to join him, and hackles rose along its spine.

"Jackson, they know you're there." There was little point in using telepathy now, especially when it was so damn patchy. "Watch your back."

"Found the spell stone," he said, either not hearing or not caring about my warning. "Any suggestions how to move the thing?"

"Find some metal or something and hit it from a safe distance. He might have put some form of protection on it after the cemetery debacle."

The weight on my shoulders grew. I tried to stretch upright, tried to deny the heaviness and remain upright, but it was useless. I dropped to my knees and, just for an instant, found relief from the pressure. It found me all too quickly, however.

I hissed and concentrated on the fire, on keeping the circle around me full and high. But the fire in the barrel was beginning to ebb, and I very much suspected the witch who'd created it was now undoing the spell that gave it life. I had a couple of minutes left, if that.

I closed my eyes, drew in a deep breath, and got

ready to rise and run. If I could get to the cage, get the door closed before they got close, I might yet survive. And surely whatever else might await in that tunnel could not be anywhere near as bad as the hounds.

Light exploded in the exit tunnel, and Jackson swore. "It's protected, all right," he said. "I saw some iron down near the cellar. Can you hang on?"

Did I have any choice? "Yes. But hurry."

He left, his footsteps echoing across the odd stillness, only to be replaced by others. I twisted around and saw more red cloaks entering the junction. Where the hell was he getting these things? The virus might be transferred easily enough, but it still took days or weeks to change—and even PIT wouldn't be able to keep a lid on things if that many people had gone missing.

Unless, of course, the city's homeless population were being used as his foot soldiers. It was a sad fact that few people took much notice of the homeless, and it was doubtful anyone other than those involved in providing services for them would actually notice a drop in numbers.

The cloaks remained near the tunnel's entrance. The hounds ignored them; two remained near the tunnel while the biggest one continued to prowl around me. His head was low, and his eyes gleamed with anticipation.

I wondered if that anticipation was his or Luke's.

My shoulders slumped as the weight grew. I shivered and slapped my hands against the cold, damp floor, trying to resist the force of it. If it didn't let up soon, I'd be squashed flatter than a pancake. But maybe *that* had been Luke's intent all along; maybe he'd decided I was far too dangerous to capture, and was simply content to watch—through the eyes of his creatures—the life being squeezed out of me.

Footsteps returned. But breathing was becoming a struggle now, and my back felt as if it were on fire. And the flames that were protecting me from the hounds were beginning to fade in and out of existence as the power began to leach out of them. There was nothing I could do to stop it. It wasn't my fire, and I had no way of shoring up the gaps that were beginning to open up.

I closed my eyes and prayed to whatever gods might be out there, listening, to give me a goddamn break. I didn't want to die—not like this. Not with Rory so far away. He'd feel it, of course, and call to my ashes, but there was no guarantee this magic would allow me through, even in death.

A rumble of sound caught my attention. The unburned hound near the barred tunnel had bared its teeth, its hackles raised. Jackson was back.

I crossed everything there was to cross and waited, my arms quivering and my breath a harsh rasp.

Metal struck stone, the sound louder than the hound's growling. The one prowling around my flickering cage paused and looked over its shoulder. Then his gaze returned to mine and promised death.

"I am not your enemy," I somehow ground out. "Hunt those who force you into this action, my lord, not those who consider you kindred."

He simply bared his teeth. Maybe he did understand me and now simply wanted revenge.

Metal struck stone again, the sound louder and drawing my attention. Sparks spun through the shadow, their color the same weird green yellow of the fast-disappearing flames.

The hound snapped at me. I raised a hand, the remnants of the fireball around my fist flaring lightly at the action. The hound drew back and resumed its pacing. It had to wait only a few more minutes, and we both knew it.

Again, the sound of metal hitting stone reverberated, but this time it was accompanied by an explosion so fierce the walls of the junction shuddered. But as dust and slime and god only knew what else rained down on me, the magic lifted and I was free.

I quickly reached inside and became spirit—and not a moment too soon, because the hound had already launched. I twisted away from his leap and threw fire toward the cloaks. I didn't have the strength to burn them all, so I simply wrapped a barrier around them and hoped like hell Luke would decide he'd lost enough people today.

When they didn't immediately test the barrier's strength, I returned my attention to the hound. It skidded to a halt several yards away and spun to face me.

"You are stronger than them, my lord." No human would understand me, but he was what I was, even if his form was different. "Do not let them destroy whatever standing you have within the mother and your clan."

He bared his teeth but didn't immediately attack. Which meant I'd been right—the dark witch might have summoned them here, but the spell had been maintained long enough that he could resist it now if he so chose.

He glanced at his companions. The one I'd burned immediately disappeared, undoubtedly returning to the mother to heal itself, but the other lunged into the tunnel, going after Jackson.

"The fae in that tunnel is my friend," I said, even as I silently added, *Jackson, there's a hellhound coming at you right now.*

"And the spirit you cindered was my brother." The hound's voice was raspy and broken, and his dialect ancient and French in origin but nevertheless understandable. "Why should I not kill both you and the fae in retaliation?"

"Because we are not the enemy. Those who called you to this place and forced you to hunt should be the ones to feel your anger. I was only attempting to protect myself." I hesitated. "I *am* sorry for the amount of damage done. That was not my intention."

"An apology comes too late when sight might be stolen forever."

"We both know the mother is generous to your kind. She would not let any of you suffer unnecessarily—unless, of course, you kill another of her children."

He bared his teeth again. I wasn't entirely sure if it was anger or amusement. "The sorceress who called us demands your death. Tell me why I should not comply."

"Because the sorcerer and the man who controls him are my enemies, and a stain on the earth itself. You saw the color of his flames—did that tell you nothing?"

"I saw the flames burn my brother. That is all I needed to see."

"I used them because the spell left me with no

flames of my own." I paused. "And be warned, the fae your third hunts has gained the flames of a phoenix. I would advise calling him off."

He didn't immediately reply, but after a few seconds, the second hound returned. It walked up to its leader, sat on its haunches, and regarded me steadily.

A good sign, I hoped.

Hound retreat, came Jackson's comment. *You okay?*

Yes. Stay there. Out loud, I added, "Lord, the will of the witch is obviously weakening. You do not have to obey him."

"The witch isn't the only one weakening, as we are both aware."

I smiled, but there was very little in the way of humor in it. "If you think I cannot harm you, then you are not as smart as I first thought."

He bared his teeth again, but I had a suspicion that this time it was amusement. "You do not mince words. I like that. We shall go. But pray we are not summoned again, phoenix, because we will kill you—especially if my brother does not repair."

I inclined my head. "Thank you."

The hounds' bodies disappeared into a swirl of black smoke. Relief ran through me, but it wasn't over yet. There were still the red cloaks to contend with.

I turned and fled toward Jackson. The cloaks immediately screamed but didn't give chase. Maybe Luke *did* have a finite number of them left. Or maybe his witch was aware just how close to breaking point his or her magic had bought me, and had informed Luke it was simply a matter of patience. Either way, I was getting out while I still could.

I flamed around the long corner and spotted Jackson about midway between the cellar exit and me. I shifted shape and hit the ground in a stumbling sort of run as my torn calf buckled and threatened to give way completely. Jackson leapt forward and caught me before I could hit the ground. For several seconds I didn't move—couldn't move. My entire body was shaking, my leg was on fire, and I would have fallen had it not been for Jackson's arms around me.

"Shit, you really *did* push the line this . . ." He stopped and held me at arm's length, his gaze on the ashes around my neck. "What the *fuck* is that?"

"The remains of the witches."

"What?"

I waved a hand. "I'll explain later. Right now, we need to move. I've stalled the cloaks with a wall of fire, but it's not going to last much longer, I'm afraid."

"And I have no intention of getting in another fight with the bastards if I can at all help it."

He scooped me up into his arms then ran like hell down the tunnel. Normally I would have complained simply because I preferred not to rely on others like this. But I was close to complete exhaustion, and we weren't out of trouble yet. I rested my face against his chest and let his body heat wash over me. It was tempting—so tempting—to reach out and feed on it, if only a little, but that wouldn't be wise right now. One us needed to be at full fighting strength if—when—the cloaks came after us.

The more distance we gained from the junction, the more it stretched the threads still feeding my firewall. As the grate leading into the basement came into view, those threads shattered. The roar of the cloaks reverberated through the stillness.

Jackson swore and boosted me up to the grate. I scrambled through and pushed to my feet. Giddiness and pain hit like clubs, snatching my breath and making my vision darken for a second. I thrust my hand against the wall and kept myself upright by sheer force of will alone.

Jackson hauled himself into the room and jumped to his feet. He didn't bother putting the grate back into place but simply swept me up into his arms and ran for the stairs. I threw fire into the air, but the orb was a pale echo of the one I'd created earlier. But it provided enough light to guide our way, and that was all that mattered right now.

He took the steps two at a time. I glanced over his shoulder; none of the cloaks had reached the grate just yet, but they were close. The sound of them scrambling over one another to be first to reach us was growing louder and louder.

We reached the top of the stairs and the black ink barrier again. The flames of my pale orb did little to lift the gloom of it, so I recalled the energy.

"You able to stand?" Jackson said.

"I'll fucking run if I have to."

His grin flashed, but the tension in his arms was echoed around his eyes. "Good. I need a free arm to ensure I don't hit anything in there."

He caught my hand and tugged me after him. The ink closed in around us, sucking away any sense of light or noise. That it was still here meant it was yet another product of the other witch. If the three whose ashes were around my neck had been responsible for it, it wouldn't still exist. Spells didn't live past those who created them.

Once again it seemed to take forever to get through the ink. Urgency beat through my brain, and it took everything I had to resist the desire to hurry. If we couldn't see in this stuff, then maybe the cloaks couldn't. Exceptions could be woven into every spell, of course, but they had to be done on an individual basis, and I doubted Luke—or whoever was creating this magic for him—would have the patience or the time to do so for every one of his infected people.

The black wall finally leached away, and true night reasserted itself. The door we'd entered through was both closed and padlocked.

"As if *that'll* stop us." Jackson wrapped his fingers around the lock and called forth flame. His fingers became molten, but the lock was tungsten steel and took a heartbeat longer to melt.

Behind us, something skidded across the concrete and clanged against a wall. Then a footstep echoed. Just one step, but it seemed a whole lot closer than whatever had hit the wall. Fire flicked through me, but held little heat. I wasn't even strong enough to form a wall right now, let alone burn the cloaks.

"Finally," Jackson muttered. He pulled the padlock free, though needle-fine strands of melted metal clung to the door, resisting until the very end.

He tossed the lock into the corner then swung the door open. "Let's go." He grabbed my hand and tugged me out into the lane. "The cloaks have to be—"

He cut the sentence off as his gaze went beyond

me, then cursed and called forth fire again. It exploded across his free hand and surged his arm, crossing his shoulders in an instant and leaping down to our clasped hands. God, it felt so good . . . I shut down the instinct to feed on it and looked over my shoulder. There were shapes evident in the ink; the cloaks were close to breaking through.

He threw his fire at the magic wall, but—like mine—it failed to make any impact. I grabbed control and smeared it across the length of the blackness, creating a fiery barrier.

"Can you hold the force of it while we run?"

It was totally possible my leg wouldn't actually stand up to running, but Jackson couldn't be expected to carry me *and* maintain a wall of fire, and I sure as hell wasn't going to hang about here. Hell, I'd damn well crawl if I had to.

"Let's find out." His voice was grim but determined.

We ran for the street and the lights. Whether we'd be any safer there given the late hour of the night, I had no idea, but at least we had more options when it came to losing them than we did this one-way lane.

A scream went up behind us, and the smell of burning flesh began to stain the air. Jackson's body twitched and danced, and it almost looked as if some invisible being were assaulting him—and if the cloaks were throwing themselves against his flames, then that was probably what it felt like. He might be well used to controlling regular fire, but the fires of a phoenix were fed from your body *and* your soul.

I glanced over my shoulder as we raced around the corner onto Little Collins Street. The cloaks had breached Jackson's barrier and were coming after us. Some of them were on fire, some of them were not, but all of them showed about as much emotion as the walls on either side of them.

"Stop feeding your firewall." The words little more than pants of air. I really *was* reaching my breaking point. "Save it for when they get closer."

"They are *not* getting any closer."

With that, he swept me into his arms again without breaking stride or speed, and raced onto Russell Street, heading away from the hotel rather than toward it. We somehow reached Bourke Street before the cloaks got to the Russell and Little Collins street corner, and went left, heading toward the mall but turning right into Swanston Street before we got there. He slowed only once we were on Lonsdale Street.

"The McDonald's up ahead is open twenty-four/seven." He carefully placed me on my feet, but kept hold of one arm as I struggled to catch my balance. "We'll hold out there until daybreak; it should be safe to go back to the hotel and collect our things then."

"Food would be good." It wouldn't help replenish my fire, but it would certainly help improve my physical strength. I pulled my jacket's zip all the way up to hide the interwoven threads of ash around my neck then gave him a quick smile. "Although what the hell they'll think when the two of us enter, all beaten and bloody, is anyone's guess. We could be the first people in the world to be thrown *out* of a McDonald's because of the state of our clothing."

He snorted and switched my grip to my elbow, lightly supporting me as we walked on. "They won't think anything. They employ teenagers at these places, and since when have teenagers noticed anything beyond themselves and their phones?"

"They're not likely to have their phones on them when they're working."

"Want to bet on that?" He raised an eyebrow at me. "Winner pays for the meal?"

I laughed. "The business pays for the meal, not us."

"True." He glanced over his shoulder and his pace quickened slightly. "I can't hear them, but I think we need to get off the street, just in case."

"Let's just hope they can't follow the scent of blood."

Jackson glanced down, his expression concerned. "Why didn't it heal when you shifted shape?"

"Because we're spirits, not werewolves, and it doesn't work that way for us."

"It really does look bad; maybe we need to get to the hospital so they can stitch you up—"

"No, because I can't risk the blood tests. I'll cauterize it when I get the chance." *I should have enough energy left to do that, at least.* I squeezed his arm. "It'll be fine, trust me."

We reached McDonald's. He opened the door and ushered me through. "Is that why your back is so scarred? Because you couldn't risk either controlling the flames or going to the hospital when you rescued the kid from the fire?"

I nodded. "I'm off to find the bathroom. Order me a couple of burgers, some fries, and the biggest damn cup of green tea they have."

I left him to it and limped away. Thankfully, the

bathroom was empty, so I tugged off my bloody shoe and sock, then undid my makeshift bandage and turned on the cold water. The wound was about eight inches long, running from the left side of my knee around my calf to the opposite ankle. Bone was evident in one section, but, for the most part, it wasn't very deep. I'd been lucky—it could have been a whole lot worse. Like one-leg-missing worse.

I shuddered and washed the wound as best I could. After padding it dry with paper towels, I called forth what little flame I had left and cauterized the wound. I'd still have to be wary of tearing it open again, but at least the bleeding had stopped for now. I stripped off my coat, tore up my remaining shirtsleeve, and wrapped the pieces tightly around the wound. Then I rinsed off my sock and shoe and got dressed again.

Jackson had claimed a corner booth well away from any of the windows. I limped over and slid in beside him. We didn't talk for quite a while, both of us too busy stuffing our faces with burgers and fries.

"I've been thinking," he finally said. "Maybe we should catch a cab to the office and wait out morning there."

"That's surely the first place Luke will look." I hesitated. "But we *could* go next door to the blacksmith's."

It was not only an option that would give us some degree of safety, but also a means by which I could replenish my flames without risking a call to Rory.

"That was also my thinking," he said, obviously catching part of my thoughts. He waved a hand at my as-yet-untouched cup of tea. "Want to bring that with you?"

I gave him an indignant look. "I'm not about to leave it behind!"

He laughed, but the sound was filled with tiredness. Creating that firewall had taken more out of him than he was admitting. "Wait here while I go find a cab."

He rose and strode outside. I picked up my tea and tried to take a sip, but my hands were trembling so much that if it weren't for the lid, the hot liquid would have splashed over my fingers. It was yet another sign of just how close to the edge I still was. The food, it seemed, hadn't done much for me physically.

I took a deep breath and slowly released it, then dug out our spare phone and called Rory. He didn't answer—no surprise given he was on night shift this week—so I left him a message, updating him on everything that had happened. I knew he'd be worried if I didn't.

Jackson appeared five minutes later and beckoned me over. It only took a few minutes to cut across to the old blacksmith's and, once Jackson had paid the driver, we headed into the rear yard. It was a sturdy-looking double-story brick building that had an almost Victorian elegance about it. A double roller door dominated the left side of the building, while there were several bricked-up arched windows on the right. He opened the door, ushered me through, and then locked it behind him. The air was filled with warmth, and I briefly closed my eyes and drew it in. It wasn't fire, but it nevertheless felt good.

Jackson caught my hand and led me forward. Ahead, in the old-fashioned brick furnace, coals glowed, casting orange shadows across the vast space. To either side of the long room was a mix of tables, cabinets holding all sorts of tools, and metal projects in various states of completion.

As we neared the furnace, he made a motion with his free hand and flames leapt to life. Their heat ran across my senses, and the part of me that was spirit and fire connected with it. The closer we got, the stronger the pull, the more I fed. It was a glorious feeling.

"Refuel, Emberly," he said as we stopped in front of the fire. "And then we'll rest."

My gaze jumped to his. "You're not communing with the flames?"

"Hell yeah." The smile that twisted his lips didn't touch his eyes. "And before you ask, yes, it'll make me hornier than hell, but I *can* assert some control when I want to. We can't risk any sort of distraction right now, however pleasurable and welcome that distraction might be."

I nodded and returned my gaze to the flames. The fire was a siren song I could not ignore, so I opened my arms and drew in its heat and power. It rushed through my body, through every inch of me, easing the trembling and refilling the well of heat deep within. It was glorious, magic, and, as my skin began to glow, I sighed in utter pleasure then reluctantly pulled free. As Jackson had said, we needed to remain alert.

I crossed my arms and stepped back to allow him full access to the furnace. Given I had no idea how long he'd be, I swung around and started looking for someplace comfortable to wait. In the far corner of the warehouse was a small office with several well-padded chairs. I dragged one closer to the desk then put my feet up and got comfortable. I was asleep in no time.

I was awoken by the noise of a garbage truck in the street outside. I opened an eye and squinted upward. There was a small window above the desk and a star-filled sky was still evident beyond the grime-crusted glass. I straightened, but that succeeded only in waking all sorts of aches. I winced and groaned as various flares of pain ran down my back and legs. Maybe sleeping in the chair *hadn't* been such a great idea after all.

Jackson, I noted, was similarly positioned in the other chair. I reached across and poked him in the side with a stiffened finger.

"Do that again and I might just bite," he all but growled.

I couldn't help smiling. "Morning, sunshine."

"Is it?" He pushed upright and scrubbed a hand across his chin. "Fuck, I feel like shit."

"Yeah, sleeping this rough isn't something I've done for a while."

"The sad thing is, this isn't actually rough." He pushed upright, glancing at his watch as he stretched his arms over his head. "Fuck, it's barely four in the morning. Why the hell are we awake?"

"Because we need to go see Grace." I rose and twisted from side to side to ease some of the kinks.

His gaze dropped to the ashes around my neck. "How long can you actually hold them?"

"Only twenty-four hours. Keeping them in close contact is helping to keep the heat lingering within them, but if it fades, they'll fall away."

"Why is it important to keep the heat within them?" He caught my hand and led the way out of the office, heading for the rear door.

"Because their spirits are still entwined within the ashes. If they are not given proper funeral rites before the heat fades, they will not move on, but rather become ghosts."

"Fuck, why?"

"Because they were killed before their time." Or, in this particular case, because *I'd* killed them before their time. But gathering the ashes of the dead wasn't something I could do for everyone I killed. It often depended on how they'd lived their lives. Fate was a harsher judge than me when it came to deciding whether or not a person was worthy of moving on.

He unlocked the rear door and ushered me out. "And does this happen to all humans who are killed too early? Because it does not apply to us. Our souls simply become one with the mother until it is time to be reborn again."

"As far as I know, it applies to not only humans but many nonhumans, like wolves and other shifters."

"But not spirits."

I shook my head. "If we die—really die—then our energy also returns to the mother, but there is no coming back for us."

He squeezed my hand. "Then I'll have to make sure you don't die for real. I'd truly miss your presence in my life if you did."

Which, given dark fae didn't really do deep emotion, was almost a declaration of love. "I'd seriously miss you, too."

"Well, *that* is only natural." His expression was decidedly cheeky. "Shall we risk heading back to the hotel to collect our things, or go straight over to see Grace?"

I hesitated. "Let's go back to the hotel. And given the rental place is open twenty-four/seven, maybe it's time to change the car over. The sindicati and probably Luke are aware we're driving it."

Of course, if the sindicati had shifted from using werewolves to using winged shifters, then changing cars wouldn't make much difference.

"Let's deal with one threat at a time," Jackson commented. "Right now, that's Luke and his cloaks rather than the sindicati."

We hailed a cab and were back at the hotel in very little time. Once we'd checked out—and after cautiously inspecting the car to ensure there were no hidden surprises waiting for us—we returned it to the rental company and got a different one. It was a subterfuge that might be pointless, but it was better than driving about in a car too many people now seemed to know about.

We found the nearest drive-through, collecting both drinks and food so we could get through the next couple of hours, and then headed through the traffic toward Sassafras. I dug out the phone and called Grace. Unsurprisingly—given the time—she didn't answer, so I left her a message saying we would be at her shop around six.

Night was still holding court by the time we got there, and the main street was quiet. Hushed. Usually places high in the hills like this were alive with birdsong at this hour, and the fact that it wasn't had unease stirring.

But maybe they knew we were the bearers of sorrow and, as such, deserved no welcome.

Aside from the streetlights, the only other lights to be seen were the ones in Grace's shop. She was waiting for us.

I climbed out of the car but didn't immediately move toward her building. I really didn't want to confront her. Really didn't want to give her the news I had to give her. I may have saved the souls of the witches, but I hadn't saved their lives, as she'd undoubtedly hoped.

"This has to be done," Jackson said, voice soft. "For the sake of those you carry as well as those who await news."

"I know."

But knowing never made being the bearer of bad news any easier. I shoved my hands into my coat pockets and led the way across the road.

Once again the bell chimed as we entered, but neither the riot of color or gorgeous scent of the place lifted my spirit as we wove our way through the organized chaos.

The curtain dividing the main room from the workshop section parted, and Grace stepped through. Like before, she was wearing a colorful gypsy skirt matched with a shirt and shawl, but this time the colors were muted, more gray and blue than cheery red, yellows, and orange.

She knew, I thought, seeing the pain etched into her features.

She stopped, one hand on the curtain and the other clenched. "You do not bring with you good news."

I stopped several feet away. Jackson halted behind me, his presence pressing heat into my spine and oddly giving me courage. "No, we do not."

"How did they die?"

I hesitated. "I cindered two. The other was dead by the time I found them. I also cindered her remains, but I cannot guarantee her soul has not become lost."

Her gaze swept me, bright with tears. "You have them with you?"

I unzipped my jacket and reveal the entwined ashes around my neck. Grace took a deep, shuddering breath. "They are all there. Come."

She disappeared into the other room. Jackson pressed his fingers against the small of my back, lightly pushing me to follow. After a moment, I did.

Grace pulled three small urns out of a small cupboard at the rear of the room then returned and placed them on the small table. All three were unadorned and made of simple clay, and were a very fitting resting place for witches who followed the earth mother.

Grace uncorked the urns, blessing each one as she did so, and then raised her gaze to mine. "Can you separate them and place each one in an urn?"

I called to the hint of fire remaining in each of the ember strands, and directed them into separate urns. Heat kissed my skin for just a moment—heat that came from the ashes themselves—then the threads that were once life unwound from my neck and disappeared into the urns.

Grace whispered a prayer as she sealed the first of

them up, but a frown creased her features as she touched the second and grew when she picked up the last one. "What happened to Rennie and Neriana? Their souls twist, as if in agony."

I hesitated, and Grace's gaze sharpened. "I must know if they are to gain forgiveness and rest in peace."

"They were all infected, as we warned," Jackson said when I didn't immediately answer. "It made each of them something of a pseudo vampire."

"That alone would not account for this." She hesitated, glancing at the first urn. "It has something to do with Angie, doesn't it?"

"Yes. I cannot say whether she was infected or not, because she was dead before I got there." I battered away the images of the other two witches feasting on her body and wished I didn't have to say what I now had to say.

"Please," Grace said, obviously sensing my reluctance.

I took a deep breath, then added softly, "She was given as a meal to the other two. They had little choice but to eat."

"He is a *fiend*." There was horror in her voice and eyes. "An absolute fiend."

"Yes. And he'll pay for his crimes, believe me."

"In this life, and in others, I suspect." She wiped a hand across her eyes, smearing tears. "Thank you for returning them, even if you could not save their lives."

I grimaced and crossed my arms, feeling cold. It had nothing to do with my failure and everything to do with the premonition that there were many more deaths to come before this was completely over. Intuition, I thought bitterly, could be a bitch sometimes. Especially when it kept hitting me with vague promises of death and destruction and yet refused to ante up anything solid in the form of a dream.

Grace scooped up the three urns and carefully placed them back in the cupboard. I suspected their final rites would be held tomorrow. The full moon was due then, and that was always a good time for such things.

After locking the cabinet, she moved across to another section of the room and picked up what looked like three simple, multicolored string necklaces.

"These are the spell blockers we promised," she said, returning to where we stood. "As I said, they will counteract only magic designed either to restrict your fire or your access to the mother, but I suspect that will be enough for now."

She dropped two of them into my palm. The energy that ran within them made my skin tingle, but it was not an unpleasant sensation. She gave the other one to Jackson then added, "We have designed them to be unobtrusive. No one but a witch of extreme power will even see that you're wearing them."

"I'm afraid there just might be such a witch in this town." I told her about the fire and the hellhounds. "Is your coven—or any of the others—missing other members?"

"Not that I know of, and we would have been informed after recent events." She frowned. "I'd suspect it might be an outsider who has been brought in, except we surely would have sensed that."

"Unless, of course, he or she is using magic to cover their presence."

"That is possible, especially if we are dealing with someone following a darker path." She hesitated. "I shall seek advice from those higher in my order. If there is such a witch in town, we'll do our best to track them down and deal with them. We cannot afford to have such a person working with those who now control Brooklyn."

"Whoever it is, it's likely they are as your missing witches were—no longer in control of their own thoughts or emotions," Jackson said. "If you do find them, it will be wiser to report their presence to PIT rather than confront them yourself."

"One witch—even a follower of the dark path—has little hope against the might of an entire coven," she said. "We can deal—"

"Yes," I cut in, "except that it's *not* just magic you're dealing with. What afflicts Brooklyn is an infection in both a physical *and* medical sense. Believe us, what happened to your sisters could very easily happen to you."

Her gaze traveled from me to Jackson and back again, and her expression became even more troubled. "If this *is* an infection in the literal sense, then I doubt the dark witch is afflicted, let alone in the control of another. Not given what you said about the hellhounds."

I frowned. "Why?"

"Because that sort of magic is extremely dangerous, and the witch would have to be in possession of all faculties to achieve the necessary control."

"Meaning he or she is working with him *willingly*?" Jackson's voice held an incredulous note. "I cannot believe—"

"Those who crave the power of the dark path are often drawn to those with similar spirits and goals," Grace cut in. "And a man with a black heart and chaos on his mind would be a beacon to those with similar aims."

I scrubbed a hand across my eyes. This was *not* what we needed. "We'll have to inform PIT," I said, glancing at Jackson.

"Yeah." His voice was grim. "They're undoubtedly under the same impression as us—that it was only the one nutter we were dealing with."

I slipped one of the necklaces around my neck and put the other safely in my pocket. "Thanks for these, Grace, and be careful out there."

"I will. And I will send a message if we do get any further information about the dark witch."

I opened my mouth to tell her to contact PIT rather than us then closed it again. Maybe the coven wanted as little to do with PIT as we did. Couldn't blame them for that.

We said good-bye and headed out of the shop. I paused on the pavement and glanced around. Dawn was beginning to spread golden fingers across the sky, but here at street level, darkness still held court, and the world remained eerily quiet. Ignoring the notion that it was the calm before the storm, I glanced up at Jackson and said, "What next?"

"I don't know. I'm tempted to go back to the office, though."

"That's just asking for trouble."

"And it would also be very inconvenient," an all-too-familiar voice said behind me. "Especially since I've taken the trouble to drive all the way out here to see you."

Chapter 12

Jackson and I swore in unison and turned around. The three men who stood in front of us were swathed head to foot in reflective blankets, and both their hands and faces were covered with heavy black material. Only their eyes were visible.

They were obviously vampires, because it certainly wasn't *that* cold up here. And while the sun wasn't yet fully up, most vamps tended to be overly cautious—not surprising when the sun's touch could at least leave them with scars and, at worst, kill them.

But I didn't need to see their faces to know the man standing slightly in front of the others was Frank Parella. He was not only a general of one of the two sindicati factions wrestling for overall control, but the man who'd shot De Luca, his counterpart on the other side.

"What the fuck are you doing here?" Jackson didn't bother smothering his annoyance. "We had a damn deal—"

"The deal," Parella cut in, "is the reason I'm here. I believe you are not living up to your part of it."

I snorted. "And you know this how? Are you psychic or something?"

"No, nor do I keep the company of witches." There was amusement in his voice, but it held little in the way of warmth. I doubted it touched his lips, because it certainly wasn't touching his eyes.

"No, you were just using the werewolves," Jackson said. "Which didn't exactly turn out well for either them *or* you."

"No, it did not," Parella said. "But it is *that* unfortunate event that has forced me out here."

"Why?" I asked bluntly. "It's not like you couldn't have sent more goons. You have plenty of them, don't you?"

"Well, yes," Parella said. "But I suspect you would have treated them no better than you treated the wolves. Besides, did you not tell them that if I wanted the damn notes that I should come and get them myself?"

Well, yeah, but I certainly hadn't thought he'd actually *do* it. "The wolves rather unwisely resorted to guns, and totally deserved what they got. I take it their actions were outside your orders?"

"Yes." That hint of amusement was back in his voice, leaving me uncertain as to whether to believe him or not. "However, you cannot escape the point that you have information you have not shared, as was our deal."

"There's nothing in the satchel of importance—"

"*I* will be the judge of that," he cut in. "The notes, Emberly, or the deal is off."

His sharp tone had annoyance flaring, but there was also a whole lot of relief. He might know about the satchel, but he was apparently unaware of the fact that we'd taken copies or that we'd found a USB in Wilson's gym locker. Hopefully, we could keep it that way. PIT were unlikely to inform us of its contents, and I certainly didn't want to lose *our* copy until we'd discovered what was on the damn thing.

"The deal was for you to stand back while we investigated," I snapped back. "Having us followed is hardly in keeping with the spirit of that."

"Given the situation and your subsequent actions, we can hardly be blamed," he replied calmly. "The satchel. Now."

I glanced at Jackson. He shrugged. *Do. Can't afford offside.*

No, we couldn't. We had enough people pissed off at us already. I blew out a frustrated breath then spun around and lead the way back to our car. There was a large white van parked behind us, which was undoubtedly how Parella and his men had gotten here. The driver was sitting inside, but he wasn't covered and none of the front windows were darkly tinted. Not a vampire, then.

I opened the trunk, pushed our bags to one side, and plucked the satchel free. One of Parella's men stepped forward and took it from me.

I scowled and returned my gaze to Parella. "Is Amanda working for you? Is that how you knew we had the satchel?"

"I believe Amanda is now under the not so tender ministrations of whoever has taken over De Luca's position."

"And De Luca's vamplings blame *us* for his murder," Jackson snapped. "Don't suppose you want to correct that piece of misinformation, do you?"

"It would not be in my best interest to do so, so no."

"It's in your best interest to keep us alive," I bit back. "Keeping De Luca's lair off our butts would be a major part of that."

"You are more than capable of taking care of yourself, young lady, and we both know it."

I couldn't exactly argue with that. And I certainly couldn't help being amused by the term "young lady." It had been a long—long—time since either of those really applied. "Then I guess it's also useless to ask you to pull the tail off us?"

"Indeed. We both know that you will not willingly hand over information. However, I am more than happy to keep advising my superiors not to kill you as long as you continue to be useful."

How nice of him. "And what about Rinaldo?"

The air got decidedly frostier. "What of him?"

"Are you working with him?"

"No, we are definitely not."

"Then why are you allowing him to gain toeholds here in Melbourne?"

"He has not—"

"He's behind a major attack on the rats," I cut in, having no intention of swallowing the bullshit he was undoubtedly about to sprout, "and he's blackmailing us to give him information about the virus research. If he hasn't already got a very strong toehold, then how the fuck is he accomplishing all that without you knowing about it?"

I could almost hear the cogs turning as he decided how much we needed to know. "It would appear you are very well informed."

"Yeah, well, when you have two sindicati factions, a madman intent on world domination, and PIT on your back, it pays to be."

"Not to mention the rats and the werewolves."

The smile that touched my lips held about as much warmth as his voice. "It would appear we are not the only ones keeping informed."

"Even the most ignorant underworld citizen would have been hard-pressed not to hear about your altercation with Radcliffe and his men. The wolves were foolish not to heed such a warning."

The wolves in general *had,* as I had no doubt *that* was part of the reason why Baker had decided to work with us rather than against us. "And Rinaldo? Or whatever the fuck his real name is?"

"Is proving rather hard to track down. We suspect there's magic involved."

Another of those prophetic chills ran through me. "The witches wouldn't work with someone like Rinaldo."

"No, but not all magic users are bound by covens, and many are far more powerful than what the witches would have the populace believe."

Two dark witches in the same city, working for different criminals? How likely was *that*? But did it mean Luke was in contact with Rinaldo, or that the dark witch working with him was actually a Rinaldo plant? Either possibility was a scary one.

If it *was* the latter, it would certainly explain how Rinaldo seemed to know so much about the virus and the research. But if it *was* the case, then why did he need us to find the missing notes when he had access to the scientists via his source in Luke's camp?

Was Luke keeping their location secret from everyone in his camp, as De Luca had kept secret Baltimore's research notes?

It was possible. Luke had never really trusted anyone beside himself. Not even his family.

Especially not his family.

"Why would you suspect magic is involved?" Jackson asked. "Why couldn't he simply be very good at hiding his presence?"

"Because between the city pack and ourselves, we pretty much own this city. Nothing goes down that we don't know about. That neither of us can find him suggests other forces must be at work."

"Even magic leaves a trail that can be followed," I commented.

"We are aware of that, but convincing the covens to work with us on this matter is . . . difficult." His gaze narrowed slightly. "You seem to be on good terms with them. Perhaps you could have a word with them?"

"Sure. As soon as you make De Luca's lair aware that we were not responsible for his murder."

He laughed. "I do like you, Emberly Pearson."

"I'm thrilled." And damn certain him liking me didn't mean he wouldn't kill me if necessary. "Is that it? Can we go now?"

He made a somewhat grand sweeping motion with his hand. "By all means, do. Just remember, keep in contact. You have my phone number."

I did—I'd grabbed it from Radcliff after one of our altercations. "Between you, Rinaldo, and PIT, it's a damn wonder we actually get off the phone and get some work done."

I slammed the trunk shut and walked around to the passenger side of the car and climbed in.

Jackson got in the driver's side, started the car, then did a quick U-turn and planted his foot. The vampires were left in a cloud of burned rubber. "Well, that was exciting."

"Yeah." I scrubbed a hand across my eyes. "Did you know they were following us?"

"No. I mean, I saw a white van on several occasions, but there's so many of the things on the road these days I didn't think anything of it."

"We'll need to be more careful."

"Is there any real point right now? It would seem everyone is aware of our damn movements."

I wrinkled my nose. "If Luke knew where we were staying, he would have attacked."

"Maybe. And maybe he's just waiting for a convenient moment."

"Luke is many things, but patient isn't one of them." I paused. "Do you think Parella is right about Rinaldo using magic to hide his presence?"

"It's possible."

"Then maybe we should go back and talk to Grace—"

"No," Jackson said, "Leave them to their mourning."

"But they might be our hope of stopping him—"

"*We* don't need to stop him." He glanced at me, expression grim. "And as long as the wolves do as they promised, we just need to keep making those calls and string him along."

"It's never wise to tease a tiger." And Rinaldo would not act favorably if he ever realized what we were doing.

"So we feed him just enough information and hope he *doesn't.*"

"Which means giving him a copy of the notes we just gave Parella."

"Why don't we go back to the office and leave our selection of pages there?"

I frowned. "Do we really want to invite him into our place again?"

"We didn't exactly invite him in the first time."

"Well, no, but that's beside the point."

"We don't have to be there. Besides, we can grab the chance to check the phones. I'm sure our other clients will be getting a little antsy about the lack of progress on their cases."

I raised an eyebrow. "I thought you rang them all and explained the situation?"

"I did. But I also didn't think this bloody thing would go on for so long or take up so much of our time."

"You could always step back and just let—"

"Not on your fucking life." He glanced at me, expression unyielding. "We started this damn thing together, and we'll finish it the same way."

"Well, technically, *you* started it. I got dragged into it when my boss was murdered."

A smile tugged his lips. "You know what I mean."

I did. And I appreciated the sentiment. I just had to hope he didn't pay the ultimate price for his determination.

"Don't worry." He briefly placed his hand on my thigh and squeezed it gently. "I'm a hard bastard to kill. Besides, there's a world of women still out there, waiting for me to discover them. I can't disappoint them, now can I?"

I snorted. "Even *you* can't possibly have the time or the energy for more women than you currently have. Or did have, before this mess all started."

He raised an eyebrow. "Is that a challenge?"

I laughed. "No, it is not."

"Shame. I would enjoy proving you wrong."

"Which you undoubtedly will anyway, given your conviction our liaison is only a short-term thing."

"I *am* hoping I am wrong—you know that, don't you?" His gaze met mine again. "But even if I am right, do not expect me to become a model of decorum. I will still flirt and tease you shamelessly."

"I'd be horrified if you didn't."

He grinned and returned his attention to the road. I flipped down the rearview mirror but couldn't see any sign of the white van. Which didn't mean they weren't actually behind us, as neither of us had spotted them the first time.

It was nearing peak hour by the time we hit the freeway, so it took us a couple of hours to get to our office. Once Jackson had parked, I climbed out and made my way up the steps to the front door. It was still locked, but that didn't mean anything when we were dealing with criminals like Rinaldo and the sindicati.

I cautiously unlocked it then pushed it wide-open with my fingertips to ensure there was no one lurking behind it. The paperwork I'd stacked on the nearby desks, ready for filing, scattered as the wind gusted around me and the air was cold—almost stale. I couldn't see or sense anything or anyone, and, after a brief hesitation, I stepped inside and turned off the security cameras. A couple of seconds later, Jackson followed me in.

"I'll check the cams," he said. "You want to see if anyone's tried to contact us?"

I nodded and headed over to the phone. Jackson generally diverted calls to his cell, but when we ditched our SIMs in an effort to stop PIT tracking us, we'd also ditched the diversion. One of the lights on the unit was blinking rapidly, and beside it a number—there were twenty-three messages waiting. I hit the REPLAY button then walked down to Jackson's industrial-sized coffee machine to make us both a drink. For the most part, the messages were either from clients wanting an update or telemarketers trying to sell us shit.

I handed Jackson his coffee then sat at the next desk as the messages rolled on. "Anything on the cameras?"

He shook his head. "Which doesn't mean they're not keeping an eye on the place."

"Why would they even need to when everyone seems to know all our damn movements?"

He grinned. "As you said yourself, if they knew all our movements, they would have—"

The next message began to play, and he cut himself off to listen.

"Mr. Miller, it's Denny Rosen Junior. Sorry for ringing you so early, but I think I need your help. I just . . ." His voice trailed off, and when it came back, it was filled with disbelief. "My father's dead—we both know that. But I just saw him in the park, and he means me no good. Please call me urgently."

As the machine beeped the end of the message, I

scrambled across to hit the REPLAY button and get the time he'd called. Eight thirty-eight. Twenty-two minutes ago. I glanced across to Jackson, but he was already on the phone, calling the number Denny had left.

"Denny," he said, a couple of seconds later. "It's Jackson—"

He stopped, his expression grave as he listened. I walked over, trying to listen in, but could hear little more than hysteria.

"Denny," Jackson snapped, voice harsh. "You need to take several deep breaths and calm down. I can't understand a word you're saying."

He fell silent again, listening, while I fidgeted from one foot to the other, desperate to know what was going on.

"Are you positive it's your father?" Jackson said eventually. "It couldn't be someone who simply looks like him?"

More silence. I flexed my fingers against the urge to rip the phone from Jackson's hand.

"Okay, okay, we'll be there ASAP. In the meantime, keep an eye on him. If he makes a move toward your apartment, let us know then get the hell out of there." He gave Denny our new number then hung up.

"He has no doubt it's his dad?" I spun, grabbed my purse then put the phone back on message.

"None." He locked the door behind us and dug the car keys out of his pocket. "And given he's psychic, I'm prone to believe him."

I jumped into the car and threw on my seat belt. "But why would Rosen want to kill his only son? It makes no sense."

"I find it interesting you haven't actually commented on the fact that he's apparently alive."

"Well, it's hardly the first time a dead man has walked out of the morgue." That's what my boss had done, after all. "What I actually want to know is how the hell it happened. Last I heard PIT was keeping his body under strict watch."

"Not strict enough, obviously."

I grimaced. "I doubt PIT would be *that* lax. Not after everything else that has gone on recently."

"Except that they're stretched to the limit—Sam said that himself."

"Even so . . ." I stopped. Arguing was pointless. If Rosen had risen from the dead and somehow gotten free, then something bad *had* happened. The only way we were going to find out was by asking PIT directly—and they'd been less than forthcoming up until now. I doubted making us "official advisors" had changed that anyway.

"What if it's a trap?"

He frowned. "Luke can't possibly be aware that we know Rosen's son."

"He could if he infected Rosen."

"But not if Rosen's simply become a vampire." He paused. "Which isn't possible given the time."

"Exactly."

Jackson thumped his hand against the steering wheel, the unexpected outburst making me jump slightly. "How many more people is this bastard going to take out before he's stopped?"

"As many as he possibly can." My voice was grim. "And let's just hope that there's no lieutenant waiting in the wings to take over as queen bee."

"Yeah." He accelerated through an amber light then said, "How are we going to play this?"

"There's only one way in or out of Junior's apartment block from what I saw. If Rosen's not in the park, then we have no choice but to go in."

"If he's in the park, I'm betting he's not alone. Luke wouldn't risk a prize like him."

"That would depend on why he infected Rosen." If he *had* infected Rosen, that is. It was always possible Denny was mistaken. I doubted it, but still . . .

We got over to Denny's place in record time. Jackson didn't stop, instead doing a slow cruise past the apartment. There was no one in the park opposite and the apartment itself was quiet. Which didn't really mean anything—after all, Rinaldo had mentioned he was having this place watched. The sindicati were probably doing the same.

"Do you think Rosen's left? Or that Denny was wrong and it wasn't his dad?"

"No." He did a U-turn at the end of the street and stopped several houses away from Denny's. "The curtains are closed upstairs."

Which didn't mean anything except for the fact that Denny had shown no inclination whatsoever to close them the last time we'd been there. And why would he, with the sort of views he had?

"If he decided to leave, surely he would have contacted us? He knew we were coming, after all."

"Maybe he didn't have the chance." Jackson leaned his arms on the steering wheel as he studied the building. "I could get into his place from the balcony next door."

"And just how are you planning to get onto that? Fly?"

He grinned. "You forget my capacity to sweet-talk."

"Hard to sweet-talk anyone if you're dealing with an empty house."

"In which case, I'll just climb the tree."

Said tree was certainly close enough to both balconies to be of use. "I'll go in the front way. If it's a trap, come running."

"You can count on it."

I climbed out of the car then slammed the door shut. The clouds hung low and made the morning appear so dark that it would be easy to believe night was closing in rather than a new day dawning. I shivered and zipped up my jacket, although I wasn't entirely sure if it was the cold or another damn premonition.

Jackson glanced at me over the top of the vehicle. "Give me five minutes, then go in."

I nodded and watched him stride away. But my gaze was soon drawn back to the park, and I rubbed my arms uneasily. Though I still couldn't see anything untoward, the notion that this was another trap was growing stronger. Whose trap, I couldn't say. If Denny *had* seen his father, then there was a good chance that Luke—or, at least, his cloaks—were out there somewhere, waiting to attack. And yet . . . and yet I suspected not.

Why, I couldn't say. Maybe it was simply a matter of timing—surely even *he* wouldn't have the ability or the people to put something else together so quickly?

I glanced at my watch and shifted my weight from one foot to another. After another minute, I pushed away from the car and walked toward Rosen's building.

It was modern in design and rather resembled a series of cantilevered glass boxes stacked on top of each other. It was the sort of design that was rather out of place in a street filled with older, more regular-looking brick buildings, and I couldn't help wondering what the hell the planners had been thinking when they'd allowed this apartment block to be built.

I opened the gate and strode up the steps to Denny's, undoubtedly looking far more confident than I felt. I might be able to defend myself against most things, but that didn't mean I was immune to danger. And I certainly wasn't immune to fear, even if I stepped into the path of dangerous situations more often than was wise.

I raised a hand to press the intercom button, only to pause midmotion.

The front door was open.

Trepidation hit like a punch to the gut. I pressed my fingers against one of the glass panels and pushed the door all the way open. The lobby was bright, white, and—like the last time we'd been here—almost entirely filled with expensive-looking bicycles and helmets. I lifted my gaze, following the glass and chrome stairs up to the first floor. Light splashed across the top couple of steps, and the only noise to be heard was the soft whoosh of air coming from the heating vents and the clacking of a fan.

I pressed close to the left wall and moved upward. The delicious aroma of bacon touched the air, but underneath it, there was something else. Something that smelled . . . not wrong, but definitely out of place.

Heat flitted across my fingertips, tiny fireflies that could at any moment become so much more. But was there anyone upstairs to even heed the warning? That was the question that now needed answering.

I slowed as I neared the top step and swept my gaze across the large open-plan living area. Like the downstairs foyer, it was all white, from the walls and ceilings to the kitchen units and furnishings. The only splashes of color came from the large photographic canvases that dotted the walls. At the far end of the room were the drawn white curtains, which hid the wall of glass and its million-dollar views of the beach.

Anything?

Jackson's question whispered into my brain and made me jump. *Nada,* I bit back. *But something smells off.*

How off? Rotten or wrong?

I stepped onto the landing, my back still pressed against the wall. *Wrong.*

Still no movement; still no sign of Denny. But there was bacon sitting in a pan on the stove, and a plate with poached two eggs already on the bench. And people didn't usually up and leave breakfast unless something untoward had happened.

Want me in?

I hesitated. *No. If this is a trap, it might be better to spring it first.*

I took a careful step forward. Tension crawled through my limbs and flames shimmied briefly across my skin. Maybe Jackson wasn't the only one needing lessons in control.

I took several more steps but kept close to the

banister—and not just so I could see anything that might be creeping up it. If I *was* attacked, then it would provide a very useful escape route.

I kept moving forward. Still nothing happened. My gaze swept to the doors leading off the main room. Both were closed, but I presumed one was a bathroom and the other a bedroom.

I didn't want to enter either.

I licked dry lips then said, "Denny? Are you here?"

No answer came, but the air seemed to sharpen and expectation spun around me.

It *wasn't* an emotion that was coming from me.

I clenched my hands against the rising heat and edged toward the first door. "Denny?"

I pressed back against the wall to the right of the door then reached across and flung it open. It crashed into the wall behind it, the handle biting so deep it sent plaster and dust flying.

The room beyond was a bathroom. An *empty* bathroom.

The fan making all the noise was above the shower, which was still running. Denny had obviously been getting ready for the day when he'd sensed his father's presence.

I glanced at the remaining door. Whatever was going on, the answer would be found in there. I was certain of that, if nothing else.

I just wasn't sure I actually *wanted* that answer.

I forced my feet forward. I'd been many things over the years—even a coward—but in this particular case, if I didn't explore, Jackson would. I wasn't about to let him step into danger just because I was afraid to.

I stopped to the right of the door again, but as my fingers closed around the handle, something—someone—stirred in the room beyond. A single footstep, one so soft I shouldn't have heard it over the clacking of the fan. But given my hypersensitive state, I'd probably hear the fluttering of a butterfly's wings.

I clenched the handle tight but got no further. The door was ripped from my fingers and a mass of hair and rage hit me hard and sent me tumbling. I came to an abrupt halt against the back of the sofa and had a brief vision of feet.

Lots of feet, all coming straight at me.

I swore and flung up a wall of fire. One of them hit it hard and his body went up with a whoosh. He didn't even have time to scream. But the heat of my flames was so fierce the fire alarms began screaming for him, and the noise was deafening.

I rose to my feet and glared at the five remaining men—and realized that at least *one* of them had been involved in the ruckus at the graveyard. Which meant they were from De Luca's lair and that my message had *not* gotten through.

There was a scrape of noise from the balcony; then Jackson stepped through the curtains. Two of the vampires reacted instinctively and launched at him. I raised a hand, but Jackson stopped me with a quick shake of his head and simply took several steps sideways—sweeping the curtains with him. The morning might not be very bright, but it was still very dangerous to vampires—and the younger the vampire, the quicker they went up.

Which they did. Like torches. It was a sickening sight to behold.

"Anyone else want to try that?" Jackson's voice was pleasant. Unfazed. "Or are we all going to be sensible from now on?"

The remaining vampires didn't actually look as if they knew the meaning of the word, but they made no further move to attack. As ashes began to stain the pristine carpet, I glanced back at the remaining lot and said, "What have you done with the man who owns this apartment?"

I didn't bother raising my voice to be heard over the still-screaming alarm; the nearest vamp was close enough to my firewall that his skin was beginning to turn pink. He'd hear me, even if the rest couldn't.

Even so, I lowered both the size and the heat output of my wall. Hopefully, it would be enough to stop the damn alarm.

The vampire didn't answer. He simply snarled, revealing canines that were not only extended, but also bloody.

"Then what about his father? The man who was watching from the park?"

No response. I flicked a hand, and a sliver of flame jumped from my wall and curled around his neck.

"Answer me, or die. Your choice." The three behind him shifted. Several more fiery leashes broke away from the wall and corralled them. Jackson's doing, not mine.

"I suggest you talk to the lady," he said. "Unless, of course, you'd really prefer an inglorious death over the prospect of living on to avenge your master's death."

The lead vampire's gaze narrowed. "You know who we are?"

"We do."

"How? We haven't crossed paths before."

"No," Jackson agreed equably, "but Emberly and I run this business together and, subsequently, share information."

"And it's not hard to remember the gritty details of idiots who attack me in a graveyard," I added.

He grunted. His expression was dark and his eyes gleamed with the promise of death. He wasn't finished with me yet. Would never be finished, not until either he or I was dead. It made me wonder why they were so convinced that avenging their maker's death would make things right again.

And why were they still running loose anyway? The elders usually jumped on this type of situation pretty fast, given the last thing they needed when human relations were already so tense was a leaderless lair raising hell.

"What about the other man?" I repeated.

"Who?"

I rolled my eyes again. "Denny Rosen Senior? The man you used as bait to get us here."

He once again played mute. I tightened the fiery cord around his neck. His skin began to blister, but little emotion crossed his face. I wasn't sure if he was simply putting on a brave face, or if he really *was* that tough.

"Answer the damn question," Jackson said. "Otherwise the police will find nothing more than ash."

The vampire's gaze shot back to Jackson. "You've called them?"

"Before we entered this building, vampire. So either speak to us or speak to them. Your choice."

"If I *do* answer your questions, will you let us go?"

"Vampire, it's daylight outside. You've nowhere to go unless you want to fry, and I've a feeling that's not on your agenda right now."

"You'd be right. There is, however, basement access."

And *that* was how they'd gotten in. It probably also meant they had a driver waiting—a very well-protected driver, if it was another of their lair mates.

"Have we a deal?" he added.

I glanced briefly at Jackson, who said, "That would depend."

"On what?"

"On whether Denny is alive or not."

The vamp snorted. "We are not so young that we cannot control our feeding."

Meaning they'd *all* fed on him. "So why is he so quiet? Are you controlling him?"

"Yes. It is not a hard undertaking with one so foolish."

I raised an eyebrow at the hint of arrogance in that reply. "Did you also force him to ring us?"

He smiled again. It was still a god-awful sight. "He was already on the phone when we entered. The hysteria you heard wasn't so much caused by the presence of his father in the park, but rather his sudden inability to say anything other than what I commanded." He paused. "Do we have a deal?"

"Answer all of our questions and we'll consider it," I said. "What happened to Rosen?"

"Nothing. We were not here for him."

"And how did you know about our connection to him and Denny?"

"We were informed."

"By whom."

He pressed the MUTE button again. I sighed and raised a hand. The cord around his neck tightened briefly. "You know, I'm told healing from a burned larynx is a long and painful process."

A remote smile touched the vampire's lips. "If I can't talk, I can't answer questions."

"No, but I daresay one of your companions will." They were, after all, looking damn uncomfortable right now—not surprising given Jackson's control wasn't as tight as mine, and their clothes were beginning to smolder.

The vampire's gaze swept my face, and whatever he saw obviously convinced him I meant what I said. Something he *should* already be aware of, given he'd been one of the vamps in the cemetery.

"The hive master told us he would be coming."

"And did he also tell when to arrive?"

"No. It was simply a matter of coincidental timing."

Luke would have known the vamps were hungry for vengeance, so I doubted that. He'd probably intended them as a form of insurance for Rosen—that we'd be so busy fighting *them* that Rosen could escape if necessary.

"What did he do when he was here?"

"He was looking for something. He didn't find it."

"And you know this how?"

"Because he opened the safe then went into a rage." The vampire hesitated, and a smile briefly touched his lips. It did nothing to alleviate the sternness of his thin features. "He kept saying, 'the bitch, the bitch.' I very much suspect he was talking about you."

More than likely, given most of the problems Luke was having of late *was* basically due to interference from me and Jackson. But why would he think *I* was responsible for the removal of whatever Rosen had been storing here? It wasn't like we'd had much to do with Denny after we'd come here to discuss the murder of his lover. But maybe *that* was enough. Luke had to be aware of the antagonism between father and son, so maybe he figured it would have been easy for us to sweet-talk the information—and whatever had been stored in the safe—from Denny. "What happened after that?"

The vampire shrugged. "He left. We did not."

Why would Luke order Rosen to leave? Why wouldn't he order him to look around for either his son or whatever he'd been sent to retrieve? "He didn't know you were here?"

"No."

My eyebrows rose. "Why are you so sure?"

"Because I touched his mind. It was weirdly empty."

It couldn't have been too empty—not if he fell into a rage when he discovered the stuff he wanted wasn't in the safe. And if Rosen *was* now a part of the hive, that rage would have been at least partially Luke's. "Weird how?"

"There were no memories, no thought, just complete and utter concentration on the task he'd been given."

"Did you feel anyone else in his mind?"

"As far as I could tell, he was not being controlled."

Meaning whoever controlled Rosen—if it wasn't

Luke—had withdrawn the second he'd—or she'd—sensed the vampire's touch. "When did this happen?"

"We weren't paying too much attention to the time, but I believe Rosen arrived about five minutes after his son placed the call to you."

Which still should have left him time to at least look around the apartment for his son or the missing items—so either Luke truly believed we'd taken the items, or he was worried about us arriving and grabbing Rosen.

"That fire engine is drawing closer," the vampire added. "We've cooperated with you. Let us go."

I glanced at Jackson. "What do you think?"

"Check on Denny first. I'm not about to trust the word of scum determined to kill us."

"I'm not lying," the vamp snapped.

Maybe not, but releasing them would only mean they were free to come after us again.

But killing them would now be a cold-blooded act, and I wasn't exactly up for that, either.

I stepped around them and walked into the bedroom. Denny lay on the bed, his eyes closed and his breathing rapid. He was as naked as the day he was born, and his neck, torso, and thighs were littered with bloody bite marks of different sizes.

A shudder ran through me. I'd experienced the bite of a vampire only once, but it was a moment in time that still haunted me. Some vampires *did* make it pleasurable, but the one who'd taken my life sure as hell hadn't. From the expression of horror locked on Denny's face, it seemed this lot didn't believe in it, either.

I knelt down beside the bed and said, "Denny, wake up."

Not even the slightest flicker of awareness crossed his features. I frowned and glanced back at the lounge room. "Release him, vampire."

A snort of amusement came from the other room. Denny shuddered and opened his mouth, sucking in a deep breath. I slapped a hand over his mouth before he could scream.

"Denny, you're okay. It's me, Emberly. You're safe. The vampires are under control."

His gaze slid to mine and, after a moment, his pupils focused and relief broke through the horror. I pulled my hand away as another shudder ran through him.

"They drank from me. The bastards drank from me!"

"I know. But I need to know—"

"Are they still here?" His horror sharpened. "You haven't killed them?"

"No. But the fire brigade and police are—"

"Why the fuck haven't you killed them?" he cut in, expression furious. He tried to sit up, but I pressed a hand against his chest and stopped him. That it was so easy said a lot about the state of his strength. Perhaps he realized it, too, because he stopped struggling and collapsed back down on the bed. "You should have killed them."

"Probably. Tell me what your father wanted."

Denny pulled a sheet over his body, although it was a little late to worry about modesty now. "He was across the road in the park, as I said. You didn't see him?"

"No. But the vampires said he came in here, looking for something. You didn't see him?"

"No. They forced me in here as soon as I'd finished calling you, and I can't remember a whole lot after that."

"So you have no idea what he was looking for?"

"Oh, I can certainly guess." Amusement briefly touched his lips. They were almost translucent, as if all the color had been leached out of him—which was unsurprising given how many vampires had fed off him. "He wouldn't have found it, though."

"Why?"

"Because I shifted the shit, that's why."

"Why were you keeping stuff for him? Especially when you two didn't get on?"

"Because, no matter what, he was still my dad, and he just seemed desperate." He grimaced. "I'm not such a bastard that I'd turn him away at a moment like that."

"When did all this happen?"

"A few months ago. He said he'd had this weird visit from some reporter, and he wanted me to keep some paperwork safe. Seemed like a whole lot of shit to me, but he was insistent that I keep it under lock and key, and even watched me put it in the safe."

"So why did you move it from the safe?" I tried to keep my voice devoid of excitement but didn't entirely succeed.

"Because it's not a huge safe, and I needed the fucking room to store an antique I bought recently."

"So where is the paperwork now?"

He pointed under the bed. I raised my eyebrows, peered underneath, and saw an old suitcase. Rosen would no doubt have been horrified, but I guessed it was as good a spot as anywhere else in the apartment that *wasn't* the safe.

"Fire brigade is here," Jackson said from the other room.

"Now is the time to let us go," the vampire said.

"We didn't actually agree to that," Jackson said sagely. "And why you'd believe otherwise given your intent to kill us both is beyond me."

The vampire snarled and surged against the leash I held around his neck. Pain rippled as the strands stretched, and, without thinking, I snapped him back sharply. There was an odd sound that reminded of bowling pins falling, and then Jackson laughed.

"Well, that's one way of dealing with a problem."

His footsteps echoed on the wooden flooring. I extinguished my flames, motioned Denny to stay where he was, and then rose to see what had happened. The four remaining vampires were lying in a clump on the floor. "I knocked them out?"

"You certainly did." Jackson stopped beside me. "In a perfectly timed piece of action, you flung the head vamp backward just as I'd tightened the leash on the others, drawing them together. The resulting crash of heads was hard enough to knock them all out."

"Brilliant, even if unintentional." I grinned. "And at least it'll make it easier for the cops to transport them."

"Yeah, but given one of them is a strong telepath, I'm betting they don't stay caught for too long."

"True, but their escape might just force the elders to get off their asses and do something about the lair." I waved a hand at the vamps. "You want to find something to tie them up with while I go meet the firemen?"

I headed downstairs. We spent the next couple of

hours dealing with not only the fire brigade, but also the cops and medical services. Thankfully, our PIT badges smoothed away a lot of awkward questions and—with the vampires taken into custody and Denny hauled away to hospital for a blood infusion—we were eventually left to lock up.

"The basement is empty," Jackson said as he came back up the stairs. "If the vamps *did* have a van waiting for them there, it's long gone."

"The driver probably put two and two together the minute he heard the sirens, and got the hell out of Dodge."

I knelt next to the bed and dragged out the old suitcase. It was padlocked, but a short lance of fire soon fixed that problem.

Jackson flipped the top open and picked up a couple of sheets. "Paperwork, as promised. This batch has a whole lot of technical jargon."

I glanced at it. "Lab notes."

"Virus related?"

"Possibly. There's a couple of terms I remember seeing in Baltimore's work."

He frowned. "But Baltimore and Wilson were working on different projects."

"Different projects but with the same end goal—to find a means of either stopping the spread of the virus or producing a vaccination against it."

I picked up another stack and quickly scanned them. Unlike the notes Jackson had, these didn't appear to be research notes, but rather a presentation of some sort. Which wasn't surprising if Rosen Industries followed the same basic procedures as the mob I'd worked for. Departmental heads had been expected to provide regular reports to both the board and to investors on the state of various projects. Baltimore's work on the virus wasn't included in those more general reports, but he'd certainly had to present his findings regularly to Lady Harriet—the harridan who owned and ran the Chase Medical Research Institute—and the most senior members of the board. Most of *these* notes contained fairly typical waffle that gave as little as possible away on whatever projects they were talking about, and it made me wonder why on earth Rosen had kept them. Then I discovered a possible reason—in among the waffle, there was some major statements. One in particular jumped out at me: *This mutation is probably the one that allows humans to become vampires. If this* is *the case, then it might one day be possible to either reverse the process or at least develop a vaccine.*

I blinked and for several seconds couldn't think of anything more than *holy fuck.*

Wilson had not only isolated the vampire gene, but had believed it might be possible to cure vampirism!

Chapter 13

That sort of information would be worth billions to anyone who controlled it. No wonder the sindicati and Rinaldo were after these damn notes. With that sort of information in their hands, they could rule the world.

Or destroy it.

"We really should burn these." Sparks danced across my fingertips. I kept them away from the paper, even though it was tempting to do otherwise.

"You found something?"

I pointed rather than answering.

He scanned the paragraph then said, "Fuck, that's *got* to be the pot at the end of the research rainbow."

"Or the spark that changes the world as we know it." I raised my gaze to his. "We can't let the vampires *or* Luke get hold of these."

"Luke has Wilson and Baltimore. He doesn't really *need* them."

"And yet he sent Rosen here to retrieve them."

"Presuming Rosen *is* one of Luke's hive members, and I'm still not convinced he is." He held up a hand, halting my protest before I could make it. "If Luke *did* send him here, then it's probably because, without the notes, they'll have to start all over again. Especially if

De Luca wasn't lying when he claimed to control all the virus research the sindicati and Luke had stolen up to that point."

"And I for one believe he wasn't." I waved the papers. "This stuff is dangerous."

"Undoubtedly, but you can't destroy them. If Wilson *did* succeed in isolating a gene mutation that accounts for the dead rising, then that gene might also be the key for a cure of the virus."

A fact I was aware of. But I also knew that until Luke was stopped, we didn't dare hand over these papers to PIT or any other government body. Because once it became common knowledge we'd found them, everyone would be after them.

"Then we stop it from becoming common knowledge."

"And how do you propose to do that? Rinaldo mentioned he was having Denny's place watched, remember, and I wouldn't put it past both factions of the sindicati to be doing the same. We can't walk out of here with a suitcase full of notes and not expect them to come after us. And my purse isn't big enough to hold the damn things."

"They don't know Denny told us about the notes."

"No, but the vamps who were here undoubtedly do—"

"How?" Jackson cut in. "Denny didn't mention their location out loud."

"No, but they could have been following the whole conversation via his thoughts. Besides, how long will it take for anyone to visit him in the hospital and rifle through his mind?"

"True." He scrubbed a hand across his jaw, the sound like sandpaper. "What about cataloguing all the notes on our phones, then picking a select—and very harmless—cross section to take with us?"

"Luke—or whoever actually controls Rosen—will know the notes aren't complete."

"*Maybe*. But to anyone else, it'll appear we've found part of what they're looking for."

"What if it's Rinaldo who controls him? He has this place under watch, so *not* mentioning the notes will only jeopardize Shona and the guard."

Jackson waved a hand. "What else can we do? As you said, we dare not risk anyone getting their hands on the full set."

He was right, and we both knew it. I guess we just had to hope that my belief that it was Luke who controlled Rosen was also right.

Of course, that still left us with the problem of Parella, who was undoubtedly also watching this place.

"We might as well call Rinaldo from the office," I said. "It's the only contact number he has for us, and I'd prefer to keep it that way."

Of course, he could always confront us in person, but I doubted he'd risk that again given he was now aware of our connection to PIT.

Jackson nodded. "Let's each photograph half the notes—that way if one of our phones is taken, no one will have the full set."

It took over an hour to photograph them all, and my phone's low battery warning light was blinking rapidly by the end of it.

"Right, you take these." I picked up the selection of reports and notes I'd placed to one side of the others. "I'll cinder the rest and flush them down the sink."

I grabbed an armful and headed for the kitchen. It only took a brief burst of fire to reduce them to ash. I turned on the tap then spun to get the rest of them. In a very short amount of time, they were on their way to Werribee with the rest of Melbourne's crap. The only difference was, this particular crap had the potential to alter many lives—for good *or* for evil.

Jackson handed me the suitcase then led the way down the stairs and back to the car. Once again there was no one to be sighted in the park, and yet that feeling of being watched came back with renewed force. I glanced upward. There was some sort of hawk or falcon circling high above. Neither was a particularly rare find in Melbourne—especially peregrine falcons, some of which can be found nesting in high-rise buildings in the city center these days—but the timing of *this* sighting had suspicions rising. Especially given that our location kept getting blown.

"And if it *is* a shifter up there rather than a regular bird," Jackson said, "there's nothing much we can do about it. Not unless you want to start taking the train."

"That's hardly practical." I threw the case into the backseat then climbed into the front. "And it's not as if a hawk can't follow a train."

"So we quit worrying and get on with business."

Which was easy for him to say—he wasn't the one getting hit by an endless stream of dire and, at least for the moment, incomplete warnings about what was coming at us. "We can't go back to our accommodation when that hawk is up there. I'm not risking Rory's life. I can't afford to."

He snorted. "I think you'll find he has *no* intention of stepping back on this one. Not anymore."

"I'm well aware of that," I snapped, then took a deep, calming breath. It wasn't fair to take my anxiety out on him. "But day-to-day stuff is vastly different from him being involved in a major confrontation with Luke."

And *that* was coming.

That and death.

I feared it. Feared it with every inch of my soul, because there was no guarantee that the person to die would be Luke.

I glanced at the side window and blinked back tears. Rory and I had often died before our time, but it never got any easier. Being reborn after such an event hurt like a bitch, but so too did having the other half of your soul being torn away.

But what if it wasn't Rory? What if it was Sam, or even Jackson? I might not have known him long, but he'd so very quickly become a part of my life, and I hated the thought of losing him.

"You won't," he said softly. "I'm not destined to die any time soon."

"You can't guarantee that." No one could. Not even someone like me, who was often visited by visions of death, and could alter the path of those involved if I so chose.

"Except that I *can*. An old witch once told me I'd be gifted with three children and live long enough to annoy the hell out of them."

I raised my eyebrows and met his gaze. "Is that why you weren't worried about jumping in front of a damn train and scaring the life out of me?"

"Precisely. It wasn't my time."

"But how can you be sure? No witch has a one hundred percent success rate, and she—"

"*He*, not she," he cut in, "and in this particular case, the witch is an air fae."

Air fae were ethereal beings who could hear the whispers of what might be in the winds that roamed the world—hence the reason they were more often than not called wind fae.

"Even *he* cannot guarantee what might be, as every action and decision we make alters the path of our destiny."

"Perhaps, but he has read the fortunes of many a fae over the centuries and, as I said, has never been wrong."

Surprise rippled through me. "So fae make a habit of having their futures read? Why?"

"Because it's always handy to know what to expect from one's life."

"But half the fun of living is the journey of discovery we take from the cradle to the grave. I'd imagine actually *knowing* would take much of the joy from life."

Although it had to be said, Jackson certainly wasn't showing any signs of *not* enjoying life.

"Exactly! It makes your experiences all that much richer, because there *is* no need to fear."

"What about death? Do you also know how or when that will happen?"

He shook his head. "Some do. My father does, for instance, but I asked not to be informed." He shrugged. "Maybe I'll change my mind once I have three children and I find myself hurtling toward old age, but for the moment, I'm simply enjoying life."

He sure was. "What about the virus, then?"

He frowned. "What about it?"

"What if I'm wrong and you *are* infected?"

"I guess that's something not even an old witch could foresee. If I *am* infected . . ." He hesitated. "I just have to hope that fate is not that cruel."

Fate could be something of a bitch at the best of times. Hell, just look at the life she'd handed us phoenixes as a brilliant example of *that*.

I guessed *I* had to hope Jackson wasn't that fae's first mistake.

It didn't take us all that long to get back to our office. Jackson repeated the process of opening the door and checking the security cams, and I headed over to the phone. The flashing indicator told me there were no new messages, so I dumped the suitcase and the extra copy of the satchel notes that we'd done onto the desk and picked up the phone. I called Rinaldo first, informing him what had happened at Denny's and that we were leaving the suitcase and the satchel notes in our office. And, in what might yet be a fatal mistake, also informed him that—given the sindicati were also tailing us—I was telling them the exact same thing. Whoever got here first could have the damn things.

"And you accuse *me* of taking unnecessary risks," Jackson murmured. "You might just have pissed him off enough to come after us."

"We held up our part of the deal by telling him about the notes. Besides, I'd rather he come after us than Shona and the guard."

I dialed Parella next, and a few seconds later, he answered. "Emberly," he said. "I didn't believe we'd be hearing from you so soon."

"Well, you did warn us to keep you updated or you'd unleash the might of the sindicati, so what did you expect?"

"I somehow doubt you are at *all* afraid of such a threat." His voice was dry. "And I very much suspect this call is related to events at Denny Rosen's."

"Indeed. We found some paperwork—"

"A suitcase full of it, in fact."

"Describing it as 'full' would be something of a misnomer. However, there's a problem—"

"If the notes have been cindered, all deals are off the table. Whether you fear us or not, we *will* come after you."

"Oh, we didn't cinder them, as tempting as it might have been. We did, however, have to inform Rinaldo of their presence."

He was silent for a moment, and a note of admiration touched his voice. "*That* was a very good move."

"Killing two birds with one stone usually is."

"Indeed. Where are said notes being left?"

"In our office. I told him whoever gets here first, gets them."

"And *that* might just be temptation enough to draw the bastard out of hiding."

"Not if he sends lackeys in."

"He has so far shown a remarkable lack of willingness to let others do his dirty work. I doubt that will change any time soon."

I hoped like hell he was right. "We've also informed the werewolves of the possibility of his arrival."

We hadn't, but it wouldn't take long to correct that.

"The werewolves are welcome to him if they get there first."

But they wouldn't, if his tone was anything to go by.

"Good. Chat to you later."

"Indeed."

I hung up and glanced at Jackson. "We'd better move. I don't want to be here when any of them arrive."

"Best ring Baker first. We can't afford to get him offside right now."

That we couldn't. I quickly dialed his number and gave him a brief rundown of events. He hung up with the promise to be here promptly.

"And with that," I said as I replaced the receiver, "all elements are in play. Anything on the security cams?"

He shook his head. "I've set them to stream a copy of all future recordings to the cloud. That way, if Rinaldo or one of the others decides to destroy or erase them, we've still got a copy."

"Not that having a copy is going to do us much good. We're already well aware who all the players are in this particular drama."

"Caution never hurts. Besides, I want to watch the unfolding drama if the sindicati and Rinaldo happen to arrive at the same time."

"Our office might not survive said drama." I slung my purse over my shoulder, but before I could follow Jackson to the door, the phone rang. I picked it up instinctively. "Hellfire Investigations. Emberly Pearson—"

"Emberly?"

The voice was sharp, cold, and feminine. It took me a moment to recognize it—not surprising given I'd only talked to her once. It was the chief inspector—Sam's boss.

My stomach suddenly twisted. "What's happened?"

"You need to get here ASAP."

"Where and why?"

She quickly gave me an address, then added, "The 'why' will be obvious when you get here."

"But surely you can—"

"No," she said and hung up. I swore and slammed down the phone.

"Another problem has just raised its ugly head, I'm gathering." There was little amusement in Jackson's expression, despite his light tone.

I stalked toward the door. "Yeah, PIT just ordered us across to Williamstown, STAT."

He frowned. "What's in Williamstown?"

"I have no fucking clue. But I'm thinking whatever it is, isn't good."

He slammed the door shut, and the sound rang across the otherwise quiet street. It sounded an awful lot like a death knell. I shivered and hoped like hell it wasn't another damn premonition, that whatever was waiting for us in Williamstown *wasn't* a dead body.

And I really, *really* hoped it wasn't the body of someone I knew.

It took just under twenty minutes to get around to the bayside suburb. Macquarie Street was blocked by police cars, so Jackson found a parking spot farther down Stevedore Street and we walked back.

"I'm sorry," a blue-coated cop said. "I'm afraid no one—"

"We're expected," I cut in, showing him my badge.

He inspected it, then waved us on. It wasn't hard to spot number twelve—the place was practically bristling with officialdom, and a mix of police and unmarked cars jammed the street in front of it.

The house itself was an old miner's cottage. Unlike the ones on either side of it, it hadn't been extended, but it had obviously been lovingly restored. The weatherboard that lined the house had been painted a lovely cream, and the single-sash windows and the door were a deeper shade of that.

A lot of people were crowded onto the small front porch. Most ignored our approach, but one—a tall, slim-built man with odd, almost hawkish eyes—stepped forward and said, "Please put these on. The inspector is waiting for you both."

He handed us some heavy-duty hazmat-type booties and, once we'd pulled them on over our shoes and the bottoms of our pants, led us inside. Like most of these old cottages, there was a central hall with rooms leading off either side. The first two were bedrooms. Then there was a bathroom and small study. None of them appeared to have been disturbed; nothing seemed out of place. My gaze went to the rear of the property, and chills ran down my spine.

Death had been here. Her scent lingered in the air.

My steps automatically slowed. Jackson didn't say anything, but his fingers pressed lightly against my spine, offering me the comfort of not only his closeness, but also the heat of his touch. I drew on it, gathering strength for what was to come—not just here, in this beautiful old building, but out there, in Brooklyn.

Because what had happened here would lead us there.

I shivered and followed the man with the shifter's eyes into the rear of the property. This section of the house had been extended and was now a large kitchen and living area. I stopped just inside the kitchen door, and not even the light pressure of Jackson's touch could force me any farther.

As I'd feared, this end of the house was where death had come to collect her souls—and she certainly would have had plenty to collect. There was blood and gore and bodies everywhere. Not just one or two, but at least a dozen. I swallowed heavily, trying to ease the sick sense of uselessness rising up my throat, and scanned the nearest corpses. On the cheeks of at least three of them was a black mark in the shape of a scythe.

Red cloaks.

My gaze finally stopped on the tall woman standing in middle of all the carnage. Inspector Henrietta Richmond, of that I had no doubt, if only because she matched the image I'd formed, right down to the black glasses. What I hadn't expected was the mane of thick black hair that was tied back loosely at the nape of her neck and the almost luminous green eyes. The inspector was a shape-shifter—a panther, if the hair and eyes were anything to go by. But I guessed it made sense that an organization whose ranks were more than half-filled by shape-shifters, vampires, and psychics would not be run by a mere human.

"Ms. Pearson, Mr. Miller, it is good of you to be so prompt." Her plummy tone was cool but not without welcome.

"I have no doubt you would have organized someone to haul our asses over here if we'd looked likely to do anything else." I waved a hand around the room. "Whose place is this?"

But even as I asked the question, I knew. God help me, I knew.

"It's Sam's." Though neither her voice nor her expression showed much in the way of anger, it burned deep in her bright eyes.

I didn't react. I didn't *dare*. If I gave in to fear now, I might not climb back out of it.

"Is he here?"

I doubted he would be, but there was always the chance that Luke had decided I wasn't worth the trouble—that it was simply easier to kill his brother and move on.

"No. He's been taken."

I briefly closed my eyes, but not in relief. He might currently be alive, but god only knew what was being done to him.

"And Rochelle?" Jackson asked.

Rather than answer, the inspector simply moved to one side, allowing us a full view of the body near her feet. It was Rochelle. She was lying in a pool of her own blood, and the knife that had been used to cut her throat lay beside her body. Two men wearing full hazmat suits were in the process of vacuuming up the congealing blood while two more stood ready with a body bag. Not taking any chances, even if they believed the virus could be spread only via being bitten or scratched by one of the infected.

"Have you got any idea who did this to her? Was it the cloaks?" *Or was it Sam?* The question hovered on my lips, but I just couldn't force it out.

"No one. She killed herself."

"Why the *fuck* would she do that?" Disbelief edged my voice.

"We have two theories." The inspector's gaze dropped to the woman at her feet. "Either she was ordered to cut her own throat, or she did it to *stop* being ordered to attack Sam."

I blinked. "So you locked the two of them in here, knowing full well that she was in contact with Luke?"

"We had little other choice." The inspector's gaze was steely as it snapped to mine. "The possibility that one or both were in contact with Luke meant neither of them could be held at headquarters, and it was impractical to place them in cell confinement elsewhere."

"Why?"

"Because both have started drinking blood to stave off the ravages of the virus. How would we have explained *that* given it's very obvious neither is a vampire?"

And keeping news of the virus secret was far more important than the lives of two agents. The inspector might be furious about events here, but she wouldn't have altered her actions *or* her decisions in any way.

"So why not hold them under house arrest in their own homes rather than together under one roof?"

"Because our manpower is stretched to the limit." She hesitated. "I also did not believe that either was controlled by the virus or the man who leads the cloaks. I guess Rochelle's actions both shatters and confirms that belief."

I took a deep breath and tried to remain calm. Rochelle had taken her own life rather than be forced to attack Sam and knowingly betray the people she worked with. It was a decision of courage, strength, and nerves of steel, and she deserved to be honored in the highest way possible. And while I might have been right about her, I was also very, very wrong.

"How long ago was the attack?"

"Prelim examinations suggest Rochelle died about two hours ago. Security footage revealed the attack happened *after* she'd died."

Suggesting, perhaps, that Luke had been well aware that his hold on Rochelle wasn't very strong. Why else would he have had cloaks standing by?

Then I frowned. "If you have this place under watch, how did all these cloaks get past?"

The inspector's expression darkened. "They didn't, at least not initially. Our people raised the alarm before they were killed."

I glanced at the carnage surrounding us again. "So Sam did all this?" Surely not. Surely even a man who'd become a pseudo vampire could not so easily tear apart flesh and bone. Not alone.

"Yes. He is . . . rather dangerous when enraged."

I'd glimpsed slivers of that rage; I had no desire to see it fully blown. Not if this was an example of it.

But then, he'd witnessed his lover kill herself. That wouldn't have exactly put him in a great frame of mind.

"Have you been in contact with Rochelle's family?" Jackson asked.

The inspector's gaze shifted to him. "No. Nor will we. Her body will be held—"

"Inspector, she's *fae*. There are ceremonies that must be performed for her spirit to find peace. You need to contact whoever she listed as next of kin—"

"One soul is not my concern right now," she cut in. "Not when I have a city full of them to worry about. Or have you forgotten what we're dealing with here?"

"Hardly," he growled, "when I could possibly face the same outcome myself."

The inspector's gaze swept him before she glanced away. "Rochelle will receive the appropriate rites as soon as possible. More than that cannot be promised right now."

"Why did you call us here?" I said quickly, before the anger and heat I could feel building in the man behind me got out of control.

Her cool smile suggested she was not unaware of what I was doing. "You're here because we had no other choice."

"Meaning what, exactly?" God, what was it about people speaking in riddles of late?

Instead of replying, she motioned us to follow. After a moment's hesitation, I did so, carefully picking my way through all the blood and body parts. The room opened out farther, revealing another large section to the right of the kitchen. On the rear wall, written in what looked like blood, was a simple message: *Emberly. Get her here. ASAP.*

Underneath the message, lying on the floor beside a bloody right arm I suspected might have been the tool used to write the message, was a phone.

Luke hadn't given up his dreams of torturing me in front of Sam. He'd just decided to up the stakes and make *me* come to *him*.

Not go alone, came Jackson's thought. *Together. Only way to kill.*

I glanced at him but didn't get the chance to reply, because at that moment, the damn phone rang. I'm pretty sure I was the only one who jumped.

The inspector dug some gloves out of her pocket then tossed them to me. "You might as well answer it. Keep him speaking for as long as possible, so we can get a location."

"He'll surely be aware you'll try that."

"Probably, but the point is not so much his current location. We need to get a lock on his phone so that we can track his movements."

Track him and kill him. She might not have said that, but that's what she intended. But Luke wasn't hers—or PIT's—to kill.

The bastard was mine.

I pulled on the gloves as I walked over to the phone, but didn't pick it up. Instead, I hit the SPEAKER button and said, "Hello?"

"Ah, Emberly, how are you this fine afternoon?" Luke's voice was loud in the sudden stillness of the room, and filled with smug satisfaction.

I clenched my fists and restrained the urge to pick up the phone and throw the damn thing. As satisfying as that might be, it'd be even more satisfying to throw the man himself—and to do that, I had to keep listening.

"Just get to the damn point, Luke," I snapped back, "what the fuck do you want?"

"You know what I want." He paused, and I could almost see the smile stretching his thin lips. "You."

"Sorry—you can't have me. What have you done to Sam?"

"Why don't you come over to my place and find out?"

I snorted. *"That's* an invitation I can definitely refuse."

"Sorry—that's not a choice you have."

"Why not? It's not like you have anything I want."

He made a low, disbelieving sound. "Your actions up until now would prove otherwise."

"Well, we all make mistakes." I paused. "How's that tame witch of yours? Have the hellhounds come a-calling yet?"

He laughed. It wasn't exactly a sane sound. "My tame witch, as you call him, cannot wait for a second encounter."

I glanced at Jackson. *Definitely male, not female.*

Need to tell witches, he replied. *Make easier to find.*

It certainly would. While male witches weren't exactly rare, most of the more powerful witches tended to be female. No one was sure why, but many seemed to think it was something to do with a more natural connection to the earth mother. Given *this* male witch had the power to call and control three hellhounds for an extended period, it surely wouldn't be hard to track down who, exactly, we were dealing with.

"Yeah, well, you might want to warn him against calling the hounds again. They weren't too impressed to discover they'd been sent against a kindred spirit." I paused. "On second thought, don't. It'll save me the problem of killing him myself."

"I do *so* love your sense of humor—and I believe it's what attracted Sam to you, too."

I smiled grimly. It hadn't taken him long to bring the conversation back to the point. "As I've mentioned before, Sam and I were over a long time ago. I'm not sure why you've got this fixation about the two of us, but you're way off base."

"And yet here you are, in his house, as I demanded."

"It has nothing to do with Sam, and everything to do with wanting to wipe the stain of your existence from our world."

"A commendable goal, but one I understandably cannot condone." Amusement touched his tone. "Shall we cut the crap, Emberly, and get down to business?"

"Please, let's." If the inspector's people hadn't had enough time to track Luke, then that was just too bad.

"Fine. I want you—and you alone—to come to the intersection where this all started. Be there by six, or Sam pays the price."

"He's going to pay the price whether or not I show up."

"Oh, true, but if you *do* fail to show, my remaining men and women will swarm into the nearby suburbs and infect as many people as possible. We both know neither you nor the inspector would want that." He paused, and a dark edge touched his tone as he added, "Do what I want, Emberly, or the world will pay the price."

I sucked in a breath and released it slowly. I was always going to meet the bastard; all his threat did was make me all the more determined to kill him.

Especially since I had no doubt that he fully intended to order the swarm and allow his people to infect as many as possible anyway.

"I'll be there," I said, voice flat.

"Good." He sounded positively jovial. He really *wasn't* playing with a full deck of cards these days. "Oh, and don't bother placing sharpshooters on high ground again. My tame witch has conjured a little spell or two to counter that sort of thing."

With that, he hung up. I blew out a breath and glanced at the inspector. "You'd better call out the military—I don't believe that threat to swarm was an idle one. It'll happen when we're meeting."

"We've already cut access to and from Brooklyn, and are monitoring all major sewer outlets. However . . ." She paused and glanced over her shoulder. "Frank, contact the brigadier immediately."

A tall, thin man with a shock of white hair spun around and headed outside. The inspector's gaze returned to mine. "What do you intend to do?"

"Meet him, obviously."

Her gaze narrowed. "And how to you intend to avoid the trap that undoubtedly awaits?"

"I don't. But I don't intend to let the bastard win, either." One of us wasn't going to walk away from this confrontation, and that person *wasn't* going to be me.

I glanced at my watch. We had two hours before I had to be in Brooklyn and a whole lot to organize in that brief time. "What I need from you, Inspector, is a map of the sewers, especially in Brooklyn. Jackson, could you call Adán and Dmitri and ask them to come here? And then call Rory, and ask him to come prepared for a firefight and magic?"

I might not want Rory near any sort of danger, but that didn't mean he couldn't help. Luke might have protected himself against any sort of rooftop attack, but I doubted he'd have afforded the sewers the same sort of protection—especially given his people were using them to move about.

Jackson left to make the calls. The inspector motioned me to follow her, but rather than heading outside, as I'd half expected, she turned into the small study. Up on the wall, above the old oak desk, was a rather detailed map of the main grid system under Brooklyn and the nearby suburbs. Beside it was a smaller map showing secondary grid systems. There were notes, comments, and various-colored circles all over both; Sam had obviously been using the sewers to get in and out of the place. No wonder he'd been so peeved that I'd simply walked in unseen the night I'd rescued him.

"What do you plan?" the inspector said.

"I once warned Luke that I'd burn Brooklyn to the ground if he didn't back off." My gaze met the inspector's. "And that's exactly what I intend to do."

She sucked in a sharp breath. "I don't think I could condone such destruction—"

"I'm not asking you to. I'm simply telling you what I'm intending." My voice was grim. "This has to stop.

If I can kill Luke, then we've at least dealt with one major problem."

Her gaze narrowed slightly, but not in anger. Her expression was more contemplative than anything else. "It is theorized that the cloaks will swarm without his control."

"They're going to swarm anyway. As I said, I don't believe Luke's threat was an idle one." She didn't, either, not if her order to warn the brigadier was any indication. "If we can cut off their underground exits and force them aboveground, then eradicating them before they exit Brooklyn will be easier."

And both PIT and the military were, after all, already patrolling the perimeter. Destroying all access points in and out of Brooklyn might raise questions from the press and public, but PIT could no doubt handle that.

"And how, exactly, do you intend to force them aboveground?" the inspector asked. "We're already monitoring all major sewer outlets, but there are numerous minor ones for them to use."

"Which is where having a couple of earth fae on our team will come in handy," Jackson said as he came into the room. He stopped beside me and studied the map for a second. "A well-planned earth shift around that entire area should take care of the sewer problem, be they major or minor tunnels."

"A quake. Interesting." The inspector's gaze swept from me to Jackson and back again. "You two do have a rather unique way of dealing with things. I can't approve of such methods, of course—"

"As I said—"

She held up a hand, halting me midsentence as she added, "But given the nature of the threat, and the fact it falls within national security guidelines, I believe that—in this instance—I cannot disapprove of it, either."

Well, good, because unless she intended on locking us up, she couldn't exactly stop us. And she'd have a damn hard time getting either of us anywhere near a cell right now.

A fact she was no doubt aware of.

I glanced at Jackson. "How long before Adán and Dmitri get here?"

"Twenty minutes. Rory will be here in fifteen."

"Good." But was it?

I closed my eyes and took a deep breath. Ready or not, we were about to go to war, and I could only hope my instinct was wrong about what was coming.

Because if it wasn't, then someone I loved would be dead by the time all this was over.

Chapter 14

The pink-and-gold fingers of sunset were giving way to night by the time I arrived in Brooklyn. The cold wind held the promise of rain, and tugged heavily at the various bits of loose boarding and metalwork on the nearby buildings, filling the silence with a symphony of creaks and groans. Plastic bags and other bits of rubbish pirouetted down the street, but little else moved.

Nothing had changed since I'd last been here—nothing, perhaps, except me.

I flexed my fingers and moved on, my gaze on the intersection ahead. That was where it had all begun for me, and that was where it would all end.

If everything went according to plan.

And really, when did anything ever go according to plan?

I ignored the fear that rose with the thought. We were as prepared as we could be for a situation such as this. We'd tried to think of every possible scenario and put countermeasures in place, but I'd learned a long time ago that it was impossible to totally predict the actions of a madman.

While there were no riflemen on high, I'd come equipped with all manner of weaponry. Whether I'd get to use them didn't really matter; the whole point of carrying was the fact it would be expected.

I glanced at my watch. Three minutes to six. Three minutes before my final meeting with Luke.

Five minutes before Brooklyn became its own little island.

I took a deep breath and tried to relax. For this to work, Luke had to believe I was here alone, that I'd done as ordered and there was no help or hope for me anywhere close. He'd be well aware that PIT and the military had fully barricaded all roads in and out of this place, of course, but hopefully he'd believe *that* was just a natural outcome of the threat he'd made at Sam's.

I continued to walk down the middle of the street. There was little point in doing anything else, because Luke had undoubtedly been aware of my presence from the moment I stepped foot in his kingdom. The buildings to either side of me continued to creak and groan, but I had no sense that anyone was near. I wasn't expecting the cloaks, given it was almost certain they were preparing to swarm, but I'd expected to see Sam. Expected to see—or at least sense—both Luke and his pet witch.

But then, while Luke wasn't playing on the same sane field as the rest of us, he wasn't exactly stupid. He wouldn't reveal himself until he absolutely believed he held all the winning cards.

As I drew closer to the intersection, the wind got stronger, tugging violently at my hair and sending chills down my spine. I thrust cold fingers into my jacket pockets and wished I could call up some heat to warm them. But I had a very tight leash on my internal fires right now, and I didn't want to waste even the smallest spark. I wasn't really concerned about my control slipping, but I needed to conserve every scrap of energy possible if I was to have any hope of making good on my threat.

Up ahead, on the roof of a building to the right of the intersection, a solitary light flared to life. It cut through the gathering shadows with cold efficiency and puddled brightness in the middle of the crossroad.

Sam stood there, untied and unmoving.

His clothes were little more than filthy rags that barely covered him, and his body was bruised and beaten. Bloody wounds marred the left side of his face and his torso, and his right arm was broken—even from where I stood I could see the sharp edge of a bone sticking out of his skin.

He had to be in a whole world of pain, but little of it showed in his expression.

That he even *had* an expression had relief sweeping through me. Whatever else might be going on—whatever other force was in play and keeping him from moving or speaking—he was at least *himself* and not under his brother's control.

My gaze rose to his. The blue depths of his eyes were filled with fury and desperation, and I knew, without him saying a word, that he wanted nothing more than for me to walk out of here and leave him to his fate. I shook my head slightly, and he closed his eyes. Just for an instant, grief touched his face.

Not the actions of a man who no longer cared.

It would be just like fate to give me a glimpse of

hope then snatch it away. And with the ever-growing certainty that someone *would* die tonight, I was beginning to fear that that someone would be Sam.

Tension curled through me, and I had to resist the urge to glance at my watch. Jackson would contact me when everything was in place. Until then, I just had to be patient.

Pinpricks of energy began to dance across my skin. It was an energy that felt dirty—unclean—but also very familiar. It was the same energy that I'd felt in both the cemetery and in the sewers before the hellhounds had attacked.

But it was also much, *much* stronger than either of those. I had no doubt the spell was designed to capture and contain a being of fire, but what else? That I could feel it this far out from the intersection meant the net was very wide indeed. It seemed neither Luke nor his witch were taking any chances this time.

I just had to hope that Grace and her people *hadn't* overstated the powers of the necklaces. If she had, then we were all in serious trouble.

The stinging got stronger. I stopped again, my fists clenched so tight my nails were digging into my palm. Surely to god three minutes had passed since I'd entered this street? Or was it another case of time slowing to a crawl, as had happened the very first time I'd come here to save Sam's life?

Arrived. Jackson's mental tones ran with excitement. *Ready.*

Dmitri and Adán?

Yes. Give word.

I took a deep breath and released it slowly. *And Rory?*

With me.

I briefly closed my eyes. While I knew the two of them were far safer underground than they would be above, the certainty of death was looming ever closer. But there was nothing I could do about it now. The game, as Sherlock had been want to say, was afoot.

Heading into the intersection now.

Say when.

I walked on, my gaze on Sam. One tiny muscle near his cheek ticked, but otherwise he was as still and silent as the rest of this place.

The closer I got to the intersection, the stronger the magic became, until it felt like my whole body burned with the unpleasant sensation. I didn't react, and I kept my flames well hidden. For this to work, Luke had to not only feel in total control of the situation *but* be totally sure I was without my fire and totally at his mercy. I doubted he'd reveal himself until that point.

I stepped into the intersection proper. For a moment, it felt like I was walking through glue—thick, scratchy glue that tore at my skin and seemed to eat into my brain. Then warmth flared around my neck, and in an instant, the sensation was gone. Grace's charm, coming to my aid. Whether it had successfully countered the fire-restricting properties of the net that now surrounded this place I wouldn't actually know until I tried to use my flames—and I couldn't do that right now. Hell, I couldn't even risk a spark.

I stopped several feet away from Sam. "We'll have to stop meeting like this." I kept my tone light and my attention on our surrounds more than him. "People will begin to think we're an item again."

He didn't respond, but just for a moment, a glimmer of amusement broke through the anger that burned in his bright eyes.

I glanced around then said, "I don't suppose you have any idea where your bastard brother is, do you?"

That cheek muscle went into overdrive again, but he still didn't move or answer.

"Personally, I'm betting he won't show up. He seems to have gained a preference of late to let others do his dirty work." I paused, and then added derisively, "But as you said at the cemetery, he always was a coward who hid behind excuses and the strength of others."

Anger surged across the night, sharp, clear, and *close*. I bit back a smile. Luke might be near enough to hear what I was saying, but he wasn't yet out in the open. Until he was, we couldn't move.

"So how is the little shit keeping you voiceless and unmoving, Sam?" I scanned him critically, my stomach clenching at the severity of some of his wounds. Dear god, he was going to have some major scarring after this. *If* he survived this, that was. "Is it magic, or some form of mental control?"

Again that muscle went into action. Not mental control, obviously, otherwise that muscle and the fury in his eyes would also be still.

I frowned and slowly walked around him. There were no obvious signs of magic etched onto the ground, and no spell stones that I could see. But as I was about to move around to the front of him again, I glimpsed something black and ugly crawling across his spine. It was gone as quickly as it had appeared, but my stomach churned. Skin runes were a particularly nasty type of magic and were generally employed when the survival of the subject was unimportant. Unfortunately, the only way to counteract them was with holy water and silver, and only then within a certain amount of time. The longer the runes were on the skin, the stronger they became, and the more they'd suck the life out of him. Given what I'd glimpsed, it was evident they'd been active for about half an hour already. He probably had that amount of time left before the runes claimed his life.

It was tempting, so damn tempting, to free him, but I couldn't risk using either the water or the knife just yet. Not until we'd brought Luke out into the open.

Frustration surged, but I kept all emotion from my expression as I stopped beside him. I wanted to reach out and squeeze his hand, let him know that it would be okay, that everything was under control. But I didn't, because it wasn't. Not yet.

"I'm here, Luke, as ordered. Are you going to show yourself or not?"

"That would depend."

His voice was coming from the right side of the road, but the waves of anger from the left. Something weird was going on.

"On what?"

"On whether you have kept your word or not."

"There are no sharpshooters, Luke. I did as you asked and came here alone."

"So it would appear—but appearances are often deceiving."

There was a scuff of sound; then Luke stepped out

from the doorway of the building that held the spotlight. He was wearing a gray cloak that hid his entire body, just as the cowl hid much of his features. Only his blue eyes were visible, so bright and so similar to Sam's and yet also vastly different. There was a spitefulness of spirit and temper evident in Luke's gaze that I'd never seen in Sam's.

"I told you not so long ago I'd burn this place down around your ears if you didn't back off, Luke—"

"Oh, you are welcome to try, dear Emberly, but I do not believe you'll have much success."

I raised a hand and let sparks dance—then die—across my fingertips. Luke laughed at the sight, the sound high and merciless. "As has proven to be the case."

A low sound of fury rumbled up my throat and in one swift motion, I reached for the gun resting against my spine and fired. The sound of the gunshot ricocheted across the night as the back of Luke's head exploded across the wall behind him.

For a moment, the world seemed to hold its breath. I didn't move, didn't relax, and kept the gun raised. As his body fell to the ground, an odd shimmer began to crawl across it, starting at his extremities then quickly spreading across the rest of his torso, until his entire being was encased. It pulsed for several seconds then disappeared, revealing what lay on the ground was a red cloak, not Luke.

A heartbeat later, Sam screamed.

I jumped and whipped around. The runes I'd glimpsed on his spine had moved to his chest and were tearing into his flesh with tiny black claws. If I didn't react—didn't stop them—they'd rip out his heart. That half an hour had just dropped to a few minutes—if that.

"Okay, okay!" I threw the gun onto the ground. "Enough. Please."

"Is that all of your weapons, dear Emberly?" This time, Luke's voice was coming from the left, from the same area as the waves of anger.

"Yes."

Sam screamed again. Blood was beginning to course down his stomach, and I could see the gleam of bone in his chest.

Fuck, fuck, fuck!

I hastily pulled a second gun and two knives from their harnesses and threw them on the ground as well. "Stop the runes, Luke, or I swear—"

"What? You'll cinder me? And how might you achieve that when your flames are now ashes and beyond your reach?"

I didn't say anything. I didn't dare. I just clenched my fists against both the fires that burned through my soul and the desire to reduce his ass to ashes. His time was coming; I just had to have a little more patience. And hope like hell that Sam could last that long.

Jackson, tell everyone to get ready.

"And I'm expected to believe that is all you brought with you, Emberly?" Luke's voice held a mocking note. "What kind of fool do you think I am?"

I undid my coat and held it open. "It's hard to acquire an arsenal at short notice."

"I find that hard to believe. Lift up the ends of your jeans."

I did so. He'd see no more there than he had on my torso. My two remaining weapons—a small extendable silver blade and the precious vial of holy water—were currently sitting inside my bra, under my breasts. With the coat now undone, I could get to them very easily.

But the scent of pain and blood and desperation was riding the air, and the vicious little runes had their claws deep into Sam's chest. If they weren't stopped soon, they'd reach his heart—and there was nothing I or anyone else could do to help him if that happened.

"Sam has, at best, a couple of heartbeats left, Luke. I thought it was your intent to make him watch me die, not the other way around."

"Oh, it is. Frederick, do please stop them for the moment."

Frederick had to be close, because that order hadn't been spoken very loudly. Energy swirled, and the runes stilled. I blew out a relieved breath, even though the danger wasn't over yet. Not for Sam, not for me, not for those who waited underground. Not when that witch was still on the loose.

I stepped sideways, pointedly putting myself between Sam and the building Luke was hiding in. And in the process, ensuring the nearest manhole cover now lay in a direct line between him and me.

"And you think that shielding him will make any difference? Surely even you are not that foolish."

He finally stepped free of the building's shadows. I watched him through narrowed eyes. After a second, I saw it. The dome that protected him sat a couple of inches away from his body and gave off a very faint shimmer every time his left leg moved. And *that* meant the charm from which it originated was either in his left pants pocket or—more likely—strapped to his left ankle.

I continued to watch him, my breath catching in my throat as he approached the old manhole cover. *Please let this work . . .*

I dropped my gaze to the nearby weapons, but he stopped too soon, and I silently swore. Three inches more and he would have been standing on that cover—that *metal* cover, made of old iron and naturally impervious to magic.

He threw his arms wide. "By all means, have a go, dear Emberly. I think you will find yourself no more successful than any sharpshooter would have been."

I didn't move. Didn't reply. I just silently willed him to take a step. Just one damn *step.*

Em, said Jackson. *Got word. Cloaks moving.*

I silently swore. *Tell Adán and Dmitri to go. We can't wait any longer.*

There was no immediately reply, but a heartbeat later, a low rumbling began, the sound distant at first but quickly gathering speed and strength. The ground underneath us began to quiver, and the old buildings around the intersection shuddered and shook.

Luke swore and looked around, his expression one of confusion. "What the fuck—"

The quivering grew more violent and—with little fanfare—the building behind him partially collapsed. A huge cloud of dust and debris rolled outward, momentarily erasing him from sight. I twisted around and threw myself at Sam, knocking him down to ground. It was a decision that probably saved both our lives, because I'd barely hit the road when something cut through the space where we'd been standing only seconds before and pinged off the lamppost on the curb behind us.

Bullets.

I twisted around and half rose, and then froze as the dust cleared a little. Luke was standing five feet in front of me, a gun clenched firmly in one hand.

And the damn sewer cover was now three feet *behind* him rather than three inches in front of him.

"What have you done?" His voice was tight with anger and madness gleamed in eyes.

"Nothing more than create a three-meter-wide trench around this entire area and, in the process, destroy all sewer access points and stop your swarm from leaving Brooklyn."

"Not even *you* can cause such destruction, Emberly. Especially not when your magic has been curtailed."

That he called it "magic" suggested that neither he nor his witch truly understood what, exactly, a phoenix was. Which was probably why I'd still been able to access the mother the last time they'd tried to contain my fire. They hadn't understood the connection and therefore hadn't built enough inhibitors into their spell.

Which *didn't* mean they hadn't learned from that experience. And I certainly wasn't about to remove Grace's charm to find out.

"I didn't have to. PIT were also listening to your call, remember, and three hours is a whole lot of time to arrange a surprise or two."

He snorted. "Not even PIT or the military has the power to cause *that* sort of destruction in a city as populated as Melbourne. They wouldn't dare."

"They didn't have to. Not when it's easier to call in a couple of earth fae to do the task for them."

For a minute, he didn't say anything. He simply stared at me, his expression cool, detached. I didn't like that look. Not one little bit.

"Clever," he said eventually. "But perhaps not clever enough."

With that, he fired. I reacted instinctively and threw up a thick wall of the mother's fire, not just to protect myself, but the man who lay helpless on the ground behind me. The bullets hit it and almost instantly began to melt; by the time they'd breach the flames, they were little more than a stream of molten metal that plopped softly to the ground at my feet.

I pushed all the way up, fire dripping from my clenched fists. Luke's eyes were wide and disbelieving. "You can't do that. You shouldn't be able to do that."

I raised a hand and threw a ball of fire. It bounced harmlessly off the field that surrounded him and spun off into the remains of the old building instead, but the power of the blow was enough to force him back a step.

"Guess your tame witch was wrong."

I hit him again. Another step back.

A scream rent the air, then another, and another, until it was a chorus of hideous cries that ringed the intersection. The cloaks weren't trying to get out of Brooklyn anymore.

They were here.

I flung out a hand; fire erupted from the earth and quickly began to surround the intersection. But even the mother's force wasn't fast enough, because there were cloaks inside her circle and they were coming straight at us.

I swore and this time raised a wall around Sam's prone body. Then I turned to face Luke—just in time to see him pull the trigger yet again. I flung myself to one side but wasn't quick enough. Not by half.

The bullet ripped through my shoulder and spun me around. I hit the ground hard and, for several heartbeats, saw nothing but stars.

Then the high-pitched screams of the insane cut through the pain and I looked to see a cloak in the air, his clawlike hands reaching for my throat.

I plucked a sliver of fire from the wall that surrounded Sam, wrapped it around the cloak's neck, and cindered him in an instant. As his soot began to rain around me, I twisted around and flung another ball of flame at Luke. Once against it bounced harmlessly off the magic that protected him, but it forced him back that one vital step.

He was standing on the manhole cover.

"Now, Rory, left leg," I screamed, and scrambled to my feet.

Fire erupted from the manhole, the force of it so strong it lifted both the cover *and* Luke high into the air. He screamed, eyes wide, as fingers of flame crawled over the metal and wrapped around his left leg. His screaming grew louder and the smell of burning flesh began to stain the air. There was a brief, sharp explosion, but then the slight shimmer surrounding Luke died abruptly.

He was mine.

As the fire still streaming from the manhole began to form human shape, I curled a fiery lance around Luke's neck and flung him roughly to the ground.

"Behind you!" Jackson shouted.

I spun and saw three cloaks coming straight at me. Fire erupted from my body, forming a wall of fire, but they were far too close, and going far too fast. They hit it hard but kept on coming, their flesh aflame and fury and determination in their eyes. Luke might be held captive by fire, but he was still very much in control of this lot.

They hit me as one, and we went tumbling in a mass of arms and legs and screaming, biting flesh. I cursed and became spirit, surging out from underneath them . . .

Only to hear Sam's scream. Fuck, the runes had been activated again.

Rory surged toward me, his spirit form fierce and bright in the night. "Go," he said. "Jackson and I will take care of the cloaks."

"Thanks."

I spun and streamed toward Sam. Several cloaks were tearing uselessly at the firewall that surrounded and protected him, not seeming to care that every time they hit the flames a little more of their flesh was cindered. I flicked several streams of the mother's fire around their bodies and quickly killed them, then went through the wall. Just for an instant, the mother's power surged through every part of me, her call evocative, sensual. Then Sam screamed again, and I was through, becoming flesh from the feet up.

There was blood everywhere, and Sam was fighting, bucking in agony as the claws reached deep inside his chest, reaching for his heart.

I was close, so damn close to losing him. . . .

I dropped beside him and pulled the blade and the water from my bra. In the depths of his blue eyes I saw a desperate battle—one I'd seen many a time over the years. It was the will to live fighting against the belief that death was the better path.

"Sorry," I muttered as I flipped the knife open. "But as I told you once before, I didn't save your ass only to have these bastards snatch it away again."

He didn't say anything—*couldn't* say anything—but the cheek muscle was in overdrive mode again and despite his very obvious agony, his eyes burned with emotion. What sort of emotion I didn't dare guess, because that would lead only to false hope.

He screamed again. I swore, raised the knife, and cut him open from left breast to right, and in the process, sliced right through the middle of the little black runes. They reacted instantly to the touch of silver, retracting into a thick ball of hissing, slashing snakes. I uncorked the vial of holy water with my teeth then poured it over both the runes and the wounds they'd created. Steam began to vent from both, and the runes screamed and twisted and slashed uselessly at the air. I sat back on my heels and waited. The seething black blob grew smaller and smaller, until there was nothing left but a tiny twisting speck. Then that, too, was gone, and Sam took a deep, shuddering breath.

"That's a fucking awesome bedside manner you have there, Red." His voice was thick and edged with pain, but never in my life had I heard a sweeter sound. "Not sure the medical board would approve the use of an unsterilized knife, though."

I laughed, even as tears stung my eyes. "Probably not."

His gaze dropped to my shoulder. "You've been shot."

"Yes." Thankfully, becoming spirit, however briefly, had cauterized the wound and stopped the bleeding.

He half raised his good hand, and I caught it in mine. Just for an instant, all the years and all the misunderstandings seemed to melt away, and we were as we had been: a man and a woman who were meant to be.

Then something flickered in his eyes and he said, "I can't—"

I pulled my fingers from his and tried to ignore the pain knifing into my heart. Damn it, when would I ever learn? "Don't move—"

"Em, it's not—"

"Medical help isn't far away," I said, ignoring him. "And I've still got cloaks and a madman to attend to."

"Luke is mine—"

"No," I cut in again. "He's not. He never was."

With that, I rose and stepped through the mother's wall. Her call was stronger this time, a warning that my strength was on the wane even if the adrenaline still coursing through my body meant I couldn't yet feel her pulling at my strength.

Both Rory and Jackson were standing in front of Luke. Around them was a sea of dead—or rather, the broken and burned remains of them, intermingled with the soot and debris of the building that had collapsed and those that still burned. I stopped beside Rory and briefly twined my fingers through his, needing the comfort and strength of his touch.

"I think you can release the mother," he said.

"What about the witch?"

"Probably long gone, if he has any sense," Jackson said. He nodded toward Luke. "What are we going to do with this scum?"

"What we came here to do."

"PIT won't be pleased."

"Like I give a fuck right now." I released the mother, felt her sigh of regret deep within as she faded away, then stepped closer to Luke. Hatred burned deep in his eyes. *That* wasn't exactly new, but the fear was. "Where are the scientists, Luke?"

He hawked and spat. It sizzled away long before it got anywhere near me. "That was decidedly unpleasant. Do it again and I'll burn your eyes out of their sockets. Where are the *scientists*?"

"Give me a decent reason to tell you, and I just might. I mean, right now I'm standing on the edge of death, and it's not like telling you will actually pull me away from that."

"No, but it will be the difference between a quick death or a long one."

"Just kill him," Sam croaked. "They have to be in Brooklyn somewhere. Without him to control the red cloaks, we can get rid of them easily enough, then search the city until we find the scientists."

"Good luck with that, brother."

There was a decidedly smug note in his tone that had my gaze narrowing. "Does that mean they're *not* in Brooklyn?"

Luke's eyebrows rose. "As I said, give me a—"

A shot rang out and, for the second time that night, Luke's head exploded—only this time, it *was* him and not a decoy. Blood and bone and brain matter sprayed across my face, and horror and fire instinctively surged. A second later, Rory hit me, pulling me to the ground as another shot rang out. It pinged against the asphalt inches from our toes and ricocheted into the night.

"Shooter, on the roof to our right," Jackson said.

I twisted around and saw the silhouette of a man a second before a huge ball of flame smothered the view and arced toward him. It hit the guttering rather than the man, and the whole building erupted into flame.

"Fuck," Rory muttered. "Jackson doesn't muck around, does he?"

"Control *has* been something of an issue." I scrambled to my feet. Jackson was already running toward the building. "Could you look after Sam for me? The two of us can hunt the bastard down."

When Rory looked ready to argue, I grabbed his arm and squeezed lightly. "Remember our vow. We've jeopardized our existence enough already."

"Agreed. Go."

I spun on my heels and ran after Jackson. The building he'd hit with his fireball burned so fiercely the glow of it lit the evening sky and heat rolled across the night. I drew it in instinctively, letting it feed my soul and energize my body. The game was still afoot, and I had a bad feeling I'd need that strength.

We ran past the building and into the nearby cross street. The fire's light turned night into day and revealed the figure of a man running down the pavement.

Jackson threw another fiery ball. It hit the concrete inches from the fleeing figure and bounced along after him, nipping at his heels, setting them alight before it fizzled out.

The figure turned, and I had a brief glimpse of a thin, pockmarked face that seemed vaguely familiar before he raised his arm and threw something. I grabbed Jackson and dragged him sideways.

"They're only fucking stones—"

The rest of his words were cut off as said stones exploded and sharp-edged little daggers cut through our clothes and across our faces, drawing blood.

"There is *never* something as simple as stones when it comes to a witch," I growled. "Be careful."

"Got it."

We continued on. The witch had gained ground on us thanks to his missiles, so I reached for the mother and sent her winging ahead. Pain slithered through me, yet another warning I was pushing the limits even though I'd drawn in strength only moments before. But weakening myself wouldn't matter—not if we caught and killed the bastard ahead.

A fierce iridescent wall of flame flared across the entire street ahead, blocking the witch's path. He swung left, into a side street, and disappeared. I swore and reached for more speed, my feet almost flying as we pounded after him.

We swung into the side street, only to discover it was not only a dead end, but also empty. I slid to a stop, felt Jackson do the same. Heard the harsh rasp of his breath and something else—a soft, almost rhythmic pulsing or slapping sound. I frowned and glanced at Jackson. He shrugged. *Worry later. Get this bastard.*

"Come out, Frederick, or I'll burn the buildings to the ground and force you out."

I didn't expect a response, and I didn't get any. So I raised my hands, called on the mother, and walked forward, streaming fire across the buildings to the left and the right. They might have been a mix of brick, steel, and wood, but it made no difference to the force I was hitting them with. They exploded into flame, lighting the sky up and quickly spreading to the rest of the buildings. I kept on walking. Sooner or later, we'd flush the bastard out.

The buildings continued to explode as we moved deeper into the side street, and that odd pulsing drew closer and closer. Nothing and no one came out of the buildings. Not even rats. But then, rats—real rats—were rather intelligent creatures, and had probably left this hellhole the minute Brooklyn had become the home of monsters.

"Movement, end building, left," Jackson muttered.

Even as he said it, a shadow scurried up the side of the building and disappeared over the rooftop.

Before either of us could react, bright light speared the night, hitting the street and blinding us in the process. I threw up an arm, trying to spot what was happening. Saw, in the edges of the light, the tail end of a helicopter.

"Fuck, go," Jackson said.

I became spirit and surged upward, even as the

helicopter banked and swept away. On the ground below, violence erupted. I glanced down and saw cloaks running out of the remaining buildings and head for Jackson. He flung fire, but it was weaker than his previous efforts and did little more than singe their clothes. And as he turned and ran, a second helicopter swept in from the left and began peppering his heels with bullets.

I glanced at the fast-disappearing helicopter that held our quarry then cursed and flung an arrow of fire at the one chasing Jackson. It banked away sharply, but I didn't go after it. Right now, the cloaks were the bigger threat. I dove down. He glanced up as I neared him and raised a hand. I grabbed him with flaming fingers and swept him up, away from the immediate reach of the cloaks.

But it wasn't easy to maintain height and speed while carrying anyone, let alone someone of Jackson's weight. My strength gave out just before we reached the intersection, and we hit the ground hard, skidding several yards farther before coming to a halt in a tangled mess of fire and flesh. I took a breath, then regained human form and rolled away from Jackson.

And heard the ominous pulsing again.

"*That* was one hell of an entrance." Amusement edged Rory's voice as he grabbed my arm and gently pulled me upright. "Did you get the witch?"

"No." Jackson's voice was tight with both anger and weariness. "We did, however, collect a tail."

Rory's gaze ran past us. "Oh, fuck. More cloaks."

"And not just cloaks. Someone is aiding the witch, and they're backed up by helicopters."

As if to confirm my statement, the bright light pierced the night and bullets peppered the ground again.

"Get out of here," Rory said, voice flat. "I'll take care of these bastards."

"You can't fight a helicopter *and* the cloaks," I said. "We need to run—"

"I know what I'm doing, Em. *Go*."

And with that, he flamed and surged upward. Jackson grabbed me and forced me forward. Sam was already struggling to his feet. His face was white, sweat beaded his forehead, and a rough bandage now protected his broken arm.

I pulled my grip from Jackson's. "Go, both of you."

"Not without you."

It was said in unison, and I couldn't help smiling. "I'm coming, never fear. I just have to set the world alight."

In skies above us, a battle raged. Bullets and fire bit through the night sky, neither one entirely catching the other. The helicopter pilot was skilled, and his machine nimble and fast. More bullets ripped through the tarmac as the second machine swept in.

And so, too, did the red cloaks.

"Go," I urged, then spun and called to the mother.

Her fire erupted through me, around me, and for the briefest instant I wavered between flesh and spirit, between the need to remain and fight and the desire to give in to the seductive song of the earth and the mother . . .

An explosion ripped across the sky, and the force of it rocked me off my feet as burning bits of metal and god knows what else rained all around me. Then fiery hands gripped me, held me, snatching the mother's force from me then flinging it outward.

The red cloaks went up in a gigantic whoosh that didn't even leave ash.

The two of us became flesh again, but Rory didn't release his grip. "Run," he said, voice tight. "There's more cloaks coming, and another helicopter out there somewhere."

We ran as fast as we could.

Fire followed us, jumping from building to building, setting Brooklyn alight just as I'd promised not so long ago. The force and heat of it rolled over us, feeding us, fueling us, but we were both dangerously low on reserves and still walking an edge that was far too tight.

The soft pulsing began to bite through the air again.

Rory cursed and increased his speed, all but hurling us through the night.

Jackson and Sam came into sight. Not far beyond them were the lights of Melbourne, a glimmer that promised safety—but only if we could reach it.

Light speared the night again, and the helicopter swept in.

"Go," Rory said and released me.

I didn't fight his decision, as much as I wanted to. I just ran on. The fire around me began to curve inward, until it had created a tunnel of flame that protected and hid our position.

As I neared the two men, they hesitated. "Go, go," I urged as bullets began to pepper the ground around us.

But they stopped almost as quickly as they'd started, and the pulsing of air altered and changed, briefly dying then coming to life again.

Again bullets peppered the ground, quickly followed by the sweep of magic.

Fear hit me, so fierce and fast I could barely even breathe. I skidded to a halt, swept a window into our protective tunnel, and looked up.

Just in time to see the whole damn helicopter explode into a ball of flame.

I blinked, my heart in my mouth, unable to take a breath. Then a fiery form pulled free from the wreckage as it began to fall from the sky. As our tunnel peeled all the way back, Rory dropped to the ground, regaining flesh as he did so.

It was done. We were safe. And despite what instinct and fear might have believed, the only ones who had died here tonight were Luke and his cloaks.

Tears stung my eyes, and it was all I could do to remain upright. The danger might be over, but we still had to get out of here, and I wasn't about to let anyone carry me.

"And that," Rory said, with a cheerful if weary grin, "should be the end—"

He didn't finish.

He didn't get the chance.

A single shot rang out and snatched the rest of his words way, along with his life.

"No!" I screamed as his blood and his brains splattered across my face.

Just for a moment, horror held me still as his body crumbled. But as flames began to consume his flesh, I spun and saw a glimmer in the distance. Luke might be dead, and his pet witch might or might not have died in that helicopter crash, but they'd left behind a parting gift, just to ensure we didn't have the final word.

I sucked in the fire, sucked in the force of the world around me, and flung it, with every ounce of strength I had left, at that building.

It didn't explode. It simply disintegrated into pieces so tiny the drifting wind caught them and flung them away.

I dropped to my knees, struggling to breathe, struggling even to remain conscious. Pain ripped through me, pain caused both by pushing myself way past any reasonable limits, and by having the other half of my soul so brutally ripped away.

Hands gripped me, held me, and warmth bled from his body to mine.

Jackson, not Sam.

I didn't say anything. I couldn't.

I simply held out a hand and called to Rory's ashes. They rose from the ground and swirled toward me, wrapping almost lovingly around my fingers and wrist, a warm caress that had tears spilling down my cheeks.

He was dead, and it was my fault. I was the one who'd called him into this fight, even though I'd feared this would be the result. Damn it, *I* should have been the one who'd died; I should be the one facing the pain of rebirth, not him.

His ashes and energy merged into my flesh, became a part of me, held safe deep inside until the time for renewal came.

Which would be soon.

And once he was whole . . .

I took a deep, shuddering breath and forced myself to move.

Once he was whole and alive once more, I was going to track down the bastard who'd killed him and return the favor.

I raised my face to the sky and drew in the heat of the day. It ran through me like a river, a caress filled with warmth and sympathy, as if the sun was aware of my reason for being in this clearing out in the middle of nowhere.

And maybe it was. It had witnessed me performing this ceremony far too many times in the past.

I closed my eyes and ignored the tears trickling down my cheeks. Rory's death was once again my fault. If he hadn't been in Brooklyn with me, he'd still be alive.

And if he hadn't been there, that inner voice whispered, *not only would it be you who was dead, but possibly Jackson and Sam as well.*

I hated that inner voice, if only because all too often she was right.

Rory had died saving our asses, and I knew he wouldn't be angry about that. He'd always had something of a hero complex and had often said that if he had to go before his allotted one hundred years was up, he'd rather do it saving someone he loved.

And he and I *did* love each other; hell, I couldn't physically survive without him, nor he me. But we weren't *in* love, thanks to the curse that haunted all phoenixes—a curse that was said to have come from a witch after a phoenix lover had left her with little more than the ashes of broken promises and dreams.

But it was a curse we could have ultimately lived with, if not for the fact that it came with one other kick in the teeth—that no matter whom we *did* fall in love with each lifetime, the relationship would end in ashes just as the witch's had.

As far as I was aware, no phoenix had ever found a way to break the curse. I certainly wouldn't—not in this lifetime, at any rate. Sam might have gotten as far as talking to me as of late, but I doubted it would ever progress beyond that. Not given what he saw as my complete betrayal of his trust—even if he now understood the reasons for it.

I drew in a deep breath and released it slowly, letting it wash the lingering wisps of regret and hurt from my mind. I needed to concentrate. The sun had almost reached its zenith and *that* meant it was time to begin.

I stripped off and folded my clothes onto the loose white tunic I'd brought here for Rory, and then kicked off my shoes. The slight breeze teased my skin, its touch chasing goose bumps across my body despite the sunshine.

Within me, energy stirred, energy that was a part of me and yet separate. Rory's soul, impatient for his rebirth. When phoenixes died—as Rory had in Brooklyn—their flesh became ashes that had to be called and then retained within the heat of their mate's body. If for some reason that process didn't happen, then there was no rebirth. And that, in turn, was a death sentence for the remaining partner, as phoenixes could only ever rise from their ashes through a spell performed by their mates.

But there was also a time restriction on rebirth. It had to be done within five days of death, or the life and the fire of those ashes would die, and his spirit and energy would be returned to the earth mother, never to be reborn.

It had been three days since Rory had passed. I was pushing it timewise, hence his impatience and, perhaps, a little fear. But I'd had no other choice—the weather in Melbourne had been so bad any fire I'd have lit would have struggled to remain alight. And while as a phoenix I could have kept the flames burning, I couldn't afford to waste energy when I had no idea how much I'd need for the ceremony. Because no matter how long I'd been doing this, no rebirth was ever exactly the same.

I brushed stray strands of red-gold hair out of my eyes as I moved into the center of the clearing and the square stack of wood I'd already piled there. The dry grass was harsh and scratchy underfoot and the scent of eucalyptus teased my nostrils.

It was a perfect day for resurrection.

I reached down to the inner fires and called them to my fingers. As flames began to dance and shimmer across their tips, I stopped on the west side of the bonfire and raised my hands to the sky. Sparks plumed upward, glittering like red-gold diamonds against the blue of the sky.

"By the dragon's light," I intoned softly in a language so old only the gods and another phoenix could understand, "and the mother's might, I beseech thee to protect all that surrounds me and the one I call to me."

As the words of the spell rolled across the silence, the air began to shimmer and spark with the colors of all creation. It was the heat of the day and the power of the mother, of the earth itself, rising to answer the call of protection.

"Banish all that would do us wrong," I continued. "Send them away, send them astray, never to pass this way. So mote it be."

The sparks I'd sent skyward began to fall gently downward but they never reached the ground, caught instead in the gentle hands of the shimmering light.

I moved to the north section and repeated the spell. The shimmering net of sparks extended and the hum of its power began to vibrate through my body. I echoed the process on the two remaining sides, until the net joined and my entire body pulsated to the tune of the power that now surrounded me.

I faced the bonfire and again raised my face to the sky, watching for the precise moment the sun reached the pinnacle of its arc. Heat, energy, and sparks ran around me, through me, a force wanting to be used, *needing* to be used.

Now, that inner voice said.

I called to my flames then stepped into the center of the bonfire. As flesh gave way to spirit and I became nothing but a being of fire, the wood around me burst into flame. I held out my hands and raised the fire to greater heights, until it burned with a heat that was white-hot.

It felt like home.

Felt like rebirth.

"I beseech the dragon that gives life and the mother that nurtures us all to release the soul that resides within."

The words were lost in the roar of the flames but they were not unheard. The ground began to tremble, as if the earth itself was preparing for birth.

"Let the ashes of life be renewed; give him hope and bless him with love, and let him stand beside me once more. By the grace of the mother and the will of the dragon, so mote it be."

As the last word was said, power tore up my legs and through the rest of my body, the sheer force of it momentarily stretching my spirit to the upper limits of survivability. Specks of luminescent ash began to peel away from those overstretched strands, gently at first but rapidly intensifying until they became a storm of light and ash. As the heat of the flames, the force of the earth, and the brightness of the day reached a crescendo of power, the motes began to condense and find form, alternating between our three—fire, firebird, and flesh—until what the earth and the day held in their grip was the spirit I'd spent aeons with.

Rory.

I thanked the earth mother and the dragon in the sky for their generosity and the gift of life, and then I reversed the spell, this time moving from south to east. The wall of energy and sparks shimmered briefly then began to dissipate, the energy returning to the mother and the fiery sparks drifting skyward as they burned out and disappeared. All that was left was the bonfire and the adult man who remained curled up in a fetal position in the middle of it.

Weariness washed through me and I all but fell to the ground. I sucked in several deep breaths to clear my head then crossed my legs for the long wait ahead. Rory might now be reborn, but physically he was extremely weak. That was part of the reason I'd piled the bonfire so high—he would need the flames to fuel his body. He wouldn't wake—wouldn't even regain his flesh form—until the ashes in his soul had refueled enough on the heat of the fire to enable full functionality. And even then, it would be days before he'd be back to his old self and fully, physically mobile.

The afternoon passed slowly. I boosted the fire a couple

of times and kept the heat at a white-hot level. It was close to four in the afternoon when his spirit form began to jerk and tremble, a sure sign that his inner fires had fully awoken. An hour later, he began to keen—a high-pitched sound so filled with pain that tears stung my eyes. Rebirth was never pleasant, but the pain was so much greater when we died before our time. I had no idea why but figured it was the mother's way of making us a little more careful about how we lived and, ultimately, how we died.

Dusk had begun to seep across the sky in fiery fingers of red and gold by the time his spirit gave way to flesh. By then the bonfire was little more than softly glowing embers, but they didn't burn him. Which isn't to say that we, as spirits of fire, *couldn't* be harmed by our element. The scars down my spine were evidence enough of that. But they'd come from a situation in which I'd been unable to either control or feed on fire, thanks to the fact I was rescuing a child and in full view of a crowd of people. Vampires and werewolves might be out and proud—and generally accepted into human society far better than most of us had ever expected—but there were still enough people who deemed them a threat to civilization in need of erasing that the rest of us thought it better to remain in the shadows.

Who knew how society would react if people ever realized just how many of us were living among them?

Even though Rory was unconscious, in rebirth the process of feeding was automatic; the bonfire continued to fuel him until the light within it was completely drained and all that remained was cold ashes.

Only then did he stir.

Only then did he open his eyes and look at me.

"Emberly." His voice was little more than a harsh whisper, but it was a sound so sweet it bought tears to my eyes. Because it meant everything had gone right; he was back and whole, and life for the two of us could go on as it always had.

I smiled. "Welcome once again to the land of the living."

"Not sure this can *ever* be called living. Not when every fucking piece of me is aching like shit."

"*That* is the price you pay for getting yourself shot."

He grunted and rolled onto his back. Ash plumed skyward then rained back down, covering his flesh in a coat of fine gray. "Did you get the bastard who did it?"

"That depends."

He raised a pale red-gold eyebrow. "Meaning?"

"That I sent every ounce of flame I could muster and every bit of energy I could demand from the mother into the building the shot had come from. It exploded into pieces so small they were little more than dust, so I undoubtedly got the shooter."

"But it's the bastard who ordered the kill we want."

"Exactly." I uncrossed my legs and pushed upright. Just for an instant, the clearing spun around me, a warning that Rory wasn't the only weak one right now. "And I thought you might like a piece of *that* particular action."

"You thought right." He scrubbed a hand across his eyes then looked around. "Where are we?"

"Trawool. Or just outside of it, anyway."

He blinked. "Where the fuck is that?"

I smiled and held out my hands. "It's about fourteen kilometers out of Seymour and about an hour from Melbourne. Ready?"

His fingers gripped mine and, after a deep breath, he nodded. I hauled him upright; ash flew around the two of us, catching in my throat and making me cough. He hissed and his fingers tightened briefly on mine as he gathered his balance.

"It never gets any easier," he muttered.

"No."

I held on to him and waited. After several more minutes, he nodded. I released one hand and shifted the other to his elbow. Just because he thought he was stable didn't mean he actually was.

"I wasn't able to drive the car into the clearing—there were too many trees," I said. "But it's parked as close as I could get."

"I'll make it." He took a determined step forward, paused unsteadily for a moment, and then took another. He very much resembled a toddler taking his first steps and, in many ways, it was an apt image. The two of us might have spent more years alive than either of us cared to remember, but each rebirth came with the cost of major muscle groups remembering how to function again. Sometimes recovery was almost instant—as had happened this time when it came to speech and arm movement—and other times it could take days. Hell, the last time I'd been reborn, it had taken close to two weeks for full function to return to my legs.

When we finally reached the edge of the small clearing, I quickly re-dressed then picked up the soft tunic, shaking the dirt and leaves from it before helping him into it. Right now, his skin was so new that it was also ultrasensitive. Anything too tight or scratchy would rub him raw.

It was only half a dozen steps from there to the car I'd rented, but by the time he'd climbed into the back of the station wagon, his body was shaking and sweat beaded his forehead.

I slammed the back door closed then climbed into the driver's seat and started the car up. "There's protein bars and a couple of energy drinks in the backpack."

He dragged it closer and opened it up. "Whatever did we do before modern food manufacturing?"

"Snacked on beef jerky and drank unrefined cow's milk boosted with raw eggs."

"Which is probably the reason I hate both with a passion today." He tore open the protein bar and began munching on it. "Except, of course, when said milk is combined with either brandy or rum in the form of an eggnog. How many days have I missed?"

I checked the mirror for oncoming cars, even though that was unlikely on this off the beaten track, then did a U-turn and headed down to the main road.

"Three. I had to wait for a hot enough day to perform the ceremony."

He snorted softly. "If Melbourne can be relied on for anything, it's weather that does *not* do what you want."

"Yeah." There were other reasons, of course, like the Paranormal Investigations Team—a specialist squad of humans and supernaturals who worked outside the regular police force to solve crimes that involved paranormals—wanting a full and detailed debriefing before they'd let Jackson and me go. Then there was the problem of ensuring we weren't being followed—one we solved by me and Jackson temporarily going our separate ways. He returned to the offices of Hellfire Investigations—the PI agency we jointly owned and ran—while I followed the example of so many of our enemies of late and used the stormwater system to get out of Melbourne unseen.

"What happened in Brooklyn after I was shot?" Rory said.

"Nothing. We just ran." Or rather, left as quickly as any of us were able, given we were little more than the walking, bleeding wounded by that time.

"And you haven't heard from either Sam or Jackson since?"

"I talked to Jackson yesterday. I'm meeting him in Seymour tonight if he can get away without being followed." I had no idea what Sam might be doing. He hadn't exactly been communicative since I'd stepped back into his life. He might be one of PIT's top investigators, and he might be chasing the same damn things we were, but he'd generally only dealt with me when and where it was necessary

"Is that wise?" Concern edged Rory's voice.

"Probably not, but it's not as if we have any other choice. There are still too many things we need to do."

And far too many people we'd endanger if we *did* stop or disappear. Hell, my vanishing for three days was enough of a risk. I was just hoping the vampire currently blackmailing us for any and all information on the Crimson Death virus—or red cloak virus, as it was more commonly known—would put our recent lack of action down to injury recovery.

Of course, he and everyone else also wouldn't have minded our finding the missing scientists who'd been working on a cure for the virus. Unfortunately, they'd been purposely infected, bought under the control of the red cloak hive "queen" and, right now, were who knew where working on god knew what.

What we *did* know was that the infected generally fell into two categories—those who became crazy pseudo vampires leashed by the will of the queen, and the ones who, while they also gained vampirelike abilities, kept all mental facilities even though they were still bound to the hive and its leader. No one really understood why the virus affected some more than others, although the powers that be suspected it very much depended on which lot infected them. The scientists were apparently in the latter category—no surprise, given the hive queen had wanted them working on the cure as much as the rest of us.

Of course, there *was* a third category, involving people like Sam who, though infected, had no attachment to the hive and did not fall under the will of its leader.

Jackson was continuing to make the required nightly call to our blackmailer, and we both hoped it was enough to keep him off our backs. Like most vampires who'd reached an extreme age, he no longer had any intimacy with his emotions and saw the world in rather simple terms. That is, things he wanted, people he could use to get those things, and people who were stopping him from getting them.

We were currently sitting in that middle class with Rinaldo, the vampire in question. I did *not* want to step into the latter.

Rory grunted. I glanced at the rearview mirror and saw he was struggling to keep his eyes open. "Don't fight it; your body needs the rest."

"You can't carry me in, and the last thing we need is you breaking your back and having us both immobile."

I grinned. "Your ass may be heavy, but I've carried it before and I can do so again. Stop being an idiot and let your body do what it needs to."

He didn't reply. He was already asleep. I hit the main road and headed toward the small holiday cabin I'd rented for the next week. It was a pretty but basic building, the interior little more than one large wood-clad room, which held a bed, a small kitchenette, and a sofa, with a bathroom tucked into one corner. But it was the open fire that dominated the main room that had drawn me there. Rory needed both flame *and* food to continue his rehabilitation toward full mobility, which is why I'd not only lit the fire before I'd left, but had also set up a bed right in front of it. No matter how long he slept, his body would automatically feed on the flames.

The moon was casting its silver light across the shadows by the time I pulled into the long driveway that led down to the half dozen cabins dotted along the banks of the Goulburn River. Ours was the very last one, situated around a slight bend in the river and out of the direct line of sight of the other five.

I reversed up to the front steps then climbed out and unlocked the front door. A wave of heat hit me and I closed my eyes, briefly drawing it into my body to ease a little of the tiredness. But this heat was not mine to enjoy.

I severed the connection and returned to the car, opened the rear door, and then dragged Rory closer. He muttered something unintelligible and half sat up, making my job a little easier. I swung his arm around my shoulder then hauled him upright, being careful not to crack his head on the top of the wagon's door.

He waved his free hand about randomly and said in a rather grand tone, "Onward and upward, my dear!"

I grinned, shifted my grip to his waist, and half carried, half guided him up the steps. His breath was little more than a wheeze by the time we made it inside, and we all but staggered over to the fire. I stripped him out of his tunic then helped him down onto the mattress. I didn't bother covering him, simply because having his entire body exposed to the flames would hasten the refeeding process.

"Thanks." His eyes briefly fluttered open. "What time are you meeting Jackson?"

I threw some more logs onto the fire then glanced at the clock on the wall. "In twenty minutes."

He grunted. "Bring back some coffee. And fries. And a big burger. Or two."

Amusement ran through me. "Like *that's* a surprise request."

I generally hungered for chocolate and green tea after my rebirths, but Rory had always preferred the fattier foods—a preference that had become much easier to fulfill when fast food had come into being. Although cheese, eggs, and milk were theoretically healthier, fries and burgers seemed to fuel him faster.

"How long you planning to be away?" he mumbled.

"Not long." Especially given he was still in such a fragile state. "But shit does happen."

Especially since I'd saved Sam's life and subsequently

become involved in the quest to stop his brother's mad scheme to spread the red cloak virus. Luke was not only one of the few infected who'd retained his sanity, but he also happened to be the queen bee of the red cloak hive and had intended to create an army with which he could rule the world. And while we'd managed to bring Luke down in the Brooklyn madness that had taken Rory's life, I had no idea how much of his army remained or if he'd had a second-in-command who could take over. He'd certainly had a witch on his payroll—one who'd been powerful enough to not only create a spell that could contain a phoenix's fire, but to call *and* control three hellhounds. That I'd survived the encounter had been due more to luck than to determination and skill on my part.

"Shit does," Rory said. "And hopefully, the next truckload will happen all over the bastard who ordered me killed."

I chuckled softly and touched his arm. His skin still held an edge of coolness, which meant there was a way to go before he was up to full strength, despite appearances. "I won't be long."

He grunted. I waited until his breathing indicated he'd slipped into a deep sleep then grabbed my coat and headed out. It didn't take me all that long to reach Seymour. Although there were plenty of good-quality restaurants in the town, Jackson and I had decided to meet at McDonald's, not only because it was easier, but because I'd have to stop by there anyway to grab Rory's food.

Once I parked, I climbed out and looked around. There weren't many cars in the lot; most customers were content to simply use the drive-through, if the long line was anything to go by. None of them seemed to be paying any attention to me, but that didn't necessary mean there wasn't anyone out there watching my movements. Which wasn't so much paranoia as past experience, given the number of people who'd been following us lately.

I couldn't see Jackson anywhere, so I headed inside. Aside from the couple eating burgers at one of the corner tables, the only other people here were the staff.

My phone—an untraceable one we'd gotten from a friend of Rory's who was heavily involved in the black market trade—beeped as I ordered a green tea, several burgers, and a bag of fries. I pulled the phone out of my pocket and glanced at the screen.

Be there in a few minutes, the message said. *Order me an espresso. A large one.*

Though there was no name on the text, it could only have come from Jackson as, aside from Rory, no one else had this number. Jackson's phone had come from PIT, though, and though they claimed it was also untraceable, they'd meant to everyone but themselves, of course.

And that was something of a problem. I trusted Sam, and I trusted his boss—the rather formidable Chief Inspector Henrietta Richmond—but that was about it. I was pretty sure PIT had at least one mole in their organization, and it didn't matter whether that person belonged to the sindicati—which was the vampire version of the mafia—or was one of Rinaldo's men. The last thing I needed was either of them getting our current location or our new phone numbers. Not when Rory was in such a weak state, anyway.

I ordered Jackson's coffee then moved across to a table that overlooked the parking lot. I demolished the burgers in record time, needing to fuel my flesh as much as I'd need to refuel my spirit with flame sometime in the next twenty-four hours. As I started on the fries, an old van drove into the parking area and stopped on the opposite side of the lot to my car. Jackson—of that I had no doubt. A few seconds later, he climbed out of the van, a lean, auburn-haired man who oozed heat and sexuality. Even from this distance, separated as we were by glass, I could feel it, a teasing but fiery river that ran delightfully across my senses, and it was something I'd never felt before. Not like this, anyway. Which maybe meant it was yet another side effect of allowing him to draw in my flames—to merge his spirit with mine—in an effort to burn the red cloak virus from his system. And we weren't even sure if we'd achieved *that.*

PIT had recently taken blood samples, but it could be days—even weeks—before we would know the test results. I seriously doubted it be the latter, though, given the fact that, to date, there was no known cure for the red cloak virus. If my flames *had* burned it from Jackson's system, then it meant the virus was at least susceptible to heat.

Not that it'd help humanity all that much. There were few races capable of withstanding the high temperatures Jackson had.

I watched him walk toward the main door. If there was one thing literature and movies had gotten wrong when it came to the fae, it was their stature. They were neither small nor winged, and the only ones who were ethereal in *any* way were the air fae.

He made his way through the tables with a lightness and grace that belied said stature, his grin easy and delighted, creasing the corners of his emerald eyes.

"Ah, Emberly." His voice was little more than a murmur, but was one that echoed deep within me. Another side effect of our merging was the ability to hear each other's thoughts. Not all the time and certainly not without some effort, but it was still there. And still developing, if that echo was any indication. "You have no idea how much I've missed you."

"Let's be honest here." The amusement that ran through me bubbled over into my voice. "You're an oversexed fire fae who hasn't had much of the intimate stuff as of late. You missed my body more than me."

"You wound me to the core with such a comment." He rather dramatically slapped a hand against his chest, but the effect was somewhat spoiled by the laughter dancing in his eyes.

I rose. "Yeah, I can see the tears."

"They are raining inside, trust me." He caught my hand and tugged me closer. "Life in the office has been seriously boring these last three days without you."

He wrapped his arms around me and held me tight. Not only was he delightfully muscular but deliciously warm. Fire fae tended to run hotter than most humanoids, and although their core temperature was nowhere near as high as ours, they did make very compatible lovers.

But Jackson was also a perfect lover in one other respect; fire fae didn't do commitment, and Jackson was never going to want anything more than a good time from me—which was just as well, given Sam was this lifetime's heartbreaker.

"You spent years in that office flying solo," I said, voice dry. "I've only been there a few weeks."

"But in those few weeks, I have become so accustomed to your presence, I cannot imagine life without it." His face grew suddenly serious. "And now, if you don't mind, I desperately need to do something that I've been dreaming about for these last few days."

And with that, he kissed me.

It was a long, slow, and extremely sensual exploration, and one that had my pulse racing and inner fires flaring. I controlled the latter, but only just—and *that* was instant cause for alarm. Because I was a phoenix, control was something I'd learned from a very young age. That it threatened to break my restraints here—with this man—was something that hadn't happened in the past and certainly shouldn't be happening now.

I abruptly pulled away. His skin was almost translucent with heat, and alarm washed through me. The lack of control wasn't mine, but rather *his*, somehow seeping through the link between us.

Jackson, I said, trying to put as much urgency as I could through our silent connection. *Control it.*

He blinked; then awareness of what was happening hit, and he cursed softly. The color in his skin immediately banked, but I could still feel the fires burning deep within him. While fire fae generally couldn't produce their own flame—they could only control fire that already existed, even if it was little more than a spark—Jackson had gained that ability when our spirits had merged.

But it was an ability he was still struggling with.

He cursed again and thrust a hand through his short hair. "Damn, I've spent the last few days practicing fire control but it looks as if the results aren't quite what I expected."

I touched his arm lightly. "It takes a phoenix years to gain full control. You can't expect similar results in a matter of days."

He snorted. "I'm a fire fae. *That* should give me some sort of an advantage."

"It will. But remember, while you're able to control fire, it wasn't an intimate part of your being until after we merged." I squeezed his arm and sat back down. "You're not used to having to control flames twenty-four/seven. Up until now, you've only had to exert control when fire was already present."

He grunted and sat down opposite me. "It's still fucking annoying. Especially if I now have to think about every little thing I do, lest I set something on fire. Or someone."

"Control *will* happen. But in the meantime, I can teach you how to leash it in more intimate moments."

He took a sip of his coffee then snagged a fry. "That sounds promising. Can we start now?"

I laughed. "Jackson, we're in the middle of McDonald's."

"And I have a van parked outside."

"I don't think either the staff or the patrons would appreciate us doing the horizontal tango out in their parking lot."

"Sadly true." He paused, and that wicked gleam reappeared. "There might, however, be room enough to do a vertical tango."

I threw a fry at him. "We haven't the time."

"It's been more than three days since my last loving. Trust me, it won't take long."

"It's a sad day when a fire fae admits to so little control."

"Woman, you have no idea just how much control I'm exerting right now." He snagged the fry from the table and munched on it. "How's Rory doing?"

"He was reborn without incident and is currently recharging in front of a roaring fire."

Jackson grunted. "How long will it take him to get back to normal?"

I raised an eyebrow. "Meaning, how long do I have to remain with him?"

He smiled. "Yes."

"It depends. Once he's fully refueled, he'll at least be capable of looking after himself even if he's still physically weak. But right now, I can only leave him for small periods of time."

"Small periods are better than nothing."

I frowned. "Why?"

"You know that itchy feeling you get? The one that says we're about to hit a truckload of trouble?"

"I get dreams, not itchy feelings."

"Same, same, just a little more detailed."

I smiled. There was a *vast* difference between getting prophetic dreams that *always* came true and simply feeling the approach of something ominous—and he knew it. "What is this premonition telling you?"

He hesitated. "Just that something bad is happening."

"Happening? As in, right now?"

He nodded, expression serious. "I don't know what, I don't know where, but whatever it is, it's bad."

"Until we get a little more detail, it's hard to do anything about it."

"Yeah." He rubbed a hand across his jaw. "Why don't we grab Rory's burgers and get back—just in case he's the reason for the bad sensations?"

"No one knows where he is, so I doubt it."

Even so, I finished off my tea and quickly rose. The drive-through queue had tapered off by that time, so it wouldn't take long to get Rory's order as well as a couple of extra burgers for the two of us.

As we headed out, I added, "It might be worthwhile leaving the van—and your phone—here. I don't want to risk anyone tracing us to the cabin."

He nodded and jogged off to the van. I climbed into my car and drove over to pick him up, then ordered at the drive-through. We swung back onto the road that would us to Trawool and the cabin.

Jackson was silent the entire trip, but I could feel the tension in him. Whatever he was picking up, it was growing in intensity. I parked in front of the door again, then grabbed the bags of food and hurried up the steps.

The heat once again surged over me as I opened the door and stepped inside. Rory was not only unharmed, but also awake.

"That was quick," he said. Though he sounded brighter, I could still feel the tiredness—the weakness—in him. Refueling was not happening at any great speed, which was damn frustrating. Not that there was anything he could do about it—it was just way things were playing out this rebirth.

"That's because I'm well aware how grouchy you get when you don't get fed in a reasonable time frame."

A smile tugged his lips. "Says the woman who once threatened to cinder me if I didn't present chocolate immediately."

"A statement any reasonable woman would understand." I squatted down beside him then unwrapped one of the burgers and handed it to him.

"Jackson didn't appear?" He took a bite then closed his eyes, his expression one of utter bliss.

"Jackson did," he said as he stepped into the room and closed the door. "Fuck, is it hot in here or is it just me?"

"It's hot." I continued on to the small kitchen table, depositing the rest of the burgers and the second tub of fries onto it before shrugging off my coat. "And I won't object if you strip down."

"I will," Rory muttered. "Keep your pants on, mate."

Jackson chuckled even as he stripped off his jacket then began rolling up his sleeves. "Never fear, I have no intentions of giving you an inferiority complex when you're still so new to the world."

Rory snorted. "Dream on."

Jackson pulled the chair away from the table and sat down, but his grin quickly faded as my phone rang. "Who's got that number?"

Tension ran through me, especially after his recent comment about something feeling off. "No one but you and Rory." I pulled the phone out of my pocket and glanced at the screen. The number was a familiar one. "It's okay. It's a rerouted call from the office."

Jackson snorted, his relief palatable. "It's probably one of our other clients, wondering why in the hell we've failed to give them progress reports in recent weeks."

"Probably." I hit the answer button then placed the call onto loudspeaker so he could hear it.

For several seconds, the only sound coming from the phone was whisper-soft breathing.

"Crank call," Jackson muttered. "Hang up."

"I wouldn't advise that," a pleasant and unfortunately familiar voice said. "Because that might have dire consequences."

Sparks danced across my fingers and it was all I could do to control them and *not* melt the phone. And this time it had nothing to do with Jackson and everything to do with anger. And, if I was being honest, more than a little fear.

"What do you want, Rinaldo?"

"You know what I want," he replied, voice urbane and ultrapolite. "And you have not been holding up your end of our bargain."

"I've been calling you every fucking night," Jackson growled.

"Yes, but your reports have been scant when it comes to information."

"Hard to give what we haven't got," I bit back.

"If that were true—and it isn't—then perhaps I might be inclined to forgive."

"Oh, for fuck's sake—"

"I told you what would happen if you failed to play by my rules, so you *will* now pay the promised price." He paused, and I could almost envision his cool, cold smile. "Or rather, your precious friends now will."